VISCOUNT
IN LOVE

"Let's do a test." He moved and sat down beside her. "A scientific test."

Torie scowled at him. "I have no idea what you are talking about."

Dominic wasn't the first man to suggest that kissing was a way to prove or disprove compatibility. Torie had always refused on principle. And because she had a horror of bad breath.

Yet she could smell faint peppermint on Dominic's breath, which suggested he used Dr. Peabody's Solution to cleanse his teeth, just as she did. She felt a little dizzy, so perhaps all the close attention he was giving her had gone to her head. Just now, his eyes were smoldering, but not with irritation.

Also by Eloisa James

ELOISA JAMES

VISCOUNT IN LOVE

An Accidental Brides Novel

AVON

An Imprint of HarperCollinsPublishers

VISCOUNT IN LOVE. Copyright © 2024 by Eloisa James, Inc. All rights reserved. Printed in the United States of America. No part of this book may be used or reproduced in any manner whatsoever without written permission except in the case of brief quotations embodied in critical articles and reviews. For information, address HarperCollins Publishers, 195 Broadway, New York, NY 10007.

First Avon Books mass market printing: July 2024

Print Edition ISBN: 978-0-06-334741-0
Digital Edition ISBN: 978-0-06-334742-7

Cover design by Amy Halperin
Cover art by Alan Ayers
Cover image © Vasilius/Shutterstock (motif)

Avon, Avon & logo, and Avon Books & logo are registered trademarks of HarperCollins Publishers in the United States of America and other countries.

HarperCollins is a registered trademark of HarperCollins Publishers in the United States of America and other countries.

FIRST EDITION

24 25 26 27 28 BVGM 10 9 8 7 6 5 4 3 2 1

This book is dedicated to my daughter, Anna,
who not only plotted and edited this novel with me,
but lent Florence her creepy tales, written at age nine.

CHAPTER 1

J'm so jealous of your sister," the Honorable Miss Clara Vetry whispered, staring across the ballroom. "Torie, do you think a gentleman will ever adore me the way Leonora's fiancé does her?"

"Absolutely!" But Miss Victoria Sutton felt compelled to add: "Though to be honest, I don't think the viscount is in love, and neither is Leonora."

Watching Viscount Kelbourne woo her older sister in the last months, Torie had seen no signs of rampant passion on either side. The viscount wore a glower, his customary expression. Leonora radiated triumph, which made sense since she had decided in the nursery to marry a mere viscount rather than a duke. Ladies of higher rank were dogged by reporters, and even back then, Leonora disdained gossip.

Romantic to the bone, Clara ignored this dampening observation. "Don't you see the way Kelbourne is gazing at her? His eyes are *blazing.*"

Torie glanced across the dance floor to where Leonora was standing with her viscount, Lord Dominic Alston Augustus Kelbourne, who was just as rigid as his name implied. "His eyes are not blazing."

"Don't be silly, Torie. The latest gossip column in *The Ladies' Mercury* named your sister's match 'the most romantic of the Season'! It couldn't be romantic without Kelbourne being in love, could it?"

Torie made a mental note to ask her maid to read that column aloud. She couldn't see any adoration in the viscount's face. The two were standing together mutely, perhaps because Leonora disliked chitchat. In Torie's jaundiced opinion, silence was an effective tool by which her sister promoted a serene and ladylike reputation.

Kelbourne would likely be surprised to meet the real Leonora, whose true temperament was akin to that of his notorious mistress, a volatile Italian lady who reportedly eschewed tea for pink champagne at breakfast.

"You aren't imagining that Kelbourne will give up that opera singer, are you, Clara?" she whispered. "Because I assure you that he won't."

"Ladies ignore such unpleasantries," Clara said, and promptly broke her own rule. "Did you hear that Lord Kelbourne's sister, Lady Dorney, has left her husband and gone to live with her latest paramour?"

"That's not true," Torie said flatly.

"She left two children behind!" Clara added with relish.

"Lady Dorney and her husband dined with us last night to celebrate Leonora's betrothal. I'm not saying the lady doesn't have a lover, because she and her husband didn't speak a word to each other, but they were there. Together."

"Disappointing," Clara remarked. Then she perked up. "Lord Kelbourne just spread his hand across your sister's back. I would *die* if he touched me like that. His hands are so large that they span her ribs."

"Likely because she rarely eats more than a few leaves of lettuce. You do not want to be her."

Clara looked back at the dance floor. "I would nibble lettuce, if that would win me such a ravishing man."

True, Kelbourne was strong and lean, with a jaw that appeared to be fashioned out of marble, and a tumble of dark hair. There was no denying that his broad shoulders and muscled body were a pleasure to behold.

Not that Torie would ever ogle her sister's future husband.

"I'd prefer my husband wasn't infamous for losing his temper and bellowing in the House of Lords when he doesn't get his way," she said. "In my opinion, Kelbourne would be greatly offended if Cupid shot an arrow in his direction. Gentlemen of his sort don't bother with love. Perhaps not even with affection."

"Yes, they do! Didn't you read *Love in Excess*?" her friend demanded.

"Novels are superficial . . . frivolous," Torie said, pitching her tone to lofty disdain.

"Oh pooh," Clara cried. "You and I are frivolous, Torie! I can't believe you haven't read it yet."

"I scorn such trivialities," she informed Clara.

Her friend narrowed her eyes. "What are you talking about? Just last week you told me that your husband would have to manage all the household expenses, because you plan to spend your spare time sorting your ribbons."

Torie staged an abrupt counterattack. "Frivolous I may be, but at least I'm not dragging a *cat* to a ball!"

Clara held up a bag fashioned in the shape of a cat's face. "Are you talking about my darling reticule?"

"Yes! Are those whiskers made of wire? Because something just poked me in the leg."

Clara started pulling the whiskers straight. "They keep getting bent and tangled, especially when I dance. You changed the subject, Torie."

Torie didn't want to talk about books or gossip columns. "Kelbourne showed no signs of infatuation at dinner last night. As for my sister, I assure you that Leonora sees him as a heap of sovereigns topped by a coronet."

"I would give anything to marry him," Clara sighed.

"The viscount is haughty—and bad-tempered. He would squish you like a bug. At dinner, he spoke of nothing other than some bibble-babble going on in the House of Lords."

"Bibble-babble!" Clara repeated, giggling. "Torie, he probably spent the day rewriting the laws of the land."

"I don't care. He's boring. And old."

"*Not* old," Clara protested. "He was at Eton with my brother, so he's not yet thirty. Twenty-seven at most."

"That's old," Torie said dispassionately. "Anyway, you can't tell me Kelbourne was more charming when he was young."

Clara opened her mouth, but Torie interrupted her. "Perhaps he cares for Leonora as much as he's capable. If you ask me, they are like two fish swimming along side by side and deciding to mate. You don't see a romantic twinkle in the eye of a trout, do you?"

Clara turned red, and a peculiar sound escaped her mouth.

"Drat." Torie willed herself not to blush as she turned about. "Didn't your nanny tell you that eavesdroppers never hear good things about themselves?"

"I'm fond of fish, so I take your remark as a compliment," Viscount Kelbourne said. "Though I agree that the eight years between us might make me appear old, or conversely, you infantile."

His expression was so daunting that Clara squeaked, bobbed a curtsy, and ran away.

CHAPTER 2

$\mathcal{T}$orie had the refreshing thought that Leonora's betrothal meant there was at least one man in London whom she had no need to please. That would be her sister's task from now on.

If Leonora bothered.

"Your frown chased off my best friend," she observed.

"I gather that you rate yourself above a trout," his lordship said.

"Actually, I don't rate myself very high," Torie told him. "The problem is that I have resolved to marry for more than my market value."

He looked gratifyingly surprised. "You are beautiful, charming, and well-bred." One side of his mouth quirked up. "I would rate you a luxury commodity."

Torie gave him a twinkling smile. "I wasn't *fishing* for a compliment."

He rolled his eyes.

"True, I am very extravagant," Torie said, thinking that Kelbourne was ten times more handsome when he was surprised out of his haughtiness. "Just look at my fichu, for example."

"If I am correct, a fichu is a piece of lace that circles a woman's neck. You are not wearing one."

"Precisely! The modiste delivered this gown with an elegant piece of Alsace lace, which as you can see I promptly discarded."

Then she winced. Somehow, she'd come close to flirting with her future brother-in-law, though his eyes didn't drop to her admittedly low neckline.

"May I escort you to supper, Miss Victoria?"

"Oughtn't you to be escorting my sister?"

"Miss Sutton plans to accompany your father, Sir William. You and I shall dine with them."

"I suppose she's trying to keep him away from the brandy."

Kelbourne's eyes didn't flicker, which meant that he already knew about her father's propensity to overindulge.

"We're family now," Torie told him, waggling her eyebrows. "You'll learn all our secrets. I promised the supper dance to Lord Paterson, so I'll have to give up the pleasure of a meal *en famille.*" She liked to throw French phrases about now and then, to counter the widespread belief that she was ignorant.

Which she was, but never mind.

"You shouldn't dine with Paterson," Kelbourne said, frowning. "The man's a ne'er-do-well."

Torie shrugged. "It's not as if I'm going to marry him."

He opened his mouth, so Torie raised her hand. "*Or* wander into the shrubbery with him. This may be my first Season, but I'm hardly a fool."

Leonora showed up at Torie's shoulder. "Of course you are not," her sister said in a sharp tone. "Any number of people can't read. I hold out hope that you might master the art before the Season's end."

Torie *felt* the viscount's surprised gaze, but she refused to flinch. At least he knew now why her market value was so low. Two gentlemen had withdrawn their proposals when her father informed them of her illiteracy.

"Another family secret, Lord Kelbourne," she told him. "My sister tears through books as if they were ballad sheets, so you needn't fear that your heir will inherit my marginal intelligence."

"Your curls are disordered," Leonora observed. "I suggest you retire and compose yourself. Supper has been announced."

Torie blew a white-blond curl away from her face. "We can't all be as perfect as you are, Nora."

"Do not call me that," her sister hissed.

"I thought we were sharing our secrets with your fiancé. When I was little, I couldn't pronounce Leonora's name," she told Kelbourne. "I shortened it to Nora, which my sister has never liked, so don't imitate me."

"I wouldn't dare," Kelbourne replied. He turned to his fiancée. "Miss Sutton, shall we find Sir William?"

"You could call her Leonora," Torie put in. "For that matter, you may call me Torie. For goodness' sake, your betrothal has been announced—even if you don't plan to marry for a year."

"I would consider such an address impertinent," Leonora said, with chilling emphasis. She tucked her hand into the viscount's arm. "Perhaps there is a children's table, Victoria."

Kelbourne nodded farewell.

"Pooh," Torie muttered after the two of them walked off.

They were both as cold and as stiff as iced-over branches in winter.

They deserved each other.

Two Years Later

After the service, mourners are invited to join the cortege that will accompany the remains to interment in the family vault at Kelbourne Chapel.

CHAPTER 3

February 13, 1802
The Drawing Room
Kelbourne House, London

*T*he twins were holding hands.

They were a peculiar-looking pair, to Torie's mind: light-framed and pallid, with pale green eyes and narrow chins, perhaps ten or eleven years old. Their black clothing made them resemble skinny ravens.

The children had not been invited to attend their parents' funeral or the interment, since outbursts of violent emotion—such as offspring of the deceased were likely to experience—were discouraged at such occasions.

In truth, they showed no signs of grief.

The girl was twisting one foot behind the other to rub her ankle; her heavy black stockings must itch. Their nanny cuffed her on the shoulder, and she subsided before switching legs and starting again. Her brother stared straight ahead, as if he were pretending to be elsewhere.

Torie could sympathize.

Viscount Kelbourne cleared his throat. "Miss Sutton, Miss Victoria, Sir William, may I present my late sister's children, Miss Florence and Master Valentine. Accompanied by Nanny Bracknell."

Neither child moved nor said a word until the nanny shoved Valentine forward. He bowed; Florence curtsied.

"They seem well enough," Torie's father said. "Not overtaken by grief, eh?"

"They have resided in the country," Kelbourne remarked.

Presumably the twins had had little acquaintance with their notorious mama, Lady Dorney, and given the scandal after their birth—when all society competed to guess which of Lady Dorney's lovers fathered the children—Lord Dorney likely kept his distance as well.

Torie looked sideways at her sister, but Leonora was twirling an emerald bracelet that Kelbourne had given her last month, after she finally allowed him to set the date for their wedding.

Torie nudged her in the ribs.

Leonora started. "What?"

"The children," Torie whispered.

Her sister jumped to her feet. "Please forgive me. I am Miss Sutton," Leonora said, "and I am betrothed to your guardian. I offer my sincere condolences."

Torie stood up too. "I am her sister, Miss Victoria. I'm so sorry about your parents' passing."

The children gave them clear-eyed looks and chorused, "Thank you."

Her sister's fiancé was regarding the orphans with the air of a man who had inherited a puzzle box without a key. His eyes were shadowed, and his face drawn.

Kelbourne had clearly loved his scandalous sister. Torie was certain that *he* had felt grief during the funeral, though the only outbursts of violent emotion came from Lady Dorney's former lovers, who revealed themselves as such by sobbing inconsolably throughout.

Whether the viscount could love his sister's orphaned children was another question. He certainly wasn't exhibiting paternal warmth now. He nodded curtly at Nanny Bracknell. One bow and a curtsy later, the woman escorted the children away.

As soon as the door closed, Sir William bounded out of his seat and headed for the brandy decanter. "The boy's a bit weedy, isn't he? Can't see a resemblance to Dorney, but that's a moot point."

"I assure you that young Valentine resembles his paternal ancestors," Kelbourne stated.

Torie winced at his lordship's grim expression. Unfortunately, her father had his back to the room.

"Of course!" he threw over his shoulder, pouring himself a drink. "Bad luck the Dorneys were in that carriage together, given that they lived apart by most accounts. You did the funeral good and proper, Viscount. The mourning coaches were a nice touch. None of the gossips can claim that you didn't give your poor sister an excellent send-off, even given her free-spirited ways. Must be a relief, but you didn't let on."

"I shall never consider Lady Dorney's demise to be a relief," Kelbourne said, his voice as frigid as arctic ice.

Sir William drained his brandy and poured himself another finger before he turned around. Even a man as oblivious as Torie's father couldn't overlook the warning note in his lordship's voice. "Damme, but I always put my foot in it," he cried. "I'll ask you to forgive me for my lack of good breeding. It's not as if we don't have free-spirited women in my own family."

Leonora looked up and then back at her bracelet.

"My wife was inclined to dance to the beat of her own drum," Sir William said. "Ah, but she was a delightful lass, high-spirited, dazzling . . .

flirtatious. She couldn't help herself. Ravishing, the picture of your own Leonora."

He finished his glass and turned back to the decanter. "Sure I can't give you a slug?"

"No, thank you," the viscount replied. Torie had a sickening feeling that Kelbourne wouldn't stand for more of her father's loutish sentiments.

Leonora was staring at the emeralds ringing her wrist with the keen attention of a jewelry merchant.

"Course, my wife *looked* like Leonora, but that was the end of their similarity," Sir William added. "It's our Torie who takes after her mama. Never met a lad she couldn't charm."

Torie managed a smile. "Thank you, Papa. It's quite untrue, but I appreciate it."

"Frivolous, the both of you," her father said. "I've always said it, especially when governesses would complain that Torie couldn't read. Why shouldn't a lady be frivolous? Why should a woman read or write? It's like asking a pig to sing opera."

Torie didn't flinch. It wasn't as if she hadn't been compared to livestock before.

Leonora cut in. "What do you plan to do with the children, Lord Kelbourne? Perhaps an aunt or some such can raise them in the country. The boy might be sent to Eton—after all, he has inherited the title—but what of the girl? What's to be done with her?"

"I am the twins' only relative," the viscount said flatly. "We have no aunts, living in the country or elsewhere. According to my brother-in-law's will, I stand *in loco parentis.*"

"Nothing much to it when they're this age," Sir William said. "Put them under the care of a good woman, and you're set. It's when they're older that they get to be a nuisance. Must be escorted to balls and such."

"Yet we see you so rarely during the Season," Leonora said, acid creeping into her voice.

Torie's heart sank. Leonora was never her best when strong emotions were being bandied about, if "her best" could be described as maintaining an illusion of docile, ladylike perfection.

"Neither of you needs me to find eligible suitors," Sir William pointed out. "I'm kept busy turning down men wanting to marry Torie." He threw Kelbourne a manly grimace. "I don't bother with balls, son, but you'll see me at the wedding. And the first christening, provided it's a child of Leonora's, naturally . . . Better get on the stick. As you can see, I ended up with two girls. Should have married younger."

Kelbourne appeared as horrified as a man with such strict control over his features could look. Torie wasn't certain if his disdain resulted from being addressed as "son" or from the implication that he might father a child outside marriage.

"Even for you, Father, that suggestion is grossly improper," Leonora observed. "Must I remind you that weddings are not conducted during mourning? Given Lord Kelbourne's tragic loss, we shall not marry for another year."

Her fiancé turned his head and looked at her beneath drawn brows. "Under the circumstances, I believe that polite society would forgive our breach of that rule."

Torie managed not to roll her eyes. The viscount didn't know Leonora if he thought she would contravene a social rule—*any* social rule.

Sure enough, her sister replied with undisguised

distaste. "If you mean to suggest that I would over-look convention and marry you in order to act the part of a mother to two orphans, you are quite mistaken, Lord Kelbourne."

There was an uncomfortable pause during which the only sound was Sir William gulping brandy.

Torie didn't know Kelbourne well, having spoken to him no more than a handful of times over the two years of Leonora's betrothal, but she didn't like the look in his eyes. He'd gone from offended to enraged.

"I am certain that your insensate manner doesn't reflect your true sensibilities," he stated.

"To be blunt, Kelbourne, given the uncertainty surrounding their paternity, it would be kindest to raise your wards with modest expectations. In the country."

The viscount's eyes narrowed. "You surprise me, Miss Sutton. I'll say again that Valentine and Florence are unquestionably the direct descendants of Lord Dorney."

Did Leonora have to discard her docile demeanor today, of all days, when her fiancé had just buried his only sister? "I'm sure you'll come to love the twins, Leonora," Torie put in.

"My affection is not the question. Society's stance cannot be overlooked. Valentine has a title and an estate, but given the late Lord Dorney's public statements regarding his marital felicity, Florence's chance of making a decent marriage is slim."

Sadly, that was true. Lord Dorney had celebrated the birth of the twins by getting drunk and announcing in his club that he avoided his wife's bed for fear of bumping into another fellow on the way out the door.

Leonora's mouth firmed. "Questions about their parentage will dog their footsteps. Florence cannot be presented to the ton."

Given the viscount's frown, he finally suspected that his fiancée's demure mannerisms were skin-deep. Leonora had spent the last two years agreeing with everything he said—while absolutely refusing to set a wedding date. That should have given him a clue about her malleability.

Torie's heart thumped into a faster rhythm. Her sister prided herself on never having met a man whom she couldn't manage—or bamboozle—but Torie had the feeling Leonora might have met her match.

"When Valentine and Florence are of age, my wife and I will introduce them to polite society as the noble members of the peerage who they are," Kelbourne stated. "I seem to have neglected a signal question during my proposal two years ago: Do you plan to mother our children, Miss Sutton? Or are they to be discarded in the country like unwanted kittens?"

Leonora raised an eyebrow. "My understanding is that children are happiest and healthiest when they are not breathing the coal dust of London, but I am happy to consider differing opinions. In my answer to your proposal, I promised you two sons. I never hesitate to do my duty, Lord Kelbourne."

Which was what?

Bear two children, or introduce said children to society? Torie was guiltily aware that Leonora considered bedding the viscount an unpleasant chore to be delayed as long as possible.

Her sister liked slender men with golden locks and winsome expressions. Viscount Kelbourne was black-haired, burly, and bad-tempered. And blunt. An alliterative plethora. *Plethora* was a word Torie had just learned in the funeral service, when the archbishop talked of a "plethora of grief and loss."

"No matter where they grow up, your responsibility as my wife will include introducing my wards to the ton," Kelbourne said flatly.

Torie held her breath while silence pooled in the drawing room. Not even Sir William's glass clinked.

Just before the stillness became unbearable, Leonora gifted her fiancé with a sweet, utterly false smile and murmured, "As I said, I shall never neglect to do my duty as your wife. Florence promises to be beautiful, and of course that will help her marital prospects."

Sir William stepped forward so quickly that liquor slopped over the rim of his glass, its fruity odor swamping Leonora's perfume. "A lady does require a nanny," he said, either missing the subtext of the conversation or ignoring it. "My household always had one, along with three nursemaids. My wife wouldn't have accepted anything less."

In Torie's opinion, the veil of Leonora's ladylike composure would shred at any moment, so she jumped to her feet. "If everyone will please excuse me, I shall greet Lord Kelbourne's wards in the nursery."

"I would be delighted to escort you upstairs." His lordship rose.

Leonora's eyes brightened. "*You* may not have an unmarried aunt in the family, Lord Kelbourne, but *we* have Victoria. She could raise those children in a cottage on your country estate."

Torie forced her lips to curl into a smile. "I am not yet an old maid."

"This Season is your third," Leonora retorted. "I have no expectation that a worthy man will overlook your inability to run a household."

"Your sister has received several proposals of marriage," their father declared, setting down his glass with a click.

"Mostly withdrawn," Leonora said dismissively. She leaned forward and gave Torie an encouraging smile. "You would do better to retire to the country, Victoria. You could indulge in your painting. Just think of all the rabbits hopping around the countryside."

"I'm afraid that I must decline," Torie said. "I am holding out for a love match," she told Kelbourne.

He gave her a disbelieving stare, but Torie shrugged. She had not yet met the man she hoped for.

Leonora finally lost her temper. "You're holding out for a miracle! A merely respectable dowry, a thick waist, and the inability to read or write . . . All the charm in the world won't win you a worthy man. You'll end up living under Lord Kelbourne's roof, so you might as well make yourself useful now."

Torie swallowed hard. Leonora was snappy when she was fraught emotionally, but she was still *Nora*, the big sister who always cuddled Torie after Nanny beat her hands with a ruler, shouted at her, and took away her supper—and often her breakfast as well—all because she couldn't learn her ABCs.

"You paint rabbits?" Kelbourne inquired, acting as if his fiancée's string of insults had not occurred.

"My younger daughter is a painter," Sir William

put in, his words slurring just a touch. "Kittens, roses, and bunnies, isn't that right, Torie? Any gentleman would be fortunate to marry her."

Torie drew herself as upright as possible, regretting that she didn't have Leonora's stature. Height made it so much easier to appear dignified. She raised her chin and met Kelbourne's eyes. "I think kittens and roses are excellent subjects for paintings," she said defiantly. "And rabbits as well, though I find their hindquarters difficult to manage."

"A distasteful remark," Leonora commented.

"You eat a rabbit leg fast enough," her father pointed out. "Would you rather we refer to a rabbit rump?" He chuckled. "Rump of rear rabbit!"

"I can find my way to the nursery without an escort," Torie said. She dropped a curtsy and treated the company to a glowing smile. "Sir William, please be so kind as to send our maid upstairs when you are ready to leave."

Leonora had insisted on Emily accompanying them to dinner on the grounds that their father might collapse into a sodden heap, at which point chaperonage would be required.

"We're supping here," Sir William reminded her, picking up his brandy snifter again. At this rate, her father would pass out before the meal commenced.

"I shall dine with the children," Torie said. She rationed the time she spent with her family members, and today's limit was reached.

Exceeded, really.

The viscount opened his mouth, but Leonora continued before he could speak. "It's best that Victoria come to know your wards, Kelbourne. One never knows what the future may hold."

Except her sister *did* seem to have a clear view of the future: one in which Torie mothered orphans and never had a family of her own.

Torie held her smile as she walked away, which felt like a triumph.

CHAPTER 4

$\mathcal{T}$orie was at the door to the drawing room when she realized that her sister's fiancé had followed her.

"You needn't accompany me," she told Lord Kelbourne, pushing open the door before he could reach over her shoulder and do it for her; that courtesy had always made her feel useless *and* short. "Your butler will direct me to the nursery."

Ignoring her, he closed the door behind them. "Flitwick, I'd like to introduce you to Miss Victoria, my fiancée's younger sister."

Flitwick was the stately sort of butler, with a melancholy face like a grasshopper's. Torie had noted that butlers often resembled their employers. Naturally, her family's butler had a red nose and a propensity to sway back and forth.

Flitwick bowed with all the elegance of a duke. "It is a pleasure to meet you, Miss Victoria."

"I prefer Torie." Her smile seemed to soften his expression, so perhaps he wasn't as rigid as his master. "Do you remain in London all the time, Flitwick, or do you travel to Kelbourne Manor when Parliament is out of session?"

"As his lordship's head butler," Flitwick said, "I accompany him to Northamptonshire."

"May I ask whether you have a family?" Torie inquired.

"Mrs. Flitwick is my housekeeper," Kelbourne put in, not hiding his impatience. "She travels back and forth to the country with us. Shall we go to the nursery?"

"In a minute," Torie told him, relishing the fact that unlike her sister, she didn't need to keep the viscount sweet. Not that Leonora seemed to bother, now that she had a ring and an emerald bracelet.

He blinked. Kelbourne was apparently unused to being contradicted. Married life with Leonora would be a revelation.

"Could you please tell us how the children are settling into their new life? My sister is most anxious that they be happily established."

She caught Kelbourne's twitch at this untruth, but she didn't take her eyes off the butler.

"The twins have settled well," Flitwick declared. "Nanny Bracknell accompanied them to London, so their education has not been interrupted."

"Not that," Torie said, waving one hand. "How *are* they, Flitwick? I'm certain that you know what I mean. It's a terrible blow to lose both parents at once."

Flitwick's stern countenance eased. "The children are very lucky to have you take an interest, Miss Torie. They are well. Intelligent, without question, and Mrs. Flitwick tells me that they have pleasant manners when they remember to use them. But they're eccentric, you might say. Always talking of the strangest topics."

"They will outgrow such foibles," Kelbourne said, frowning as if he had been informed that all the butter in the house was rancid.

Torie had the distinct impression that "eccentric" was anathema to his lordship. After all, he had chosen to marry Leonora, the epitome of an English lady.

On the surface.

"Lord Kelbourne, please do rejoin your guests in

the drawing room," she told him. "Flitwick will escort me upstairs."

"I haven't yet visited that floor, so I might as well make certain the children are comfortable."

Torie stared at him. "You have not visited the nursery at all?"

"As I said." Kelbourne's expression was always closed, but his mouth got a little tighter. He clearly didn't like criticism, even the implicit sort.

"Their parents died a week ago," she pointed out. "And they arrived at your house when?"

"Four days ago," Kelbourne said stiffly.

"Has anyone lived there in the nursery since you were a baby?"

"It was hardly the Middle Ages."

"I can assure you that the mattresses were aired, and the rooms recently cleaned," Flitwick put in.

"Of course they were," Torie said. "But if Lord Kelbourne means to be *in local parentis*, he must be hands-on." She began to climb the marble steps leading to the first floor.

"*In* loco *parentis*," Kelbourne corrected, following.

"I took your use of the term to mean that you plan to be a father. You could stow them in the country, as Leonora suggested. She comes by that model honestly: after our mother died, we were sent to the country estate, and Sir William never darkened the door of the nursery again."

"Was his absence significant to you as a child?"

She glanced over her shoulder, and then quickly turned her head forward again. Kelbourne was altogether too handsome for normal life. His profile belonged on a Greek coin. "A father's attention would have been helpful. Our nanny was as cuddly as your Nanny Bracknell."

"No nanny is cuddly," his lordship said.

They reached the landing. Generous corridors stretched left and right, caramel-colored floorboards shining in the afternoon sunshine. The wallpaper featured brilliantly colored, improbable birds.

"I adore this paper," Torie commented, stopping to admire it. "Peacocks *and* parrots!"

"My sister chose it just before she left the house to marry." His voice softened. "Hand-colored and a ridiculous expense for a mere corridor. Letitia was extravagant." He glanced down at Torie but held his tongue.

"A 'luxury,' like myself?"

Kelbourne's eyelashes flickered. Torie let her smile widen. She always enjoyed it when she could interpret her acquaintances. Clara bounced on her toes when she was excited. Her future brother-in-law's eyelashes fluttered when he was irritated.

"I particularly like these cranberry-colored birds," she told him, tapping one. "I would like a reticule in precisely that color."

He frowned at the wall. "The red ones?"

"They're not red!" Torie protested.

"They look red to me."

She held out her skirts. "I suppose you think that my gown is merely black?"

He looked at the fabric she was holding up. "You must be jesting."

"I spent the best part of a day in Partlet's Emporium finding just the right shade of mourning bombazine," she told him. "This black has a touch of silver that complements my hair."

His gaze went from her hair to her skirts and back.

"Don't you dare look disdainful," Torie cried. "The silver streaks in my hair would be garish against matte black. You're going to be my brother, so you'll have to trust my opinion."

His eyes returned to her face. "Are you sure you want a brother? Your sister exhibits a remarkably dismissive opinion of your worth."

When Leonora's feelings were ruffled, she lost her temper and got snappy, but her sister never meant it. "That's merely Leonora's way," Torie said airily. "I don't take it seriously."

His eyes were blue-gray with a black rim around the irises. "Is it merely your father's way to compare you to an opera-singing pig?"

Torie cleared her throat. "Sir William loves me, if that's what you're wondering. As does Leonora."

"Hmmm."

She fidgeted, fluffing her skirts. "Shall we continue?"

"Why is your sister so brusque with you?"

"Leonora thinks . . . no, she is right. I *am* flighty and frivolous. I truly can't read or write, which makes me fairly useless. I can count, but calculations are above me. I have a veritable passion for expensive silks; if I were Eve, Adam would likely scold me for overindulging in fig leaves and leaving none for his breeches."

He took her hand in his. "I don't think you're flighty. You seem loyal and kind." Warmth spread through her body from the large fingers wrapping around hers.

"I don't mind the word," she said, summoning up a smile. "We can't all be in the House of Lords. I may be useless, but I am very ornamental. Rather like this wallpaper." She was rattled—she shouldn't be holding hands with her sister's fiancé!—and so the next sentence just rolled out of her mouth, unprovoked.

"Or your mistress."

CHAPTER 5

$\mathcal{D}$ominic could scarcely believe his own ears. He dropped Torie's hand and said sharply, "My mistress?"

He didn't want to think about Victoria Sutton in the same breath as Gianna. Torie was charming, fresh, and funny. Useless, perhaps, but enchanting. Especially when she was facing down her father and sister with that beaming, courageous smile.

His mistress was . . . Well, Gianna was a tempestuous Italian with the propensity to throw crockery at the servants.

His future sister-in-law bit her plump lip, a wash of pink rising in her cheeks. "I shouldn't have said that," Torie whispered. "Could we pretend I didn't?"

"No."

"Why not?"

"Because I am appalled," Dominic said grimly. "A gentleman's private arrangements are never to be discussed in polite company."

"You're unreasonable," Torie countered, raising her chin. "Why should I pretend not to know of Miss Peccati? She is reportedly ravishing, if temperamental, and the two of you are a favorite subject of gossip. Moreover, my sister told me that you had been remarkably frank with her on the subject."

"Leonora told you about our conversation addressing my *mistress*?"

"Of course she did! I'm her sister. In my opinion, you distinguished yourself by scrupulous truthfulness. You informed her that you sought to marry an excellent hostess who could soften your reputation and improve your standing in the House of Lords—not the most romantic of reasons, but refreshingly direct. You promised never to betray her with another lady but specified that a mistress doesn't count as adultery. Once again, applause for your candor, though I would have kicked you and your proposal out the door." She grinned and added, "To be honest."

Dominic was nonplussed. It was as if Torie didn't understand the nature of marriage at their rank.

"In case you're wondering," she continued, "Leonora is an excellent hostess, and she will never take a cicisbeo. She is ruthlessly conventional and will give you two sons of your own bloodline. Did I miss anything?"

"No." He made the word as forbidding as possible.

Torie rolled her eyes. "You're not a prudish dowager, so why should I pretend that I don't know of the existence of your mistress? Or my father's mistress, for that matter?"

"Such indelicate matters should never be bandied about."

"You and Leonora are a match made in heaven: she too likes to proclaim rules as if airing her opinion will make people agree. All I meant to say is that according to the gossip columns, Miss Peccati reportedly drinks pink champagne for breakfast, which I applaud. Pink champagne is *much* prettier than plain wine, in my opinion."

"Such details appear in newspapers?" *Appalled* didn't cover his feelings.

"Regularly. Bellowing in the House of Lords wins you frequent notices as well. You weren't aware?"

"I've never seen such a column."

"You are right to ignore them," Torie said blithely. "I won't bring Miss Peccati up again since you don't wish me to. There's nothing worse than being teased about one's secrets, don't you think?"

"Are you referring to your inability to read?"

"Pretty much," she confided. "After everyone learned the truth in my second Season, life became easier. The year before, I was always dodging comments about the latest novel."

Dominic drew in a deep breath. No one had ever spoken to him in such an impertinent fashion, but it was clear that Torie meant no disrespect. Instead, she was explicitly disregarding convention on the grounds that they were family. It was as if she were an American. He'd once spent a few months in Boston and had conversations with forthright ladies that would never occur in polite society on this side of the Atlantic.

At his silence, Torie gave a little shrug before she turned and headed for the stairs to the second floor. "My sister and father will be displeased if you don't return promptly."

Victoria Sutton was shorter than Leonora, and yet her personality was far larger. She was bursting with life. Even her laugh was vibrant; he felt her deep chuckle in his bones.

At that thought, he had a sudden sharp realization: thank God he hadn't betrothed himself to a woman like her, someone flamboyant and irritating and far too sensual. He pushed that ridiculous thought out of his mind and followed her up the stairs. They creaked under his tread, and the walls were still painted olive-brown.

Torie reached the landing and paused to wait for

him. "Come along," she said, diving at the nursery door before he could touch it.

The occupants of the room didn't look up. Florence was seated on a settee that Dominic recalled from his childhood as having cushions like rocks. Valentine was lying on his back on the floor, his booted feet propped on the seat beside his sister. The room was clean enough, but dreary.

Just as he remembered.

Two beds, the hard settee, a tin tub surrounded by a yellow curtain hanging from clattering iron rings.

"Has it changed since you were a child?" Torie whispered.

"It is precisely the same." Just as depressing. He could feel his spirits sinking.

"'As for the severed heads, he had placed them amongst the items of the rest of his collection, in a line of almost military perfection along the window-sill,'" Florence read aloud from a sheet of foolscap.

Torie caught Dominic's arm and put a finger to her lips. Her eyes were dancing with laughter.

"I like that line," Valentine said, staring up at the ceiling. "Where'd you get the idea of the severed heads?"

"In the drawing room," Florence replied. "The way they all stared at us. Next line: 'I could imagine him, late at night when his mistress had gone to sleep, rustling their hair with all the strength in his long fingers until the heads crumbled.'"

"Mistress?" Dominic muttered in disbelief. Even children knew what a mistress was? Then it occurred to him that severed heads were more problematic. Shouldn't his niece be writing a story about fairies and frilly ball gowns?

"I'm not sure I like what comes next," Florence continued, scribbling. "'The fresher heads were brushed to one side as they lay before the open window.'"

"You need to set the scene. . . . 'Before the open window, bathed in steady flows of moonlight,'" Valentine amended.

"Personally, I think that 'bathed' and 'flows' are jarring in the same sentence," Torie put in. Weathered floorboards squeaked as she walked into the room.

Florence jerked upright and stood, dropping her pencil and sheet of paper to the ground. Valentine twisted his head about to see who had entered, then pulled his feet from the settee and rose.

"We just met downstairs," Torie said. "I am Victoria Sutton, and I'll be your aunt one of these days, since your uncle is marrying my sister."

Florence dropped a curtsy. Valentine bowed. "Good afternoon," they chorused.

Dominic suddenly realized that Florence was wearing neither slippers nor stockings. He could see pale ankles below the hem of her black dress.

Torie sat down opposite the twins. "Let's talk about severed heads."

Dominic froze on the spot. What had seemed like a simple matter—house his sister's children and raise them to adulthood—abruptly felt impossible. Florence's ankles were as thin as a bird's. Was she ill-fed?

What about those severed heads? Did that reflect a diseased imagination? He could imagine the distaste on Leonora's face if she heard about this story. Ladies didn't write about severed heads or greet visitors with bare legs and toes.

The twins didn't seem to notice that he hadn't greeted them or seated himself. No match for Torie's charming smile, they dropped onto the settee and tumbled directly into a tangled description of a story short on plot but rich with horrific details.

Why hadn't his brother-in-law sent his son to Eton? Valentine didn't seem to have any understanding of gentlemanly behavior. Even if settee cushions were rocklike, one didn't prop one's feet on them. Florence was equally oblivious. As he watched, she pulled up her thin legs and hugged her knees, wiggling her bare toes.

What in the hell was he going to do with them?

CHAPTER 6

*T*orie generally liked everyone she met unless they tried to pinch her bottom or made an overt joke about her intelligence. But these children?

She *really* liked them.

She had grown up in a nursery with Leonora, who by the age of six already knew how to keep her curls tidy, sew a straight seam, and write all her letters.

Torie's crimes began with unmanageable curls and went downhill from there. She was personally responsible for several nannies and two governesses being dismissed after they had failed to teach her to read.

Which led to a deep, abiding fascination with books. With words. With people who could make up stories.

The twins were tripping over each other, explaining that Florence was writing the story while Valentine was helping. "He's not as good a writer as I am," Florence pronounced. "He's overly flowery."

"I like 'bathed in flows of moonlight,'" Valentine protested. "It has *gravitas*. Don't you think so, Lord Kelbourne?"

Their guardian had finally seated himself but still hadn't said a word. He looked as if he'd undergone a severe blow—not the first of the day, Torie reminded herself. The poor man had apparently believed that his private affairs weren't of interest to everyone capable of reading a gossip column, just as he thought his future wife was a docile, fragile flower.

The children stared at their uncle, waiting for him to respond.

Torie took pity on the viscount and intervened. "Does your character have fangs? Because I have the inkling that this man would have fangs overhanging his lower lip. They could shine in the moonlight. Or—be *bathed* in moonlight."

"I like that!" Florence exclaimed, scribbling on her foolscap.

"Where's your nanny?" Kelbourne asked, ignoring the moonlit fangs.

"Downstairs with the housekeeper," Valentine said. "Nanny Bracknell finds us very tiresome, and we feel the same about her."

His sister elbowed him. "Don't be such a frightful snob, Val."

"Snob?" Torie asked.

"Valentine thinks that he's smarter than everyone he meets," his sister disclosed.

"That's not true," Valentine protested. "You are smarter than I am."

"He walks around making judgments about people based on the last book they read. Nanny likes to read the Bible, and even then, only the New Testament. Beware: if you admit to not having read Plutarch, my brother will dismiss you as an idiot."

"I might as well be frank with you, Valentine," Torie said. "I haven't read a single book."

The children's eyes widened. "Whyever not?" Florence gasped.

"I am unable to read or write."

"*Read?*" Valentine was seemingly too appalled to be snobbish. "You can't *read?*"

"Shall we teach you?" Florence asked, leaning forward, eyes shining. "I began reading at three years old, and after that, I taught my brother *and* the milkman. So I could teach you."

"It won't work," Valentine said flatly. "It's not like when you taught Puffer to read. If she doesn't know by now, there's likely something wrong with her brain, Flo. Pulling out a slate board won't help."

Kelbourne cleared his throat. "A gentleman should not be so blunt. You might hurt Miss Victoria's feelings."

The twins' eyes moved from him to Torie. "Did I?" Valentine asked.

"No," Torie replied. "I'm used to being the dunce in the room."

"It would be interesting to dissect your brain," Valentine observed. "Do you know about dissection?"

Torie shook her head. "My ignorance knows no bounds. What is it?"

"Cutting up a dead body to see what it's like inside," Valentine said. "When I'm old enough, I mean to cut up many people. I expect your brain looks differently than mine."

Torie almost said "smaller," but caught back the word. She was trying not to disparage herself, given that the world so often did it for her.

"This is not a proper subject for conversation. Ladies are horrified by the mention of dead bodies," Kelbourne announced. If he was thinking of Leonora, he wasn't wrong. Torie's sister would expire from shock if she heard about Florence's story.

The twins glanced at him, unimpressed. Torie had the feeling that any number of people had tried to steer them into being more conventional.

And failed.

"Ladies prefer more delicate subjects," Kelbourne continued, an edge in his voice. "For example, Miss Victoria is an excellent watercolorist. We could discuss her paintings of kittens and flowers."

"I paint in oil. And you have no idea if I'm excellent," Torie said, wrinkling her nose at him.

"Well, are you?"

"Yes," she admitted.

"Except for the rear ends of rabbits," the viscount qualified, the faintest glimmer of laughter in his eyes.

"I could try to write a story about a rabbit," Florence said dubiously.

Torie choked back a peal of laughter. "How many stories have you written?"

"Loads. Especially lately. We like to read, but Nanny wouldn't let us bring any books. So in the last few days, we've been writing instead."

"Why weren't you allowed to bring your library?" Kelbourne asked.

"She wanted us to try to be normal children," Valentine explained. "Or at least appear so."

"Too late for that," Torie said, grinning. "'Master Valentine' is such a mouthful. May I address you as Val?"

Val nodded, but Florence said, "I do not wish to be addressed as Flo."

"My usage is grandfathered in," Val said.

"Florence is more dignified," his sister explained. "Also, it's a city in Italy that I mean to visit someday. Have you been there?" she asked the viscount.

"Yes, I have. Florence is a charming city, full of art."

"I shall go there on tour," Valentine announced. He turned to Kelbourne. "Since you're our new father, you might as well know now that we'd prefer that Flo marry young."

The viscount blinked. "Father?"

"Our first father told us that in case of his death, you would be our second," Valentine explained. "I gather that Miss Sutton is to be our new mother."

Kelbourne had the stunned look of a man recognizing that his life has just changed profoundly. Torie jumped in again. "Why do you wish to marry young, Florence?"

"So that she can accompany me on my Grand Tour," Valentine explained.

Torie couldn't help smiling. "And her husband? Will he accompany you as well?"

"Of course. It's called a honeymoon."

Kelbourne's dazed features eased into something like amusement. "A honeymoon is generally a trip conducted by a new husband and wife alone."

"Not in our case," Florence said with utmost confidence. "We're twins, you see."

"Flo must marry so she can come with me. First she has to master the arts of enticement." Valentine eyed Torie. "Perhaps you could help her."

"'Arts of enticement'?"

"The phrase comes from a really interesting sermon about sinners," he explained. "Preached after a 'mortal and bloody duel.'"

"You're reading Joseph Sewell's sermons?" Torie asked, recognizing the author from his sermon given at Westminster Abbey.

"I found it in Father's library," Valentine said. "Someday I might have to fight a duel, so I hoped the sermon would include useful information, but it did not."

Kelbourne frowned. "No pastor knows anything about dueling."

The twins ignored him, which Torie thought he'd better get used to.

"You will need to dress like her and walk like her," Valentine told his sister, nodding at Torie.

Torie glanced down at herself. Her black bombazine had none of the ruffles, lace, and ribbons she adored. She preferred to be one of the widest ladies in any room, but her mourning dress was designed for small panniers. Moreover, the bodice touched her collarbone, whereas most of her gowns showcased her breasts.

She did not feel enticing.

"I can already wiggle," Florence said. She hopped up from the settee and walked across the room, her narrow hips swaying from one side to the other. "Good afternoon, Lord Whatsit," she cooed, bobbing a curtsy.

"You look like a duck crossing the road," her brother observed.

"Miss Victoria does not move in that exaggerated manner," Kelbourne said.

Florence turned around, hands on her hips, and swished left, then right. "Enticing ladies wiggle!" she informed the viscount.

"Yes, Mother wiggled," Val agreed.

A glance flashed between the twins, something that Torie couldn't interpret.

Florence returned to her seat and tucked one bare foot under her. "I'm only eleven. I have time to learn how to entice a husband."

"Very true," Torie agreed.

"I suppose you haven't found one because you can't read," Florence said, giving her a sympathetic look. "You could live with me once I'm married, if you wish."

"To be quite frank, the idea of marriage turns my stomach," Valentine said. "I think I'll avoid it. You never truly know who you're marrying, do you? Flo wrote a story about a man who killed *several* wives. Each one was terribly surprised when she discovered a chamber full of legs and arms and such."

"Why did he chop up his wives, let alone kill them?" Torie asked.

Florence shrugged. "I got the idea from an item in the newspaper about Lord Adolphus Bufford, who had three wives. All of them died, so obviously he killed them."

"I am acquainted with Lord Bufford," Torie said. In fact, he had been one of Kelbourne's rivals for Leonora's hand in marriage. "I've danced with him numerous times, and I assure you that he is a perfect gentleman."

"Dancing is not the same as marriage," Valentine pointed out, with some justification. "His homicidal tendencies wouldn't be obvious in a ballroom."

"Lord Bufford is an elderly peer, well respected in the House of Lords," Kelbourne said sharply.

"*Three* wives," Florence reminded him. "Respect from his peers is hardly likely to stifle bloodthirsty impulses. Just look at Lady Macbeth! She was probably ladylike until she bathed her hands in blood."

Torie was thoroughly enjoying the fact that neither child was intimidated by the viscount. Lady Dorney's interesting romantic life had apparently kept her so busy that she had neglected to teach her children to respect their elders.

Or, like Leonora, she might have considered her mothering duties completed after she dropped her children in the country. Torie had the distinct impression that the twins had raised themselves with the help of their father's library.

"Two dead wives might be regarded as misfortune, but three smacks of homicide," Valentine put in, grinning.

"This is a most improper subject for conversation," the viscount pronounced.

"You wouldn't want Miss Victoria to keep dancing with Bufford, would you?" Valentine asked. "What if he began courting her? What if he proposed?"

"No worries about that," Torie said. "He would never choose someone like me."

"Because of the reading problem," Valentine said, nodding.

"Partially, but more likely on the grounds of character. Lord Bufford is very worthy, and wouldn't want someone as frivolous as I. I combine illiteracy with a passion for painting flowers, remember?"

"You're very pretty, though," Florence observed. "We look wretched in black, but it makes your skin look as white as . . . as wallpaper paste."

"Wallpaper paste!" her brother exclaimed with disgust. "*Moonlight*, Flo! Or milk. Or lilies. White lilies!"

"Thank you both," Torie said, desperately trying to stop herself from bursting into laughter.

"I wouldn't mind marrying you," Valentine observed. "I could read aloud to you."

"Perhaps you could read to me even if I don't marry you? I am rather old for you, though I do appreciate the compliment."

"Age is merely a number," Valentine said with a

wave of his hand. "If not me, why don't you marry our second father?" He nodded toward Kelbourne. "He's older, but we sweeten the bargain."

"He can't. He's marrying her sister," Florence pointed out.

Torie didn't dare glance at the viscount.

"It would be easier to read to Miss Victoria if she were living with us," Valentine said.

"She's going to be in our family, so we *can* read to her," Florence said. "We'll start with fairy tales. You'll like them," she told Torie. "Witches who eat children, evil stepmothers, et cetera."

Torie had a dizzyingly joyful feeling that she had found some family members who liked her, even given her deficiencies. "Please call me Torie," she said warmly. "As we're family."

Kelbourne threw her a reproving look. Unsurprisingly, given that she had suggested that he address her as such two years ago, and he was still parroting "Miss Sutton" at her sister.

"All right," Valentine agreed, obviously having no idea how unusual it was to address an adult by her given name.

"Only when we're in private," Torie clarified, because Leonora would have a fit of vapors if she overheard him.

The twins nodded. "Would you like to read a book now?" Valentine asked. "I think that Father likely has some good ones in his library."

There was a moment of silence before Kelbourne woke up to the fact that he was the father in question. He cleared his throat. "Yes. I do."

"I suggest you only address Lord Kelbourne as your father in private as well," Torie said. "*We* may all understand that your first father intended him to be your second, but 'Lord Kelbourne' is the most polite address."

"My fiancée is Miss Sutton." Kelbourne hesitated. "Never address her as 'Mother,' even in private."

Florence's lips rounded into an O, and her eyes lit up.

"My sister will *not* be an evil stepmother," Torie said hastily. "Leonora is simply quite proper."

"Disappointing," Florence remarked. "I'd like to prove myself against an evil stepmother. I would never allow myself be put into an oven." Turning to Kelbourne, she added, "Will you marry soon? Shall we continue to live with you, and will Torie join us?"

"If we are to live with you, can we *please* have some books, or at least borrow them from your library?" Val chimed in.

"You will live wherever I live," Kelbourne said. "You may have as many books as you wish, and I shall immediately send for those left behind. I shall not marry Miss Sutton for at least three months, since we are in mourning for your parents."

"We do recognize the fact that we ought to be in torrents of tears," Valentine disclosed.

"We're not good at crying, and unfortunately, we didn't know either of them very well," Florence said.

"Moreover, they didn't like us," Valentine added.

"Your parents loved you," Kelbourne stated firmly, much to Torie's relief. She was feeling out of her depth, having only met the Dorneys once, at Leonora's betrothal dinner. Neither Dorney had frequented the same parties as debutantes.

"That's not the same as 'like,' is it?" Valentine argued. "The last time we saw Mother, she fired our governess, saying we were akin to barbarians.

We think she forgot to hire another, because a year went by, and no one replaced Miss Biddleton."

Kelbourne's jaw tightened in response to this artless depiction of his sister's cavalier mothering. "You're too old for a governess, so I will hire a tutor. The three of us will live here in my house in London when Parliament is in session and retire to Kelbourne Manor in the summer. Once we are out of deep mourning, you shall go to Eton, Valentine."

Valentine shook his head. "No, I shall not. Father considered that as well, until I explained that I could not be separated from Flo."

"Father was surprisingly persistent," Florence added. "He stayed in the nursery for at least an hour, trying to persuade Val. We never saw him again. Would you live with us once your sister marries our father?" she asked Torie. "You seem to like us. At least, you don't appear to be hysterical, and you're not shrieking."

Leonora *would* be shrieking. Torie was still trying to get her head around the idea of her sister having regular conversations with these two. "I shall happily visit, if his lordship approves. My father's house is only a few blocks from here."

"We must read to Torie, even before you marry Miss Sutton," Val said to the viscount. "You must see that. Likely she doesn't know *anything*."

"I'm an expert in ribbons and gowns. And painting roses."

Val closed his eyes, looking for all the world like an exasperated sixty-year-old peer, then squinted at her disbelievingly. "No Plutarch?"

"Who?"

He sighed loudly. "This is a disaster."

"Miss Torie may visit the house whenever she

wishes," Kelbourne said. He had the stern, some-what pallid countenance of a man trying to recover from a severe shock. Or influenza.

Torie gave him a thankful smile. His gaze remained cool. Even stuffy Lord Bufford had responded to her charm, but not the viscount.

Not that it mattered, of course.

He would be merely her brother-in-law. His hard jawline was Leonora's problem, not hers.

"Would you like to hear more of the story I'm writing?" Florence asked.

"Absolutely!" Torie said.

"Another day," Kelbourne said. "Miss Victoria and I must return to the drawing room."

"Why don't you call her Torie?" Florence inquired. "She's to be your sister."

"Sister-in-law."

"Please do," Torie said, mischief prompting her to poke at the viscount. "I believe I asked you to do so two years ago. And I shall address you as . . ."

"Dominic," he responded after a chilly pause.

"Dominic it is. Or perhaps Dom?" Torie chirped, enjoying the way he recoiled slightly on hearing his first name. He was a stick, but she felt sympathy for him. This nursery visit must have been a blow to his constitution, from being addressed as "Father" to being cheerfully informed that Eton was out of the question.

"Surely it's time for your supper," he said to the twins. "Does your nanny appear regularly with meals?" His voice had taken on such a forbidding edge that both children blinked at him in surprise.

"Nanny Bracknell will bring up some food when she gets around to it," Val said.

It couldn't have been more obvious that neither child paid attention to mealtimes.

"Must you leave with Father?" Florence asked, her pale green eyes fixed on Torie's face. "I can add fangs to my story!"

Torie had the distinct sense that the children were desperate for attention. "I shall dine with you, but Lord Kelbourne must return to the drawing room," she said, rising to her feet. "On your feet, twins. We shall bid your"—she faltered—"his lordship farewell."

"Dominic," he reminded her. To her surprise, a smile lurked in his eyes. "Perhaps I might share your meal?"

"I'm afraid not," Torie said. "You are hosting my sister and father, if you recall." Though she was certain Sir William had passed out by now.

A bow and two curtsies later, the viscount walked out the door, promising to dispatch a footman with an English translation of Homer's *Odyssey*. He had looked surprised on being told to leave, but Torie had no wish to find herself berated by Leonora for boring her fiancé.

"You must remember that trivialities are mind-numbing to men of substance," Leonora often told her.

So: off with the man of substance.

"We can read Homer over our meal," Val proclaimed.

"We should work on my story first!" Florence argued. She picked up the page again. "'I could see him enjoying their company across the dingy room from beyond the dead, unlit hearth where spiders set up camp and trapped only dust mites.'" She paused. "What do you think?"

"I like that the 'spiders set up camp' trying to trap flies but only caught dust mites," Torie said. "Whose company are we talking about?"

Val had dropped to the floor the moment the door closed behind the viscount. He put his boots up on the settee next to his sister.

"The severed heads," he said, rather dreamily. "They wouldn't be nearly as good as mere 'heads,' would they? The word *severed* makes all the difference."

CHAPTER 7

Over the course of the next two months, Torie's life fell into an agreeable pattern. Every morning, she paid a visit to the Kelbourne nursery, taking lunch with the twins if she wasn't otherwise engaged. In the afternoons, she painted in her studio, a room at the rear of the house overlooking the back garden. In the evenings, she sallied forth to the theater or a ball, escorted by one of her suitors and chaperoned by Leonora, her maid Emily, or Clara and her mother.

Despite Leonora's ominous prophecy regarding Torie's future spinsterdom, she had several new suitors, one of whom was the Duke of Queensberry. During their most recent dance, His Grace had cheerfully told her that no bluestocking's brains could compare with a complexion like hers.

Torie wasn't thrilled to be courted for her complexion, but beggars couldn't be choosers . . . and he was a duke.

One day Florence asked to see Torie's painting studio, so Torie walked the twins to her house and brought them directly upstairs since Leonora was receiving callers in the drawing room.

She and the viscount had tacitly agreed that the twins weren't ready for a prolonged conversation with her sister. Kelbourne had instituted a Prohibited List, an index of topics to be avoided in polite conversation.

Rather to Torie's surprise, the list kept growing. She had not considered how many topics were never discussed by gentlefolk. The viscount's command,

"Put *that* on the list," had become a joke amongst herself and the twins, with imitations of his growl leading to peals of laughter.

In years gone by, her studio had been her mother's sewing chamber, but three years ago, Torie had claimed it due to its west-facing window. She hadn't realized until she escorted the children through the door how messy it had become. The bare floor was splattered with paint in every color, and jars of paintbrushes bathing in solvent sat next to empty teacups. Their butler's inept household management meant that servants avoided the studio altogether.

"I adore this room!" Florence squealed, clapping her hands. "Why do you have two easels?" she asked, walking over to a still life made up of billowy roses.

"One captures morning light, the other afternoon," Torie explained.

"I see what you're doing here," Valentine said, rather surprisingly. He was standing before her morning easel. The nearly finished painting depicted a rabbit family gamboling in a clearing flooded with sunlight.

"You do?" Torie asked. Half the time she wasn't sure what she was doing; she was simply compelled to try to master an idea.

"Dawn light is burnishing the rabbits' ears," Valentine said. "Do look at this, Florence." His twin promptly came to stand beside him.

The children were still dressed in deep black, but Torie had dispatched a modiste to Kelbourne House so they at least had touches of white at the neck. They'd gained some weight after the viscount imposed regular mealtimes.

Torie couldn't help thinking they were utterly adorable, especially when they stood shoulder to shoulder, their hands clasped behind their backs.

"I think she smiled while painting these bunnies," Florence told her brother.

"I see what you mean," Valentine replied, once again sounding as judicious as a sixty-year-old man. "These rabbits are joyous, though I'm not sure how the emotion makes itself known."

"Look here," Florence said, pointing at one of the babies. "The way his ear flops and his head is bent. He's so happy to be with his brothers and sisters. And his mama."

Valentine leaned in, squinting closely at the canvas. "How did you make these whiskers, Torie? I can scarcely see them."

"A pin," she explained. And then, since they were interested, she told them all about painting rabbits. "The hindquarters are the most challenging, not because of their shape—that's easy—but because a rabbit is almost always in motion and springs from its rear legs."

Florence mimicked her brother, peering closely at the painting. "I see it in the rabbit in the air." She traced its legs with her finger. "He went up and twisted. I expect it was hard to portray him in motion like that."

"It's taken me years," Torie said simply.

"Perhaps you could teach us to paint," Valentine suggested. He moved from examining the rabbits to the woods behind them. "I like the way you used indigo blue to make the woods seem so deep."

Torie laughed aloud. "You're the first who's noticed that trick. I learned it from an Italian painter whose paintings are displayed in the permanent exhibit of the Royal Academy of Arts."

"We should go see his work," Valentine declared. "I want to learn to paint rabbits. Perhaps not roses, though."

"They're not merely roses," Florence objected. "There's a ladybug on one leaf."

The upshot of the twins' visit was that the viscount had a great deal of paint and two easels delivered to the nursery. "Try to paint something monumental, like the Tower of London," he advised Valentine. "Roses and rabbits are for ladies."

Torie swallowed back a wave of irritation.

"Because they are as delightful as women," Kelbourne added quickly, eyeing her face.

The viscount's condescension was no worse than that of other men in her life. After seeing one of her paintings hanging on the wall of a friend, the Duke of Queensberry informed Torie that it was marvelous she had a hobby, and that the roses were as pretty as she. "The female vision is attuned to sensual particularity," he had opined.

Trying to create the depth of the room behind the bunch of roses thrown carelessly on a table had taken four months. She didn't think her eventual triumph had anything to do with "sensual particularity."

Valentine gave his uncle a clear-eyed look and said, "I shan't paint a tower because I'm not interested. It doesn't sound very challenging."

A week later, Torie decided that the twins were ready to meet Leonora. The Prohibited List was several pages long—and memorized. A placid conversation over a cup of tea would hopefully lead to her sister reconciling herself to the idea of having wards, which might stop her from grumping about the time Torie spent at Kelbourne House.

"You are so rarely at home," Leonora complained. "Lord Bufford paid us a morning call yesterday, and you were nowhere to be found. I had to summon Emily to chaperone. I could almost think that you deliberately avoided him."

"You would be correct," Torie confirmed. She had glimpsed Bufford's carriage trundle to a stop before the house and promptly slipped down the back stairs. "Given that Lord Bufford just escorted us to the theater, I didn't expect to see him the very next day. Besides, he only comes to see you."

The elderly baron hadn't given up hope of winning Leonora from the viscount and had been taking full advantage of Kelbourne's withdrawal from society due to mourning to escort her to balls and the theater almost every night.

A faint smile touched Leonora's lips. "His lordship is remarkably persistent, isn't he? Yet he's such a gentleman that he never makes me feel uncomfortable. I feel safe in his company even without a chaperone."

To Torie's mind, ravishment was unlikely, because Bufford had to be past sixty and walked with a cane. "Does being in Kelbourne's company make you uncomfortable? We haven't seen much of your fiancé in the last month."

She kept to herself the fact that she often met Kelbourne coming or going from the nursery. They'd even shared a few meals, chaperoned by the twins and the *Odyssey*, which had proved bloody enough for Florence and eloquent enough for Val.

Leonora shrugged. "The viscount is in mourning,

Torie. It would be most inappropriate for him to attend the theater, let alone a ball. As you know, I am besieged by invitations and in need of a companion. Lord Bufford is a godsend."

"Mourning wouldn't prevent your fiancé from taking you for a drive in the park," Torie observed. She was slightly worried that Leonora would change her mind about Kelbourne and decide to marry someone more manageable. Thankfully, no other viscounts were available for marriage.

In the depths of the night, Torie had started to imagine raising the twins, as Leonora had suggested. Perhaps if they moved to the country, she might meet a farmer, preferably one who couldn't read. A broad-shouldered man without pretensions, but with burly thighs.

Kelbourne's thighs were far more muscled than those of the Duke of Queensberry. According to Leonora, her fiancé's daily rapier practice had resulted in swollen muscles, which she found most distasteful.

Torie would never look at her sister's future husband with desire, of course, but she had to admit that she liked swollen muscles.

"I might summon Kelbourne for a drive in Hyde Park," Leonora said, sounding distinctly unenthusiastic. "He's getting impatient about our delayed wedding."

"That's fair, given the two years you put him off even before he went into mourning."

"I certainly couldn't have married him within months of his proposal. Hasty weddings give entirely the wrong impression."

Such as the impression that two people couldn't wait to be together? But then Torie realized her sister was talking about the overly prompt appearance of babies.

"Last year was extremely crowded with events," Leonora continued. "The celebrations following the conferral of Prince Augustus Frederick's dukedom, for example. The wedding of a viscount should be the premier event of the Season."

"You could meet Kelbourne in his own house while visiting the nursery," Torie suggested. "Once you are better acquainted, I am certain you will grow fond of Valentine and Florence."

"I don't wish to be acquainted with them, let alone feel a warmer emotion," Leonora stated. "Fairly or unfairly, they carry the blemish of their mother's shameful reputation. I can't imagine why Kelbourne hasn't dispatched them to the country, but I think less of him for it. It is not fair to them to raise them in the environs of polite society when they will never find a place amongst us."

"You sound remarkably uncharitable," Torie observed. Sometimes her only defense was to attack Leonora for unladylike comportment. "Shouldn't you be more loyal to your fiancé?"

"I am being practical. Reputation aside, can you imagine me introducing that strange-looking girl to society? Her eyes are the color of gooseberries."

"Florence is beautiful!" Torie protested. "Her hair curls most attractively."

Leonora wrinkled her nose, so Torie added cunningly, "If we made a brief visit to the nursery, you could take another look at the grand salon. If you recall, you decided that it needed renovation."

When Leonora finally agreed, she insisted on taking the carriage all of three blocks and sending in her card. Flitwick himself came out to the carriage to say that the viscount was in attendance at the House of Lords, but he implored them to enter for a cup of pekoe tea and a few of Mrs. Flitwick's freshly baked lemon scones.

"No scones," Leonora stated, descending from the carriage.

"Yes, scones," Torie said, jumping down. "Flitwick, we'd like to see the children, so perhaps we could take tea in the nursery."

"First, the grand salon," Leonora said, making her priorities clear.

She spent the next hour directing Flitwick to strip the oak paneling and create a serene and symmetrical space. "I prefer quiet colors. Those crimson draperies are horrendous." She gave a dramatic shudder. "This room must be completely refurbished before I live here. The cacophony of color is most disturbing."

Flitwick assured her that work could begin immediately.

"We shan't marry for at least six months," Leonora told him.

Torie managed not to raise an eyebrow, though she was certain that the viscount planned to marry as soon as he was out of deep mourning.

The first thing she saw on opening the nursery door was Florence atop her bed, twirling a leaky pillow while feathers eddied around her like a snow shower. "Avast ye, scurvy dog, you beetle-browed dolt!" she shrieked.

Both children had repurposed their mourning armbands as eye patches worn diagonally over their foreheads. Pillows had turned to weapons. In short, they were pirates.

"You bilge-sucking, lily-livered scalawag!" Valentine shouted. His hair had grown long enough to snare feathers; they ringed his dark curls like a ragged halo.

"Pirates, ahoy!" Torie said briskly, diving into the room and snatching Flo's pillow before it lost any more feathers.

"Sink me, 'tis me auntie!" Valentine said, hopping off his bed.

"Torie!" Florence shrieked. Torie had just enough time to drop the pillow to the floor before the girl hurtled off the bed. She threw her arms around Torie's waist. "Hello!"

From the door, Leonora cleared her throat. "Good afternoon, Miss Florence, Master Valentine."

The twins' heads swiveled to the door in unison.

Torie held her breath. Most of the time Leonora showed the world an inflexibly decorous façade, maintained by rigid attendance to rules such as *Laughter is immoderate.* Very occasionally, Nora—the sister who used to love nursery games—would reappear.

"Or am I addressing two pirates?" Leonora added, smiling.

Torie sighed with relief.

"Would you like to play with us, Miss Sutton?" Florence asked excitedly. "We have more pillows."

"Oh, no," Leonora stated. "Miss Victoria and I are too old for such games. When you're a grown lady, Miss Florence, you won't wish to be buffeted by a pillow, will you?"

"I believe I wouldn't mind," Florence said thoughtfully. "Especially if I am doing most of the buffeting."

"She's remarkably violent for a member of her sex," Valentine said. He was plucking feathers from his hair and throwing them in the air. "Look at this, Torie. The draft in this room runs east to west."

"I would be an excellent pirate," Florence said.

"How so?" Torie inquired. She felt a pricking unease at the expression on Leonora's face; her sister may have accepted the pirates, but by addressing Torie with her nickname, Valentine had just breached a cardinal rule: *A well-bred lady encourages no one, including her spouse, to address her in a casual or informal manner.*

"I am free from sentimentality," Florence explained. "Pirates are not mawkish while making fellows walk the plank, for example. I feel certain I could dispatch them with aplomb. Isn't that a lovely word? *Aplomb* means 'assurance.'"

"No woman is a pirate, or at least, no *lady* could be a pirate," Leonora said, distracted from the issue of Valentine's informality. "Ladies have a natural sense of delicacy, a sensibility that defends them from bloodthirsty practices."

Florence regarded her with distinct aplomb. "Perhaps I shall grow into sensibility, although I don't hold out much hope."

"You can feign delicacy," Valentine called encouragingly from the window, where he was trying to coax feathers to float in the draft coming from the closed window. "Just look how well I can bow. Though frankly, if I wanted to finick about like a heron, I'd live in a stream." He looked to Torie. "To *finick* is to 'affect extreme daintiness or refinement.'"

"Thank you," Torie said. "On that subject, Val, you have neglected to bow to us. 'Sink me' is not an appropriate greeting."

Valentine walked forward, clutching two feathers

in his left hand, and bowed with a finicking flourish of his right. "Good afternoon, Miss Sutton. It is indeed a pleasure to meet you again." He bowed. "Miss Victoria."

Leonora nodded a greeting. "Master Valentine. I hope you find the nursery comfortable."

The room had transformed from Torie's first visit. Two desks now stood side by side against one wall. The easels were positioned before the window, and new beds lined another wall. A painted screen in the corner had been left folded open, and behind it she could see a gleaming brass bathtub. Finally, comfortable chairs and a sofa were arranged before the fireplace.

"It's rather cramped for two of you, is it not?" Leonora continued, without waiting for Valentine's answer. "Miss Victoria and I grew up in a nursery in the country, where there was enough room for my sister and me to have our own bedchambers."

Torie cast her sister a jaundiced glance. Of course Leonora would champion the pleasures of country living.

"We wouldn't care to sleep apart," Florence said. "Fa—Lord Kelbourne has refurbished the room since we arrived. Do you like the wallpaper?"

"No," Leonora said, before Torie could catch her eye. "I find it chaotic and overly colorful."

"The children's mother chose this paper," Torie said.

"For the nursery?" Leonora asked incredulously.

"Oh no, for the downstairs corridor," Valentine explained.

"This paper would be just right in a corridor," Leonora said immediately. "One would pass by and be left with an impression of beauty."

Torie took a relieved breath. Her sister was a kind

person, as long as emotions were muted and propriety observed.

"We didn't know our mother very well," Florence said, "but Lady Dorney was rather peacocky, like this paper. We think perhaps seeing it every day will make us care for her more."

"*You* think that," her brother said. "I find it most unlikely."

Leonora opened her mouth and shut it again. "Just so."

She cast a somewhat wild look at Torie. The twins never said what one expected, and Leonora was particularly wedded to the expected. She undoubtedly felt that Lady Dorney's children should refer to their late mother only in saintlike terms.

Sir William often described his dead wife as "lively"; Leonora had always told Torie—who couldn't remember her mother—that their mother had been a paragon among ladies.

"When you marry Lord Kelbourne," Florence continued, "perhaps you could choose new wallpaper, Miss Sutton. That way we will come to be fond of you."

"Affection comes with time, not with wallpaper," Torie said.

Leonora nodded. "I would be happy to replace this paper, perhaps with a paint that promotes tranquility, such as alabaster. Master Valentine, shall we summon your valet to remove the feathers from your hair?"

"I don't have a manservant of my own yet," Valentine replied. "I may never have one, as I believe our father left us impoverished. Are we allowed to discuss gambling or is that prohibited?" he asked Torie.

"Since your father has passed from this world, his memory must be honored," Leonora said firmly.

"I could speak on the subject with reference to your father, who is still in this world," Valentine said agreeably. "His recent wager, as I'm sure you know, was covered on the front page of the *London Times*. Well, Torie wouldn't know, because she can't read."

Leonora cleared her throat.

Valentine disregarded this warning sign. "It was quite foolish to wager eight thousand pounds that a curricle could not circle the Tower of London ten times in thirty minutes, especially given that Sir William's confidence in his bet manifested after a pigeon shat on his shoulder."

Catching Leonora's shocked expression, Torie said quickly, "Ladies' sensibilities are offended by mentions of excrement."

"I'll add *shat* to the Prohibited List," Valentine said, throwing both feathers into the air at once.

"List?" Leonora repeated in a stunned voice.

Florence offered helpfully, "Subjects such as flatulence, loins, rogering . . . oh, and bastardy. I can tell you more of them, if you wish. I have an excellent memory."

Leonora's eyes widened, though she probably didn't know what "rogering" was. Torie didn't. Certainly no one had mentioned flatulence or bastardy in Leonora's presence in years. If ever.

"Nanny said she would feed you to a cat if you mentioned rogering again," Valentine said to his sister. He turned to Torie. "*Rogering* is vulgar slang for—"

"Best not," Torie said, interrupting.

"As I *am* a lady, those are words that offend me,"

Leonora pointed out. "They should never be uttered in my presence, and you would offer myself and Miss Victoria a further offense by explaining a vulgarism."

"I do see that you're very ladylike," Florence said. "We said that, didn't we, Val? After we were in the drawing room, where we first met you both."

"Perhaps you would be more comfortable living in the country, where you needn't mind your tongues as much," Leonora said. "Countryfolk are not overburdened by sensibility as we in London are."

"Really?" Valentine asked with interest. "Because we have heard some extraordinarily vulgar phrases since we arrived in the city. The other day—"

"Valentine!" Torie cut in. "Why don't we all sit down? Tea must be on the way."

"I could read to you from the *Odyssey*," Valentine offered.

The children dashed to their favorite seats: Valentine to a large chair by the fire with a towering stack of books nearby and Florence opposite, with a stack of foolscap, a half-written story of severed heads, and a lap desk that Dominic had given her a few days ago.

"A gentleman never sits when a lady is still on her feet," Leonora barked. "Obviously, your comportment lessons haven't been detailed enough."

Val didn't move.

"Master Valentine!"

He startled, looking up from his book. "What?"

"No gentleman sits in the presence of a lady."

Valentine muttered something that sounded perilously like "Bollocks," but he rose, book in hand.

Thankfully, the door opened behind Torie's back, and she turned toward it, smiling valiantly. She didn't care who it was—Flitwick, Mrs. Flitwick, Nanny, the cook, a nursemaid, *anyone*—because Leonora was winding up like a top. One more vulgar word and she would spin out of control.

Well, anyone . . .

Except perhaps the viscount.

CHAPTER 8

$\mathcal{D}$ominic walked into the nursery and instantly realized that he had strayed onto a battlefield. His fiancée's cheeks were flushed and her eyes wrathful, which wasn't particularly surprising if she'd been in the twins' presence for long.

Torie took severed heads in stride, but Leonora? Unlikely.

"Good afternoon, Miss Sutton, Miss Victoria," Dominic said, bowing. "Children."

Torie dropped into a curtsy. The twins chorused, "Good afternoon, Lord Kelbourne," followed by a creditable bow and curtsy.

Leonora bobbed and then folded her arms over her bosom. "Kelbourne, your wards have offended me in more ways than I can enumerate. I am sadly convinced of my original judgment. They can never—"

Before Dominic could speak, Torie intervened. "*No.* Whatever observation you are about to make should be expressed in private."

"We don't mind," Valentine offered. "We have both concluded that Miss Sutton doesn't like us." Without a trace of embarrassment, he added, "I fear the feeling is mutual."

Bloody hell. One should celebrate honesty in children, but the twins were honest to a fault.

"How dare you!" Leonora retorted. "You are a vulgar, impudent little boy, and you will *never* be accepted in polite society!"

"I could say the same to you, but I gather you have managed to disguise your nature," Val remarked dispassionately, "which suggests I could do the same."

Leonora's cheeks turned from pink to purple as she drew in a harsh breath.

"We could try to like you, Miss Sutton, if you choose new wallpaper," Florence said quickly.

Dominic tried to make sense of that, but quickly discarded it.

"I cannot introduce these children to the ton," Leonora said shrilly. "They mentioned flatulence, and something I suspect refers to fornication. She . . . the girl spoke of bastardy when . . . You cannot expect it of me or any lady, Kelbourne! The task you envision is impossible. They have no grace, politeness, gentility, *nothing* that becomes their supposed rank."

Dominic turned to the twins. "I am disappointed. We've spoken about appropriate topics for conversation. What happened to the list?"

"In fact, they were exhibiting their newfound knowledge," Torie said wryly. "My sister's injured sensibilities stem from a misunderstanding."

The children surveyed him with clear eyes. "Florence assured Miss Sutton that we realize some topics of conversation should not be aired among ladies," Valentine explained. "We did not broach those topics. Florence listed three only after the lady expressed interest."

"Four," Florence corrected him. "I can whisper them in your ear, if you wish, Lord Kelbourne." She trotted over and came up on her toes, whispering audibly, "Flatulence, rogering, bastardy, loins. Three nouns and one verb."

Dominic's heart sank. Leonora wasn't wrong. No lady of his acquaintance—except for Torie—

could have heard that list without taking grave offense.

"You see," his fiancée said, her voice crackling with rage. "Moreover, she—they—spoke insolently of their dead parents. And my own father!"

"Where is your nanny?" Dominic asked the children.

"The nanny is irrelevant," Leonora spat. "We have come to an impasse, Kelbourne. You must face reality. These children display none of the qualities required of those of gentle birth. Their behavior is a mark of their parentage."

"No, merely lack of education," Torie cut in. "They are making great strides."

"Nanny Bracknell is belowstairs," Florence reported.

"Do not speak unless you are spoken to," Leonora spat.

"I was spoken to," Florence objected. "My father asked me a question, and I responded."

"Your—father. *Father*? He is, at best, your guardian." Leonora looked to Dominic. "Fix this, if you please."

Dominic felt a surge of raw anger at her rudeness, which he instantly quashed. In time Leonora would come to terms with the twins' place in her life. "The situation does not require repair. The children were given to me and rightly consider me their second father. I am raising them."

"In the *Odyssey*, Penelope raises Telemachus by herself," Valentine said. Meeting Leonora's uncomprehending stare, he clarified, "Telemachus is the son of Odysseus." And then, when she still didn't respond, he added with painstaking emphasis, "Odysseus is the subject of a classic epic, the *Odyssey*."

"A non sequitur," Florence observed. She turned to Torie. "A *non sequitur* is a statement that doesn't logically follow from what came before."

"I believe that Valentine means to applaud Lord Kelbourne's parenting," Torie said. "Leonora, I assure you that the twins are learning the rules of conduct at an extraordinary rate. Valentine has taken interest in the pianoforte, and—"

"He is a *boy*," Leonora gasped. "Are you planning to teach him to embroider?"

"I shouldn't care for it," Valentine said thoughtfully.

"Do not speak unless addressed!"

Dominic made the unwelcome discovery that his fiancée's eyes had an uncanny resemblance to a hawk's. He moved to Leonora's side and held out his elbow. "May I escort you downstairs, Miss Sutton?"

She cast a look at him, walked to the door, wrenched it open, and left.

"To return to the *Odyssey*, Telemachus turned out fine with only one parent," Valentine said.

Torie moved to his side and plucked two feathers from his curls. "My sister was shaken, but she will be an excellent guardian to you both, once she gets used to the idea."

"You told us she was a reader," Valentine said.

"She is," Torie insisted. "Ladies are not offered the *Odyssey*, so she's had no opportunity to read it. You must be fair." She sat down on the settee, and Florence immediately nestled beside her.

Dominic ought to follow his fiancée out the door, but instead he walked to the fireplace and dropped into a seat. "What am I to do now?" he asked bleakly.

Perhaps if he'd met Torie before Leonora—but that was inconceivable, even if Torie was kind to the children. Beloved by them, if truth be told.

He had chosen Leonora for her intelligence, ladylike grace, and acumen. They had been first introduced in an interval during a performance of Molière's classic play *Tartuffe*. Leonora had decried the vulgar plot, while noting that the English translation had neglected to reproduce Molière's twelve-syllable lines. Dominic had decided in that moment to make her his bride.

Now the very reasons for which he had chosen her had come into conflict with his loyalty to his sister's children. Tempting though it was to break the betrothal, as a gentleman, he could not. This situation was not Leonora's fault.

Opposite him, Torie drew in a deep breath. "I'll take them."

Dominic's mind muddled as her bodice strained—and somehow did not slip below her nipples. Torie's bodices were so low that no man could stop himself from picturing her naked. Her sister was near prudish in her dressing; Torie was the opposite.

"What did you say?" Florence asked, looking up at Torie. "Take us where?"

"Would you like to live in the country with me?"

He felt the shock of that question down his legs. Almost without noticing, he had accepted the twins' claim that he was now their father. No one would take his children from him, no matter how peculiar and outspoken they were. *Especially* not a woman who couldn't even read.

"No," Dominic barked. "They live with me. They are mine. Besides, they are . . ." He hesitated and then said it as kindly as he could. "They are more gifted than most children. I hired their tutor from one of the Oxford colleges." He hated the stricken look that crossed her eyes, but his first responsibility was to the twins.

"Of course, I understand," Torie agreed instantly.

"I don't think we're gifted," Florence put in. "I'd quite like to live in the country with Torie."

Whether or not Val attended Eton, he had a great deal to catch up on, not least Latin and Greek. The children didn't need a cuddly nanny, as Torie had suggested. They needed stimulation, knowledge, and intelligent conversation. Plus . . . they were *his*.

Torie would have her own children soon enough. She could not have his.

He shook his head. "I'm your father, Florence, and so you live with me."

"As a point of fact, our first father never lived with us," Valentine remarked.

"Shall we join Miss Sutton downstairs?" Dominic asked, feeling strongly disinclined to discuss Lord Dorney's household arrangements.

Torie stood, giving Florence a squeeze and reaching over to pluck another feather from Valentine's hair. "All the feathers must return to the pillowcase, after which it should be sent downstairs for mending," she ordered.

Dominic glanced about and discovered white drifts under the settee and around Florence's bed. "Every feather," he agreed.

"Good afternoon, children." Torie went to the door.

"Wait!" Florence called.

When Torie turned, Florence dropped an elegant curtsy, deep enough for a royal greeting, and

Valentine bowed with a flourish of his hand. "Good afternoon," they chorused, straightening.

"Excellent!" Torie called.

"We're not done. Don't leave, Torie!" Florence called. "Come on, Val."

They moved apart, facing each other, and then slid into a graceful minuet, marred only by Valentine calling out the paces. "Lead-in, right-hand turn, left-hand turn, two-hand turn closing."

Torie started laughing. She was enchanting when she smiled, but when she laughed? Her eyes turned as deep and blue as a mountain lake.

"There!" Florence cried as they finished the measure.

"Remarkable," Dominic said, meaning it.

"Miss Sutton said that we have no grace, politeness, or gentility," Valentine said, grinning widely. "But Mr. Petre is most pleased by our prowess."

"I apologize for my sister's unkind remarks," Torie said. "She spoke in the heat of the moment."

"Perhaps Miss Sutton is experiencing her monthly courses," Florence said with interest. "The governess that Mother fired said that women become quite heated at that time and are not responsible for their outbursts. That was after the governess threw an ormolu clock at Valentine's head." She turned to Torie. "*Ormolu* is—"

"I do know that word," Torie said. "I find gilded clocks to be gaudy but charming. I trust the governess didn't strike your head, Valentine?"

"Oh no, she never managed to hit either of us, no matter the time of month. We became excellent dodgers."

"I'm glad to hear it," Dominic bit out, a surge of anger almost blocking his throat. If he'd known that the twins were being neglected, he would have taken them from his sister years ago. His brother-in-law wouldn't have given a damn; the poor man was humiliated by persistent speculation about which of his wife's lovers fathered his heir.

"Thank you for demonstrating your excellent command of the minuet," Torie said, curtsying. "Please put 'monthly courses' on the Prohibited List."

"That's an odd addition, given that—as I understand it—ladies are universally plagued by the event," Florence observed. "Next time, perhaps the four of us could dance together? Mr. Petre could play the pianoforte."

Dominic fleetingly met Torie's eyes. He had never danced with his future sister-in-law. He had asked her once, years ago, but she had turned him down for some reason he'd forgotten. He had already been betrothed to her sister by then.

If he was honest with himself, of course, he had *noticed* her. He had watched her dance and seen her smiling under her eyelashes at captivated gentlemen. No man could be in her presence and not find himself dazzled by the way her unruly curls invited a man to—

He cleared his throat. "Miss Sutton is a remarkably graceful dancer, and I expect she would be very pleased to dance with us."

Torie smiled and vanished through the door.

A small hand touched his elbow. "Must you?" Florence whispered.

He didn't pretend not to know the real question. "Yes. A gentleman never betrays those to whom he has made promises. Nor does a gentlewoman."

"But Mother—" Florence broke off.

"We understand," Valentine said.

CHAPTER 9

Torie woke up in the morning with a terrible feeling of foreboding. What would happen if the twins were wards of a man with no connections to her family other than a broken betrothal to her sister?

Moreover, a man who didn't seem to like her very much.

The idea of not watching them grow up was heartbreaking. She felt swamped with sadness.

The day before, Leonora had brooded in a corner of the carriage the whole three blocks from Kelbourne House before accompanying Lord Bufford to a musicale in the afternoon. After that, she claimed to have a headache and took her supper on a tray in her room.

Leonora almost certainly intended to return Kelbourne's ring.

Torie couldn't argue with her sister's decision. She'd never understood Leonora's ruthless adherence to social rules, but there it was. Kelbourne would have to find a different viscountess to introduce the twins to society.

The ironic thing was that in Torie's opinion, Leonora was wrong. Seven years from now, Florence and Valentine would stroll into London ballrooms and effortlessly command attention. They had easy confidence, a quality that could not be taught. Their *aplomb*, as Florence called it, was innate.

Torie was more observant of that quality than most because she did not have it. No one who'd spent her life so aware of failures could.

In short, she was addle-headed.

She'd never felt more addled than in the aftermath of the moment when she blurted out that offer to "take" the children. Even thinking of it made her hands curl into humiliated fists. How could she have been so stupid?

Lord Kelbourne had been appalled.

Appalled.

She'd seen it in his eyes. And he was right. Florence and Valentine were extraordinarily intelligent and deserved to be cared for by someone who was as brilliant as they.

Never mind her instinctual feeling that the twins just needed to be loved. Kelbourne did love them, in his own way, but he showed it by expressionless nods and frequent additions to the Prohibited List—with the best motives, of course.

Florence and Valentine needed someone in their lives who'd put them *first*. Before society's rules, before the House of Lords, before lovers (in the case of their mother), before their reputed paternity (in the case of their father).

If Torie had taken the children to the country, she would have put a minuet low on the list of skills to be mastered. The pirate game was the first time she saw the twins playing. They needed to learn to have fun outdoors.

Who better to teach that than Torie? She'd spent her childhood dodging nannies waving books that she couldn't understand. Leonora may be able to read, but she'd never walked through Torie's favorite glade, where the wild bees thronged and rabbits raised their kits. Torie had climbed trees to peer into robins' nests, and clung to a tall elm in a windstorm, pretending to be a ship's boy. More than one summer had been spent trailing after the estate gardeners. When she painted roses, she knew their names; when she painted rabbits, she knew the precise pink of their velvety noses.

Now she folded her arms behind her head and stared up at the gathered draperies over her bed. If *she* had Valentine and Florence, she'd take their books away after breakfast and chase them out of the house.

Florence would soon have more to write about than severed limbs. Or they could make her descriptions more realistic by dissecting a dead squirrel. If Leonora hadn't started screaming when Torie cut open a dead frog, she would have extracted all its bits and pieces for a closer look.

The bedchamber door burst open while she was imagining a daily picnic. She and the children could lie on their backs in a field of cow parsley and watch starlings circle. Or listen to Val read the *Odyssey*.

Emily dashed in, threw open the curtains, and screeched, "Miss Sutton is *gone!*"

Torie sat up. "What?" She squinted at the window. It couldn't be more than nine in the morning. Her heart sank; she could guess where her sister was. "I expect Leonora is calling on Lord Kelbourne before he leaves for the House of Lords, Emily. She likely slipped out of the house and walked there."

"Miss Sutton doesn't walk anywhere," Emily retorted. "No, she has left for good!"

"If you are suggesting that my sister has eloped, you are mistaken. She would rather die."

"She rang for me at dawn," Emily said dramatically. "I dressed her in that new gown, the one with hand-painted flowers."

Torie nodded.

"I had no idea, but Sir William's valet had dressed him early as well! He and Miss Sutton left together without breakfast. And now the master's returned alone and announced that Miss Sutton won't return to the house—*ever*!"

"I doubt that very much," Torie said, swinging her legs out of bed. "Did Sir William have brandy with his morning tea?"

Emily shook her head. "He was sober as a judge, though now he's in the library with the decanters, so who can say? He's in a regular snit, I can tell you that. Sent for Lord Kelbourne, or so the butler says."

Torie winced. Apparently, Leonora had left the unpleasant business of breaking off her betrothal to their father. "I suspect my sister has traveled to Wales to stay with my uncle for a few months, until the gossip about breaking her engagement dies down."

Emily gaped. "Miss Sutton jilted the viscount?"

"I think so," Torie said.

Leonora's flight to Wales was a remarkable concession, given that she disliked their uncle to the point of refusing to be in a room with him. In fact, it suggested that her unwillingness to settle on a wedding date reflected genuine reluctance to marry Kelbourne. After all, if the viscount had insisted on keeping the twins in London, Leonora could have just pretended that the nursery didn't exist, a time-honored practice amongst noblewomen.

Torie suspected that Kelbourne was too male for Leonora, with his blunt mannerisms, his burly physique, and his obsession with rapiers, as her sister had acidly put it.

"Wouldn't Sir William have sent Miss Sutton to

Wales in the barouche?" Emily asked. "If she is paying your uncle a visit, I mean."

Torie frowned. "Perhaps the barouche is not equipped for such a long journey, and the threat of scandal forced her onto the stagecoach. Leonora loathes gossip, and she's certain to be on everyone's lips this week. She may have demanded to leave immediately. You know how she is."

"Stubborn as a stone," Emily agreed. "But Miss Sutton on a common stage without a maid? I can't imagine it. And if she's paying your uncle a visit, why's the master in such a canker, saying that she will never return?"

"He doesn't mean it. Sir William is enraged because Leonora instructed him to break her betrothal," Torie surmised. She stood up, feeling foolishly near to tears.

No more twins, at least until they were old enough to debut in society.

The Duke of Queensberry had been angling for a kiss, and she should probably indulge him. As a duchess, she could ensure that Florence was a success among the ton.

"Please call for a bath," she said dully.

Emily rang for hot water while Torie brushed her teeth.

"Lord Bufford is going to be so disappointed," Emily said, clicking her tongue as she pulled Torie's nightdress over her head. "The gentleman actually thought Miss Sutton might accept his proposal. *He* thought to lure the most beautiful lady in London away from a viscount, though he's old as the hills and likely takes his teeth out at night!"

In her bath, Torie resolved to pay a visit to Kelbourne House to say goodbye to Florence and Val.

She didn't have to worry about running into the jilted bridegroom; the viscount would hear the bad news and go straight to the House of Lords. He wouldn't allow a broken engagement to come between him and the laws of the land.

She refused to be another person who simply disappeared from the twins' lives. If only she could write, she would correspond with Florence. She pushed that wish away with a practiced grimace.

Forty minutes later, she was laced into her favorite *robe à l'anglaise*, strawberry pink with a deep green hem trimmed with white ruffles. Emily darted forward to position the matching ruffled hat with a playful tilt to the left before pinning it in place.

"It's odd to think of Miss Sutton without a maid," Emily said, stepping back to check every detail of Torie's appearance. "How will she dress herself?"

"My uncle will assign her one of his upstairs maids. I'm sorry about how the jilting affects you, Emily. You deserve to be the personal maid to a viscountess." Torie hesitated and then added, "I am certain that Lord Kelbourne's household would have been far more comfortable than ours."

Emily's sigh took in their oft-drunken butler and equally inebriated master. "You are a pleasure to dress, Miss Torie. Your sister always demanded a fichu wound halfway up her neck, and I couldn't persuade her to raise her hems, despite fashion's demands."

Torie cocked her hip and slid forward a darling slipper so she could see the strawberry ribbons that crossed over her ankle—which brought a rueful smile to her face as she remembered Florence wiggle-waggling across the nursery.

Somehow, she *would* remain friends with the

twins. Even if Lord Kelbourne took a justified dislike to her entire family after being jilted.

Torie drew a deep breath and prepared to go downstairs.

Beside her, Emily gave a little squeal. "Pray take care!" She reached over and tweaked the ruffle that adorned Torie's low bodice. "Your nipples will be served up on a platter if you aren't cautious."

"I'll breathe shallowly," Torie promised, picking up her reticule. Perhaps she'd go to Delbart's Book Emporium before visiting the nursery. Mr. Delbart had become quite good at advising her about books the twins might like. Florence had adored *The Necromancer; or, The Tale of the Black Forest* and had promised to read it aloud once Odysseus finally found his way home.

No *Necromancer*.

No more *Odyssey*, either. Though to be honest, she had started to find Odysseus frustrating. If Torie had a loving family waiting at home, she wouldn't skip from island to island, seducing witches and letting her men be eaten by cyclopes and turned to pigs.

Achingly empty days and months without the twins stretched ahead of her. Of course, she had her painting. She'd been working on the cabbage roses forever, and the piece was finally coming into focus. She tried to muster some enthusiasm for finishing it.

"I shall work in my studio this afternoon," she told Emily. "I promised to join Clara for the evening meal, but under the circumstances, I will remain home. Will you please send her a note?"

One of the more humiliating aspects of her illiteracy was that her maid wrote all her messages and read aloud any responses. "I'm sorry that Leonora changed her mind about marrying the viscount, but I *am* glad that you're staying with me," Torie said, dropping a kiss on Emily's cheek.

Her maid nodded. "If Leonora had become the viscountess, I would have had to leave you as you are . . . It didn't feel right."

As you are: a delicate way of classifying an addled brain.

"Please let Roberts know that I shall visit the bookstore, so he should bring a purse," Torie added. Even though she was certain she could manage such a simple transaction, well-bred ladies never touched coinage.

Not unusually, no footman was to be seen when Torie arrived at the bottom of the stairs. In their household, staff invariably needed to be rousted from belowstairs. She turned to enter the breakfast room but froze when she heard her father's raised voice coming from the library.

"You drove my daughter away!" Sir William thundered. "Leonora had no choice but to break her betrothal."

It seemed Viscount Kelbourne had responded to her father's summons and was now being informed of his fiancée's departure. Torie sighed. Sir William was hardly presenting Leonora's decision in a tactful manner.

Long experience of judging Sir William's voice suggested he was mildly tipsy. But—and this was unusual—he was genuinely enraged. Her father was an amiable drunk who could be compared to a lady prone to fits of vapors: at some point in the evening, he would collapse on a nearby couch.

But now he was furious. Of course, Leonora's

betrothal, celebrated far and wide as a brilliant love match, had done much for the family's consequence. In contrast, Torie's betrothal—if there ever was one—would be followed by animated speculation about the intelligence of her offspring.

A low rumble from the viscount followed, interrupted by her father.

"Leonora is *delicate*, with a gentlewoman's sensibilities. You allowed her to be insulted by your wards and, not content with that, indulged them as they disparaged my St. Paul's wager!"

It was unclear which was the greater affront: the disrespect to his daughter or to his most famous bet.

"You made unreasonable demands," Sir William continued. "No lady would want to introduce those young fiends to polite society, and you oughtn't have asked it of her."

Torie scowled and headed toward the library door. Val and Florence were not fiends, and she wouldn't allow anyone to say so.

When she entered, Kelbourne was standing before the window, light glazing his hair to the color of blackberries. He was at his most autocratic, jaw stony, eyes ferocious. She had to stiffen her knees; some cowardly part of her saw raw emotion in his eyes and wanted to soothe his irritation.

Which would be precisely the wrong way to respond. He was far too used to having his own way when people cringed before his temper. It wasn't good for him, any more than it had been good for Leonora.

"Good morning, Father," Torie said, dropping a curtsy. "Lord Kelbourne." She dropped another.

The viscount gave her a forbidding stare and bowed. Her father just glanced at her. His cheeks were adorned with purple circles, like a lady whose face was inexpertly painted.

"My children are not fiends," the viscount stated. His voice was calm but all the more threatening for it. "I take offense, Sir William."

"*I* take offense," Torie's father snapped. "I gave you my daughter, the most beautiful debutante in all London, and you failed to tie the knot for *years*."

"Your daughter refused to set a date for our wedding," Kelbourne retorted. "Am I to understand that Miss Sutton now refuses to marry me at all?" His voice was even, but Torie had learned to read his expressions over the last few months.

He too was outraged, which was somewhat surprising. After all, he'd had a taste of Leonora's temper.

He must have truly loved her. Guilt flashed down Torie's spine. Of *course* Kelbourne had loved—still loved—Leonora. She was lovable. Rigid, but lovable. Not to mention beautiful and intelligent. Ladylike most of the time. She would have been a practically perfect viscountess, if the twins hadn't come along.

"Leonora cannot marry you," Sir William said, following the declaration with a hearty swallow of brandy.

"Oh?" Kelbourne asked.

"This morning she married someone else."

CHAPTER 10

Rage exploded through Dominic's body.

He had hoped Leonora would break off their engagement; he had acknowledged as much to the twins yesterday. The last thing any man wanted was a reluctant bride.

But abruptly marrying another man was grotesquely improper and would open both of them up to unpleasant blather. Leonora should have explained her feelings, whereupon he would have expressed graceful, untruthful regrets and placed an announcement in the *Times*, informing all interested parties that the wedding was off.

Instead, she made a fool of him by eloping while they were still betrothed.

A new wave of anger broke over him. "Whom did my fiancée marry?" he demanded.

"Leonora would *never* elope!" her sister cried at the same moment. Torie's eyes were round with shock. At least she hadn't schemed to bring him low.

"Leonora did not elope," Sir William clarified. "Married by special license this morning to a decrepit old goat—entirely *your fault*," he thundered.

"Not Lord Bufford!" Torie gasped.

Dominic blinked. His fiancée had run off with an elderly man with three dead wives in his past. Unbelievable.

Still—he felt better. Leonora must be deranged. If asked, his only comment would be well wishes for the newly married couple.

Of course, now he had to start the entire process

over. It had taken him several months to find a lady who could be a true partner and offer an intelligent assessment of current events. Most ladies fell into Torie's camp. Granted, she kept the nursery laughing with her wry observations about Odysseus's adventures, but that wasn't the same as sharing lucid analysis.

"Aye, she's Lady Bufford now," Sir William said heavily. "Presented me with a special license and threatened to run to Gretna Green if I didn't accompany them to a chapel. To think I should see such a day! Bufford is well enough in his own way, but aged. Older than I am." He tugged his vest down over his belly.

"Sir William, I offer my very best wishes for your daughter's married life," Dominic said, realizing a beat too late that given Bufford's dead spouses, his congratulations could have been better worded. "I shall take my leave."

"Lord Kelbourne, may I say goodbye to the twins?" Torie asked, stepping toward him, her hands twisting together. "Please?"

"What?" Shock turned his voice to a growl. "Why would you say goodbye?"

"You are no longer a family member," Torie explained. Her eyes seemed twice as large as normal. "It would be most improper for me to visit the house of an unmarried man."

Of course, that was true.

But Torie had never bothered about being chaperoned before. He felt an instinctive dislike of the idea that he wouldn't meet her regularly, not to mention sharing an impromptu meal or two.

"No one could imagine you compromised by visiting a nursery," he stated. "The three of you formed strong bonds during my betrothal to your sister. Florence and Valentine wait every day for your arrival, and they would be heartbroken never to see you again."

"My daughter is no nanny to your misbegotten wards," Sir William snarled. "Leonora never should have aired that crack-boned scheme to send Torie to the country to care for your children. Torie shall not enter your house again, now that you've chased off Leonora." His thick brows drew together. "Put my darling daughter off so much that she married a geriatric Scotsman!"

"I do not think of Miss Victoria as a nanny."

"You have used her as one," Sir William retorted. "No daughter of mine will dwindle into a spinster, caring for orphans." He turned to Torie. "Which reminds me that I accepted a proposal on your behalf last night at the club. Didn't have a chance to tell you."

Torie's mouth fell open. "You did? Without asking me?"

"No need for that, since it came from the Duke of Queensberry. No one refuses a duke. The ton will be 'Your Gracing' you within the month. I specified a short betrothal," Sir William said smugly, muttering, "Nanny my arse," as he knocked back a large swallow of brandy.

A feeling akin to panic shot through Dominic's body. He barely stopped himself from barking a refusal, though he had no right to do so. The Duke of Queensberry was a decent fellow but not right for Torie.

"He doesn't mind my illiteracy?" Torie asked.

Dominic *hated* the catch in her voice, the uncertainty.

He'd been taught that intelligence was evidenced by book-learning. Val needed to learn Greek in order to take his place in society. But Dominic was beginning to understand that Torie was an exception to the rule.

Sir William nodded. "Said you were the prettiest, silliest, most affected husband-hunting butterfly he'd ever met, and he couldn't wait to make you his duchess. Doesn't give a damn about whether you can read. In fact, he said that he'd prefer a wife who didn't neglect him for a novel, since I gather his sisters are avid readers. Haven't I told you that the right man would come along?"

Queensberry called Torie a "butterfly"? Not to mention silly and affected. Unfamiliar emotion was churning in Dominic's stomach. He felt ferociously protective, which made sense. They'd spent so much time together in the nursery that she was akin to a little sister.

"Best be off with you, Kelbourne," Torie's father said, moving behind his desk and sitting down. "We have a wedding to plan. Bit tricky, given the scandal that's about to break. I must let Queensberry know." He pulled a piece of stationery from a stack on top of his desk.

Dominic's pulse was pounding in his ears; he was caught in a maelstrom of fury, as fierce as he had ever felt in the House of Lords. He leaned over the desk. "What's the going price for a bride?"

CHAPTER 11

Torie was reeling from the news she was to be married to a man who had described her as silly and affected. The whole of it—Leonora's jilting and her own future—collided in her brain. She and the duke had shared a few suppers, but she hardly knew him. He seemed well enough, but in her current state, she couldn't bring his features to mind. Chestnut hair and a blunt nose . . . perhaps?

Lord Kelbourne's words filtered through her bewilderment.

"What is the viscount talking about?" she asked her father, swallowing convulsively. She might throw up on his desk, which was odd, since she also felt as hollow as a drum.

"He is talking nonsense. I've no need to sell my daughters," Sir William blustered. "You and Leonora are dazzling, dowered, and delightful in every way."

Torie's heart plummeted to her toes. She knew the sound of her father's lies all too well.

"To the contrary, you informed me that Leonora's dowry had been spent," Kelbourne snarled, moving closer to the desk.

Her lips rounded, and she whispered, "No dowry." Then, in a louder voice, "What happened to my dowry?"

"I suspect it was gambled away," Kelbourne said, his voice sounding like that of a judge instructing the jury to find a prisoner guilty. "Two years ago, Sir William requested ten thousand pounds for the privilege of marrying Leonora."

"Why shouldn't I have?" Torie's father asked pettishly. "I had the goods, and you wanted them."

"Do I have a dowry, Father?" Torie asked. And when her father looked down at his desk rather than meet her eyes, she asked again, her voice rising: "Do I still have a dowry?"

He shrugged. "You don't need one. The duke wants you with or without funds. He was most gracious about it." He picked up a quill as if the conversation was over. "I'll send His Grace a notice about Leonora's love match. Aye, that's how we'll present it." He threw the viscount a surly look. "There are those who will think she had a fine escape."

"I shall need the fortune I paid to marry Leonora repaid immediately," Kelbourne stated, rapping his knuckles on Sir William's desk.

Torie swallowed back a string of unladylike curses. Could this get any worse?

"I'll wager you didn't get nearly that amount from Queensberry," the viscount added. "His annual income is insufficient to put his hands on ten thousand pounds."

Sir William sniffed. "So he claimed."

Kelbourne leaned forward, looming over the desk. "Perhaps you didn't understand me, your lordship. I expect my money to be repaid immediately. You could take it from Bufford's payment, though he may have declined under the circumstances. In her haste to escape the horrifying prospect of raising my wards, Leonora likely begged him to take her."

"Papa, did you really take money from the viscount?" Torie could feel a scream rising in her chest.

"This subject is not for a lady's ears," Sir William chastised the viscount.

Kelbourne snorted. "I assure you that your youngest daughter has a remarkable tolerance for unladylike conversation."

Torie's father threw down his quill and slammed to his feet. "Just what do you mean by that? Have you debauched my innocent daughter by word or deed?"

"Absolutely not," the viscount responded dispassionately.

Disinterestedly.

Torie sighed. "I didn't faint when Florence broached the subject of flatulence."

"That's right, Leonora complained of that. Nervous farters, are they?" Sir William asked, sitting down again. "Likely too much milk. Hopefully they'll outgrow it. I'll bid you good day, Lord Kelbourne." He uncapped his ink bottle.

"Father, you must repay whatever money Viscount Kelbourne gave you," Torie insisted. She kept a hand on her stomach because her gut had clenched at the beginning of this nightmarish conversation, and it wasn't calming down.

"Can't," her father said, tapping surplus ink from his quill. "He's right about Bufford, and I've placed a few bad wagers lately. I'll pay when I'm back on my feet. It's the viscount's own damn fault for scaring off Leonora, forcing her to marry a man with a foot in the grave."

"I did nothing to scare her off."

"Oh? Because Leonora doesn't want you, Kelbourne. I argued with her, promising on your behalf that you'd banish the fiends to the country. She told me the thought of your wedding night made her want to vomit."

Dominic had never attempted to kiss his fiancée. Perhaps he should have.

He barely resisted the impulse to plant his fist on Sir William's chin. He had struggled with his temper as a boy, although these days he rarely lost control. Yet now he was vibrating with an inarticulate rage . . .

That had nothing to do with Leonora. He took a deep breath and realized it also had nothing to do with the ten thousand pounds.

It was about Miss Sutton . . . Victoria . . . *Torie*.

To be clear: his anger was the result of her father's careless treatment, casually betrothing her to a man who mocked her as foolish. The duke thought it was *better* that his wife couldn't read?

Torie touched his sleeve, and he glanced down at her. He knew precisely why Queensberry didn't care about his future duchess's literacy: he wanted a wife with soft white-blond curls, a delicious mouth, generous breasts . . . but more, a wife whose joy bubbled up in her eyes, no matter how often the world seemed to kick her in the arse.

From what he'd seen, Torie's own family had been so routinely unkind that she was surprised by decency.

Having been betrothed to her sister when they met, he had never allowed himself to consider Torie's appeal. He had deliberately ignored such shallow traits when looking for a wife. He'd even told himself that he didn't care if his fiancée was plain, as long as she had the attributes he considered essential to a partnership.

Staring down at Torie, he felt the long-nosed bluestocking of his imagination slipping away. "Leonora mentioned that requests for your hand in marriage had been withdrawn on being told of your illiteracy," he told her. "I think it more likely that the men in question couldn't pay your father the amount he demanded."

Her hand dropped from his sleeve, and she swiveled to face her father. The blustery defiance on Sir William's face spoke for itself. Torie's whole body flinched. She turned away and looked back up at Dominic.

"I am truly sorry about your ten thousand pounds, Lord Kelbourne. I will speak to the Duke of Queensberry. Leonora can speak to her husband, now that she is Lady Bufford."

"Aye, there's a plan," Sir William said, putting down his quill before he'd written a word and pouring another measure of brandy. "Bufford will be as dead as the Roman Empire in no time. You can have your ten thousand out of Leonora's widow's portion."

"No, I'll take your daughter instead," Dominic stated.

Torie gasped. "What?"

"Bufford ain't dead yet," Sir William snapped. "Even a viscount can't get around the law."

"Not Leonora," Dominic said, matter-of-factly. "I want Victoria in her stead."

Sir William laughed aloud. "My feckless illiterate? Even if I hadn't promised her to Queensberry, I'd judge you mad." The edge returned to his voice. "You'll get your reparations—the new Lady Bufford will use the wealth of her estate to see you made whole, and we can put this unpleasantness behind us."

"You can't promise that Leonora will repay that sum, Father," Torie said hollowly. "At least, not without speaking to her and her husband. Where are they now?"

"Bufford's estate in Scotland," her father said. "He's got a castle there or some such. He told me that they'll wait out the scandal and return to England in the fall."

"Bufford also has an heir who might decline to pay a widow's share to her father," Dominic pointed out. "Moreover, his lordship shows no sign of dying in the near future." He leaned a hip against the desk, arms folded over his chest. "We're at an impasse, Sir William. I want restitution—*now*." He glanced around the room. "You could sell these furnishings, but they can't be worth more than a hundred pounds."

"You wouldn't!" Torie cried.

"I would," Dominic replied. A feeling of satisfaction was tearing through him. Torie needed protection from her grasping, unkind father. He needed a mother for the twins. True, he had hoped to marry a woman who would challenge him intellectually, but he could reconcile himself.

Hell, he had all the challenging conversations he wanted in the House of Lords. For a moment, he pictured the despicable faces of the men opposing the current bill against slavery in the colonies. He didn't need a wife to point out their avaricious motives. He could do that himself.

"Both my father and I are sorry that Leonora impetuously broke your betrothal without having the courage to tell you herself," Torie said, her eyes shining with earnestness.

"Oh, aye," Sir William said. "I've always thought

Torie was the fool in this family, but it turns out that Leonora takes the crown. I flatly told Bufford that if his fourth wife dies before her time—that is to say, before *he* does—I'll be at his front door with a cocked pistol."

"Torie is not a fool," Dominic stated. "I'll take her in lieu of the debt you owe me, Sir William."

Torie was shaking her head. Dominic ignored it. She'd be under his protection, and anyone who spoke slightingly of his wife would answer to him.

Given his skill with a rapier, a single duel would ensure that no one ever, *ever* called his wife stupid. In fact, he'd probably challenge any man who mentioned Torie's inability to read.

Perhaps he'd challenge the Duke of Queensberry first, on general principles.

Unfortunately, he couldn't challenge Sir William, but he would make his opinion clear later, in private, when she wasn't within earshot. He didn't want her lummox of a father to ever hurt her feelings again.

"Torie, I told you once that you were a luxury commodity, and still you persistently undervalue yourself," he said. "You cannot marry a man who thinks you silly and speaks of you so disparagingly, even if he is a duke." He turned away from the desk. "So you might as well marry me."

"*You* think I'm silly," Torie retorted, her scowl deepening. "When I pointed out that Odysseus was a terrible leader because he lost so many men, you said that I didn't understand a Homeric hero's thirst for glory. Frankly, I thought you proved my point in labeling his motive, but you blathered on about courage and intellect."

Dominic raised an eyebrow. "You're refusing to

marry me based on an interpretative point in a Greek story? I didn't say *you* were silly, though I do think your argument is irrational."

"When I said that a man who sacrifices six men rather than risk a bad sea voyage is a rotten leader, you said that I had a schoolgirl's understanding of a great epic."

Dominic frowned. "I don't remember saying that."

"Torie remembers everything," Sir William commented. "Can quote me back chapter and verse on every Sunday sermon too, not that I'd ever ask her to. Frankly, I agree with her about the *Odyssey*. The man came far too close to allowing a woman to turn him into a pig."

He dipped his quill in the inkpot again. "I suppose that was a whatsit . . . a metaphor. In fact, I shouldn't be surprised if a witch turning men to swine isn't a metaphor for marriage," he mused. "Didn't understand that when I was a boy, of course."

The fool was ignoring Dominic's demand and scratching out a greeting to the Duke of Queensberry.

"Torie is often surprisingly astute," Sir William said chattily.

Dominic reached over and tweaked the quill from his future father-in-law's hand. Ink splattered across the desk. "I'll take Victoria in lieu of my ten thousand pounds."

"You just ruined a perfectly good piece of parchment," Sir William snarled. "Do you know what your trouble is? You're too used to having your own way. The money is lost. Accept it. If I have a string of good luck, I promise to think of you."

Torie cut in before Dominic could respond. "Lord Kelbourne, I will not marry you under any circumstances. As of last night, you were betrothed to marry my *sister*. And since both of my prospective husbands think I'm silly, obviously I'll choose a duke who has not already proposed to a family member!"

"The Duke of Queensberry is no great shakes himself in the intellect department," her father said encouragingly. "Your children might be a bit muddled, but one never knows. Perhaps the heir would be a throwback to some Oxford-educated chap. I never made it there myself," he said to the viscount.

"If Torie doesn't marry me, I shall sue you for breach of contract," Dominic stated, cutting to the chase.

"I don't want to be sold to Dominic or anyone else for ten thousand pounds!" Torie cried.

He saw her fingers trembling before she curled them into fists, which made him feel a flash of shame—but no. She needed him to save her.

"You're already calling him by his first name?" Sir William said. A calculating expression crossed his face. "Perhaps you should marry him, Torie. He's rich as bejesus. Since I don't have the ten thousand pounds, I'd take it as a courtesy."

"No, I am betrothed to a duke," Torie reminded him.

Dominic thought fleetingly of the hundreds of ladies who had made it clear by word, deed, and fluttering eyelashes that they would love to marry him. The desperation in Torie's voice wasn't very complimentary.

It stood to reason he'd decided to marry the one woman who didn't want him. His father had pointed out years ago that Dominic always chose the hardest route to success.

Sir William shrugged. "Marriage will cost you more than ten thousand pounds, Kelbourne. You'd have to match the duke's offer—nay, exceed it, because your title isn't as high or as old as his."

"I'm rich as bejesus, and that's more useful to you," Dominic reminded him.

"You would be paying exorbitantly for the nanny you want, but there's no accounting for taste. I will say that Leonora was far more likely to turn you into a pig. My youngest has a sweet nature."

"None of this matters since I refuse to marry my sister's leftovers . . . her *slops*!" Torie cried.

Not the most positive word she could have chosen. Pink had surged into her cheeks. Unlike her sister, she was not a woman who would ever be able to hide strong emotion. "Perhaps you could think of me as a legacy, a gift from Leonora," he suggested.

"You may not have noticed, but she and I are nothing alike," Torie retorted. "I have no interest in marrying a man who seems to have forgotten how to smile and is best known for shouting in the House of Lords." She folded her arms over her chest. "I won't do it."

"In that case, I shall remind you, Lord Kelbourne, that you cannot sue me for breach of contract, as we had none," Sir William said, rising to his feet. "I'll ask you to leave my house directly. You want a nanny? Hire a nanny. We will bid you good day." He bowed.

Sir William was right. Dominic's demand for repayment wouldn't hold up in court; it had been a gentleman's agreement.

Sir William was no gentleman.

From the corner of his eye, Dominic saw Torie curtsy, her mouth still pressed in a tight line. He bowed. "Good day, Sir William." He turned and bowed again. "Good day, Torie."

What neither of them understood was that when Dominic made up his mind . . . he made up his mind. The twins were *his*.

And Torie was *his*, even if he had to pay out another ten thousand pounds.

He wasn't certain where his conviction came from. Likely it was because she'd been so kind to the children. When he visited this morning, rather than writing about severed limbs, they were both painting misshapen rabbits.

Perhaps because she never bothered to flatter or agree with him. Leonora had agreed with any opinion he aired, which seemed peaceful at the time, but now . . .

Boring.

He had been introduced to Leonora; they had conversed; they had understood without words that they would marry. He couldn't even remember whether he actually proposed to her. Once he paid her father, the deed was done.

Now the exhilaration of a hunt sparked in his chest.

Torie didn't escort him from the study, so the last glimpse he had was of her mutinous scowl.

He found himself smiling as he let himself out the front door. There was no sign of the hungover butler, who was probably lying down with a wet cloth on his forehead.

Once home again, he bounded up the stairs. The twins were still painting. Valentine's rabbit had a grotesquely enlarged eye but was recognizable. Florence's was not.

"Did you see Torie?" his niece asked, whirling to face him. She had flecks of paint in her curls and a splash of pink on her chin.

"Yes. She won't be coming to visit today."

"You're smiling," Valentine observed in a surprised tone.

"Miss Sutton married another man this morning."

When the twins smiled back, Dominic discovered that Valentine had inherited the dimples he loathed. Or rather, the dimples his father had despised and mocked him for.

On Val, they were endearing.

"Now you're free to marry Torie!" Florence cried, clapping.

"I asked, but she turned me down," Dominic said.

Valentine frowned. "I thought that might happen."

Dominic raised an eyebrow. "You did?"

"She'd have to balance being our mother against becoming a viscountess," Valentine explained. "We never managed to enchant our own parents, let alone a fairly new acquaintance."

Florence came over and stood beside her brother. "I don't agree. If Torie won't marry you, it's not because she doesn't care for us, because she does. More than she cares for anyone. Her father isn't nice to her at all." Her chin jutted out, surprising Dominic with its resemblance to Torie's. "You'll have to try harder."

The twins fixed him with their pale green eyes. "Put your best foot forward," Valentine advised. "Flowers and such. It's a pity that codpieces are no longer in fashion."

Even given that the twins regularly surprised him, this comment was startling. "Add codpieces to the Prohibited List and never mention such articles of clothing before your sister," Dominic ordered.

"I already know what a codpiece is," Florence reported. "I do not think that an adornment of that nature would win Torie's approval. You have to be *nicer.*"

She put her hands on her narrow hips and fixed Dominic with a look verging on a glare. "You are not nice enough. I've seen you look at Torie in a haughty way, and doubtless she has noticed too. You look as if you're scowling even when you are just waiting for a cup of tea. You were rude when we discussed Odysseus."

"I could write you some poetry or a love letter," Valentine offered. "Torie gave me a rhyming dictionary."

"That is very kind of you, but I'm confident I can court Torie on my own." He hesitated, remembering the impassioned way she'd labeled him "slops," as in scraps thrown to pigs. "I will do my best. I know how much you love her, but unfortunately, she is being courted by a duke."

"That's a better title than viscount," Valentine said. He looked Dominic over. "It's a pity you're still in deep mourning. Black isn't very flattering, is it? Do you think if you stopped eating scones for tea, your legs would shrink?"

Dominic spared a moment to remember the life he had imagined, with a flatteringly adoring wife and children. "No," he admitted. "These are muscles, not fat."

"Our father wore horsehair pads on his thighs," Valentine told him. "At least you don't do that. Imagine if your wife caught you taking them off at night."

"Torie would be the very best mother for us," Florence said, palpable longing in her voice. "She *likes* us."

"Flattery is key to courtship," Valentine said.

"Remember when Homer said Circes was 'lustrous'? Actually, don't use that word until we have a chance to define it for Torie."

"She knows it already, because we read it aloud," Florence said scornfully. "Torie remembers *everything.*"

"Well, I suggest using a more approachable word, like *lily.* For example: 'Your skin is as white as a lily.'"

"And *you* are very silly," his sister retorted.

CHAPTER 12

In the following week, Dominic endured any number of impertinent inquiries about his emotional state in the aftermath of his fiancée's scandalous marriage to Lord Bufford. Infuriatingly, Sir William proved correct in that many interpreted her flight not as a love match, but as an escape from his foul temper.

Several guessed that the scandalous Dorney children had something to do with it, which resulted in gratuitous, unwelcome advice about how to stow embarrassing relatives out of sight.

Dominic gritted his teeth, indulged himself in a bout of scathing rhetoric in the House of Lords defending the antislavery bill, and sent Torie two bunches of flowers.

Both of which were returned by an unkempt footman wearing Sir William's livery, his coat visibly patched at one elbow.

Rather surprisingly, Torie's betrothal to the Duke of Queensberry hadn't yet been announced. Perhaps His Grace and Sir William hadn't agreed on an appropriate payment, or they were waiting for the scandal to die down.

Thinking to woo Torie, Dominic walked into Almack's and saw the Duke of Queensberry gazing at her with an absurdly infatuated smile. Simultaneously, he was assaulted by greetings from two marriageable ladies apparently ready to overlook his temper. He left immediately, realizing that he couldn't court Torie while society watched.

Not given his history with her sister. She was right about that.

He had to find a way to speak to her alone. His returned flowers suggested that she would flatly refuse a morning call. Besides, what if the Duke of Queensberry had arrived before him? The man who thought Torie the "silliest, most affected husband-hunting butterfly he'd ever met"? Also the "prettiest," but Dominic didn't like that, either. She wasn't pretty; she was beautiful. Far more so than her sister, given that Leonora was as thin as a stalk of celery.

It wouldn't help his courtship if he succumbed to irritation and dealt His Grace a blow to the jaw.

The next morning, when he strode into the nursery before leaving for the House of Lords, Florence danced up to him and said, "Valentine and I would like to go to this exhibition later today."

She handed him a notice cut from the *Times*.

> The Duke and Duchess of Huntington are honored to present the newest iteration of the highly original ducal steam-engine-powered locomotive, fitted with a new bent chimney designed by Her Grace. The public is welcome to examine the new clack box feed pipe and speak to the inventors. Those interested in steam power are particularly welcome. The locomotive will be available at Buckingham House on April 28 from 4 o'clock to 6 o'clock.

Her Grace? He knew about Huntington's obsession with steam, but his duchess designed a chimney?

"Of course you may attend," Dominic said, rather

grateful to discover they wanted to go to a wholesome event. So far, Valentine had asked to attend a lecture about Egyptian mortuary rituals, and Florence had wanted to visit a Hammersmith churchyard at midnight in hopes of seeing an infamous ghost. "You may inform your tutor that I approve."

"No, *you* should take us, because we believe Torie will attend," Florence said.

"Why would you think that?"

"She's interested in steam engines. She has a friend, Lord Lusker, who told her all about his investment in a Scottish locomotive. She says that someday they'll overtake carriages as a mode of transportation."

Dominic could imagine Lusker telling Torie "all" about steam engines. He'd seen the way she soaked up knowledge, her eyes shining at whomever was telling her about . . . anything, it seemed. In the last few months, she'd shown interest in every subject the twins brought up, including those on the Prohibited List.

It was only the work of the House of Lords that she dismissed as fiddle-faddle. Or was it bibble-babble?

Valentine wandered over and stood beside his sister, their shoulders brushing. "A duchess designed part of this steam engine, although generally ladies aren't allowed to invent anything. If Torie could read, she would make a better chimney than the duchess's."

"She could make one now if she wished," Florence said, scowling at her brother. "Don't make the mistake of thinking that book reading equates to intelligence, Val."

"I shall return at four o'clock," Dominic said,

escaping the nursery to the sound of inelegant whoops of joy.

Since it was a sunny day, he drove them in his low-slung, open curricle, the twins crowded on the seat beside him, excitedly pointing out an apple seller, St. Paul's Cathedral, and an elderly man whom Florence declared possessed by a devil based on his "pitch-black eyes."

Dominic added "possession" and "possession by a devil" to the Prohibited List.

"At this rate, we shall have nothing to talk about at all," Florence observed dolefully.

Which was precisely why Dominic had tried to find a wife with whom he could converse. Thankfully, they arrived at Buckingham House before he had to reveal the unfortunate truth that most conversations were as sweet and empty as spun sugar.

"We can always discuss steam engines!" Florence exclaimed as they turned from Marlborough Road into Pall Mall and saw an engine on a large cart, surrounded by people.

Dominic had the idea that decorous women like Leonora probably didn't celebrate the Duchess of Huntington's inventions, but steam engines were certainly better than codpieces. "You might begin a list of approved topics, to balance the other," he suggested.

"The locomotive is beautiful," Valentine observed, hanging over the side of the curricle to see better. The machine had a cherry-red cylinder for a body and a chimney that bent to the side, just as noted in the newspaper.

"What peculiar-looking wheels," Florence observed.

"Torie said they will run on steel rails, remember?"

her brother replied, leaning even farther as he craned to see underneath the locomotive. "Of course, it arrived here on a farm wagon, as London streets have no rails."

"Don't fall out," Dominic barked. His groom leaped from the stand behind the curricle and moved to the horses' heads.

"She's here!" Valentine crowed.

Dominic glanced over the crowd and immediately saw Torie. No one could miss her, since she was wearing a bright orange hat with a distinct resemblance to a steam pipe, along with a darker orange, extremely tight walking costume. Most of the men who'd come to see the locomotive were staring at her curves rather than the puffs of steam emerging from the engine.

Torie was listening intently to a stout, middle-aged woman with a monocle—likely the Duchess of Huntington, since the lady was gesturing toward the engine.

"Don't be rag-mannered when greeting Miss Sutton," Dominic told the twins.

"Don't you mean Miss Victoria?" Florence asked.

"As her older sister has married, she is now Miss Sutton."

"She's still Torie to us," Florence said with certitude. "Oh, now I see her!" She pointed in an extremely inelegant fashion and seconded it by giving her brother a shove. "Do get out, Val!"

Her brother pushed open the curricle door and jumped down. By the time Dominic came around to lift his niece from her seat, she had already plummeted to the ground and toppled forward to her knees. Florence popped back up, gave her dusty skirt a perfunctory brush, and dashed after her brother, who was weaving his way through the crowd.

Dominic strolled after them, consciously putting a sardonic twist on his mouth because otherwise he might grin in an entirely uncharacteristic fashion. Torie had made it clear that she didn't want his title or his temper.

What she didn't realize was how much he relished a challenge.

When he reached his niece and nephew, Torie was introducing the twins to the Duchess of Huntington. He made a mental note to congratulate their tutor; Valentine's bow was a thing of beauty, and Florence sank to just the right level for a duchess, undismayed by her dusty skirts.

Actually, she had probably forgotten the state of her dress.

"Ho, Kelbourne," the Duke of Huntington bellowed from where he was standing on the wagon, lecturing the crowd. His Grace refused to waste time in the House of Lords but had promised to appear on the day of the antislavery vote. Dominic had a whole list of lazy lords to whom he would send a summons on the morning the bill was—*finally*—forwarded for a vote.

"Good afternoon, Your Grace," he called. And turning: "Miss Sutton." Torie was hard to take in with one glance: her insouciant hat, her generous lips, her figure, enhanced by her exquisitely tailored costume.

He'd like to greet her with an open-mouthed kiss. Just looking at her made lust boil up in him.

Despite lecturing the twins on proper comportment, he didn't feel proper at all.

He had discounted the role of lust in his marital plans, never expecting to feel it for his wife. No longer. Not when he could barely take his eyes off Torie's mouth. He felt like an adolescent trying to quell a throbbing groin.

"We asked Lord Kelbourne to bring us," Florence said to Torie, beaming as she hung on to her hand.

A reluctant smile tugged at the side of Torie's mouth. "I understand. Your Grace, may I introduce Viscount Kelbourne?"

The Duchess of Huntington picked up the monocle pinned to her chest by a ribbon, screwed it in place, and said, "Kelbourne, is it? The unconscionable delay in passing the slavery bill reflects our country's debased values."

"I agree," Dominic said, rather taken aback by the way her monocled eye appeared twice as large as the other.

"Please, let's go look at the engine," Florence cried.

"I have a girl just your age whom I've been trying to interest in locomotives to no avail," Her Grace commented. "My son, Silvester, is even worse and pretends they don't exist."

A crafty smile spread over Florence's face. "I would be so grateful if *you* showed me the engine," she cooed. "Showed me and my brother, I mean." Valentine was watching starlings circle overhead. She kicked him in the ankle.

"As would I, Your Grace," Valentine said, bowing.

"Our guardian, Lord Kelbourne, will entertain Miss Sutton," Florence announced.

The duchess was likely startled to find herself walking away with two children, but Florence had a way of presenting her wishes in a manner that stifled protest. Dominic regularly found himself doing things he wouldn't have imagined only months earlier, such as courting a woman who couldn't read and scowling at men oozing desire for her—at least, until he terrified them by putting a hand on his rapier.

The public had been corralled behind a rope, but Her Grace pulled it back and ushered the children through to greet her husband.

"I hope she keeps Florence's skirts away from the coal box," Torie said. She dropped a curtsy. "Lord Kelbourne. It's a pleasure to see the children outside the nursery."

He removed his hat and bowed. "Miss Sutton." The crowd eddied about them, pushing them so close that he could see the raspberry sheen on her lower lip and the black color she'd smudged in a narrow line under her eyelashes. Since he'd warned off lecherous louts, no one was paying them any attention.

"Have you rethought your rejection of my proposal?" Not that he actually had hope, but it was worth a try.

Torie shook her head.

She was trying to work out why the twins had forced Dominic to attend the demonstration. In Torie's opinion, Florence would only be interested in a locomotive if she added a ghost, turned it into a haunted steam engine, and described it running amok and killing any number of innocent bystanders. Valentine was gazing blankly at the machine, either making up an overwrought sonnet or doing mathematical figures.

Which meant the twins were forcing Dominic to renew his lukewarm proposal.

She summoned up a sympathetic but firm smile. "While I cannot marry you, Lord Kelbourne, I do promise to keep close contact with Florence and Valentine."

"Dominic," he corrected her. "Or even Dom, if you please. No one is listening to us. Is betrothal to the Duke of Queensberry standing in your way?" His tone was amiably polite, as if he were offering her a choice between a scone and a lemon tart.

"No, I am refusing you on your own merits," Torie said, succumbing to irritation. Even a woman being proposed to as payment for ten thousand pounds would prefer her wooer didn't appear so nonchalant. "Frankly, I don't understand why you persist in your proposal, given your freely expressed horror after I offered to care for your wards in the country."

"You offered to 'take' them, but they're *my* children," the viscount replied, his eyes sharpening. "No one can take the twins from me." He took a step closer, but Torie stood her ground. She couldn't think clearly when he crowded her, but she knew instinctively that she couldn't quail at all this . . . this maleness.

Standing right in front of her. Throwing himself about and making irrational decisions based on irrationality, looking as bullheaded as an ancient Greek soldier.

His appearance at this event meant that his proposal had nothing to do with the money her father demanded. It was all about Valentine and Florence, who surely missed her. Likely he missed her too, given that in the last few months she had arranged decent menus for the children, ordered new clothing, taught them to paint, and more.

"I can help you find a good nanny," Torie offered. "Once I'm a duchess, I will spend every morning with the twins again. I miss them horribly." Relief spread through her as she realized the implications of marriage to Queensberry. A married woman—a duchess!—could certainly remain in contact with orphaned children, even treat them as if they were her own young relatives.

Dominic was staring at her with more attention than he had ever paid her, except perhaps that time when she beat him playing Riddles. He wasn't used to losing and had started glaring at her with hawk eyes.

"Even a duchess cannot visit the house of an unmarried man without causing a scandal," he said. "Given my sister's affairs, I am well aware that gossips eagerly condemn married as well as unmarried women." The biting note in his voice spoke for itself.

"I shan't mind a few dents to my reputation," Torie assured him. "When I am a married woman, no one could claim I was compromised and force us to marry. Don't you see that it solves our problem, Dominic?" She curled her hand around his forearm, feeling his muscles flex with a little thrill.

His brows drew together, and she dropped her hand.

"Duchesses appear in the gossip columns no matter what they do," she insisted, falling back a step. "That's why Leonora decided to become a viscountess." She snapped her mouth shut.

Too late.

"'Leonora decided to become a viscountess,'" Dominic echoed, his eyes cooling. "She *decided*?"

"Well, yes," Torie admitted. "In the nursery. My point is that duchesses are always chattered about, so I shall have to reconcile myself to being the subject of gossip." A happy thought occurred to her. "I can also help you find a new fiancée! I will be in an excellent position to survey the available ladies and find one who will understand Val and Florence."

Not that she'd met such a woman yet, but there was always next Season.

"Let's go back to your sister. How old was she when she decided to become a viscountess?" Dominic asked.

"That's no longer relevant," Torie replied. "In the end, Leonora chose a lord over a viscount. Her marriage to Lord Bufford must be true love."

"I doubt that."

"Well, you would doubt it, wouldn't you?" Torie asked. In her experience, men rarely accepted logical conclusions. "What other explanation is there? Don't bring up the twins, because Leonora could have forced you to put the children in school."

"She never wanted to marry me, just the title," Kelbourne said, acting as if he'd received a blow to the gut.

Torie sighed. "Surely this isn't the first time you noticed the appeal of your title?" Then she felt a twinge of guilt. "Or were you in love with her?"

He shot her an incredulous glance. "I chose your sister carefully."

"A face that inspired poetry, together with the promise of ladylike docility. You weren't the only man to fall for it," Torie said. "You don't seem to have given any thought to the attributes *she* might have been looking for in a spouse."

"The title of viscount," he snarled, all too obviously wallowing in a feeling of injustice.

"True, you were lucky that Viscount Cornwell married the year before," Torie said. "Leonora would have chosen him over you." She was starting to enjoy the conversation. "Because of the attributes she would have preferred in a husband, given the chance. The ones you never considered."

"Which are?"

"Golden locks and slender limbs."

Dominic's mouth curled with distaste. "She wanted a man who would 'caper nimbly in his lady's chamber to the lascivious pleasing of a lute'?"

She looked him over slowly, registering not for the first time that *her* list of attributes would include burly thighs and intense eyes. "You're no Richard III, so Shakespeare's next line is entirely inappropriate." Heat came up in her cheeks; a lady shouldn't mention bawdy innuendos, but her dratted memory had served up the speech in its entirety.

"Being 'shaped for sportive tricks'?" Dominic's slow smile was a triumph of sensuality. "I may not be good at capering, but I'm dead certain that I can manage 'sportive tricks.'"

"Your future wife will be happy to know it," Torie managed. "Can we please return to the subject of this conversation? We are planning how I, as Duchess of Queensberry, will help you raise the twins. For example, I would be very happy to chaperone Florence's debut, if you haven't married by then."

"I would prefer that you chaperone my daughter as her mother," Dominic said, one side of his mouth quirking into a smile. His eyes glittered at her from under heavy lids.

Torie decided to ignore that stubborn comment—*and* the smile. Though she was amazed at how the expression changed his face. One might think that such a bold profile would be feminized by dimples, but Torie found the opposite: they made her imagine that he might smile, even laugh—in bed.

"By the time Val and Florence are sixteen," she said quickly, "the twins will have perfected the arts of enchantment. Further, as a ranking duchess, I will be able to secure their invitations to all of the Season's premier events. They will rule polite society. I am certain of it."

After a pause, Dominic conceded. "You are right."

Torie drew a breath of red-hot air into her lungs. Of course she was happy that he had reconciled himself to the inadvisability of marrying her. She would never suit him. Even this . . . this *tension* between them was evidence of that.

She couldn't be this close to him without catching a whiff of bergamot and clean man that made her body prickle awake. Leonora would have been horrified by the sensation, whereas Torie felt yearning surge inside her. She and her sister were as different as chalk and cheese—yet Leonora was the kind of woman whom Dominic wanted to marry.

He could find another bride who was both ladylike and tolerant of his condescending manner. And of the twins.

And of his thighs.

"There's Florence now!" Torie said brightly, shoving away her irrational feeling that a woman who married him for his title wouldn't make a good wife: a category that included her own sister.

Apparently, Valentine had been converted to steam engines, because Florence grabbed Torie's hand and said, "You must come and extract Val. He just offered to help His Grace with some calculations. He's forgotten that he's only eleven!" The duke had hoisted Valentine up onto the farm wagon beside him and was talking energetically.

Dominic watched as Torie turned her back and walked away with Florence. Perhaps he shouldn't have made that jest about being shaped for sport.

But she brought up the Shakespeare line; he didn't. She had never seemed prudish before, but suddenly her cheeks had gone red, and she'd thrown him an irritated glance. He'd blundered.

Or had he?

He could swear there was desire in her eyes when she looked him over. Leonora might have wished for a husband with slender limbs—which was true of Bufford if you overlooked his barrel-shaped middle—but Torie didn't. She liked the muscular shape of his legs.

A cautious optimism filtered through him. He could use that to his advantage. No bride *wanted* to vomit on her wedding night.

The Duchess of Huntington had escorted Florence to Torie's side, but rather than return to the locomotive, she nodded. "Odd children you have. I like them."

"So do I," Dominic said.

"Someone told me a few years ago that you were betrothed, but Florence says she hopes you marry Miss Sutton."

"My former fiancée chose someone else. After she fell in love," Dominic added, disliking the duchess's shrewd gaze. Like everyone else, Her Grace probably thought that the jilting was the fault of his temper.

"In my day, happiness in marriage was a matter of chance," Her Grace observed. "I got to know my husband in the carriage after our marriage ceremony."

She couldn't possibly mean what he thought she meant.

The glint in her eye suggested that was *precisely* what she meant.

"I expect marriage is always a gamble," Dominic said cautiously.

"Domestic fetters are hard for a woman to accept," the duchess told him. "You could do worse than Miss Sutton."

"Thank you for the advice."

"I suppose you want to be worshipped? Revered? Treated as a mystical being? I doubt she'll do that. She's not the type."

"I have no such expectations," Dominic said, starting to feel distinctly nettled.

The duchess picked up her monocle again and gave him a long stare. "I suspect you chose your previous fiancée based on some fool notion of a good wife."

He managed not to flinch.

"Tried to find a woman with ladylike skills," she chortled, pleased with herself. "The ability to stitch a sampler and paint a watery landscape doesn't help a marriage thrive."

"Not everyone can design a chimney," Dominic said, dimly feeling he should defend Torie. "Miss Sutton is an excellent painter who works in oils rather than watercolors."

"Good," Her Grace said, distracted by the new subject. "I shall commission her to paint the steam engine. It's our fourth iteration, and only oils can do justice to its red hue."

"I think she mostly paints flowers, not engines," Dominic said.

The duchess's preferred mode of communication

seemed to be a snort. "Because the woman's never been allowed to paint anything else." *You dunce* hung in the air, unspoken. "I don't suppose you've escaped the House of Lords long enough to attend one of the Royal Academy's exhibitions?"

"I have not," Dominic replied.

"Still life is the lowest genre," she told him. "Biblical paintings are highest, because men love to spy on Bathsheba unclothed, or depict Judith serving up Holofernes's head on a platter. After that comes mythological, portraiture, landscape, animal paintings . . . with still life at the very bottom of the list. So, what are women allowed to paint? Anything that doesn't move!" She snorted again. Loudly.

"Torie also paints rabbits," Dominic said.

"If you manage to persuade her to marry you, get her a tutor, for God's sake. We're taking a trip to Venice, and I'd like to give a painting of the locomotive to my husband on our return."

"I shall do my best to convince Miss Sutton to become my viscountess," Dominic said, accepting the duchess's point about a tutor. Certainly Sir William wouldn't have bothered to pay for one.

"I have faith in you, viscount. I'll wait a year or so and commission it then."

"Miss Sutton, whether or not she becomes my wife, will paint only what she wishes," Dominic said with frosty emphasis. "She has no need to take a commission."

Her Grace's lips parted, and he braced himself for a ducal setdown. Instead, she bellowed with laughter, her monocle spinning at the end of her ribbon as her bosom heaved.

He caught a whiff of Torie's honeysuckle scent

and turned just as she arrived at his side, Florence in tow. "I had no idea you could be so entertaining, Lord Kelbourne," she murmured.

"I have moments," Dominic said. Sunlight turned her curls to beaten silver. "You'd have to marry me to benefit from them." He leaned over and muttered, "And my sportive tricks."

Torie rolled her eyes at him.

"I should like you to pay me a visit in the country," the Duchess of Huntington said to Torie. "You could bring your easel and paint some roses, though I admit that the flowerbeds at Huntington Grange have run to weed."

"Dandelions?" Florence asked with interest. "Do you know what a dandelion is?"

"A weed of some sort," the duchess replied.

"No, a dandy-lion is a big cat wearing a dapper hat!"

Torie broke out laughing.

"I miss that," Florence said, slipping her hand into Dominic's.

He looked down, eyebrow raised.

"Her laugh. Torie laughs better than anyone in the world."

CHAPTER 13

The next morning, Dominic made up his mind to pay Torie a call, no matter what Sir William thought of it. Besides, he had a shrewd feeling that his lordship rarely emerged from his darkened bedchamber before afternoon.

He had to bang the knocker several times before the butler appeared, looking as if he'd slept in his slovenly attire.

"I wish to pay a call on Miss Sutton."

"She isn't taking callers," the man said, pushing the door closed with one hand as he straightened his toppling wig with the other. "She's busy."

Dominic shouldered past and walked through a beery cloud wafting from the butler into the entry. "Is she in her studio?"

"Aye, but she's not chaperoned—"

Dominic cut him off. "Show me to her studio, if you please."

The butler thought about that for a while, brow furrowed, before he began trudging up the stairs. Dominic followed him, thinking that even if he wasn't set on marrying Torie, he'd want her out of this ill-regulated household.

Was it possible to feel well-intentioned concern—and raging desire?

The butler rapped on a door and then stood aside to let Dominic enter the room before backing out without a word. The man was remarkably thoughtless. What if Dominic had designs on her virtue?

Which he did.

Torie was standing before an easel positioned

in such a way that morning light poured over her shoulder, illuminating a vase of big, fluffy flowers. She wore a simple cotton gown, covered by a canvas pinafore smeared with every paint color imaginable. Her hair was caught up in a chignon, curls escaping to frame her face.

She was exquisite, even when scowling at her easel.

"Good morning, Torie," he called, realizing she hadn't heard the door open.

She glanced over and groaned. "Go away, Dominic. I don't want to marry you."

"But I want to marry you," he argued. He walked forward so he could see her painting, instantly grateful that the Duchess of Huntington had decided not to commission a painting for at least a year, after Torie had some tutoring.

The cut flowers were fresh and colorful, but Torie's depiction was muted and not nearly as pretty. In her depiction, the vase sat on a checkerboard table that was slightly distorted, as if she had problems with perspective.

He cleared his throat, trying to think of what to say. He wasn't a man who attended art exhibitions, but anyone could see that Torie could benefit from a tutor.

She stuck her brush into a can of solvent and pulled off her pinafore, dropping it on a paint-splattered stool.

"Your flower painting is very nice," he commented. That didn't sound praiseful enough. He noticed the three fallen petals, each curled in different directions, so he added, "Meticulous and graceful."

She had been moving toward a group of chairs

on the other side of the room; her shoulders froze, and then she kept walking, throwing an amused comment over her shoulder. "I am confident of my ability to paint flowers, Dominic. You needn't strain your vocabulary."

Feeling a flash of remorse—but honestly, what *could* one say about wilting flowers?—Dominic seated himself opposite her.

"I don't understand your persistence," Torie said, without preamble. "Can you ill afford to lose ten thousand pounds? Marrying me won't bring back the money. Even if my first action as your wife—which I will never be—was to fire Nanny Bracknell, you wouldn't save much."

He shook his head. "That's not a problem. Your father would like to screw me out of another fifteen, which I can afford, if need be."

Torie bit her lip.

Dominic was wearing his most autocratic expression, the one with which he likely bullied members of the House of Lords into doing his bidding.

Obviously, Florence and Valentine were still pushing him to propose. She was touched, not just by the fact that the twins cared for her, but that he cared for them enough to make repeated attempts after being rebuffed. She couldn't imagine he'd ever had to implore a woman to pay him attention.

Just now he was giving her that intensely observant look again. As if he were truly interested in her thoughts. As if she were the only woman in the world.

She probably found it so seductive because no man had looked at her that way before.

But she did not want to marry her sister's fiancée out of fondness for two children, finding herself relegated to a nanny and tied to an irascible peer who thought a painting that had taken her months was "nice."

"I do feel guilty about my father's demand," she said, clearing her throat. "Perhaps if I weren't so extravagant, Sir William wouldn't have exacted money for Leonora's betrothal. I have a weakness for colored silk, in particular, and it's horrendously expensive."

Dominic shook his head. "If you'll forgive my bluntness, your father is a rogue, not to mention an inveterate gamester."

"Be that as it may, I still refuse your proposal," Torie said, trying to ignore the fact that her heart seemed to have migrated into her throat and was threatening to suffocate her. She couldn't imagine how his opponents in the House of Lords withstood his demands. Against all her best instincts, some errant part of her wanted to throw herself into his arms and breathe "yes" in his ear.

"Why?" Those blue-gray eyes were known for terrifying opponents during debates. Just at the moment, they weren't fierce as much as—as confused. "True, Queensberry has a higher title, but I have Valentine and Florence, and surely you agree that the twins trump any benefit that a higher title might bring."

Torie swallowed convulsively. "Because you were going to marry my sister! You were betrothed to Leonora for over two years. Can't you see how humiliating it would be for me to marry you?"

"No," he said, uncompromisingly. "I feel I am an excellent marriage prospect."

"I promise to remain friends with the twins," she offered.

"Only my wife can see Valentine and Florence both morning and night," he replied, a distinctly calculating tone to his voice. "Only my wife can be there if they fall ill, or . . . or begin missing their dead parents. Grieving for them."

He caught her expression. "Fine, the last is unlikely. I need a wife who will love the twins and help me talk Val into going to Eton, rather than banishing them to the country."

She felt as if her heart was being torn in two. "I wouldn't do that unless Eton opens its doors to girls. I do love them. You know that."

"I do."

"However, I think of you as my brother-in-law. Can you imagine the gossip if I married my sister's fiancé?"

He shrugged. "Who cares what people think?"

That was easy for him to say. The viscount reportedly shouted at anyone who dared disagree with him. Shaming remarks would follow her around a room, and she couldn't bully the gossipers into silence.

It was one thing if a duke was infatuated enough to overlook her deficiencies. People seemed to find it particularly romantic that Queensberry proposed despite her addled brains.

It was quite another if she ended up married to her sister's jilted fiancé. The duke looked at her with adoration, the viscount with calculating interest.

Everyone would be certain that Torie had been forced to accept him. That money had been involved somehow. And they would talk . . . oh, how they would talk. Most of the shame would fall on her, but people would mock him as well.

"I care," she told him, embarrassed to be revealing the truth, because generally she pretended to blithely ignore insulting chatter. "Leonora loathes gossip, but I think I hate it even more. People have always chattered about her because she's beautiful and intelligent. That has not been my experience."

"No one will say disparaging things about my wife." Dominic folded his arms, looking for all the world as if he could stop the tide from coming in to shore.

"In case you're hoping, you will not be able to teach me to read. It won't work. I cannot read. I will never be able to read."

"I understand."

"No, you don't," Torie said. "It's not merely the question of accepting me as a substitute for my more desirable sister. They'll mock you for marrying me. If we ever have children, they'll be judged witless before they speak their first word. What's more, I can't cipher, so you'd have to hire someone to keep the household accounts."

"My steward keeps them now, and he can continue. You're overlooking a key point."

She frowned at him. "Which is?"

"Your family should have been defending you. Instead, they left you to face society alone. In fact, they *joined* in the mockery. That will not continue when you are my wife."

Torie couldn't hide her curiosity. "Just how would you hope to suppress belittling on the part of non-family members?"

"Do you see this rapier?"

Since he was still in deep mourning, Dominic was clothed in black; his black sheath lay almost invisibly against his leg. When he drew out the blade, it wasn't a gleaming silver color, but black as midnight.

"Is that a *mourning* rapier?" Torie asked, rather fascinated.

"Dull black for the first stage of mourning. I have five rapiers for the various stages."

"You must be joking."

"I never joke about rapiers."

"Leonora said—"

"She thought I should give up the practice as it was causing my muscles to be 'gracelessly bloated,'" he said dryly. "A direct quote. Added to your revelation about admiration for golden lads with slender thighs, my deplorable physique presumably led to her hysteria regarding our wedding night."

"My sister can be very blunt at times," Torie murmured. "Are you proposing to slash your way through polite society in defense of my wits?"

"I won't stand for anyone hurting my wife's feelings," Dominic said, sliding the blade back into its holster. "A duel or two will solve that problem. I won't fight to wound but to make myself clear."

He was mistaken—such a duel would cause gossip to flourish—but Torie rather liked the idea of someone offering to defend her. She habitually fended off mockery through charm, humor, and self-deprecation, but the experience was never pleasant. She'd rather not label herself silly and frivolous.

"You will marry me because you love Valentine and Florence." There was a surprisingly warm glint in Dominic's eyes, given that he usually looked as chilly as the north wind.

Torie shook her head, somewhat regretfully. "As I

said, I do love them, but I cannot give up my life for them. You want a nanny, not a bride."

"We can have our own children, and by then the twins will be yours too." He hesitated. "Though I do intend to send them to school."

"I have different ideas about how to raise Valentine and Florence. My ideas do not involve Eton, Latin, Greek, astronomy, or ciphering half the day, as they are doing now."

He frowned. "They need to be stimulated. They are brilliant."

"And quite bizarre," she pointed out. "I know something about being strange in the midst of polite society. It is *not* a pleasant feeling."

Dominic's eyes softened. "I'm sorry. But taking away their books won't make them any less intelligent."

Torie suppressed a snappy observation about the fact that her intelligence was constantly in question merely because she had no book-learning. "They are suffering from lack of attention. You should eat with them every single day."

"In the nursery?" He seemed dumbfounded.

Torie belatedly realized that she did sound like a nanny. She shook her head. "Becoming a nanny would be so belittling, don't you see? As if I was inadequate to be someone's wife. As a duchess, I'll know my husband prized *me*, not my child-raising skills."

"You wouldn't be a nanny," he said stubbornly. "You'd be a viscountess."

"You wish to marry me for one reason. No, for ten thousand *and* one reasons, but mostly for one. The duke will marry me because he's infatuated, and everyone knows it. That's an emotion celebrated by society." She took another deep breath, because she still felt as if the room was short of air.

Rather than accept her logic, Dominic started smiling in the brash manner of men who think they know better. "You're leaving something out of the calculation."

"What?"

"Let's do a test." He moved and sat down beside her. "A scientific test. Val would approve."

Torie scowled at him. "I have no idea what you are talking about."

"I never kissed your sister. Had I tried, I would have uncovered her inclination to vomit while contemplating intimacies with me. She wouldn't have fled to the dubious protection of Lord Bufford, because we would have mutually agreed to end the betrothal."

Dominic wasn't the first man to suggest that kissing was a way to prove or disprove compatibility. Torie had always refused on principle. And because she had a horror of bad breath.

Yet she could smell faint peppermint on Dominic's breath, which suggested he used Dr. Peabody's Solution to cleanse his teeth, just as she did. She felt a little dizzy, so perhaps all the close attention he was giving her had gone to her head. Just now, his eyes were smoldering, but not with irritation, as when she won at Riddles.

Lust, she registered. It wasn't her first experience with male lust, but the first that her body had acknowledged. Her breathing sped up again, and a wave of heat swept down her legs.

"Kissing won't change my mind," she said, trying to stick to the main point. "I would still be a gossiped-about nanny."

He frowned. "What role do you envision playing in your husband's life?"

"I'm holding out for a love match."

"Although you'll drop that ambition for the title of duchess?" he said with an edge.

"Queensberry adores me, and love will come in time," she said equally sharply. "The bride you want doesn't resemble me." She cleared her throat. "To put it a different way, you are planning to fight duels with your oh-so-black rapier because you are protective of your family, not because you think society's assessment of me is incorrect."

"I shall always be protective of my wife. You may be unable to read, but I see no reason why that fact should be repeated within my or anyone else's earshot."

Torie drank in the intensity of his gaze, reminding herself that her response was a reaction to novelty. Her head was spinning because Dominic looked interested in her, in her opinions and desires. It was unsettling.

Well, that and his sheer physical beauty.

But this was her future they were discussing. Her happiness. Her whole life from now on. "What were you looking for in a bride?" she asked, taking another deep breath.

She followed his gaze to her breasts. Thankfully, her morning gown had a sensible bodice, but he made his point. Apparently, her bosom qualified for spousal status. Right now, he needed help with the twins, and he liked her appearance, but what would happen in a few years?

Her deficits would sink in.

"You said that my sister fulfilled your every requirement for a wife," she prompted.

His eyes were suddenly wary. "Yes."

"Do I have *any* of the attributes you were looking for?"

She had learned a great deal about Viscount Kelbourne in the last months. He didn't lie. He was brusque, impolite at times, but never false.

"No," he said with obvious reluctance. "You do not." He stood up and brought her with him. "My idea was misguided. It didn't include *this*."

"What?"

"Your appreciation of my shape, as Shakespeare had it," Dominic said, his voice lowering to a rasp. "My body and the way it's 'shaped for sportive tricks.'"

Torie scowled at him. "Perhaps I too like golden-haired men."

He shrugged. "I can wash my hair in lemons."

She managed a wry smile, eyeing his black-as-midnight hair. "My point still stands. You've only changed your mind about what you want in a wife because of the twins. In the long run, you would do far better to marry someone who is your ideal. The twins will grow up and leave, and you'll be stuck with me." She hesitated. "I really can't bear being a disappointment again. For the rest of my life, in the case of marriage."

CHAPTER 14

$\mathcal{D}$ominic never liked those moments in the House of Lords when an opponent brought up a good point. In a perfect world, his would be the only valid arguments, and compromise would mean that he had squashed the opposition. In other words, they would agree to his logic, and he would generously concede something to assuage their loss.

Very occasionally, he was wrong.

"Stop standing so close to me," Torie demanded. She put both hands on his chest and gave him a little push. "We have no need for a 'test.' I understand that you and I—"

Her voice broke off.

"You and I *what*?" he asked with interest.

Torie cleared her throat. "I wouldn't vomit on our wedding night. Probably."

Dominic had never stolen a kiss. In fact, he'd never contemplated such a breach of etiquette. When an unmarried lady tilted toward him with pursed lips, he looked around for the chaperone sure to erupt from a corner and scream about a compromised reputation. When married ladies did the same, he backed away, having an innate distaste for adultery, compounded over the years by his sister's blithe disregard for marital vows.

He would have expected to enter Leonora's darkened bedchamber on their wedding night, introduce her to marital intimacy, and hopefully leave before she lost her supper. Not that they had discussed it; he'd never bothered to imagine her response or lack thereof.

As he saw it, Torie's promise not to vomit on their wedding night was practically an invitation.

He leaned in, quick as lightning, and brushed his lips over hers. How did he catch an impression of tart sweetness in a mere second? He *felt* the shock of that kiss. He went rock-hard, and his heart started up a wild drumbeat.

Torie shook her head. "What on earth are you doing?" she inquired. "You can't run around kissing random women to make up for your mistakes with Leonora."

"You are not random. You're the woman I wish to marry."

She sighed. "Look, if I put my mind to it, I can find you a bride within the month. Tell me the attributes you're looking for, other than beauty and ostensible docility."

Dominic swallowed back his frustration. "It wasn't a list of attributes as much as a wish. Or two."

"Such as?" Torie demanded, folding her arms over her chest, which plumped her breasts in an extremely desirable fashion. "I know I don't meet your standards, but I always hope to learn from my failures."

"It wasn't a matter of success or failure!" he protested.

His conscience prickled to life. Was that the case? Didn't he separate the wheat from the chaff by questions aimed at discovering whether he and the lady in question would be suitable for each other? Able to successfully converse over the breakfast table?

"I hoped that my future wife and I would have something to talk about in a few years," he explained. "So many couples sit silently together, even after they've watched a play. It looks depressing."

It looked, though he would never say so, like his parents' marriage. Chilly silences had been the norm.

"I'll give you that," Torie said. "So ask me one of the questions with which you tested my sister for compatibility. Just so I understand," she added.

"Did you see Molière's *Tartuffe*?"

"The French play? Of course I did. Along with most of London, since it was the hit of the Season."

The way her mouth turned down at the edges suggested she shared Leonora's opinion of the performance.

"What did you think of it?" he asked.

She burst into laughter. "You chose your wife based on literary criticism? Leonora's response to a revived French play?" Her eyes lit up. "You must have agreed with her. Which explains precisely why we would never get along, given our disagreements over the *Odyssey*."

"I didn't look for agreement."

Torie nodded. "I think you missed the mark with Leonora. I don't suppose you noticed her avoidance of idle chatter?"

"Too late," Dominic admitted. He hadn't let himself dwell on it, but he had been disconcerted by the way he and his fiancée would stand silently together, gazing over a ballroom of babbling guests. Still, she readily offered intelligent opinions if asked a direct question, and a gentleman never reconsidered a proposal of marriage once a lady had accepted it.

"My sister likely proved her intelligence by offering a sanguine comparison of the performance and original script. I'm sure she had read the play in French. She adores the language."

Any defense would be foolish, so he held his tongue.

"Unsurprisingly, I haven't read *Tartuffe*. But I'll tell you what I enjoyed about the performance," Torie said, her eyes mocking him. "I liked the young fellow playing Damis, especially the scene after he was disinherited, when his shirt ripped in two. I considered that an excellent directorial choice. My friend Clara sat through the play three times merely to watch Mylchreest prance across the stage half-naked."

"Mylchreest? Who's that?"

"The actor playing Damis."

"I see," Dominic said. If he recalled that scene correctly, Mylchreest's physique had more in common with his own than that of the Duke of Queensberry, who was on the weedy side. His Grace wore narrow-cut coats with embroidered trim and considered his rapier an embellishment rather than a weapon.

No one would buy tickets to see the duke half-naked.

"I'm sure my sister offered intellectual commentary," Torie prompted.

"Miss Sutton thought the translator should have retained Molière's twelve-syllable line," Dominic confirmed. "She found the performance unconscionably lewd."

"Whereas I enjoyed the half-naked actor. The difference between myself and my sister in a nutshell." Torie stood and went to pick up her pinafore before hanging it on a hook next to the window. "I think we've been unchaperoned for long enough. I should probably locate my father and make sure he eats something before his morning brandy."

Dominic didn't like her dry tone. Or the fact her

father was a drunk. Or . . . or anything about her circumstances.

"What of you?" he asked. "What are you looking for in a husband?"

She turned around, mischief sparking in her eyes. "Could I choose the actor? Just think of the fascinating questions we could have over breakfast about the intricacies of French medieval drama! I can scarcely imagine the pleasure."

"I was a fool," Dominic conceded.

"Yes, you were. Still, you knew what you wanted: a sweet, gentle maiden who was your intellectual equal. I couldn't read *Tartuffe,* so I know nothing about its syllables. I didn't agree with Leonora's stance that the plot was immoral. I thought the half-naked man strutting across the stage was delightful. In short, I don't fit any of your parameters."

He opened his mouth, but Torie held up her hand. "Don't lower your standards, Lord Kelbourne. The difference between you and my other suitor is that the Duke of Queensberry has only one. He cheerfully informed me last night that what he wants from his marriage is a bedfellow able to take a joke."

Rage consumed Dominic like a bonfire. "'Able to take a joke' about your illiteracy, you mean?" His hand went naturally to the handle of his rapier before he stopped himself. He could deal with Queensberry later.

"No. The duke is a kind man. He will never mock me. He merely recognizes that marriage is more successful if both people have a sense of humor."

The implicit reproach spoke for itself. Dominic had no way to defend himself. He didn't grow up in a household that prized cheerfulness. His father's taunts about his dimples had eradicated any impulses Dominic might have had to smile, let alone laugh.

Torie bit her lip. "I'm sorry, but I can't let you think that my refusal is a matter of not loving Florence and Valentine enough. I am attracted to you, but I too have ideas about my spouse."

"You want him to be able to jest," Dominic said flatly.

"And *have fun*, simply put."

Dominic repressed an impulse to inform her that he could ensure she had fun in the bedchamber. "My work is serious, not the bibble-babble you labeled it. What do you mean by fun?"

"A picnic, for example."

"Eating on the ground, sharing food with insects? Picnics are nursery fare. Though not the nursery I grew up in," he added.

"Nor the nursery run by Nanny Bracknell," Torie pointed out. "That woman is as cold as a gravestone, which may explain why Florence is so obsessed by ghosts."

"My niece is obsessed by graveyards because her parents are dead," Dominic said, giving a bite to his voice.

"Florence scarcely knew them. Thus her easy ability to consider you her father. She has no understanding of the word *father*."

"I don't want to marry to 'have fun,'" he said. "I'd like a partner with dignity enough to prefer not to sprawl on the grass and share meals with ants."

Her eyes narrowed at his tone. "You prove my point. Sprawling on the grass is one of my favorite activities. Moreover, I would like to marry someone who isn't cold, self-absorbed, and serious. Need I continue?"

Silence fell as Dominic weighed various rejoinders. Usually he aligned his facts and formulated a plan of attack long before he entered a debate, but Torie's arguments constantly shifted ground. Her latest accusation was a facer.

He couldn't counter her requirements because he didn't know a single jest. He didn't think he was self-absorbed, but he wouldn't, would he?

"I shall keep your ideal in mind while finding you a bride," Torie promised. "You'll be glad to know that the Duke of Queensberry has no objection to my visiting your nursery after we marry. His mama supports parentless children as well, the only difference being that she visits orphanages."

The blasted duke was fighting dirty, giving his future duchess permission to visit another man's house.

"You will visit the nursery, because you'll be living in my house," Dominic stated. But he already knew that such statements had no effect on Torie. She had to be the most stubborn woman he'd ever met.

At this rate, she'd end up married to a duke simply because she refused to marry *him*. Frustration leaped through him before he had an idea.

He did have assets that the Duke of Queensberry did not.

He pulled off his coat and tossed it on the couch, followed by his cravat.

"You have an astonishing belief that if you simply *say* that I'll marry you, the ceremony will miraculously occur," Torie said, before she noticed what he was doing. Her eyes widened as he unbuttoned his waistcoat. "What on earth are you doing? I've made up my mind to marry the duke."

"Your betrothal hasn't been announced. I mean to convince you otherwise." Dominic untied the knot behind his neck and then reached backward and wrenched his shirt over his head, dropping it to the floor.

Torie's lips rounded, but he saw no apprehension in her face. She trusted him. He put his hands on his hips, letting her look her fill. Some women in polite society wanted their men to resemble reeds. Others did not. He had more breadth in his shoulders than the young actor in *Tartuffe*.

Torie appeared to be struck dumb.

Remembering the scene, he pulled out his rapier before he dropped onto a chair, throwing his leg over an arm precisely as Mylchreest had in the play. "Close enough?" he asked Torie, waggling his eyebrows.

Some women liked rippling muscles. He swung his rapier in case she was one of them.

Torie made a choking sound. "You are cracked." There was a giggle in her voice—and more than that, an undertone of raw desire.

Dominic slung one arm on the back of the chair in case she'd like to assess his biceps. His tailor regularly grumbled that he was built like Hercules.

He looked over to assess her reaction—and froze. She was standing in front of the window, and her cotton gown followed every line of her body. The dress was caught up just under her breasts in the new style, designed without the panniers.

Desire roared through him. Every inch of Torie was perfection, from those glorious breasts to the natural curve of her lush hips, to the surprising length of her legs, given how petite she was.

"Are you having fun yet?" he asked, threading a sensual invitation through the question.

A tide of color swept over her face. "Put your clothing back on," she hissed.

"We haven't finished that scene," Dominic objected. "Though I'm not going to strut across the stage."

Then he rethought it, bounded to his feet, and sauntered toward her. All the time her gaze flicked over him, watching the play of muscles in his chest. When her teeth bit down on her bottom lip, he knew he had her.

Caught like a fish—his lure being the body Leonora loathed. Not that he really cared about his former fiancée's distaste, but no one wanted to be told that a woman anticipated gagging after he took off his clothing.

Once he was standing just before Torie, Dominic drawled, "I do know how to have fun, Torie. I have many sportive tricks to show you."

Her pupils were dilated. She was definitely not queasy.

"I will laugh at your jokes, but never at you," Dominic promised. "I will strut across the room without my shirt whenever you ask, with no need to purchase tickets. We will have a good marriage, Torie. Better for not agreeing about play productions. Do you know what I think of that scene?"

She shook her head. He flexed his chest muscles, which made him feel ridiculous but gave her something to look at.

"That actor's shoulders were twice the width of His Grace, the Duke of Queensberry, and mine are broader than his. Perhaps you didn't consider such shallow traits when imagining yourself a duchess?"

She dragged her eyes away from the trail of hair that disappeared into his breeches. "Certainly not."

She almost managed to sound disdainful, but her voice was too breathy to achieve it.

"I didn't when proposing to Leonora, either. She and I would have had a wretched marital life, our intimacies limited to unhappy encounters aimed solely at creating an heir."

Torie cleared her throat. "Clothe yourself, if you please. What if someone walks in?" Her eyes narrowed. "Don't think I'll marry you because you compromised me. I won't, even if you stroll out of here naked as a jaybird."

He put his hands on his waistband and waggled his eyebrows. Thereby proving he did have a sense of humor.

"I wasn't suggesting that!"

"I would never coerce a woman to marry me," Dominic said.

"A terrible basis for marriage," she agreed.

"In choosing Leonora, I was stupid enough to think that the kind of affinity you and I share was unimportant."

"Affinity?" she repeated.

"Desire. Your sister looks like a toothpick," he said, deciding that only brutal honesty would prove his case. "You"—he let his eyes caress her generous curves—"don't. Ours won't be the marriage I foolishly thought I wanted. It will be better." He reached out and took her hands, drawing her slowly toward him before he turned her palms against his bare chest.

She startled, so perhaps she felt some of the visceral shock that exploded in his body at her touch.

"We'll be true partners," Dominic said, his voice rough with desire. "I don't need a wife who can read in French or English. I've no interest in syllabic lines. I don't care if you have no idea of the prime minister's name."

She had been staring at his chest, but she looked up at him, frowning. "As it happens, I have met him several times. Did you actually have *requirements*?"

"No," Dominic said. He hesitated, but then decided to be honest. "Leonora impressed me with a coherent discussion of the latest farm bill, as reported in the *London Times*. Obviously, you can't do the same, but it's not your fault."

"Do you know how condescending you sound?" Torie demanded.

"I suspect that marrying you will knock that out of me." A sense of well-being spread through him, and his arms circled her waist. "All we have to do is show the ton precisely how we feel about each other, and no one will mock our marriage. Do you know how few married couples—in polite society, at least—have any fun in the bedchamber?"

"Queen Charlotte and King George," she said instantly. "All those children."

Dominic bent toward her and brushed his lips over her generous mouth. "I don't mind having fifteen children with you. I think it would be f—"

She cut him off. "Don't say it."

"We could conceive one of them on a picnic," he said, running his tongue along the line of her bottom lip. "Surrounded by ants."

She giggled even as her flush deepened. "You can't— We couldn't—"

"I'd prefer a blanket to sprawling in the grass, but Torie? I'll make love to you anywhere you'll have me."

"Outside the bedchamber?" she asked, apparently flabbergasted by the notion.

Of course Torie was a stranger to passion; she likely believed lustful acts could only be performed on a marital mattress. Her mother was long dead, and Leonora was hardly the sort of woman to discuss connubial matters. He shelved that problem for another day. "May I kiss you?"

"Oh, bloody hell," she muttered. "This is going to happen, isn't it?"

Dominic froze and let the words filter through his mind two or three times before he allowed himself to recognize that she had just accepted his proposal: not gracefully, but resignedly.

They were getting married. He'd won the argument with a strategy he'd come up with at the last moment.

He wanted to snatch her up and take her back to the couch to engage in debauchery that most ladies wouldn't abide before marriage, and perhaps even after marriage. He had the feeling that Torie would match his inventiveness, if he didn't scare her off before the altar.

Not that she was at all like Leonora.

"Yes, this is going to happen," he stated. "You're mine." Still, one thing was making him uneasy, and he had to bring it up to ease his conscience while she still had a chance to turn him down. He frowned, considering how best to phrase it.

"Something is bothering you. My children may be unable to read," Torie said, her voice brusque.

"I had no intention of asking that!" Dominic said, startled.

"Like me, my mother couldn't read. My father had no idea until she signed the parish register with an X."

Despite himself, his jaw tensed. The idea of a Viscountess Kelbourne signing the family Bible with an X was daunting. On the other hand, that X would have made his father burn with rage, which was an excellent reason to marry an illiterate woman.

"I can sign my name," Torie snapped.

"That wasn't what was bothering me," Dominic said. "My question is about what you want in a husband. You told me that you wanted to marry for love, and I am not a man who falls in love," he said, trying to be as clear as possible. "I doubt it's in me."

Torie's eyes lightened to an exquisite cornflower blue. "*That's* your oh-so-important concern in response to my acceptance of your proposal?"

"You didn't precisely accept," Dominic pointed out. "I would describe your comment as a disgruntled recognition of reality. Not a desirable reality, apparently."

"I am putting away childish things," Torie told him.

"Did you mean to quote Corinthians?"

Her mouth tipped up on one side. "Chapter 1, verse 11. 'When I was a child, I spake as a child, I understood as a child, I thought as a child: but when I became a man, I put away childish things.' Let's turn that from 'man' to 'woman,' and define 'childish things' as the dream that someday I would fall in love."

Dominic raised an eyebrow. "But the duke loves you, no?"

"His Grace did tell me I was driving him mad, and his insanity could only be cured by marriage."

What an idiot.

"His adoration didn't spur yours, I gather?" Dominic asked.

"No." She gave him a rueful smile. "This is my third Season, and I've seen the best that London has to offer along with a great many of the worst on offer. I haven't felt the slightest pang of love, let alone come close to madness."

"Neither have I," he offered. He grinned back at her, thinking that he had found just the right woman. How often had he silently rolled his eyes when gentlemen claimed to be in love? "After the disaster of my first betrothal, there's only one thing that I desire in a wife. Honesty."

Her forehead pleated. "Fidelity?"

"No, honesty. Just being yourself as opposed to the proper lady you think I want."

"As it happens, I am not good at being anything else. My defects are far too well-known for me to fool you or anyone else," Torie said with a distinctly happy note in her voice.

Dominic picked up her hand and regarded it: slender fingers, fine bones, speckles of paint, a callus. He rubbed it.

"From holding a paintbrush," she explained.

He kissed her hand. She smelled of turpentine and paint.

"This is going to happen, isn't it?" he drawled.

CHAPTER 15

Sir William was not happy with Torie's announcement. "What am I to tell the duke?" he grumped at luncheon. "What's more, you're asking me to give up the eight thousand that His Grace offered."

Torie rarely flatly contradicted her father, but this time she leaned across the table and said fiercely, "The viscount will *never* pay you for the honor of marrying me. You may consider yourself lucky that he is not demanding that immoral payment you extracted from him two years ago."

"Christ, you look like your mother when you go all disproving," Sir William snapped. "You shouldn't interfere in men's business."

"You shouldn't have gambled away my dowry," she retorted.

"I suppose you'd better tell Kelbourne to come over tomorrow morning," her father said, ignoring her reproach.

Out of her earshot, Sir William wouldn't hesitate to renew his demand for money. "I shall invite him for dinner, and you may offer your congratulations then," Torie said coolly. "I shall write to the Duke of Queensberry and inform him of my decision."

"His Grace won't like it," Sir William said, with some truth. "The man's infatuated. You'll never be able to control Kelbourne that way. You're making a mistake, mark my words."

He wasn't wrong about His Grace's feelings.

Queensberry arrived a mere hour after delivery of her note—written by Emily, of course. He im-

plored, begged, and generally made it clear that he
would be a most amenable husband.

Torie felt genuinely sorry. But at the same time, she
couldn't help comparing the two men. The duke was
a perfectly fine specimen of his lineage. He spent his
days in his club when he wasn't visiting his tailor.

Moreover, though she hadn't noticed until Dominic pointed it out, Queensberry's legs were tooth-
picks. White silk stockings with clocks up the side
together with red-heeled shoes were not flattering.

He finally left with tears in his eyes; her father
stomped into the drawing room as the ducal carriage pulled away and indulged himself in a long
rant on the idiocy of his daughters. Having heard it
before, Torie let the words flow over her while she
considered how to break the news of her betrothal
to the ton.

Dominic was right: they had to *show* everyone a
motive for marriage. Yet she didn't want anyone to
think that Leonora had married Bufford because
her younger sister had been bedding her fiancé.

It was a conundrum.

They could not circumvent the banns with a marriage license. They would have to wait the full three
weeks and then at least two more, marrying in the
cathedral, with all the pomp and circumstance of
a royal wedding, albeit royalty in half-mourning.

Her father finished his first diatribe and started a
new one to do with his wretched luck as displayed
by a wager that a goose wouldn't eat strawberries.
Apparently, the bird in question had gobbled down
an entire quart.

Torie ignored him, trying to imagine Dominic
looking at her with Queensberry's adoration. He
wouldn't.

He *couldn't*.

She had the feeling Dominic was constitutionally unlikely to fall in love and certainly would never reveal the feeling. He'd consider it akin to an embarrassing illness. In fact, he would probably be outraged if he felt a prickling of adoration or, even worse, devotion.

Which was fine, because she didn't adore either of her suitors. She was making a rational decision, considering each man on his merits.

Emily was in a flutter of excitement. "I just can't believe it!" she kept exclaiming over and over as she was dressing Torie for dinner. "Of course, he is *that* handsome, isn't he, miss?"

"Yes, he is."

"How lucky that new evening dress was just delivered."

"You don't think that it's too risqué?" Torie asked doubtfully. Her new gown was in the very latest fashion, a design taken from a French fashion magazine and worn without panniers or stays, merely a small, unboned corset to support her breasts.

"For whom would you wear it, if not for your future husband?" Emily answered, reverently placing the gown on the bed. "Lady Bufford would *never* have worn this gown. You must set yourself apart from your sister, Miss Torie."

It still felt strange to think of Leonora as Lady Bufford. She had the feeling that her sister would consider their engagement entirely her doing, given that she'd suggested Torie mother the twins. But Dominic desired her; he wasn't marrying her only for the sake of Florence and Valentine.

The gown had blush-colored skirts and an overskirt of "silver spot lace," or so the modiste called it. Torie had never seen fabric painted with metallic silver paint before. She'd bought the entire roll, thinking that she would drape a table and throw roses carelessly on top, resulting in the kind of still life that Clara adored.

Emily piled Torie's hair atop her head and bound her curls with three silver bands, adding a pearl necklace and earrings, and finally, white silk gloves. "You are late downstairs, but Lord Kelbourne won't mind once he sees you! Would you like lip color?"

"Not tonight," Torie said, which made Emily dissolve into naughty giggles. Lip color was for display rather than kissing, since it tasted like fish oil.

Torie walked down the stairs, smoothing her long white gloves. It was absurd to feel nervous. She wouldn't if the Duke of Queensberry had arrived to dine. But Dominic was . . . so much *more*. More powerful. More male.

The sheer force of his masculinity swirled about him like a windstorm.

When she walked into the drawing room, their butler was nowhere to be seen, and Dominic was gazing out the window. He turned and froze.

"You have dimples when you smile," she said, walking toward him.

Dominic hadn't even known he was smiling.

He started toward Torie, forcing himself to look at her face rather than the rest of her. Her gown was somewhat gaudy, painted with odd metallic circles that sparkled under the chandelier. But he didn't care, not when it skimmed her curves so beautifully.

"I shouldn't worry that others will discover your secret dimples, given that you smile so rarely," she told him as they met in the middle of the room.

"I've hated them since I was but a boy, yet I can't stop smiling around you," Dominic said, capturing Torie's lips with his own.

She tasted of peppermint and tea. Fire exploded in his loins as her tongue met his with sensual joy, her arms winding around his neck.

He brought up his hands to cup the back of her head, plunging greedily into her honied mouth as his tongue dipped between her lips over and over in a carnal dance, a seduction, an erotic invitation.

"God, I want you," he muttered, words erupting in a husky growl. "I want to throw you on a couch and rip off your dress. I want to kiss you for hours, licking my way down your body."

Leonora—and most other ladies, for that matter—would have fainted at his hunger to bed her, let alone his frank expression of desire.

Not Torie. Her inarticulate gasp encouraged him to deepen the kiss, turn it hotter, rougher, less gentlemanly. It turned to a possessive statement, a silent way of informing her that now she was his. She was *his*.

"May I unbutton your gloves?" he asked hoarsely.

She nodded, and he slowly peeled them back and then kissed every bare finger before pushing back his coat and flattening her palms against his linen shirt. "I am not wearing a waistcoat," he told her. "Just in case I was lucky enough to feel your touch."

When he finally pulled back from that kiss, Torie's hands were roaming his chest, leaving trails of fire in their wake.

She let out a low, breathy sigh as his hands slid around her head to frame her face while he waited for her to meet his eyes. Long lashes finally swept up. "We'll be incredible in bed," he told her, low and deep. "I'll work you until we're both covered with sweat, and then I'll lick your sweat from your body. You'll ride me until you're panting and my heart is about to burst from my chest."

"Dom!" Torie sounded outraged, but her eyes betrayed fascination. She didn't squeal and run from the room.

"No one has called me Dom since my sister died." He loved hearing the name on Torie's lips.

"You said . . . Those things you just said were vastly improper." Torie kept her voice steady, but an aching undertone betrayed her.

"You are no lady," he said, nipping her lower lip.

"I am," she retorted, slinging her arms around his neck and, to his infinite delight, nipping him back. "I know everything about being a lady. How to curtsy, how to giggle, how to paint roses."

"Ladies kiss by pursing up their lips as if they were hiding a treasure behind their teeth."

She wrinkled her nose. "I kiss like a man?" He loved her wry tone.

"You kiss like a woman." He put his hands around her waist, allowing his thumbs to caress the generous swell of her breasts. "No stays? No whalebone?"

"These new French dresses are worn with a little corset." She blinked. "Surely ladies' undergarments are on the Prohibited List?"

"Miraculously, they haven't come up in conversation yet. I thought you weren't wearing stays yesterday." He knew his smile was wolfish, but on the other hand, she liked his dimples.

"I don't wear one while painting," Torie confessed. "No one can see under my pinafore."

Jesus. Lust coursed down his limbs, sanity lost.

"I shall put a couch in your painting studio in our home," he promised hoarsely. "I'll come back from the House of Lords at luncheon just to see you. Throw you on your back and wrench up your gown."

Torie bit her lip.

"Watch you sprawl before me, laughing. Push your legs apart and lick you, because I'm so hungry for you that I've had a cockstand all morning."

She made a stifled sound, somewhere between a gasp and a laugh. "I've never heard of such a thing."

Dominic nodded, seeing an opening for a question he'd wanted to ask. Torie couldn't read; her mother was long dead; her sister had fled. "What do you know about copulation?"

She frowned.

"About 'having' in the Biblical sense?" he amended.

Her eyelashes fluttered, but being Torie, she didn't gasp with ladylike horror at the question. Instead, she met his eyes with her clear gaze. "I've watched animals . . . rabbits."

If he grinned this often, it might become a habit. "How do rabbits mate?"

"The male rabbit grips his mate's throat with his teeth," Torie said primly, but her eyes were dancing.

"Like this?" He pulled her more tightly against his stiff cock and nipped her neck.

A shiver went through her. "Yes," she said breathlessly, pulling away. "Then he passes out."

"*What?*"

"It's true! I've seen it several times. He falls unconscious and topples to the side."

"Bloody hell," Dominic muttered, feeling sorry for males of the *Lepus* genus. Poor blokes.

"I have wondered if that was true of men, but

I haven't had a chance to clarify it, for obvious reasons."

"Not in my case," Dominic said. "Perhaps I can give you so much pleasure that you pass out. We'll have to test the hypothesis that men and women are like rabbits. Scientifically, by repeating the test many times. Of course, we may end up with fifteen children, like Queen Charlotte."

"As do rabbits!" Torie said, gurgling with laughter.

Dimly, amid one of the most scorching kisses of his life, Dominic realized that he didn't give a damn about theatrical criticism or parliamentary debates. Or anything other than her, the woman standing before him smelling like honeysuckle, her fingers leaving an impression like hot coals on his chest.

They should have a short betrothal.

Very short.

"Is Sir William joining us?" he asked.

"He is supposed to chaperone us," Torie said, catching her breath. "Which brings me to an important point, Dom. There will be no preempting the wedding night." She fixed him with an uncompromising gaze.

"Of course," he said readily. "I suggest we marry by special license." He could buy one in the morning; they could marry in the afternoon.

She shook her head. "Absolutely not. If we intend to . . . to give the polite world the impression that we are happy to marry—"

"Because we are," he growled, snatching her into a kiss.

Later, Torie said breathlessly, "We can't marry by special license."

Dominic tried to look inquiring rather than aggravated. The marriage date was a lady's purview, which had proved problematic during his first engagement, although in retrospect, Leonora's hesitation had been for the best.

"Don't scowl at me like one of those tigers in the Royal Menagerie!"

Apparently he hadn't achieved placid inquiry. "I'd like to marry you tomorrow," Dominic said, somewhat surprised by the desperation in his voice.

"I thought about it most of the night," Torie told him. "If our marriage is to be accepted as an affair of the heart—as per your idea—then our betrothal must be conventional and include the reading of banns."

Affair of the heart?

Dominic flinched. He was going to disappoint her.

"Don't be so silly," Torie said, rolling her eyes. "I'm not in love with you. I'm merely asking you to perform not *Tartuffe* but *Romeo and Juliet*. Supposedly the greatest love story ever written. We can pretend to be lovesick fools, because we can scarcely tell society the truth, can we?"

"That I want to smoke your chimney and ring your chimes?" He grinned because, damn it, he did have a sense of humor, albeit of a particular sort.

She raised an eyebrow.

"I'll explain at a later date," Dominic said, deciding the drawing room wasn't the place to inquire about her orgasmic experiences, if any.

"If we wish to convey the idea that you are overlooking my deficits due to infatuation, we have to kiss in front of a great many people."

"You have no deficits," Dominic said instinctively.

She didn't roll her eyes, but the feeling hung in the air.

"We're giving them a reason why you're marrying me, other than that you need a nanny or my father owes you money. Yet we can't risk people thinking that Leonora fled with Bufford because her younger sister shamed her by seducing a viscount. *Her* viscount."

"Ah. I see that," Dominic conceded. "At the moment, they think that she fled my temper."

He no longer cared what they thought about his broken engagement. He wanted Torie, and if he had to wait to marry her, he would.

"No rabbiting?" he asked, just to be clear.

"None."

"When do we perform *Romeo and Juliet*?"

"Tomorrow, because the play is opening at the Theatre Royal Haymarket." She laughed. "I know that Clara will attend as Mylchreest, the actor she likes, is playing Romeo. She'll certainly be surprised by our kiss."

"I have no box at Haymarket," Dominic remarked. "My father preferred Drury Lane."

She flicked him a look from under her lashes. "Then you'll need to take a box by tomorrow night, won't you?"

Dominic nodded. "You should wear this gown. The spots will glitter under the candelabra and catch every eye."

"Do you like it? I've never worn it before."

"Yes, certainly the . . . the shape of it," he said cautiously. "No stays. Every man in the theater will celebrate French gowns. The fabric? Not as much."

Torie narrowed her eyes. "Your honesty is refreshing, *sometimes*."

"It's a bit gaudy."

She folded her arms over her chest. "Like a circus costume?"

"I've never been to the circus. I don't care what you wear to the theater," he said with rough sincerity, drawing her back into his arms. "Wear nothing at all," he said, kissing her neck. "Please."

When Torie laughed, Dominic couldn't believe that he hadn't grasped two years ago how sensual she was.

"This gown will scandalize half of London, but there's no need to send them into apoplexies with nudity," she said.

"Kissing me in front of everyone will scandalize the other half," he pointed out. "I'll have the banns read for the first time on Sunday, and for two consecutive weeks . . . and then we marry, Torie."

"At least two weeks after the third banns," she said firmly. "I shall wear a gown in this style, making it clear I am not carrying a child." She looked down. "Not that my stomach is as flat as yours."

"If we don't have a child for nine months after marriage, no one can possibly think I married you for that reason."

"As long as there's no rabbiting," she said. "I attend performances at every theater, by the way. So we can polish our roles every week before our wedding."

Thankfully, he caught back a stupid question just in time. Of course she went to the theater weekly. Unless someone read aloud from the *Odyssey* or another book, she lived in a world without stories.

"It's acceptable for a betrothed couple to attend the theater without a chaperone, but I think it would be wise if we were prudent," Torie added.

"I'll invite the Duchess of Huntington and her husband to join us at *Romeo and Juliet*," Dominic said.

"The two rarely visit London, and their presence in our box will ensure that all eyes will fix on us."

"Very clever," Torie said approvingly.

"Husbands and wives don't only dance the horizontal jig in bed, you know." He brought her hands up to his mouth and kissed first one, then the other.

"Oh?"

"A husband could read aloud to his wife in bed. Not epics or gossip columns, but perhaps novels?" He scoured his memory. "Florence likes *Castle Rackrent*, which I believe you gave her."

"You would read that aloud to me?"

He nodded. He would do almost anything to make her happy, but he quickly buried that thought.

Torie's soft mouth trembled before curving into a smile. "Bed may become my favorite place," she whispered.

Dominic groaned, the sound torn from deep in his chest. "Until now, the debating floor of the House of Lords has been mine."

CHAPTER 16

*W*hen the door to the drawing room finally opened, Dominic lifted his head quickly from Torie's mouth and looked around, thinking to see Sir William.

"His lordship has taken ill," the butler said without preamble. "Dinner is served."

Torie grimaced.

"Does this happen often?" Dominic asked, reaching down to entwine her fingers in his. After all, they were betrothed. They could be improper, especially when the only audience was a butler walking so unsteadily that he might crash into the wall.

"More often than one would wish," Torie replied.

In the dining room, Dominic moved to sit beside her rather than at the far end. He waited until they'd been served before he jerked his head, sending the boozy butler out of the room.

"Did you tell the twins about our engagement?" Torie asked him, poking her fork at an anemic pile of green beans on her plate.

"They are wildly happy," Dominic said, taking a bite of greasy duck. Sir William's cook was as inept as his butler. "I received extravagant and surprised congratulations. They had no faith that I'd be able to persuade you."

Torie raised an eyebrow.

"I had been advised to wear a codpiece and offer poems in praise of your skin, to be written by Valentine."

She laughed.

"You do know what a codpiece is," Dominic said

with satisfaction. "I am never sure about items on the Prohibited List."

"Codpieces feature largely in portraits of Henry VIII," Torie told him. "The king had endless creativity in that respect. His codpieces were not merely embroidered, but tasseled, tinseled, and bejeweled."

"Perhaps I've underestimated your knowledge of the male physique," Dominic said, thinking of ancient sculpture.

"Greeks were fond of depicting men in their entirety," Torie said, turning a rosy color. "I understand." She waved her hand in the vague direction of his waistline as she took a swallow of wine.

Dominic had been dragged in front of a few ancient statues back when he was at Eton; amongst him and his lustily minded classmates, the primary fascination was why gods would be portrayed with such insufficient private parts. "That part of a man changes when he is aroused."

Torie looked blank.

"Private parts look like unhoused snails in Greek statues," he said.

She nodded. "I know just what you mean."

Dominic stood, walked to the door, and told the footman leaning against a wall to bring a pencil and paper. When he returned to the table, he sat down and made a rough sketch. "Unlike you, I have no skill, but I have tried to draw an adult man, aroused. There. I did my best." He gave her the paper.

Torie looked down, and her mouth fell open.

"I hope you're not offended," Dominic said, squinting at his lamentable drawing. "I simply thought that if I were you, I'd rather know more about the male body than can be gleaned from ancient art."

His future wife was staring down wide-eyed at his illustration. "This is a man?" she asked with uncomplimentary doubt.

Dominic cleared his throat. "Schoolboys draw these diagrams all the time."

"They do?" Torie's finger landed in the middle of the sheet. "He appears to have a clothes-peg where a Greek statue might have a fig leaf. Or an unhoused snail."

"As I said, statues are notably deficient with respect to the male organ."

"Interesting," Torie said. "I don't always see line drawings very clearly," she added, folding up the sheet as the butler returned with a second course. "I shall look again tonight."

"My drawing skills are extremely poor."

"Your motive is generous," she said, smiling. "People say that you are uncaring and unkind, but that isn't true, is it?"

Personally, Dominic thought that judgment wasn't incorrect, so he changed the subject. "I also have this." He pulled an emerald ring from his breast coat pocket and placed it on the table before her.

"Was it your mother's?" Torie asked, picking it up.

He couldn't tell from her expression whether she hated it. "No. I bought it this morning."

She pushed it on her finger and held it up to catch the light. Dominic had a surge of pure male satisfaction. She was his, and now everyone would know it.

"Did you give your mother's ring to Leonora?"

"My mother didn't wear a betrothal ring, since my

parents' marriage was arranged when they were still in the cradle." It occurred to him that she might be comparing the rings—*of course* she was comparing the rings. "I bought Leonora a diamond, but I found you an emerald because I thought you'd love the color. It's not just green. There's blue as well."

"And a touch of purple," she said. Then she leaned over and initiated a kiss of her own volition for the first time.

"We picked it together," he said, reining in a wave of lust. "Valentine and Florence and I."

Her smile was like sunshine, warm and blessed.

Dominic Kelbourne rarely did anything without a plan. He didn't trust things like *instinct*. In his experience, people used instinct to explain ill-thought-out impulses with the potential to harm others.

But pulling his fiancée onto his lap? Kissing her in between bites of food, and sending the butler away because privacy was all the dessert they could ask for?

Instinct.

Pure instinct.

CHAPTER 17

May 1, 1802
Theatre Royal Haymarket

The opening night of *Romeo and Juliet* starring Mr. Mylchreest as Romeo drew a crowd of hundreds, given the growing notoriety of the handsome actor.

That morning Emily had read aloud a report that predicted Mylchreest would remove his shirt. "I cannot wait!" she squealed. One of the underfootmen had cleverly managed to buy tickets in the pit, winning his first evening in Emily's company.

"Are you sure you don't wish to accompany me in the box?" Torie asked. "I shall be chaperoned by the Duchess of Huntington, but you are more than welcome to join us."

Emily scoffed. "With all of you sitting up there looking so high and mighty? The pit only costs six shillings, and it's so much fun. Everyone is talking, of course, and sometimes throwing veg, though no one would *dare* throw anything at *him*."

"Him" was Mylchreest, the talk of London.

Torie waited until she was in the center of the crowded theater entry before she removed the swath of silver silk around her shoulders and revealed her French gown. After that, it was hard to say whether startled faces had more to do with her costume or the man beside her.

Ranks of boxes covered the walls of Haymarket; Dominic had taken one in the very best position, on the lower level close to the stage where anyone looking to the front would see them. She seated herself and saw with satisfaction that the dot-lace was sparkling before she flipped open a fan of mother-of-pearl inlaid with silver.

A marquess and his wife sat to their left. The marchioness was one of Torie's friends; she waggled her eyebrows and cried, "Ooh, la la!" To the other side was an elderly couple; the lady was apparently offended by Torie's gown, as she made a point of turning her head away. When her husband showed no signs of following suit, she forced him to move his chair until both their backs were to the stage.

When Dominic sat down, a ripple of excitement went through the theater. Torie glanced at him from behind her fan. He was dressed impeccably in black, with touches of white to indicate that he was now in half mourning.

"Are you wearing a different rapier?" she asked.

"Yes," Dominic said, drawing out the blade.

"It's sparkling!" Torie exclaimed.

"Diamond-cut navy-blue glass," Dominic said, turning the hilt so she could see.

"You thought *my* gown was garish?" She couldn't help laughing. Before he could respond, a brisk knock sounded on the door to the box, and the Duchess of Huntington and her husband surged into the small enclosure.

"Hello!" the duchess boomed.

Torie jumped to her feet and curtsied. "Your Grace!"

"We've finished the steam engine tour and are taking a few days in London to relax," the duchess said, dropping into a seat.

"How gracious of you to join us," Torie said.

"Lots of fool gossip going about saying this and that," Her Grace commented with disdain. She pulled out a lorgnette and surveyed the theater. "Course, now they've seen you in that gown, they'll know precisely why Kelbourne—and any other unattached male—would be lucky to marry you."

Torie straightened her back, suddenly wishing there were a few whalebones between her breasts and the eyes of the audience.

"I like it," the duchess said. "Wouldn't suit me, of course. I couldn't do without stays."

"I couldn't wear more than a small corset," Torie confirmed, thinking that perhaps she should take up the duchess's offer to bring the twins to the country. It would be refreshing for them to spend time with someone who scorned a Prohibited List of conversational topics.

"This play is Shakespeare at his most ridiculous, wouldn't you say?"

"I don't know more than its reputation," Torie admitted.

"That's right, you don't read." Her Grace glanced over. "Take that expression off your face, girl. Do you think I bother with feeling belittled just because I can't see without a lorgnette?"

"No," Torie said.

"I'll give you a sense of the plot, so you can follow along. Two fool adolescents meet and fall in love while dancing. A ball can be dangerous for headstrong youngsters. I'll watch my gals carefully once they reach that age, not to mention my eldest, Silvester. I've an inkling that he could be as idiotic as Romeo when it comes to women. Entirely too charming for his own good."

"I shall do the same with the twins," Torie said.

"You'll have to. Your Florence will be trouble. At any rate, the boy ends up killing the girl's relative.

Then there's a lot of crying and carrying on. She pretends to be dead, ends up in a tomb. He kills himself, and so does she."

Torie turned to her other side. "Dom, did you know that this play is a welter of violent deaths?"

"*Welter.* Good word," the duchess grunted. "Despite your illiteracy, I expect your vocabulary is better than most. Likewise, I can see better through my lorgnette than other people do with both eyes. People don't bother to look carefully, because it's so easy for them."

Torie had a feeling that she was making a friend, perhaps her first friend after Clara—though Dom had become a friend as well. She gave the duchess a beaming smile.

Her Grace squinted through her lorgnette. "Can't imagine why all London isn't at your feet."

"A duke was," Dominic said from her other side.

"Just look how they're craning their necks now," the duchess said, waving her lorgnette over the audience. "There's a fool rumor going around that Sir William owes Kelbourne here a gambling debt, and that's why he's handing over another daughter."

Torie sucked in a breath of air.

Dominic's warm fingers curled tightly around hers under the edge of the box, where no one could see. "I would never take a wager from Sir William. In fact, I never gamble."

"Neither do I," His Grace put in. "Idiotic way to lose money."

"If you must lose money, why not throw it away on a steam engine?" his duchess agreed.

That started a lively discussion of the future of travel. Torie thought that the entire United Kingdom

would be connected by steel rails in a decade;
Dominic was more cautious. "A network of canals
already exists," he pointed out. "I believe in steam,
but in addition to current means of travel."

"Locomotives will be faster than canal boats,"
Her Grace told him. "Once we solve a few more
mechanical problems."

By the time the curtain rose, Torie was certain
that everyone in the theater had registered that she
and Dominic were seated together, in company
with the famous inventive couple who were so
rarely seen in London.

Within one act, it was clear that she and her fiancé
would not agree on the quality of the production.

Torie was swept away by the beauty of the language; Dominic was irritated by the bungling
portrayal of sword fighting in the first act.

The curtain fell after a glorious bedroom scene in
which Mylchreest strode around the stage without
his shirt. Dominic and the Duke of Huntington immediately turned to each other and began tearing
apart the tragically bad swordsmanship on display.

For Torie, the only tragedy had happened on
stage. She sat quietly, trying to stop herself from
crying.

In the end, her public kiss with Dominic happened naturally. He turned to her and frowned,
seeing her eyes brimming with tears. He ran a
thumb under one of her eyes and bent toward her
inquiringly.

"Mercutio was my favorite character," she told him.

"Even though he remained fully clothed?" Dominic
asked teasingly.

"'I talk of dreams, which are the children of an
idle brain, begot of nothing,'" she quoted. Another

tear escaped. "He was so funny and brave while he was dying."

Dominic frowned. "I didn't catch it. What did he say?"

"'Ask for me tomorrow, and you will find me a grave man.'"

"I like that pun on 'grave,'" the duchess said, rising. "We're off to greet a few friends."

"You quoted those lines word for word," Dominic observed.

Torie shrugged. "I have that sort of memory."

"The bedroom scene was very erotic." He bent his head and gave her a feather-soft kiss on the cheek, which was improper enough.

Awash in glorious love language, Torie turned her lips and caught his mouth in an open kiss that could never be mistaken for a peck from ladylike pursed lips.

When she finally drew away, flushed and breathing heavily, the first thing she heard was Dominic's rumbling laugh. "That will put paid to those absurd rumors."

"I forgot," Torie gasped. Looking around, she thought every eye in the theater was on them. People down in the pit were craning their necks as if one of Lunardi's great air balloons was drifting over the audience.

"I'm the luckiest man in London, and now they all know it," Dominic said with satisfaction.

Torie dropped her hand below the edge of the box and took his hand. It curled around hers like a bulwark against the world's contempt.

CHAPTER 18

May 16, 1802
Kelbourne House

$\mathcal{T}$wo weeks later, a groom in majestic livery appeared in Torie's studio. "His lordship the Viscount Kelbourne, Miss Florence, and Master Valentine request the honor of your presence at the evening meal." He paused and added with emphasis, "To celebrate the third reading of the banns pursuant to your upcoming marriage."

"All right," Torie said, amused. Presumably that meant the twins' table manners had finally met their tutor's exacting standards. The children were being allowed to eat in the dining room.

He bowed again and retreated backwards, leaving her to wonder how such a stately household would feel the first time she rose at midnight and went to her studio, bundling a pinafore over her nightgown.

Perhaps she could paint in a room next to her bedchamber, so the household staff wouldn't be aghast to find the viscountess downstairs at dawn, unkempt and half-dressed. Of course, the chamber next door would presumably be her husband's . . .

Their marriage was only two weeks away, which meant that Dominic would soon sleep in a bed close by. A mind-boggling thought.

She was prying open a tin of oil-resin gel when a thought struck her, a natural segue from the question of bedchambers. Should she have declined his invitation to dinner on the grounds that she would be unchaperoned? She had been blithely visiting the nursery, but a formal dinner with an unmarried man, albeit one's fiancé, was decidedly more audacious.

Yet did anyone really care?

Biting her lip, Torie ground crimson powder into the "gumtion," as her chemist called the gel. Her sister had left without bidding her goodbye. Her father was meandering along in the pleasant life he'd chosen, all the hard edges rubbed off by a golden haze of brandy.

The gumtion dried faster than she liked, and her fight to get the luminosity of a petal just right made her late to dinner. When she finally walked into the drawing room—unchaperoned—she found Dominic seated in an armchair, with Florence and Valentine perched on the sofa opposite him. The twins were immaculately dressed and obviously on their best behavior.

"'Trifle not,'" Florence intoned with a dramatic shudder. "'Hasten to tell me what you saw in the great chamber upon opening the door.'"

Torie waved at Florence as she walked in, mouthing, *"Don't stop."*

"'Tell me, I adjure thee by the souls of my ancestors, what thou seest? What hath thou heardst?'" Florence demanded.

"I don't like 'heardst,'" Val objected. "Anyway, I think it should be 'heardest.'"

"Never mind. She's finally here!" In moments like this, when Florence's arms wound tightly around her, Torie knew deep inside that she was right to marry Dominic. Her girlish dreams of marrying for love?

She *was* marrying for love.

The conversation at dinner turned to the *Odyssey*, specifically the Greek idea of Elysian Fields, the afterlife peopled by golden-haired, welcoming nymphs.

"It's only for heroes? What about Odysseus's wife, Penelope?" Florence demanded, her little mouth turning down in disgust. "Where will she go?"

Torie let Dominic take the lead on that tricky issue. He floundered about, explaining heroic traditions rather than answering Florence's question.

"Not good enough," Florence retorted. "If Odysseus is married, he shouldn't be with anyone else." Her voice was ferocious.

"Neither of us thinks adultery is a good idea, given our mother's behavior," Valentine remarked.

From Dominic's appalled expression, he had had no idea that the twins were aware of his sister's reputation. He looked to Torie in desperate appeal.

"You and I are not yet married," she reminded him. "Surely this is a moment for paternal advice."

"Please." Dominic so rarely admitted a need for help that she gave in.

"Your mother's behavior does not reflect on you," she told the children. "We try to think kindly of the dead, so let's concentrate on Lady Dorney's best characteristics."

Dominic was supposed to leap at her prompt, but he just dragged a hand through his short curls, which gave him an adorably rumpled appearance.

Very unlike the Viscount Kelbourne of debating fame.

Florence kicked the table leg so hard that the wood groaned. "I still don't understand why Odysseus would bother with these golden-haired nymphs. He had Penelope."

Once again, Dominic didn't respond, so Torie tried to explain. "Some people feel that a spouse isn't enough. They dream of variety."

"Variety in appearance? Was Penelope described as having yellow hair?" Valentine asked. "I can't remember."

"Homer describes her as loyal and intelligent, which is far better," Torie replied.

There was a brief digression after Florence uttered a comment that she'd overheard in the stables, which was instantly added to the Prohibited List.

"Odysseus had connubial relations—Torie, *connubial* refers to the marital bed—with all sorts of women," Valentine pointed out. "He wasn't faithful to Penelope. He was the sort of man who prefers variety."

Dominic promptly added "connubial relations" and "marital bed" to the Prohibited List. Torie was growing distinctly irritated by the fact that her fiancé seemed to consider the censorship of improper words his sole responsibility, as if Val could discuss adultery without them.

"Some men view infidelity as an ambition rather than a prohibition," she said. "And now I think we should talk of something or at least some*one* else. I'm tired of Odysseus."

That led, as she expected, to a firestorm of protest, taking the conversation in a different direction.

After the twins returned to the nursery, Dominic escorted Torie back to the drawing room, where Flitwick offered her tea, sherry, port, or hot chocolate.

"A cup of sherry would be lovely," she said, drifting across the room to look over a stack of books.

"You should never have said anything so inappropriate about infidelity," Dominic stated once

Flitwick left the room. "In fact, you should have headed off the entire unseemly conversation."

Rumpled and adorable as he sometimes appeared, he had a positive gift for chilly observations. *Rude* observations. That tight jaw wasn't adorable at all.

Just as she had feared, it seemed a nanny's twill dress and apron had dropped over her head.

"I would have preferred that you step forward and manage that conversation yourself, given that your sister's behavior was at the heart of the matter," Torie said, keeping her voice cordial with an effort. "But one grows used to male cowardice."

"Cowardice had nothing to do with it!" he snarled.

Torie leaned back against the mantelpiece, rather enjoying herself. "Yet the great debater of the House of Lords, the man famous for his withering setdowns— not to mention his bellowed retorts—couldn't steel himself to answer questions about a Greek epic?"

"Valentine referred to my sister's infidelity. What in the hell was I supposed to say? How did they know that?"

"The whole world knows of it, unfortunately. Having met Lady Dorney only once, I was unable to list your sister's better qualities, so I gave you the chance to do so." She took a sip of sherry and raised an eyebrow.

Dominic's mouth tightened.

"Oh, for goodness' sake," Torie cried. "*Your* only knowledge of your sister springs from her dalliances with men? Or you were so overwhelmed by her sins—which gentlemen of every stripe indulge in daily—that you have forgotten who she was as a person?"

"I didn't know her," he said.

Torie found herself, for the first time in her life, thinking that she might sketch a face rather than a rose, trying to catch the interesting panels of Dominic's cheeks, the curl on his broad forehead, his dark eyes. *Offended* eyes.

"I was sent to Eton at the age of seven, and even before that, we had little contact."

"You must have overlapped in the nursery," Torie said.

"She was sent to seminary when I was five."

"Then you should make something up. Those children need to know more of their mother than her scandals."

"My point was not in reference to my sister's lamentable marriage, but to your remarks about infidelity."

"Ah," Torie said sweetly. "You didn't care for my observation that men consider fidelity a vague suggestion rather than a commandment? After all, I have heard it said that sleeping with a courtesan doesn't count as adultery. Yet I believe that Exodus 20:14, also known as the seventh commandment, would not concur that payment creates a special exception."

Dominic put down his sherry with a click. "The subject is unsuitable for children."

"One could say that Odysseus *earned* the nubile nymphs in the afterworld by right of his meandering heroic adventures with various goddesses, pigs, one-eyed giants, et cetera," Torie continued, ignoring his sour comment. "But is that the same as the hero offering coin to such a nymph? Or a husband to a mistress?" She tapped her chin with one finger.

Dominic looked furiously annoyed—and then suddenly amused.

Torie's heart thumped. He was handsome when he lost his temper, eyes flaring and all the rest. But when his face softened into laughter?

"Thankfully, I am not in charge of legislating morality within marriage or literature. But I do remember a story that I could tell the twins about their mother."

Torie picked up her sherry and let a spicy swallow course down her throat. "Yes?"

"One Christmas, I was home from Eton and she from seminary. I must have been seven, so she was around nine. She was looking out the window of the nursery at the drive before the house when she suddenly turned around and bolted out of the room."

"Did you follow her?"

"I? No. I was memorizing Latin verbs."

"Of course you were."

"She returned to the nursery with a soggy young rabbit in her apron. She'd fished it out of the Italian basin that marks the center of the shell drive."

"The rabbit was in the basin?" Torie repeated, fascinated.

"It's a large fountain that my mother had imported from Florence, with a looming statue of Poseidon with two hippocampi."

"Which are?"

"Sea horses spewing water."

"Did the rabbit survive?"

"Yes. My sister dried him out by the fire. He spent two days in the nursery."

"Your sister was heroic," Torie said with satisfaction. "She rescued that poor animal from the grim fate of drowning. Did she give it a name?"

"Parsley," Dominic said, frowning at the floor.

"Named for his favorite food, I assume. She was softhearted and loving. What happened to Parsley?"

"We let him go in the woods when Nanny refused to let him stay another night in the nursery. I'd forgotten . . . She cried for hours that night."

Dominic's hand was clenched around his sherry glass. Torie walked over to him. "I like to think of the two of you setting Parsley free."

"I was afraid of the dark woods, but she wasn't. She was never afraid."

He looked wary and uncomfortable, as if he'd surprised himself with that memory.

"Another quality to share with her children," Torie pointed out.

Dominic gathered her into his arms, even though they had no audience. "You smell of soap and turpentine."

"I had a bath, but the fragrance lingers. Do you find it bothersome?"

He started kissing her neck. "I shall require closer proximity to reach a conclusion."

Torie relaxed against him. For all her middle-of-the-night fears about this marriage, there were moments—during Florence's hugs or Dominic's kisses—when she was surprised by happiness.

Before her betrothal, joy came after a painted rose petal finally caught the light the way she had imagined: a private emotion based on satisfaction.

This was altogether different, and yet the intensity, the utter concentration, felt the same. If a painting was going well, the image was all she thought about. She ate absent-mindedly, thinking how to give a petal the luminosity of silk. When she was kissing Dom, the world faded away in the same manner. Instead of petals, she focused on the silk of his tongue, the rasp of his voice, the rising heat in her body.

She drew a line with one finger from his forehead, down his nose, to his lips. "I'm about to say something shocking."

"Go ahead." Why should two words, two small words, make her flush and imagine all the many ways she could *go ahead*?

Torie cleared her throat. "I am looking forward to marriage, especially that . . ." She couldn't bring herself to say it.

"Especially, I hope, to the marriage bed?"

"Yes, to the marriage bed," Torie said. She cleared her throat. "That."

"Yes, *that*."

"When you smile like this"—she touched his bottom lip again—"no one in the House of Lords would recognize you."

"Good." His lips drifted along her jaw. "No one has ever seen this expression on your face before, either."

She wondered dimly what he saw, but his lips covered hers in a deep, open-mouthed kiss that burned away her focus—and bubbling up in its stead?

Happiness.

CHAPTER 19

June 1, 1802
Vauxhall Gardens
Two days before the Kelbourne wedding

$\mathcal{M}$iss Clara Vetry considered herself a sunny person by nature. She hated to think poorly of acquaintances, and always did her best to consider their point of view. When someone made fun of her darling reticules—the one shaped like a mouse's head seemed to draw particular scorn—she dimpled at them forgivingly and straightened its wire whiskers.

So often criticism was the result of being accidentally poked in the leg, and one couldn't blame them for being irritated. Whiskers were a signal characteristic of her reticules, and she couldn't give them up.

Viscount Kelbourne, for example, had smoldered at her in a most unforgiving manner when the whiskers on her darling black-and-white skunk reticule snagged his silk stockings. He went so far as to suggest that skunks didn't have whiskers, which she could have vigorously contested—except he made her far too nervous, so she had done nothing except whisper apologies.

The skunk-hating viscount was marrying her dearest friend in the world. She wanted to think well of him, even given his dislike (and ignorance) of whiskers.

Yet Clara could think of nothing that would excuse his behavior at this very moment. Nothing. She could only thank her lucky stars that Torie hadn't accepted her invitation to join them at Vauxhall.

"Do I believe my eyes?" her Aunt Marigold said in an escalating whisper, staring across the dance floor into one of the open boxes under the Pavilion.

"I can scarcely believe the exquisite decoration on the Pavilion," Clara cried, suddenly realizing that Kelbourne's appalling behavior would be of interest to others. "Aunt, do let us go around the other side and examine that eggshell blue more closely."

"What lechery, virtually on the eve of his wedding," Aunt Marigold breathed. "Vile *lechery*, performed before the eyes of the world!"

Aunt Marigold was devoted to the teachings of a minister who regularly portended the end of the world due to human misbehavior, which had a dampening effect on her mental state.

For a moment, Clara entertained the wild notion of begging her aunt to pretend she'd seen nothing, but since Vauxhall did not offer dancing on Wednesdays, the floor was thronged with people who would be just as interested in Kelbourne's activities as Aunt Marigold—who was now tugging on Clara's mother's sleeve.

The Right Honorable Lady Vetry turned, her mouth tight as a drawstring purse. Clara's mama had been chatting with a countess, and though the Vetrys traced their ancestry—albeit with a few creative embellishments—to one of Henry VII's trusted courtiers, she was clearly not be pleased to be interrupted while speaking to those of higher rank.

"May I be of assistance, Marigold?" she asked with acid emphasis.

"Look who is seating himself in the box to the left," her sister hissed.

Lady Vetry pointedly rearranged the stiff brocade of her sleeve. Her gown harked back to the days of Queen Elizabeth, a fashion she preferred to the present. Queen Charlotte's towering wigs? Heaven forbid.

Her eyes widened as she followed Marigold's gaze. "Two days before his marriage!"

Clara's heart was hammering, but she could already see that there was no way to head off a scandal. All the world that hadn't attended Vauxhall this evening would learn everything by the next morning, when the gossip columns rolled off the press, bundled for delivery while their ink was still wet.

Her darling Torie's fiancé—that beast—was seated in an open box with his flamboyant mistress, the infamous opera singer Gianna, to his right. The lady had piled lightly powdered dark hair atop her head. She wore one of the new chemise gowns; tawny silk clung to her curves.

It hardly needed to be said that Lady Vetry would never allow Clara to order a garment so scandalously revealing. Even now, in Clara's third Season, her mother scarcely allowed her to wear white silk instead of white dimity cotton, let alone any of the more exciting fabrics and shades.

Gianna—as the world knew her—wore the gown so well, Clara thought with a pang. Even if her mother did allow a dress like that, Clara was too short and squat to be flattered by it.

"If I've told you once, I've told you a hundred times," Aunt Marigold rabbited. "Vauxhall is no place for ladies. I shall not join you again. A lady of quality should *never* rub shoulders with the demimonde."

"Don't be silly, Marigold," Lady Vetry said. "The

pleasure gardens are the pinnacle of the fashionable world. One cannot afford *not* to be seen here, no matter whom one rubs elbows with."

"But she's just sitting there, as if she has every right to be in our presence!" Marigold cried.

Gianna was indeed looking over the crowd, her gaze cool and impertinent. Clara had the feeling that Kelbourne's mistress never suffered from the sort of anxieties that plagued her own mind every day.

"As Mama just said, she has every right to be here," Clara pointed out. "Could we please not make a fuss about it? Torie will be so horribly embarrassed."

"That poor girl," her mother said. "That poor, poor girl."

People often talked of Torie that way, as if she had been staked to a rock and fed to a dragon. That was dramatic, but Clara adored fairy stories, and her mother always acted as if Torie was on the point of death. Which she wasn't.

"Gentlemen of quality do have mistresses," Clara said. "We all know that. When Kelbourne was betrothed to Leonora, he told her as much himself. I fail to see why we should decry *her*, rather than condemn *him*!"

"Clara Vetry!" her mother cried in ringing tones, dropping the languid pose that she affected in public. "I am appalled that you would mention such a dreadful subject."

"We are all talking about that subject, Mama," Clara objected.

Aunt Marigold was still gazing contemptuously at Gianna. "The waiters just delivered two bottles of pink champagne," she reported. "She drinks it

like water, so they say. Instead of breakfast tea."
Her voice grated with horror; that choice might be
more offensive than the lady's profession.

Lord Kelbourne had to know that someone
would tell Torie. But would he care? Presumably,
darling Torie already knew of the woman. After all,
she was the one who had told Clara years ago that
the viscount would never give up his mistress.

All around them, chatter kicked up as people
scanned that box and then made sure their neighbors did as well.

Kelbourne was staring blankly at the dance floor.
Clara thought he didn't even see all the people
peering at him.

She had a strong feeling that he wouldn't give a
damn. Not given that sardonic tilt to his lips.

"She should jilt him and marry the duke," Clara's
mother said. "I heard on the best authority that the
man's brokenhearted. His mother ordered him off
to Bath to take the waters, as she feared his liver
would give out from distress."

The rigid line of Aunt Marigold's mouth opened
just enough to intone, "That woman is a jezebel.
The viscount is a devil." She was likely scanning
her memory for applicable Biblical verses.

"Kelbourne bellowed at Lord Peyrenes in Lords,
saying he was as greedy as a hog," Lady Vetry put
in. "As a hog! Can you imagine? Everyone knows
that Lord Peyrenes lavishes attention on his six
spaniels; they sleep in velvet beds. That is *not* the
action of a greedy man!"

"Gentlemen have mistresses," Clara insisted.
"Are all of them devils?" She would never say as
much to her mother, but surely Lady Vetry knew of
her husband's paramour. Clara had seen the lady

in question in Hyde Park, driving in a smart two-wheeled cabriolet presumably paid for by Clara's father. Her father's mistress had been driving herself, while his wife wouldn't even walk down the street without a groom and maid in attendance.

"Gentlemen may do as they wish in their private time. They do not make a performance of themselves, parading a doxy in public," her mother replied, very much on her dignity. "Out of respect for their wives. Viscount Kelbourne is behaving with what one can only describe as *contempt*."

The countess with whom she had been talking earlier turned around and said, "Lady Vetry, I agree. I expect it is because he is being forced to marry. I heard that he owes Sir William a great deal of money."

The woman beside her ladyship looked like a frog but cackled like a goose. "It's the other way around. Sir William owes Kelbourne money, and the man has taken his daughter in payment. Of course Kelbourne doesn't respect Miss Sutton." After a pause, she added delicately, "For more than one reason, of course."

Lady Vetry glanced at Clara, but thankfully she held her tongue. Over the years, Clara had made it clear that no one in her family was allowed to make disparaging comments about Torie's intelligence.

In Clara's opinion, her friend was smarter than any of the women who clustered around them, their only claim to cleverness being the ability to read the gossip columns over their breakfast tea.

She stole another look. Now Kelbourne was speaking with more animation on his face than she'd ever seen before. More than she'd ever seen when he talked to Torie.

Her heart throbbed with sadness. When the viscount kissed Torie in front of the whole theater, she'd actually believed he was infatuated. It seemed so romantic, kissing his fiancée in the middle of a performance of *Romeo and Juliet*, as if the play had stirred his heart.

Men were a conundrum. She absently straightened the whiskers on her kitten bag until her mother's voice caught her attention again.

". . . diamonds!" Lady Vetry was saying, her tone exhilarated. There was nothing that Mama loved better than a scandal.

"What diamonds?" Clara asked.

"The ones she's wearing. A circlet worth a fortune."

"Payment for the wages of sin," Aunt Marigold said sourly. Her forehead was still pleated in shock; although she was always looking for evidence of sin, her aunt was—to Clara's mind—absurdly astonished when she found it.

"I would guess that the diamonds were a gift to reconcile the woman to his coming marriage," Lady Vetry pronounced. "Not that she could have hoped to marry him, being a woman from the gutter, but she has been under the viscount's protection for some time."

"Years," the countess put in.

They were all silent for a moment.

Clara didn't know about the rest, but without locking a man into a marriage, she thought she'd be lucky if a gentleman stayed with her for a year. She couldn't even find one who liked her enough to propose, let alone one who would *pay* for her company.

Not that being a mistress was merely a question of companionship, of course. She knew that.

"I think it's a crying shame," the countess said, finally. "Kelbourne seems to be doing this deliberately to humiliate Miss Sutton, which is so unkind. I agree with you, Lady Vetry. She ought to jilt him."

"Surely . . . surely he isn't," Clara stuttered. She couldn't bear it. Poor Torie had already put up with so many insults since everyone found out that she couldn't read.

"I'd wager he doesn't give a damn because she's addled," someone else said.

"Don't forget the Dorney wards," the countess put in, a malicious glitter in her eyes. "A ninny for a nanny—that's what my husband said."

"Torie is *not* a ninny!" Clara burst out. "He couldn't be so cruel as to do this deliberately."

"If that's the truth, then he simply doesn't care for her feelings," her mother retorted. "Look at the way he kissed his fiancée in front of the whole theater—as if she were no better than a courtesan."

They were all chattering, humming like a beehive in summer, some arguing for Torie's deliberate humiliation and others that the viscount was an uncaring lout. At the same time, they kept peeking out of the corners of their eyes, hoping Kelbourne would pull his mistress into his arms and give them a show paralleling the one he put on during the interval of *Romeo and Juliet*.

Clara turned her back and desperately thought about whether Torie would want to know. Thankfully, her friend couldn't read the gossip columns. Since Leonora left for Wales, the scandal sheets were presumably not delivered to the house any longer, so her maid wouldn't read them to her either.

"Showering her in diamonds," the countess said,

catching Clara's attention, "while his poor fiancée has a paltry emerald for a betrothal ring."

"Poor woman" seemed to be the general summary of Torie's plight.

Torie could jilt him at the altar, and after this evening, not a person in polite society would blame her. The scandal wouldn't affect her marriage prospects since she could send a groom to Bath and retrieve the liverish duke.

But she had only one day to make up her mind. On Friday morning, Torie would walk down the aisle of Westminster Abbey, and after that?

In the eyes of society, she would be a ninny *and* a nanny for the rest of her life.

CHAPTER 20

The next morning, Torie twisted the large emerald off her finger and put it on the windowsill where it didn't risk being dabbed with paint. She was trying to decide if she'd made a terrible mistake.

The twins were so happy. And so was Torie—when she was in the nursery, or when she was kissing Dominic. The rest of the time she was plagued by serious doubts about how well she and her husband would get along.

She couldn't help thinking that the Duke of Queensberry would have acquiesced to any reasonable request she made. It wasn't just that His Grace was malleable: he was *ready* to get married. He wanted a partner in life.

Dom? Not so much.

The more time she spent with him, the firmer her impression that her future husband envisioned his life unchanged by the addition of a wife, other than in the bedchamber and, of course, the nursery.

The problem wasn't so much that she and Dominic together were as combustible as kindling, but that he really did consider her primarily a nanny, not a wife.

Perhaps due to her inability to take over the household accounts, Dominic hadn't introduced her to his steward. Although he had chosen Leonora for her hostessing skills, he had told Torie that she needn't fuss if he invited a few people to dinner, because Mrs. Flitwick knew his preferences. Moreover, he noted that he would frequently dine out and she could al-

ways eat with the twins. Clearly dinners together as
husband and wife were not a priority.

Dominic followed that patronizing announcement by giving her such a scorching kiss that she
temporarily forgot to challenge him.

Did he imagine she would dine in the nursery,
waiting with bated breath for the moment when
her lord and master strode through the door?

He wouldn't have assumed that attitude with
Leonora. Torie's sister would have demanded companionship most evenings. She would have insisted
her husband accompany her to balls and musicales
and all the social occasions that the Season offered.

For some reason, he assumed that Torie would
rather stay at home, even though she distinctly remembered telling him of her love for the theater.

Putting that irritating thought away with her betrothal ring, she pulled on her pinafore, enjoying
the familiar smell of paint. At least when she was
in her studio, no one thought she was *less* than a
lady. She had mastered ladylike subjects such as
roses and rabbits.

A half hour later, she was staring blindly at her
canvas, a paintbrush dripping burnt sienna onto
the floor, thinking about the outcome of their
wrangle the night before. Dom had given her one
of his rare smiles, pulled her into his lap, and said,
"Can't you guess why we argue so much, darling?"

"Because you are wrong?"

"Because I want to claim you as my own. To toss
you onto a bed and lick you until you are hoarse
with pleasure." He kissed her. "And you want the
same," he added, his voice dark with anticipation.

Of course Torie's mouth had eagerly opened to

his kiss. To her surprise, every kiss seemed more intimate than the last, as if they carried memories of all the previous kisses with them.

Her fiancé only had to look at her, and the feeling of his hands caressing her breasts made her breath catch. A whiff of his citrusy soap made her legs quiver. She tasted his mouth and stopped thinking altogether.

When she was in his arms, the rest of the world fell away; she could imagine herself married, able to kiss him wherever she wished, rather than in carriages and dark corners. In truth, kissing was the backbone of their relationship, the only activity during which Dom stopped being argumentative and snobbish and became abruptly enthralled, looking at her with utter fascination.

The viscount *talked* in the grip of desire. He groaned words into her mouth, whispered them against her skin, even growled them hungrily in her ear while they were dancing: what he wanted to do, what he planned to do, how she made him feel.

It was all amazingly educational. At home in bed, she puzzled over his promises until she figured out the postures he described.

Luckily, she had discovered one thing that she instinctively knew how to do well. Painting was hard work; seducing Dom was not. She needed no instruction to run her hands over his nipples, drawing a low groan from his throat. When he traced her bottom lip with a finger, she nipped it—and then sucked. After that, he kissed her so fiercely that heat pummeled her body—specifically her most private parts, the ones no one had glimpsed except for her maid.

Around Dom, she was addled not by words, but

by feelings. Though he had only taken off his shirt once, in her studio, her hands often slipped under that garment. Touching his hair-roughened chest made her head swim.

She couldn't wait to bed him after their wedding tomorrow.

The only problem was the rest of the time, when he stalked around as if the world was his castle, and his pronouncements had the magical ability to become fact.

Those pronouncements brought out the worst in her, Torie had to admit. She fought the impulse to counter *whatever* he said, whether it was as simple as a dislike of picnics, or as complex as an assessment of her relationship with her sister. One bitter argument had broken out when Dominic announced that he didn't want Leonora invited to the wedding.

He had demanded with raw anger that Leonora not "sully" the ceremony.

"Because she jilted you?" Torie had choked out, appalled to think he cared.

He had barked with laughter. "Hell, no. I won't have her in the church, putting you down. That is not negotiable, Torie!"

How many things would he decide were not negotiable? Would he domineer over all aspects of her life?

Torie had a nauseating feeling that the answer was yes. Dominic always thought he knew best, even when his ideas were based in ignorance. He didn't understand the relationship she had with Leonora, the sisterly bond that he would never grasp.

On those nights after their nanny withheld Torie's

supper because "only lazy children refused to read," Torie would climb into Leonora's bed. Her big sister would give her a roll that she had hidden in her pocket and then read aloud the book that Torie had been instructed to read for the next day. Torie's memory was such that she could "read" perfectly for some time, but inevitably she would continue when she should have turned a page, and Nanny would erupt, instructing her to hold out her hands, palms up.

With a violent shake of her head, Torie dismissed those bad memories and turned to her painting, drawing her brush again across the cake of burnt sienna.

Two hours later, the door swung open. Out of the corner of her eye, Torie saw Clara close the door in the butler's face.

"Hello, darling," Torie said absent-mindedly. A glow of satisfaction was humming through her body. After months of work, the painting was finally coming together. It was done. She squinted. Almost done . . . perhaps a bit more sienna in the lower right.

Clara moved to stand next to her. "Torie, it's . . . well, it's not precisely lovely. It's—it's so *sad*," she burst out.

Torie dropped a kiss on her cheek. "You think so?"

"Anyone would."

"Dominic described it as 'nice.' Oh, and 'meticulous.'"

"Men are philistines," Clara said. "I haven't met one who understands my darling reticules. If not sadness, what were you aiming at, Torie?"

"I was trying to capture a feeling of time."

"Because the flowers are dying?"

Torie nodded. "A vase of flowers exists for a

flicker of time in my life or yours. Think how many blossoms wilt and are thrown away before we even notice a new bouquet appearing on the sideboard. We have so many days, and flowers have so few. Yet we discard them as soon as their petals begin to discolor."

"Not just sad but tragic," Clara muttered, staring at the painting.

"In my painting, at least, the flowers exist for themselves, in their own time," Torie said, knowing her objectives made no sense to anyone but her.

"It makes me think how fragile everything is. These are beautiful still, even while dying."

"The ironic thing is how many flowers have wilted and died in the months I've been working on the piece, just so I can get the details right."

"Absolutely worth it," Clara said. "Is this one good enough to hang on your father's wall, or will you give it away?"

Torie gave her a one-armed hug. "I thought I might give it to my husband."

"He'd better treasure it."

"If he doesn't, I'll take it away and send it to you. It's just as well the piece is finished, given the wedding tomorrow."

"I have to tell you something," Clara said, her face suddenly pinched with worry.

"Is your family all right?"

Clara's words tumbled out. "It's Kelbourne, Torie. He took Gianna Peccati to Vauxhall last night. She was wearing a ravishing diamond necklace, and people say it was a gift to convince her to forgive his marriage."

At first Torie couldn't understand; Clara's words had jumbled in her brain as if they were written down on paper. Then she turned away sharply, realizing her hands were shaking as she took off her pinafore and hung it on the wall.

"Did you know he still had a mistress?" Clara asked. "Because, of course, many women don't care about such matters."

Torie looked blindly out the window rather than at her friend's face. "I didn't."

She hadn't believed his dictum regarding his mistress pertained to her, to their marriage. Not given the way they were together. The things he said to her. Their kisses.

She had assumed . . . *assumed*! What an idiot she was. His life was continuing in its usual path, marriage or no. Obviously, that life included a mistress, just as Odysseus's afterlife included a nymph—never mind the fact that Penelope had waited all those years for his return.

"Kelbourne wouldn't have paraded that woman in front of all society if he were marrying Leonora!" Clara said, spitting with rage like a wet cat. "He wouldn't have dared. He disrespected you, Torie. It wasn't a masquerade night, and no one was wearing masks. He sat there beside her in the open, eating ham and drinking pink champagne."

"Apparently her tastes haven't changed," Torie said, grimacing. She walked over to the sideboard and began to rub speckled paint from her fingertips with an oily rag. She felt sick with anger—at him and at herself. Leonora had clarified the question of faithfulness when she planned to marry him, so why hadn't she?

She knew the answer. It was her own bravado. She had spent her time worrying about whether she would be enough for him—smart enough, interesting enough—but she assumed that she would be enough in *bed*, because she walked away from their kisses tingling all over, longing for their wedding night.

Now that emotion sickened her. Perhaps he had been kissing her and then taking his carriage over to Gianna's house and—

Torie wrenched her mind away. She couldn't bear to imagine him in bed with another woman. It wasn't just that the Italian woman was reputedly so beautiful. Gianna was brilliant; she spoke three languages and could sing in several more. She was everything Torie wasn't, except Torie was a lady. A possible viscountess.

Obviously, Dominic would have married Gianna, if his mistress had a claim to gentle blood.

"I'm so sorry," Clara said miserably. "I hated to tell you, because I know you genuinely like Kelbourne. But I thought . . . it's not too late to rethink this marriage, Torie." She paused. "There's a rumor going around that your father owes him ten thousand pounds, and you are being forced to marry him rather than the Duke of Queensberry as a result."

Torie sank onto the sofa and put her face in her hands.

"It isn't true, is it?" Clara asked. She plopped down beside her and started rubbing Torie's back. And then, when Torie didn't answer, she said dismally, "It *is* true. No wonder Leanora ran away! It's so unfair, Torie. Why should you pay Sir William's debts? It's grotesque, like the old stories of wives sold at Bartholomew Fair to the highest bidders!"

Torie choked back tears until she trusted herself to lift her face. "That's not true about my father's debts."

Clara pulled her into a hug. "Gentlemen aren't supposed to behave like this, especially not when they're about to be married. My father probably accompanies his mistress to Vauxhall, but only on a masquerade night when he couldn't be recognized. Could you persuade Kelbourne to behave with more decorum after the wedding?"

"I doubt it," Torie said, sitting upright again. "Remember, he told my sister that he would never be unfaithful with a lady, but that a mistress doesn't count as adultery. Maybe he takes her to Vauxhall every week."

"Poppycock!" Clara growled, her face as bulldoggish as was possible for someone often compared to a cherub. "What if you and I went to the gardens one evening, and there he was? Eating ham with *her*? Could there be a more humiliating moment in a woman's life?"

Torie sighed. "Many men have mistresses. The practice is widespread, Clara. You know it."

Sickeningly, this shame felt worse than being called addled. She was used to that. Starting in her second Season, she had stopped hiding her illiteracy, admitting her failures with a chuckle.

But this?

True, gentlemen had mistresses, but those men didn't flaunt their coquettes before their wives—or almost-wives. How was she supposed to react? Was she supposed to chuckle when her husband strolled by, arm in arm with a diamond-clad woman?

He was the one who suggested they befuddle the ton by kissing in public, but how could she claim to be marrying him for any reason other than coercion when he paraded his mistress before Torie's acquaintances two days before their wedding?

"*Please* rethink your betrothal. I have a terrible feeling about your marriage." Clara clasped her hands together. "I know you didn't read *Castle Rackrent*, but there's a cruel husband named Sir Kit Rackrent who reminds me of Viscount Kelbourne."

"Dominic is not cruel. He can be very kind."

"Kind! Did you hear that he lost his temper the other day and shouted that Lord Bellybrook was 'false as Hell'?"

"I expect that Bellybrook is one of those people arguing against the antislavery bill."

"Yes, he does have sugar plantations, so my father says," Clara agreed. "Bellybrook is despicable. But *shouting*? In the House of Lords?"

"Dominic is passionate. He *cares*. The bill is important to him."

"I wish he cared as much for you," Clara said flatly. "That you were as important to him."

Torie swallowed hard. No matter how ignorant Dominic was about gossip columns, he had to have recognized numerous acquaintances last night; Wednesdays were the most popular night of the week to visit the pleasure gardens.

He surely knew that the truth would filter back to her.

Even worse than not caring for her reputation, he didn't care about her feelings.

"Now everyone in London is whispering about your wedding again, and not in a good way," Clara said.

"Luckily, my entire life has prepared me to walk down an aisle tomorrow morning with mocking whispers on both sides." Torie managed to keep her voice steady.

"Oh, please, won't you jilt him?" Clara implored.

"I don't believe you about your father, Torie. Even I know that he gambles to excess. Why should your life be sacrificed as a result?"

If it was just a matter of money, she *would* jilt him. She would walk the three blocks between their houses, scream an insult or two, and throw the emerald ring at his face, hopefully taking out an eye.

"The Duke of Queensberry has fallen into such a melancholy that he's fled to Bath," Clara continued. "He would marry you by special license, and you'd be a duchess. Just think, Torie: yours would be the romance of the Season! No one could call you 'poor woman' then."

"I can't jilt the viscount," Torie said heavily. "It's too late."

She felt the truth of that statement in her bone marrow. Since their betrothal, she had spent time every day with the twins. Her feelings for them when Leonora ran away to Wales were nothing to how she felt now, after accepting them as *hers*, her children. She had so many plans for their happiness and well-being. The morning after the wedding, Torie planned to fire their grumpy nanny.

As if she were Persephone, she had eaten the pomegranate seeds and doomed herself to the underworld. She would do anything for Valentine and Florence.

"Pooh!" Clara cried. "Even my mother, who loathes a scandal, thinks you should jilt him. No one would blame you."

Likely that was true. She would only blame herself.

"Shall we go have a cup of tea?" Torie asked, desperate to end the conversation.

Clara waved her hand before her nose. "*You* have need of a bath, my dear. All I can smell is turpentine. I'll leave you to think about it. I don't like Kelbourne, but please know that I will stand with you no matter what you decide."

Perhaps no one liked him. Dominic wouldn't give a damn.

After Clara trotted down the stairs, Torie sat down and tried to think clearly. She didn't have to accept public humiliation. She could demand that her fiancé dismiss Gianna. Thinking about the woman's neck glinting with diamonds made her feel positively feral.

She didn't care for diamonds, but she'd turned into a possessive wretch.

Yet if she demanded that he let the woman go, issuing an ultimatum—*keep her or marry me*—what would happen?

Dominic was not a man who would respond well to an ultimatum. He didn't like to be told what to do. He'd made it clear in small and big ways, in complaints and growls. So far, she had stubbornly growled back.

Her stomach screwed into an even tighter knot. If she gave him an ultimatum, he might choose Gianna. After all, they'd been together—if that was the proper term—for years. At least four years. Quite probably he loved her.

He was merely fond of Torie. His quixotic plan to fight anyone who humiliated her signaled affection, yet the shallowness of those affections was evident in the fact that *he* was the one who had humiliated her.

His actions told the world that he not only didn't love her, but he had no respect for her.

After Torie took a bath to wash off the turpentine, Emily helped her put on a promenade dress, burnt sienna just like the final dabs on her painting.

"The color turns your hair to burnished silver," Emily said, handing her a lacy parasol. "Are you certain you don't wish me to accompany you, Miss Torie?"

"I'm only walking to Kelbourne House," Torie said, looking in the mirror. "I think a bolder lip color, Emily, to balance the color in my gown."

Emily darted over to the dressing table and came back with a round box. Popping open the cover, she proclaimed, "Love's Last Sigh. Deep red."

Brilliant.

Just brilliant.

CHAPTER 21

$\mathcal{T}$he whole three blocks to Kelbourne House, Torie counseled herself to keep her temper. She would calmly explain that her husband could not shame her by keeping a mistress in public or private.

Ever. Never. Not at all. In fact, he had to go over there and get rid of that horrible diamond-bedecked—

No.

She took a deep breath. She was used to charming men, so why couldn't she seem to do it with Dom? With him, she lost her temper in a moment, and then he started kissing her, and then . . .

He got his way, all too often.

The Kelbourne butler opened the door with gratifying speed before she reached the top of the steps. "Miss Torie," Flitwick said, welcoming her inside. "May I take your parasol? Lord Kelbourne is in his study, if you'd like to greet him."

"Good morning, Flitwick," Torie said, handing him her gloves and unpinning her hat. "How are the twins?"

"They spent the morning in Hyde Park, as you suggested. Miss Florence brought home several earthworms, much to Nanny Bracknell's disapproval."

"What does Florence intend to do with them?"

"Paint them," Flitwick said, his eyes twinkling. "She has decided to eschew rabbits and try an animal that remains on the ground."

"A very sensible decision," Torie said. "I shall greet Lord Kelbourne. You needn't announce me, Flitwick."

When she pushed open the door to Dominic's study, she froze for a moment, trying to determine why a mere glimpse of the man had such a heady effect on her. He was seated behind a huge walnut desk, his head bent over a letter.

True, he was unfairly beautiful; his cheekbones made him look as sensitive as one of the carved stone angels she stared at in church.

Sensitive? Ha. She couldn't have found someone more insensitive. More bellicose.

Just now he was writing quickly because he was also so *competent* at everything he did. As well as passionate and self-assured.

"Are you coming in?" he asked, finishing his line.

"Yes," she said shakily, moving away from the door and shutting it behind her.

He jumped to his feet, his eyes hungry. "I thought you were Flitwick," he said, moving around his desk.

Torie instinctively reacted to his expression— and then loathed him, and her own response. How could he feel scorching lust for two women at once? Was she benefiting from Gianna's sensuality, or was he taking all the desire that flared between them and returning to Gianna's bed?

How could she want a man who was bedding another?

She forced herself to smile and curtsy. "Dom."

He bowed. "I thought we'd moved away from formal salutations."

"I did call you Dom," she murmured, allowing him to steer her to a couch. As they sat down, he brushed tendrils of hair from around her face and dropped a kiss on her nose.

"May I kiss you?"

"I'd rather not," she said, looking at her hands as she reminded herself not to lose her temper, remain calm, be charming, be . . .

All that.

For the first time in her life, she wished she'd asked Leonora for lessons on pretending to be a lady.

"What's the matter?" He shifted closer, his hip touching hers. "Where's your betrothal ring?"

Torie blinked. "I left it on the windowsill because I was painting this morning. I'll retrieve it as soon as I go home. No need to worry, as servants never enter my studio."

"I shall be very glad when you are living under my roof with servants who *will* enter your studio," Dominic said.

Torie edged away from his hip and said, "I realized that before we marry, we should have the same conversation you had with Leonora."

"Which conversation?"

"Don't you remember how horrified you were that she shared details with me?"

Dominic was having trouble paying attention.

Torie was wearing crimson lip color, precisely the same shade her lush mouth turned when reddened by his kisses. Less than a day until they married. Hardly more than twenty-four hours. Then he'd have her in his home, in his bed. His arms.

Making that needy sound in the back of her throat as he put her on the bed and worshipped her body.

He had never found himself in the grip of a craving this intense. He no sooner began listening to a speech in the Lords before his thoughts were interrupted by an image of the two of them entwined on white sheets, his hand woven into her thick hair as she—

"I apologize," he said, clearing his throat. "What conversation did I have with Leonora?"

"Regarding unfaithfulness," Torie prompted.

He frowned. "What about it?"

"I won't countenance adultery," she said, casting him a glance from under her long lashes. "By which I mean," she clarified, "I would feel hurt and angry if you had an affair. Everyone would . . . everyone would talk."

"I agree," he said.

"If you're going to strut around half-naked, you'll do it in front of me and no one else."

Lewd thoughts flashed through Dominic's head. "Agreed," he growled. "The same is true for you. You'll be faithful to me."

It was a statement, not a command. Torie was infuriating, mischievous, exquisite—*loyal*. He was pretty sure that she was marrying him out of loyalty to the twins, out of love for them. He respected that.

Perhaps even loyalty to her father. He didn't respect that, but he'd take it.

He had a bone-deep belief that she would never break her vows.

"I will be faithful as long as you are," Torie agreed. "But what about your mistress?" She raised her stubborn little chin and fixed him with an imperious glare. "You told my sister that a mistress doesn't count. I think a woman such as that *does* count, as I made clear in our discussion of Odysseus's infidelities."

Dominic felt a flare of irritation at her presumptive tone. She didn't understand the private life of gentlemen. "I have never visited a brothel—"

Incredulity flickered across Torie's eyes. "Am I supposed to celebrate your self-denial?"

He cleared his throat. "There are illnesses—"

"Syphilis, for example," she cut in. "Otherwise known as the pox. Which, by the way, is not limited to the women who work in brothels. Mistresses are just as vulnerable. As are *wives*." She spat the last word.

This conversation was getting out of hand, and Dominic could feel his temper flaring. The last thing he wanted was a wife who told him what to do, who curtailed what he did or who he spent time with. Who sought to control his behavior. He'd had enough of that from his father, and from the moment the former viscount died, Dominic had never again allowed himself to be leashed.

"The Duke of Queensberry has a mistress," he said flatly. "Did you have this conversation with him?" The moment he asked, he realized that the duke would promise anything to marry Torie. The man was absurdly infatuated.

"If you keep a mistress, I shall take a lover." Her blue eyes darkened to a seething lavender. He recognized that sign from the months of their betrothal: his fiancée had a temper like a bonfire.

"My wife will *never* take a lover," he told her, keeping his voice even. No one—*no one*—sparked his temper the way Torie did. Those idiots in the House of Lords had nothing on her.

Torie shrugged, fanning his irritation. "It's up to you. If you satisfy yourself in someone else's bed, why shouldn't I? It's only fair. Logical."

"That isn't how it's done."

"I don't give a damn how it's done," she flared. "When you tire of our bed and *caper* in some other woman's chamber, you can be damn certain that I will issue an invitation to mine."

"We will share a bedchamber," Dominic snarled, his voice ragged. "You'll sleep with me every night, so I know where you are."

She scowled at him. "I'm not the unfaithful one. You are."

Dominic was fighting the conviction that no wife should command her husband's private life. It was shameful. Raw emotion caught him by the throat, an offensive experience.

"No one tells me what to do," he stated.

Torie raised an eyebrow. "Maturity often brings new experiences," she said coolly. "I am merely informing you of the consequences of your own actions, so you understand them." She leaned forward and caught his eyes.

"If you *ever* humiliate me the way you did last night, flaunting your diamond-clad mistress before my acquaintances, you will never know who fathered your children. I am not my sister, reluctant to damage her reputation as a perfect lady. Think of me as more akin to *your* sister!"

Dominic's face closed like a steel trap. "Humiliate you?" he repeated, his voice grating.

"Vauxhall?" she demanded.

His heart skipped a beat, curses rocketing through his head.

"Those gossip columns you claim to know nothing about?" she fired at him. "You and your Italian friend will be front and center in every single one this morning. Luckily for me, I can't read them—but then, I have no need to. I've already heard from one friend, and I'm sure many more will give me their condolences. They will wait until tomorrow, at our *wedding*!"

Dominic digested that with a stab of remorse.

No, a tidal wave of remorse. He'd been an idiot. Again.

"You were intentionally disrespectful of me and our impending wedding," Torie said scathingly.

"I had no such intention," he said, voice rasping. "I suppose people showed particular interest because of the wedding." What in the hell had he been thinking? He hadn't been thinking. Hadn't thought clearly in days, to be honest. He had been too focused on Torie, which was ironic now.

"Precisely the same interest they paid us at the theater, so don't pretend that you didn't anticipate it," she retorted. "I told you long ago that reporters dog your mistress." Fury vibrated in her voice. "The fact that you bedecked that woman in diamonds and took her to Vauxhall—which is regularly attended by the fashionable world, including myself—was fascinating to all."

Color had ebbed from her face, leaving crimson lips against skin that was the precise shade of wallpaper paste.

Gianna had summoned him to Vauxhall, and he had thought . . . well, it didn't matter what he thought, because he hadn't considered the consequence. Torie was furious, but more than that, she was shamed, her eyes raw with humiliation.

"Yes, this does feel worse than being labeled a silly butterfly," she said, confirming his thought. "Oh God, I wish I had married Queensberry. He would never have done this."

The longing in her voice shattered Dominic's haze of self-condemnation. His brain snapped into cold calculations, precisely as it did when he was thwarted in debate. He'd *fucked up*. For a moment, he considered Gianna's motives for asking him to meet her in Vauxhall—and pushed that thought away.

Torie was looking at him like an enemy. That skewered him through the gut. In the last few months, he'd felt as if he'd made a friend for the first time in his life. They didn't agree on much, but he enjoyed skirmishes over the *Odyssey* far more than fights over moral issues in Lords that felt, to him, as if only one side was ethical.

Now that friend was justifiably looking at him with a combination of distaste, disappointment, and rage.

"We are due to marry tomorrow morning," she told him. "I'll offer you a choice. Either we break it off here, or we wait to consummate the marriage until you are finished with your other relationship and free to concentrate on your wife."

His eyes narrowed. Choice? It was an order. That maddening thought battled with the equally maddening hunger for her that turned his bones to molten lead. The pulse of it beat in his blood, in his bones—in his groin.

At the same time, his pride was outraged. His manhood. He could hear his father's harsh voice in his mind, squawking with laughter at any man who let himself be dictated to by a woman, especially by a wife.

"That is not a choice, but an ultimatum."

Her chin took on the challenging slant that had grown familiar. Her willful mouth tightened in the corners.

"An ultimatum would be if I insisted you discharge your mistress before we marry. I am giving you a choice. At some point, you may become tired of champagne for breakfast and feel like joining your wife for a simple cup of tea. Or you may not. Until then, I shall remain your nanny, which is, by the way, how you treat me when you aren't kissing me. There will be *no* kissing the nanny in dark corners."

She pressed a hand to her waist. Dominic knew that gesture; Torie's stomach was churning with the strength of her feelings.

"You don't want to consummate our marriage?" he demanded, incredulous.

"I will never share my husband with another woman," Torie stated, her eyes glittering at him. "You scarcely envision me as a wife anyway. Face it: in your mind, I'm a glorified nursemaid, albeit with some extracurricular capering. Except that now I understand that you have other bedrooms to caper in."

"I do not think of your role in my life that way!"

Her lip curled. "As your wife, I am supposed to make no demands and set down no rules. We might occasionally entertain, but the invitations would come from you, and the arrangements needn't strain my pitiful brain. You'll be out most nights, so I should feel free to 'join the children in the nursery,' which implies you think that I will be humbly waiting at home for you." She laughed.

Her hand slipped away from her stomach: not calm, but better.

"I didn't mean it that way," Dominic said, trying to remember precisely what he'd said.

"Yes, you did. Really, you must stop denying statements for which there's so much evidence," she retorted. "I don't blame you. You find me addled, but you're fond of me, and protective too. I learned long ago to separate people's motives and their assessments."

"You are completely misunderstanding my opinion of you."

"My point is that you have declared over and over that you don't want me to be ashamed. You insisted my own sister couldn't attend the wedding in case she said something slighting to me. And yet *you* arranged it so that the entire congregation of the cathedral—every single person—will be tittering about your relationship with Gianna while you vow, supposedly, to be faithful to me. That was worse than anything my sister could have said!"

Dominic wanted to thunder a denial—but he was the one in the wrong. He didn't have the moral high ground the way he did in the House of Lords.

"You shamed me just before we are to marry," Torie said, her voice breaking. "That says to me that your relationship with Gianna is stronger than ours." Her eyes were shining with tears. "It says that your fondness for me is as shallow as a puddle."

"That isn't true," Dominic said hoarsely, feeling as if he were drowning. "I do care for you, and I am deeply regretful of my thoughtless behavior last night." He took her ringless hand in his, hoping that it wasn't a sign. "Please believe that I had no intention of disrespecting you. I didn't think of the consequences, or I would never have agreed to go to Vauxhall."

Her eyes searched his face, and to his relief, they softened. "People thought you were deliberately humiliating me, but I hated to believe it."

"I would *never* do that," he growled.

"You are too fond of me to be so cruel. I told Clara that."

The words stabbed him. "I apologize."

He was solidly on the wrong side of the moral fence, and it felt—horrible. "My only excuse is that I didn't think about gossip. Or reporters. The opinions of ladylike matrons are meaningless to me. They don't matter."

"My feelings matter to me," Torie said, her hand going back to her stomach.

"Of course," he said raggedly. He'd done it *again*, said the wrong thing. Defended the indefensible. "I didn't mean that."

"At least we're being honest with each other now, more than we ever were before." Her voice had a jaundiced undertone that he hated. "I suspect that your relationship with Gianna is the longest and deepest you have had in your life."

Dominic's lifelong dedication to honesty stifled his response. She wasn't wrong. He and Gianna went back years.

He had never made male friends the way other gentlemen did. His father had been a beast and kept him away from boys his own age. His sister had flitted here and there, unable to stay in one place. They'd had no real bond.

When he couldn't bring himself to lie, Torie said heavily, "I do know that you have been together for more years than I've known you. I always thought men liked variety in the bedchamber, but you have been faithful to her, presumably."

"Yes."

His father's commands were clashing with the disdainful expression in Torie's eyes. Her ultimatum was unacceptable. Giving in would be shaming.

But then, he had shamed her . . . His mind went into a dizzying spiral, trying to calculate the best option, the argument that would satisfy her and preserve his integrity.

"Since you're referring to your mistress, I shall not congratulate you for your fidelity," Torie said with devastating frankness.

"I am not yet married," Dominic said, his father's barking voice echoing in his head so strongly that he fancied it could be heard in the room.

"As of tomorrow, your relationship, if one can call it that, will become adulterous," she retorted. "Vows are vows. I've never heard a proviso in the Anglican marriage ceremony excusing paid intimacies, have you? 'With my body I thee worship' doesn't have the addendum, 'except when I'm worshipping someone else's body.'"

"You've made your point," Dominic said. He was hanging on to his temper by a straw, aware it was flaring high out of guilt. Because *he* was the villain. He was the man whose wife would be mocked all over London. The cathedral would indeed be crammed with people coming to whisper, gloat, and laugh.

"You and I will not sleep together until you agree to stay out of Miss Peccati's bedchamber," Torie repeated.

Dominic opened his mouth to tell her—

She cut him off. "Furthermore, if I ever discover you have taken another mistress, I shall take a lover, whether or not I have provided you with heirs. As I already informed you."

A low growl came from his chest. He had to leave the room; he was about to erupt, and when he lost his temper, he invariably said things he didn't mean. It had become the hard and fast rule of his adult life: leave before you shout.

Unless in Parliament, of course.

"If you don't agree to that, I will jilt you here and now. I will take it upon myself to explain it to Florence and Val. It will break their hearts, but they will understand—and after that discussion, we can return adultery to the Prohibited List, if you'd like. It's bad enough that I'm agreeing to marry someone like you, but if we don't even begin with an even playing field? I simply can't do it. I don't think I could ever love you."

What did she mean by "someone like you?" Cold, self-absorbed, and unfaithful, presumably?

He didn't want her to clarify that sentence.

"What's more, if we consummate this marriage, I can't promise that we'll have two sons. I don't know how Leanora thought she could. We might have two daughters. We might have only one. We might have seven."

"Seven!"

"Or none. People never seem to consider the fact that some couples are not immediately fruitful." She narrowed her eyes. "It might be *years* until you are free to buy yourself variety in the bedchamber. You might want to keep that in mind when making your choice, as well as the possibility that I may prove to be barren, which would curtail any *cavorting* in other women's chambers."

Dominic was a consummate debater, skilled at knowing when to hold his fire. There was no point in arguing until they were able to consummate the marriage. Tomorrow.

Part of him couldn't believe that she hadn't already jilted him. If he let go with the howl in his chest . . . His blood was pounding through his veins so hard that he could hear it in his ears. He had to leave the room.

She'd jilt him if he shouted. He knew it.

"I agree to your terms," he said abruptly. "Your ultimatum," he added, just so they both knew he'd given in under protest.

He had to make certain that didn't become a habit. He certainly wouldn't obey her routinely.

Just now and then, since conceding a losing battle was sometimes the best way to win the war.

CHAPTER 22

June 3, 1802
Westminster Abbey

$\mathcal{T}$he following morning, Torie walked the long aisle of the cathedral on her father's arm, each step closer to the altar sending a fresh wave of terror through her body.

Ahead of her, Florence was prancing along, throwing rose petals left and right. Dressed in delicate violet for half mourning, curls bound by a circlet of rosebuds, the girl was utterly adorable, and the audience had audibly sighed at the sight of her.

Clara followed Florence, serving as Torie's witness since her sister remained in Scotland. Dominic waited at the altar, Valentine at his side.

Torie's heart pounded like thunder in her ears. She wasn't taking the easy option, which would have been to jilt Dominic and marry the Duke of Queensberry.

But Queensberry didn't have Valentine and Florence. Of course, he also didn't have a temper.

Dominic would explode if she began visiting another man's house every day. He would be a prickly and possessive husband. Even worse, he had turned her into a prickly and possessive woman, with a temper to match his.

"No one questioned Leonora's ability to manage the viscount," Clara had said that very morning, in a last-minute plea that Torie jilt her fiancé. "I am genuinely concerned for you. Apparently his roars can be heard all down the corridor in the House of Lords!"

Even from several pews away, she could see a glitter in Dom's hooded eyes as he waited at the altar. She knew him well now: that ferocious expression signaled intense focus, not rage. His jawline was clenched because he wasn't sure what marriage to her would be like. He hated the fact that she'd given him an ultimatum.

She understood his dislike. *Neither* of them had taken the easy option. He could have found another lady to marry. Torie had none of her sister's docility, the air of fragility that Leonora put on so well.

What sort of marriage would they have if they fought over every aspect of their marital life? If he didn't give up that mistress . . . If she took a lover?

Deep inside, she was praying that he had dismissed Gianna. Perhaps he wasn't experiencing the same sensual hunger Torie was. Or perhaps he *was*, but it was directed at all women.

Or—a sickening thought—just at Gianna and her.

Florence reached the top of the aisle and dropped into a curtsy before Dominic, who bowed—and then kissed the top of her head. Her back to the audience, Clara scowled at Dominic before whisking Florence to the front row.

Torie's hands were visibly trembling by the time she joined Dominic at the altar. She couldn't help thinking of the dreams she cherished: visions of a man who would love her for what she was, rather than forgive her for what she wasn't. Dominic had promised not to humiliate her ever again, but that was a long way from respecting her.

Throughout the marriage service, she kept peeking at the viscount's face, hoping to see an emotion that she could interpret as loyalty. His eyes crackled with intensity as he listened to the minister, whose words she couldn't comprehend.

Why listen? Vows were for people who planned . . . well, who were vowing fidelity. Which neither of them was.

"I do," she said huskily, madly regretting her acceptance the moment she uttered the words. From the corner of her eye, she saw Dominic's large frame relax. So he hadn't been sure whether she would humiliate him by running screaming from the altar, playing her sister's role but with a crueler twist.

The ironic thing was that she cared about Dominic too much to do that to him. She was a fool when it came to him. More than a fool.

The twins would still have loved her if she married the duke.

Too late now.

Thoughts chased each another around in her head like the horses of a carousel. She was going to have to stand up for herself, or she'd be walked on. Not deliberately, but because Dominic always thought he knew best. It was a constitutional part of his character. She could not allow herself to be squashed beneath the foot of a man who was so forceful and sure of himself.

"I do," Dominic said in a deep rumble. She heard Florence give a little whoop from the front seat, where she sat beside Valentine.

Walking back down the aisle, Torie kept sucking in shaky breaths, telling herself that she had made her bed, and now she had to lie in it. Throughout history, countless women had survived loveless marriages. An Oxford professor had once regaled her with information about ancient ancestors who "lived in caves" and were uninterested in fidelity, or so he'd said.

She should have married him. He could barely afford a cave, let alone a mistress.

Sickeningly, she still faced the challenge of signing the parish book validating her wedding. Emily met her at the end of the aisle, murmuring congratulations as she discreetly handed over a reticule containing a bottle of ink.

Once Torie, Dominic, Clara, and Valentine joined the archbishop in the sanctuary, Dominic signed the parish book and stepped away. Torie moved forward with her ink bottle, but His Excellency turned obstinate, insisting that she sign the parish book in black ink rather than something as "newfangled" as blue.

Clara leaned toward the archbishop, and suddenly the man gave a little shriek and jumped away, as if he'd been stuck with a spit.

Torie quickly scrawled her name in blue. Acting as Dominic's witness, Valentine smirked at her as he signed his in blue; Clara snatched her quill and did the same.

They arrived at her childhood home to find that Sir William had put on a lavish wedding reception complete with a cake soaked in marsala and covered with sugar icing, brandied chocolate, and every kind of breakfast food from buttered toast to coddled eggs.

Torie drifted around the drawing room, Florence hanging on one hand, accepting congratulations and the occasional hushed commiseration. She seemed to instinctively know where her husband was, enabling her to stay far away from him.

Would that be the future of their marriage? The thought was enough to make her despair.

When a second wave of food—ranging from stuffed crane to beefsteak—was shepherded in by the redoubtable Flitwick, Florence ran off to find Valentine, leaving Torie chatting with friends. Dominic was on the other side of the room, his eyes glinting at a hapless lord who was apparently daring to disagree with him. Later he began talking to a beautiful woman who looked vaguely Italian. Of course, not Gianna. There was no mixing between ladies and women of the demimonde except at Vauxhall.

He looked . . .

Well, he looked precisely as he always did. Broody and bloody-minded, iron-willed and—so handsome. Torie's stomach curled into a painful knot, but she couldn't let herself put a hand to her stomach in case it was taken as a sign of pregnancy.

"Time to leave," Dominic said a half hour later, appearing at her shoulder. "Twilight has fallen. Valentine had three pieces of wedding cake along with a handful of olives, and I think he's going to be very ill. Your motherly skills are required."

Clara kissed her, glanced at Torie's husband, and stamped away without bidding him farewell.

Dom's eyes glittered derisively from beneath lowered lids.

"You make her nervous," Torie said defensively.

"The woman's addled," he retorted. "Did you see that absurd reticule she was carrying? She stabbed the archbishop with it."

"Clara designed it herself," Torie muttered. He was just voicing the same unkind things he thought of *her*. She and her best friend, both addled and shallow as puddles.

They located the twins, who looked rather more pale than usual. "We tried champagne," Florence reported. "The monk who made it said it tasted like stars, but we don't agree." She swallowed. "Or the olives don't agree with the stars."

"We've never had olives before," Valentine informed them. "Or boiled tongue, stuffed crane, and coddled eggs. Or wedding cake, brandied hot chocolate, and cheese straws."

"I gather you tried them all?" Torie asked. "Where is Nanny Bracknell?"

"We sent her home," Florence said. "After all, our parents are here." She swallowed convulsively again, and Torie made a mental note to inform Nanny that the twins were not in charge. Along with the news that this had been her last day of employment.

Dominic's coach was waiting on the street, but he refused to allow the children to enter, which was a good decision since Florence was sick after walking one block.

Strangely enough, that brought on one of Dominic's rare smiles. "I am lucky that you have such a strong parenting instinct," he commented, watching Torie hold back Florence's thick curls as the girl threw up in the gutter.

A block later, Valentine turned green and gagged, so Torie chirped, "How lucky I am that you . . . what was the rest of that sentence?"

He eyed her. "You never forget anything."

She handed him a handkerchief.

Later that evening, Torie allowed Emily, bubbling with naughty laughter, to dress her in a silk nightdress. She climbed into bed and waited, gnawing her bottom lip. They had agreed not to consummate the marriage, but would Dominic pay her a visit for the sake of appearances?

She was just beginning to fall asleep when the sound of her bedroom door opening jolted her back to wakefulness.

"Good evening, viscountess."

CHAPTER 23

Good evening," Torie choked out, feeling extremely awkward.

Dominic sat down at her dressing table. "We have much to discuss."

She didn't care. How long did he have to stay in her bedchamber in order to convince the household that the marriage was consummated? Torie hadn't slept more than an hour the night before and spent the day being buffeted by emotion. She was desperate to sink into sleep and forget her marital state altogether.

"Most guests assured me that you will be a marvelous mother," Dominic continued, stretching out his legs.

"Yes, they seem to have settled on that as your motive for marriage," Torie said, twisting a piece of fine linen sheet between her fingers. She had no intention of telling him about the condolences she received.

At least from now on no one could warn her that she was making the mistake of her life. She had already made that mistake.

"Sir William graciously informed me that he considered my ten thousand pounds repaid."

Torie grimaced. "You didn't give him any more money, did you?"

"No. Just so you know, he requested another eight thousand, but I informed him that his daughter had forbidden it."

That explained why Sir William had been more acerbic than usual. It also explained why he had banged on her bedchamber door in the wee hours of the morning and drunkenly advised her not to marry that "ruthless bastard."

"I did pay for the wedding breakfast," Dominic added, with the air of someone confessing one of the seven deadly sins. "I had the distinct impression that otherwise Sir William might entertain our guests with stale bread and water. No, I take that back: bread and brandy."

Torie began pleating the hem of her sheet, trying to suppress her conscience's insistence that she'd been sold. Or bought. How different were these payments from a dowry and jointure, after all? Women were traded on a market basis, and she should be grateful that her price was anything close to her sister's.

The silence between them felt as thick as a brick wall.

"Did Mrs. Flitwick give you a tour of the house?" Dominic inquired. And at her nod, "Was the room designated as your studio acceptable? Flitwick had your paint and easels moved while we were at church."

"I'm afraid that I need a room with a better light," Torie said. "Flitwick was most understanding and plans to move everything again tomorrow. We must sacrifice the breakfast room, but Flitwick tells me that the dining room is more convenient for him and the footmen."

Beginning tomorrow, she would focus on raising Florence and Valentine. She might even begin a new painting in her series of "time" still lifes: dead flowers this time. Withered, dead flowers, thanks to Persephone's time in the underworld.

That subject could qualify as "mythological,"

which was more highly regarded than simple floral arrangements.

"The servants have migrated to your camp," Dominic said. "This morning Flitwick came damn close to giving me some sort of paternal advice, which would have had him fired on the spot."

"You cannot fire Flitwick!"

"Why not? You plan to fire Nanny Bracknell."

Torie choked back a retort. Dominic's face was etched with lines of exhaustion and savage tension, so she wasn't the only one who'd had a hard day. A rotten wedding day.

"Would you like a drink?" he asked.

She swallowed hard, trying to keep pent-up tears from falling. "Yes, thank you."

Dominic pulled a flask from the pocket of his dressing gown. "Your father handed it to me before the wedding. He did the same thing before telling me of Leonora's flight, so I decided he was boozing me up before you jilted me at the altar. Making his daughters two for two." He poured golden liquor into her water glass. "I was certain that you planned to jilt me, to be honest, but I owed it to you to show up and let you do it."

She frowned, trying to make sense of what he was saying. "I suppose I could have run away last night with the Duke of Queensberry, as Leonora did with Lord Bufford."

"No, in fact you could not." He handed her the glass and sat down again at her dressing table.

"You couldn't have stopped me." At his silence, Torie sat bolt upright. "Dom, what did you do?"

He regarded her with a mutinous expression. "I would have done anything to win you. To keep you."

Her eyes widened. "He isn't in the river, is he?"

Dominic cocked an eyebrow. "You think me capable of murdering an innocent man? Well, he did have designs on my betrothed, but you were fair game. If he tries wooing my wife, he might end up in the Thames."

"I think you are far too used to getting your own way," she snapped.

"I paid off his tailor's bill, in return for which he has been enjoying a prolonged visit to Bath," Dominic said without a flicker of remorse.

Torie swallowed hard. "The duke agreed to that?"

"There was no coercion involved, if that's what you mean." His eyes softened. "Queensberry is genuinely infatuated with you, Torie, but he was at that performance of *Romeo and Juliet*. He watched us kiss. I offered him an escape from the pity he was being served at his club. I don't blame him for taking it."

"I blame him! And I blame you, too! How dare you move us around like chess pieces?"

"I can't help being the sort of man who plans ahead," he said coolly. "I didn't want to make it easy if you lost your nerve. I'm aware that Bufford was escorting Leonora hither and yon in the weeks before she ran off with him."

Torie put the glass on her bedside table and went back to pleating her sheet. Humiliation was burning down her spine. Her husband had essentially paid off the man whom she might have married in his stead. "How much?" she asked.

"Pardon me?"

"How much did it cost to send the duke to Bath?"

Silence, then: "Are you sure you want to know?"

"Oh, definitely. A woman should always know her value, don't you think? We're trained to evaluate each other by our dowries, but I have been startled to learn that unreported rates are so significant."

"The duke owed his tailor three thousand," Dominic said. "He complained that his pink embroidered coat alone cost eight hundred guineas. Sewn with glass diamonds, apparently."

"Charming," Torie said, keeping her voice steady. "You did this before the Vauxhall incident? In other words, while we were still getting along?"

She stole a glance at Dominic from under her lashes.

He was watching her steadily. "You were having second thoughts before I went to Vauxhall."

True enough.

"I never felt more grateful in my life than when you said 'I do' at the altar. Sir William had had time to convince you otherwise, and I was handicapped by my promise not to pay him off."

"So you paid off the duke instead."

He nodded.

"Actually, my father isn't very concerned either way," Torie said, still fussing with the sheet.

"Were you aware of the betting books?"

Torie looked up.

"Your father bet fifty-to-one that you would leave me at the altar. I'm afraid he's considerably poorer this evening."

"Extraordinarily offensive," she muttered, feeling her gut twist. None of the men around her gave a damn about how much they embarrassed her.

"Other wagers followed that pattern, but at least they weren't made by family members."

"Did those wagers agree with my father?"

"The odds were in favor of your flight, which made sense since gossip has been focusing on my temper as the reason for Leonora's marriage to Bufford."

"How do you know?" She couldn't imagine him sharing a cozy chin-wag with friends in his club.

"I told my valet to round up all the relative news-papers and summarize what was said of us."

"When?"

"When what?"

"When did you order your valet to collect the gossip sheets?" Torie asked.

"Three weeks ago."

So he had to have known that reporters would cover his outing with Gianna.

He shook his head at her angry look. "I was a fool. The fact that they would report my appear-ance at Vauxhall never occurred to me. How close did you come to leaving me at the altar?"

"Not close. I had made a promise."

"So did your sister."

"Not to *you*, to the twins," she said miserably. "I couldn't bear to let them down."

She picked up the glass he'd given her, but after years of smelling brandy on her father's breath and clothing, the smoky, spicy scent nauseated her. She put it back down. "I would never have left you at the altar. I would have informed you in person so that you could send a notice to the paper."

He nodded, his stubborn jaw relaxing, appar-ently happy to hear that she avoided publicly hu-miliating the people in her life. "Thank you. Did Florence tell you that she would like to pay Leonora a visit? One of the servants told her that all three of Bufford's former wives haunt his castle."

"I received a kind letter from my sister this morn-ing," Torie said.

"What does my former fiancée think of our wedding?" His voice was so derisive that if Torie hadn't known better, she would have assumed that Leonora had broken his heart. But no, she had just wounded his pride by choosing an elderly peer and a castle crowded with ghosts over his magnificent person.

"Leonora was surprised to learn that I had received a proposal from a duke."

Dominic's eyes took on a sardonic gleam. "I hope you told her that you took her nursery lessons to heart and refused the duke for the better title."

"Of course I didn't!"

"Is she happy up there in Scotland?"

"She says so."

He took a swallow of brandy straight from the flask, since she only had one water glass.

"Would you mind not drinking that in my room?" Torie asked. "I'm afraid that the smell brings back bad memories."

Whatever Dominic saw in her face must have been convincing, because he walked over to pick up her drink. "I forgot that I have a wedding present for you." He pulled a folded sheet from his coat, dropped it in her lap, and then went to the window and poured the contents of her glass and the flask into the street.

Torie opened the page, thinking he might have drawn another sketch. But no, it was a letter. As usual, the writing was unintelligible, made up of shapes running in wavy lines like childish depictions of the sea coming to shore.

"I hope you find him satisfactory, because I've already hired him," Dominic said, seating himself again. "Langlois trained at the École de Mars in Paris, which is supposedly a good place. Should be able to teach you how to paint any number of things other than rabbits, perhaps even people."

"Dom," she said, and cleared her throat, folding the sheet back up.

"You don't care for him? I can find someone else."

"I can't read this," Torie said. In the silence that followed, she added, "I gather it's a description of a Monsieur Langlois?"

"What an idiot I am," Dominic breathed, his voice rough with regret. He came over and sat down on the edge of the bed. "I muffed it. I'm sorry. I was thinking about how difficult your father's love of brandy must have made your childhood, and I didn't consider what I was doing."

"It's all right." She had learned long ago that there was no point to whining about honest mistakes. "Do tell me more about the painter." Her voice sounded husky, thickened not by tears but by the fact Dominic had seated himself so close to her. His hair was still damp from a bath, and he wasn't wearing a nightshirt, given she'd just glimpsed his chest through a gap in his robe.

Perhaps he was naked. Her imagination rocketed into improprieties.

"May I sit beside you?"

She silently moved over, watching as Dominic kicked off his slippers and sat down, atop the sheet rather than under it. His feet were strangely sensual, with powerful toes. Hers were like pink snail shells in comparison.

"The man's name is Eustache-Hyacinthe Langlois," he said. "Well-thought-of in France, and here in London due to the wars. He's happy to tutor all three of you to paint more than rabbits."

Torie ground her teeth. Her husband didn't mean

to be so condescending. He didn't know that a lady unable to read from a book or sheet music might focus on painting as the only ladylike skill available and make it the linchpin of her . . . of everything.

She murmured something vaguely grateful.

"He'll sup with us," Dominic said. "He's the son of a baron, so we can't have him belowstairs. Have you seen Valentine's latest attempt? It looks like a clamshell with long ears. I think part of the problem is that he's never seen a rabbit."

Then: "What's wrong?" he asked, tilting his arrogant, beautiful head to the side.

"Nothing," Torie said lightly, employing skills gained by years of disguising embarrassment. "It will be a pleasure to be tutored by Monsieur Langlois. When will we meet him?"

"In a week or so."

"I don't have a formal wedding present for you, but perhaps you would like the painting that I just finished. You thought it 'meticulous,' which I take as a compliment."

"I meant it as such. Your petals, the fallen ones, were very precisely detailed. I am honored by your gift."

Torie raised an eyebrow. "Truly?"

"Of course."

She looked back at the linen sheet. "A number of my friends have hung my pieces, but my father has always declined."

"I couldn't paint a daisy," Dominic said. "I don't know how to talk about art, but in my life, 'meticulous' is high praise."

"Because you place such a premium on honesty," she guessed.

"One must be meticulous in presenting facts that

might change a nation's course." He hesitated. "Can you tell me about the blue ink at church?"

She might as well disclose every wretched short-coming. "I can only sign my name in blue ink. I cannot make my signature intelligible in black." A ragged breath escaped her mouth.

If she'd had any inkling of the multifold humiliations involved in marriage, she would have happily jilted him and chosen to be an old maid.

"And you couldn't read the parish book," Dominic said, working it out in his head. "Can you read your own name?"

"No. I cannot read anything. That includes signatures."

Thick silence descended between them again.

CHAPTER 24

*D*ominic had had every intention of seducing his wife—until he saw Torie's white, weary face. He might be a bastard in the eyes of most of the cultivated, refined guests who clustered at their wedding breakfast like pigs at a trough, but he tried not to be cruel.

Though he couldn't stop himself from desiring her.

Torie's nightgown would have tempted an octogenarian bridegroom. The entire bodice was made of pure lace, flirting with pale nipples that he craved to touch.

They sat silently for five minutes before she drowsily told him to close his door on the way out. When she fell asleep, he drew her gently toward him until her head rested on his shoulder.

She was less formidable with her eyes closed. In fact, she looked sweet and delicate, although when awake, she was far from fragile. He liked that. She wasn't afraid of him. In fact, she was stubbornly fighting for dominance in their marriage. He couldn't allow it, but he respected it.

It even occurred to him that he'd never had a better-matched opponent. Her scathing looks felt as if they searched the bottom of his soul—and found it lacking. Perhaps they could be partners, though he'd never imagined such a marriage.

A few minutes later, he guided her head to the pillow. His blood was literally sparking in his veins, imploring him to wake with a kiss.

He should leave.

They hadn't had an honest conversation—or

rather, an honest conversation in which he didn't lose his temper—but there was time for that tomorrow. Hell, they had a lifetime together. The thought eased the tightness in his chest that had come on the moment she snapped at him about Vauxhall and remained, even after she promised in front of God and man to become his wife.

He couldn't get over the fact that *he* had humiliated her more than her father had. He had sworn always to protect her, and then irrationally, carelessly, injured her.

Taking a deep breath, he stood up, tossing his robe to the side, and slipped under the sheet beside her.

He couldn't sleep, so he lay awake and picked through the problems keeping them apart. There was Gianna and the question of mistresses. Other wives barred their husbands from the bedchamber after a child or two, but why should that apply to Torie? Nothing he knew of "ladies" as a species seemed to apply to her. Her dislike of his "cold, self-absorbed, and serious" personality was more difficult to overcome.

Then there was his temper. *Her* temper.

His mouth eased into one of the smiles she prized as he thought about their arguments. Conflicts in the House of Lords left him feeling enervated and full of bile. He would go to White's, his club, and then leave directly because he couldn't bear to be in the room with his peers. At least, not those with whom he disagreed.

Arguments with Torie just made him want to get closer to her. When color rose in her cheeks, he wanted to lick her stubborn lips, steal the air she was using to shout at him. He had fantasies about tupping her in every one of the places they argued:

his study, her studio, the dining table . . . hell, even the theater box. If he caught her hand and drew her to the very back, they could slip behind the velvet curtain.

In the last weeks, it hadn't mattered how often he took himself in hand to quell his lust. He was never satisfied. It had become something of a routine: argue with his fiancée, return home, hurtle into the water closet, lean against the wall with a groan escaping his lips . . . finish.

Only to visualize her lips and find an erection bobbing against his belly again.

At last he picked up her left hand, the one that wasn't tucked under her cheek, kissed her palm, and curled her fingers over the kiss.

Dominic woke hours later to find shocked blue eyes staring at him. Thankfully he had turned on his side in his sleep, which hid his morning erection.

Behind Torie, morning sunlight was pouring in, tinting her rumpled curls the milky color of opals. Somewhere close by, a swallow was fretfully singing like a child playing with a pianoforte.

He pushed himself up on his elbow. He considered kissing his wife good morning, but decided he'd better wait.

"Dom!" Torie hissed. "This is taking verisimilitude too far!"

He thought for a moment about the fact that her vocabulary was better than most of his acquaintances'. "Do you remember every word you hear?"

"No." She sat up. "I can't ring the bell for my maid while you're here. In my bed." She poked him. "You'd best be gone now. I need tea."

"So do I," Dominic said, leaning over to pull the

rope hanging by his side of the bed. "Married people have tea in bed together."

She chewed on her lower lip, looking unconvinced.

Every time she moved, her breasts shifted unsteadily, setting his blood on fire. He glanced down: his personal clothespin had tented the bed, though Torie apparently hadn't noticed.

Leaving it to fate, he crossed his arms behind his head, ridiculously pleased by the way his wedding ring looked on her finger.

"Why is it so light in here?" Torie asked crossly, avoiding his eyes.

"No maid drew the curtains, since we were supposed to be engaged in the all-important activity of validating our marriage with bodily union." Dominic felt awash in affection for his wife, which was a good start to a marriage—especially combined with the undertow of desire that nearly crippled him whenever he was in her presence.

A gentle knock on the door signaled the entrance of an upstairs maid, carrying a tray with a teapot and a bunch of bluebells. The trays he'd been sent up till now had no flowers, so presumably they were a delicate recognition of his married state.

"Good morning, my lady, my lord," the girl murmured, placing the tray on Torie's side.

"She never looked at the bed," Torie observed after the door closed. "My maid, Emily, could never have been so circumspect." She cleared her throat. "Emily would have been scandalized."

So she *had* noticed the clothespin.

"Flitwick's staff is excellently trained," Dominic said. "May I have a cup of black tea?"

When Torie turned to pick up the teapot, the

delicate silk of her nightgown pulled against her breasts. His erection throbbed against the sheet. He felt like a boy again: any moment he'd start to doodle nipples the way they used to. Breasts and nipples in endless variation.

"They've marmaladed our toast," Torie said, handing him a thick linen napkin, followed by a cup of tea and a plate with two pieces of bread.

He spread the napkin over his crotch, pressing downwards in a silent reminder to his body that he was a grown man and fully in charge. "That's the way I like it, but you can ask for plain butter tomorrow."

"Don't you think this is going a bit far in convincing the household that our marriage has been consummated?" she burst out once she sat back against the headboard, tea in hand.

"I've never shared a breakfast tray with a woman before, but now I look forward to marmalade toast with you for the next eighty years." Dominic couldn't help his cheerfulness. Even though they needed to have a serious conversation, and he had to apologize *again*, he was happy.

Full of happiness as a cistern after a rainstorm, though that wasn't a poetic phrase.

His wife's eyes flashed at him, and he could almost see her building up a "head of steam," as the Duchess of Huntington had said of her engine.

"How interesting! I would have imagined you and the lovely Gianna sharing many such meals, given her famous propensity for drinking pink champagne for breakfast."

"Never with me," he said, taking a bite of toast. Then he added, "Gianna enjoys embroidering the facts, and apparently she sees reporters as fair game."

"Let me explicate something for you, Dominic," Torie said. "I do not want to know anything about your mistress, not a detail, not a word. I am merely your nanny at the moment. We will *not* sleep together again until you—"

"She's gone," he interrupted.

Torie blinked. "No— What? Gone?"

"Has been gone," he said, not smugly, because he should have told her the moment the subject came up yesterday.

"After our conversation?"

"No. Months ago, she sold the house I bought her and moved back to Italy."

Torie choked on her tea. "What?"

"Before you ask, I did not replace her."

No one—*no one*—greeted his statements with such an expression of incredulity. His opponents hated his passionate arguments, but they respected the facts he brought forward. They didn't question that he offered the truth.

Perversely, Torie's skepticism and her temper-filled eyes aroused him even more than the sight of her erotically clad in lace.

"Here's the kicker," he said, a trace of satisfaction leaking into his voice. "She's newly married to an Italian conte. A count."

"Right." Her tone was laden with skepticism. "What were you doing at Vauxhall with a newly married contessa?"

"The gossips apparently didn't notice that Gianna and I shared the box with a dapper Italian," he said, taking a bite of toast. "The newlyweds were in London on their honeymoon, touring its attractions, which included Vauxhall. She asked me to join them there, and I stupidly—I can never apologize enough, Torie—I stupidly agreed. The reporters who stalked us ignored her husband."

Dominic had spent the last months reading Torie's expressions more closely than he ever did a legal document. Sea-blue eyes darkening to navy? She was curious, even bewildered. Well, the truth was confusing.

"The diamond necklace was a wedding present from the conte, who was so jealous, by the way, that when they arrived in London, he demanded to meet the viscount who had supported his dear wife for several years, this kindness being entirely due to said viscount's childhood friendship with Gianna's dead brother."

"That's . . . that's mad," Torie stammered.

"Gianna takes a flexible approach to the truth, never more so than when she wove the story of how a storm of fraternal kindness led me to give her a house in London. I must have loved her brother dearly." He took another bite of toast.

"The conte cannot have believed her!"

Dominic finished his tea and put it to the side. "All signs were that he did. The brother, by the way, may or may not have existed. I never got around to asking. Gianna simply gave me my script and demanded I join them at Vauxhall."

"That story is almost mad enough that I believe it," Torie breathed. Then: "You bought her a *house*?"

He raised one shoulder. "We were together for five years."

She eyed him over her toast. "Is that normal? I'm sure that my father hasn't bought anyone a house. He's lucky to have inherited the one I grew up in."

"The only person I've ever spoken to on the subject was my father," Dominic said. He heard amusement fall from his voice. "The late viscount was miserly in thought and deed. Consequently, I have made a rule of generosity."

Torie glanced at him. "That explains your willingness to throw pounds at problems, but I don't know whether I believe you about the contessa. The story is too incredible."

"We could drop by the newlyweds' palazzo in Florence during the honeymoon that the twins are planning for the four of us. After I paid for several bottles of champagne, mostly consumed by the conte, his lordship issued an invitation to me and my future bride. You do know that the twins plan to join us in Italy, don't you?"

Torie ignored that digression. "Just to summarize: you went to Vauxhall two days before your wedding because your former mistress asked you to convince her new husband that you had never been more than a generous friend of her brother, who may or may not be fictional."

"It didn't take any skill on my part to act completely indifferent toward Gianna," Dominic said. "By the end of the evening, the conte was probably grateful to escape my soliloquy about your paintings of rabbits, your sense of humor, your opinions of classical texts, your kindness to my orphaned niece and nephew, and your overall perfection."

He eyed her. "I told him that you were the most beautiful woman in London. Gianna scowled, but she could hardly complain, given the tissue of lies she'd told him."

"You could have told me this before we married," Torie said hoarsely. "You let me think that you had been kissing me—and then going to *her* bed!"

Dominic nodded. They'd reached the sticky part. "I was furious."

"Because I had the temerity to ask you to be faithful to your wedding vows?"

"Because of *this*." He plucked the last bite of her toast from her fingers and threw it on the tray before he rolled on top of her, bracing himself on his elbows. His heart was hammering in his chest.

It was all so disconcerting. Why was he feeling scorching desire for a woman whom he'd hardly noticed a year ago?

Torie stared up at him, her eyes defiant. But she wasn't saying no. She wasn't keeping him at a distance or shouting at him. It was just the two of them in a silent bedchamber smelling of marmalade and buttered toast.

"I likely wouldn't have gone to Vauxhall, but the only thing I could think about was going to bed with you. I lost my train of thought talking about the farm bill in Lords and had to sit down in disgrace."

He dropped a small kiss on the corner of her voluptuous mouth. Then, as her lips eased open, he nibbled on her lower lip. Finally their tongues met in a sensual dance that sent hunger raging down to his groin.

She tasted like sweet, sticky, jammy woman—like every idle dream he ever had about making love. He suspected Torie didn't even like him, and she certainly didn't approve of him, yet she was kissing him back with a burning intensity that matched his own.

They were matched in lust, he thought dimly.

She pulled away. "Not yet," she said breathlessly. "I still don't understand why you didn't just tell me the other day that you weren't *with* Gianna at Vauxhall? Why didn't you just say that she hadn't been your mistress for—for how long?"

"Since the fifteenth of February."

"It would have been so easy."

Dominic rolled over on his back and repeated, "I was infuriated."

Her silence did a good job of conveying incredulity.

"I don't take ultimatums well," he admitted. "My father was dictatorial, and I find it very difficult to obey commands."

"I deliberately did not issue an ultimatum," Torie said.

He tried again. "I have a temper."

She snorted, reminding him of the Duchess of Huntington. "More people know of your temper than your former mistress—and she is known throughout polite society."

"When I feel my temper slipping, I leave the room. It's a hard and fast rule."

She cast him a skeptical look. "May I remind you that you're famous for bellowing insults in the House of Lords?"

"That doesn't count. I must catch their attention, or they just wallow in complacency or fall asleep, especially after lunch. They serve too much port in the Lords dining room."

Torie came up on her elbow. "You could have come back to me that evening, after you'd calmed down, and explained. Did you *want* me to jilt you?"

He glanced over and found her eyes narrowed. "No!"

"Poppycock. You did, didn't you? Why didn't you simply break the engagement?" Her eyes took on a bruised pansy color that he'd never seen before.

"I did want to marry you!"

She rolled to her back. "You should have been

honest, Dom. You're stuck with me now. I could be married to a duke, and you courting a docile lady."

Fuck.

"I was afraid," he said, the words coming roughly from his throat.

She didn't look at him, but her lips shaped the word *poppycock*.

"I didn't want you to jilt me, but I thought you had the right." The words came deep and rough from his chest. "I was horrified to think that you were humiliated by my being with Gianna. That I had inflicted that pain. I'm not used to being *wrong*."

She propped herself on her side again, close enough to him so that her legs almost touched his. "Hmmm."

"I know you've been thinking about jilting me ever since you put that emerald on your finger. Half the time you don't even wear it. Why do you think I paid the Duke of Queensberry to leave London? I wouldn't have bothered if I wanted you to jilt me, would I?"

"Once again: Why not just tell me the truth?"

"I was about to tell you, but you interrupted me by announcing that you cheerfully would take a lover. After you left, I decided you had the right to jilt me at the altar. Your father's wager seemed proof that you planned to."

"Did you care?"

"God, yes." The word was fierce. "I had made an ass of myself at Vauxhall, and I would have deserved it if you fled before the wedding or left me at the altar. But make no mistake, Torie: I would have come after you. Even before that night, I got rid of Queensberry to give myself time to persuade you."

He paused, and then added for the sake of honesty, "Or seduce you, whatever it took."

A knee nudged his leg. "You truly don't have a mistress? Any mistress?"

"No. No one." He took a deep breath. "I dismissed Gianna the night after we first spoke about her. I didn't think twice about having a mistress when I spoke to Leonora about it." He turned his head and met her eyes. "Then you told me that you would have kicked me out, and it made me rethink the kind of marriage I wanted. I gave Gianna enough money to return to Italy in style, which allowed her to snag the conte."

A smile touched her lips. "I like that."

"I thought you would."

"You still should have told me earlier."

"I felt trapped, and I never behave my best in that situation." He cleared his throat. "I shall try, but we both have tempers."

"We do, don't we? Do you know what I think of this, viscount?"

He shook his head.

"I think the conditions of my ultimatum have been met."

Dominic couldn't suppress his smile. "I thought you didn't offer an ultimatum?"

"Well, it might have been something in that genre. The Kelbourne dimples have made an appearance," Torie said with dramatic emphasis. "Have I told you how much I like your smile?"

He shook his head.

"So . . . smiling husband."

"Yes?"

"Shall we consummate this marriage?"

CHAPTER 25

Torie sank backwards as Dominic rolled over, one thick leg pinning down both of hers. Neither her nightgown nor the sheet caught between them disguised the hard thrust of his arousal against her thigh.

She was about to begin asking questions—which was how she usually found her way through new situations—but he bent his head to kiss her. No questions presented themselves, not in the middle of ravishing kisses. What was there to question when her body was shuddering with desire?

He pulled the sheet away and tossed it to the bottom of the bed. His hands slid up her leg, and Torie stilled in sudden anxiety. Only her maid had seen her unclothed. Morning light was pouring into the room.

"Aren't we supposed to do this in the dark, at night?" she asked, her voice cracking. "Under the covers?"

Dominic shook his head. "There's no *should* about it. I would like to make love to you at every time of day." His dimples appeared. "We should test every hour of day and night to determine which is your favorite."

Torie gulped. "At the moment, this room is very bright." She pushed her nightgown past her knees. Her body was besieged by feelings she had no words for. Her breasts felt heavy, and her nipples felt oddly tight. She wasn't stupid enough to ignore the craving sensation, but she was trembling half from desire and half from fear.

"I don't like being a virgin," she said crossly.

Dom threw back his head, and there were those dimples again, because he was laughing, actually laughing. Torie found the sound intoxicating, likely because he was so sober most of the time. She found herself leaning toward him, tracing the generous outlines of his bottom lip with her finger.

"Why don't you laugh more often?"

His dimples vanished. "Men don't," he said simply.

"You seem to me to have far too many ideas about what men can and can't do," she said, allowing him to suck the tip of her finger into his warm mouth.

"I promised you a body made for sportive tricks," he growled in her ear. "A male one."

Torie took her finger out of his mouth and then slipped it in her own, hollowing her cheeks. "You taste delicious," she murmured, pouting.

"Hell," he groaned, his eyes blazing with intensity. He swung off the bed, stood up, and stripped off his robe, moving back to the bed naked.

Dom's chest muscles brought back the moment when he first stripped off his shirt. But a furrow of silky hair pointed down, and there weren't any breeches blocking Torie's view this time. Seeing his thighs in breeches wasn't at all the same as when he was kneeling on the bed in front of her, letting her look her fill.

She looked down again, felt her eyes widen.

He was . . . big.

Not that she knew much about sizes, but there wasn't a lady in the ton who hadn't experienced an idiot in silk pantaloons accidentally brushing her hip and cackling because he apparently thought she'd be overcome by desire, by—

By what she realized now had been impoverished

versions of her husband's hard flesh. It was smooth and looked almost painfully rigid. She cleared her throat. Dom was grinning at her again. Not boastful, the way those foolish boys were, but openly.

He was big everywhere.

Her eyes went back to the muscles in his thighs, and she discovered that she had been correct about her affinity for a farmer's body. "I meant to . . ." she said with a gulp and stopped.

"What?"

"I thought of marrying a farmer," Torie murmured, her eyes eating up the way Dominic's muscles bulged as he shifted his weight. His limbs weren't furry, but they were roughened with hair. Her prickling skin informed her that she would enjoy the sensation of his legs against hers.

"A farmer?" He sounded bemused.

"Who would have legs like yours," she managed. Dom had been honest with her, so: "I made up my mind about the farmer back when you were betrothed to my sister, though I never looked at you with desire then, I swear it!"

The dimples came back. He wrapped a hand around her cheek and bent to kiss her. Torie put her hands on his shoulders, loving the way he twitched under her fingers as if he were excited by that simple touch.

"May I lie beside you?" he murmured against her lips. "You probably have questions. I would be the first to say that my sketch was insufficient. The legs were just sticks, after all."

After he threw that big powerful body down onto the sheet, arms crossed behind his head, Torie couldn't think of a single question. Not when she could caress him until a rough groan escaped his lips, and then rub more to see whether she could produce that sound again.

Which she could.

His fingers clenched in the sheet, and he started talking, muddled, broken half sentences coming without forethought from his throat. Even though, she dimly realized, she would have said that every word Dom spoke came with forethought.

He walked out of rooms to protect himself from spontaneity.

Not now. Not here.

He raggedly told her exactly what her touch was doing to him, especially once she slid lower in the bed and draped one of her legs over his, her fingers dancing down his ridged belly.

She hesitated until he wrapped his hand around his tool, showing her how to slide along its length with a twist. When she imitated him, he wrapped his hand over hers and pulled in a way that made him throw back his head with a groan.

It gave her a deep stab of satisfaction that the man who prided himself on keeping a remote, somber expression couldn't do so now. Every time her hand moved, he grimaced, eyes gleaming under half-closed lids, gripped by desire that no one could mistake, even someone with as little experience as she.

That is, no experience at all.

"I like your clothespin," she murmured.

He wasn't paying attention, lost in a sensual fog. So she tightened her hand and edged closer, examining the ridges that marked his stomach. When she licked them, he shuddered and wrapped one of his hands around the other wrist over his head, as if he were only barely able to restrain himself from touching her.

Torie felt an errant spark of laughter.

This was *serious*. This was marital consummation, marital intimacy, and all that. But the idea that Viscount Kelbourne had to physically restrain himself in order not to leap on her? That was funny.

It was also funny to watch his stomach muscles jump when she ran her tongue across them, especially when she edged farther down. A smile was fluttering in her heart, curling her mouth. It was an important moment, but it was also . . . funny.

Fun.

Her tongue touched the mushroom head of his tool. He gasped and arched his back, a silent plea, except that Viscount Kelbourne would never lower himself to plead.

She hummed, deep in her throat, and then licked him again.

A sound broke from his throat.

Perhaps she could make him *beg*.

Torie was rarely confident. But doing this? Making love to Dom? She knew what she was doing, without written instructions, without experience.

Just by touch and feel.

She dipped her head and took the fat head of his clothespin into her mouth. Didn't he mention this at some point? Or perhaps not. Perhaps he only talked about licking her. But sauce for the goose, et cetera.

"How's that?" she asked cheerfully, letting him go with a pop of her lips.

"My God," Dom said, eyes wild. "Bloody hell. Fucking hell."

"Tsk, tsk, do please keep in mind the Prohibited

List," she chuckled. And bent over him again. He tasted musky and clean, so she sucked until a need for oxygen made itself known.

"Still good?" she asked, more huskily.

All the time he had been talking, telling her to suck him down, telling her how it felt when her tongue wrapped around him, telling her she was sinful, delicious, everything he wanted.

"I've been longing for months to see you kneeling in front of me." Dom's voice was a throaty promise.

"I hope you're planning to kneel in front of me too," she told him.

Having this large male body laid out for her pleasure was intoxicating. Her tongue wrapped around him once again. He groaned deep in his chest and said, "I can't take it any longer."

A moment later she was under him again, snug beneath his heavy weight. It felt lovely. Safe and sensual, as if she could melt into him, and he would never mock her.

His body shifted. She was suddenly aware that, games aside, there was much she didn't know. That she wanted to know.

But he was in charge now. His jaw was set, and his eyes blazing into hers as he moved her legs so that his fingers could slip up her thigh.

Celebrating in a gruff voice when she was wet and tender. Cursing when she relaxed her legs and smiled at him. Turning the air blue when she wound her fingers into his hair and pulled him closer, his mouth crashing down on hers.

"What next?" she asked at some point, catching her breath. She had no fear, just joy in her veins.

"This . . . that," he said, losing all the eloquence

that he usually had. His eyes were strained, his voice savage.

"Well, then," she said, schooling her voice to be demure. "This, that, you, me?"

"Tell me," he said, his eyes on hers. "Tell me what you want, Torie. What you need."

The answer was simple, of course. She'd known the truth even when she thought that Gianna was in her way. "I need you," she breathed. "Please, Dom."

She almost forgot what came next, except his hand slid up her hip and then pulled her gently into place so that—

She expected a thrust. To be honest, she would have welcomed a thrust, because there was a tingling emptiness between her legs that was making her shift restlessly beneath him.

Instead, he entered her slowly and tenderly, his eyes asking over and over if the pain was too unpleasant. The feeling wasn't all that good. But there was a beat underneath every movement he made that sent a promise down her legs.

When he finally sank in all the way, he grunted, and the sound felt right. When he withdrew and plunged in again, that felt right too. It all felt right, especially when sensation began to spiral up her legs, and her nails dug into his arms.

He was throbbing inside her, and she could feel some sort of storm rolling toward her on the horizon when he withdrew.

Torie gasped. "No!"

His heated gaze met hers. "I have to lick you. Have to taste you." His voice was hoarse, drenched and heavy with lust.

A quiver went through her. "I don't think that is something I will enjoy."

"Please."

The man who never begged was close to it. "All right," Torie whispered. Light was still pouring into the room. She would feel better in the dark, under the covers. He was going to . . .

He was doing it.

Looking at her. Pulling her legs apart and *looking* at her. Torie felt scarlet color flooding her cheeks. She let out a shaky breath, searching his face.

His eyes were wide. "So pretty," he growled.

She glanced below his waist.

"I'm not pretty. Hard and waiting for you," he said, following her gaze. "I need to taste you, Torie. I've been thinking of these rose petals for months. Desperate for you."

For months? And she was worried about embarrassment? She smiled and widened her legs.

"All right," she agreed. "All yours."

She melted into the sheets, melted into his expression, squeezed her eyes shut, and trusted. And waited, as if she were at the top of a steep hill in a runaway carriage.

Big hands caught her legs, gently, and pushed them even farther apart. A ravenous groan sent warm breath over her most intimate part, making her shudder.

Suddenly his tongue ran up her in a wide swipe that felt like nothing she'd ever imagined. She could never have imagined.

Of course, he talked. "You taste like flowers and the sea. So soft." The bed rocked, and she could tell, even with her eyes closed, that he was shoving his hips against the bed because he was greedy for her, for more of her.

All the time his tongue was dancing over her

folds, and then his fingers joined in, a gentle touch after a rough stroke, a sweet caress followed by a thrust of a broad finger.

If she thought she was excited before . . . She began crying out, sound breaking from her chest without volition, her eyes still squeezed shut. Dominic groaned and kept licking, muttering disjointedly that she was so sweet and tight, hardly big enough for his finger.

What did shame matter, when this man, this man, *Dom*, was unashamedly grinding against the mattress because her taste was driving him wild?

Finally Torie succumbed to the storm barreling toward her. It swept up from her ankles, perhaps from her toes. It turned her hot and liquid, and when it reached the place where two of his fingers were thrusting . . .

She exploded.

Helpless, crying out, shuddering. A little afraid, because surely this wasn't natural. Normal. In the daytime? Her mind skittered again.

Dom dropped his grip on her thighs and rose over her, thrusting inside in one swoop. There was the thrust she wanted, the wildness that answered her own hunger. A broken cry in her throat, matched by his ragged groan.

For a moment, it was too much, too overwhelming. The feeling was maddening but elusive.

"I got you," he growled, taking her mouth. "I have you, Torie." His kiss claimed her, and she tasted him, the same man who had kissed her for months. That did it: calmed her spirit if not her thundering heart.

He slipped one hand under her hip and began thrusting in a rhythm as steady as waves coming in to shore. Her mind blurred, and everything slipped away except the shattering sensation unfurling in her body.

It wasn't enough, not deep enough, so she arched against him—at the same moment that he ground down, shuddering, thrusting deep, emptying himself into her.

His eyes blazed into hers, and she didn't cry out. She screamed as pleasure washed over her again.

"Are you knocked unconscious?" she asked drowsily, a moment later. His heavy body had slumped onto hers after the arms he'd braced by her ears relaxed.

He turned his head and kissed her ear. Nipped it. "Like a rabbit? I didn't faint, but it was damn close. A man can go much longer on the second round."

"Second round?" she echoed.

When rabbits did it, the male fell off on the ground. His mate hopped away and started chewing grass again. There was no second round.

Something stirred against her leg. "I'm going to wash you," Dom said. "Then I'm going to lick you from your earlobe down to your tiny toes. I'm going to drive you to incoherent bliss, as is my husbandly duty."

"Oh." Torie thought about it. "I think I was there already. Twice."

"Two or three more times," Dom said, moving down so that he could press kisses on the slopes of her breasts. "The sunshine makes your breasts look as if they're shimmering. Or perhaps that's because I'm drunk."

Torie was rather surprised to see her nipples respond to a delicate flick of his tongue.

"Dew-crumpled rose petals," Dom muttered

with surprising eloquence. "No, the color isn't quite right. Strawberry pink." He tapped her nipple, sending a zing of pleasure straight through her. "Darkening to strawberry pink."

Torie squirmed under his investigation, filled with delight, her breath coming faster. Bedding was a messy, intimate business, but she loved it. "You did say that we are validating our wedding with bodily union," she reminded him.

"We need more union, more validation. I didn't get enough time with these beauties," her husband murmured.

"I feel as if our bodies united," she said thoughtfully.

"We're married now. No escape." He got up and came back with a wet cloth. "Are you sore from all the bodily uniting, Torie?"

She glanced down, and then came up on her elbows. "Is this you?" She swiped a finger through the pearly liquid running down her thigh and stuck it in her mouth.

Her husband dropped the cloth and bent over, groaning as if he had taken a blow to the stomach. "You," he said. And then nothing else.

So Torie took the wet cloth and wiped away the evidence herself.

CHAPTER 26

When Torie woke up again, hours later, her husband was nowhere to be seen. Would he go to the House of Lords the day after his wedding?

She rolled over and looked up at a ceiling painted with fat cupids, analyzing the painter's use of perspective before deciding that yes, her husband had almost certainly gone to Lords.

What Dom was fighting for wasn't bibble-babble. He'd explained it to her. Still, she wished he had stayed home for the day. After three "bouts," as he called them, she felt sore and a bit fragile, as if she had overused muscles that hadn't existed before she married.

But she had to get up, so she pulled the bell cord and let Emily's familiar energy swirl around the room and get her into a hot tub of water. Her lady's maid was feeling particularly dramatic due to being in a new household. Mr. Flitwick apparently ran his household like a king governs his court.

"We stand until he seats himself," Emily explained, shaking her head—not negatively, but in surprise.

Torie sank a little deeper into the hot water. "The maid who brought our tea was very well trained."

Emily giggled. "Betsy came back down and said that she'd never seen the viscount looking so dazed. He's that in love."

"I thought she didn't even glance at the bed!"

Emily scoffed at that. "That's what eyelashes are for, aren't they? Before Betsy was in service with Lord Kelbourne, she served a countess who had a stream of men coming in and out of her bed at all hours. This house is so much better. For one thing, she's in the bedchamber next to mine. Not one of us has to share a room!"

"Marvelous," Torie said.

"She's infatuated." Emily lowered her voice. "You'll never guess who."

"I only met the grooms and footmen briefly yesterday."

"Mr. Flitwick himself!" Emily said, giggling madly. "He has to be thirty years older than she, and married in the bargain."

"Surely he's not—"

"Of course not," Emily said. "Never. Not him. Right proper he is. Fair, too. One of the footmen dropped a tray of madeleines coming into the wedding reception yesterday. His shoe caught on that uneven board outside the drawing room, the one that's sprung a nail."

Torie groaned. "Father kept saying he would summon a carpenter."

"The sweets were ruined, but Mr. Flitwick didn't say a cross word. He just sent the lad back here, to Kelbourne House, because his knee breeches were scuffed. No one can have even the smallest smut or stain on their livery. It isn't allowed." Emily smirked. "He mentioned that I was perfectly attired."

As a lady's maid, Emily didn't have to wear a snowy apron or livery; just now she was wearing a violet morning gown to which she'd added a black neck bow in recognition of the household's half mourning.

"I always said you should be a viscountess's maid," Torie said, floating in the warm water and wishing she could stay there all day. If not in bed, then bath.

"Well, you didn't marry him for the title!" Emily said with another spate of giggles. "What would the viscountess like to wear today?"

"Six weeks of half mourning remain," Torie reminded her.

"I suggest the white satin morning gown. It has that trim of black chenille."

Torie nodded, standing up and accepting a length of toweling. "I'll paint this morning."

"No," Emily said decisively. She was stripping the bed, but she turned around. "You'll need to assert yourself in the household today, my lady. Mrs. Flitwick is nice enough, but she's used to having her own way. Last night, she told me that I should choose a French name, as a true lady's maid to a viscountess had to be Frenchified." She snorted. "I told her that Emily was good enough for my mother, and good enough for you too."

"Perhaps just—"

"No," Emily said, shaking her head. "I know how you feel about your paintings, but you're the *viscountess* now."

Torie sighed.

"Of course, you will spend time with Master Valentine and his sister."

"I plan to fire Nanny Bracknell," Torie remembered.

"Excellent," Emily said. "Assert yourself!"

Picturing Nanny Bracknell's sour face made Torie want to crawl back into bed, but Emily was bundling up sheets stained with blood.

"These will stop anyone in the household thinking there'll be a six-month baby," she said with satisfaction. "Not that Mr. Flitwick would countenance an ill word amongst us, but he did have to fire a footman who was selling information to one of the gossip columns! News gets around, as we know."

"His lordship does *not* have an Italian mistress," Torie said. "I know everyone is chattering about it, but it's not true."

"*We* know the truth of it," Emily told her. "Last night Mr. Flitwick said that he doesn't condone evil gossip, particularly about the family, but he felt it behooved him to clarify that issue. Isn't *behoove* a lovely word? He meant that he felt obliged to tell us the truth. Lord Kelbourne dropped that Italian woman long ago. Months ago."

"How on earth did Mr. Flitwick know that?" Torie asked.

"The household knows everything, my lady. You'll have to remember that. Not that you'll be behaving like that countess with a swinging door."

Torie digested that in silence. "I suppose they all know that I can't read, then."

"Indeed they do, because his lordship told them himself, the afternoon before the wedding. He said that if anyone made you feel ashamed, they'd be dismissed without their last week's wages." Emily chortled. "Nicer than Sir William, I must say."

When Torie didn't answer, she added hastily, "Though Sir William was sometimes befuddled by drink and didn't know what he was saying. Would you like to see Nanny Bracknell before Mrs. Flitwick?"

"Yes," Torie decided. "Give me five minutes to get my thoughts in order, and then send her to my sitting room."

"No one in the household likes the way she slaps

the children, but his lordship didn't want to cut the twins' last tie to their parents. Mrs. Flitwick is looking forward to going over the linens and preserves with you. Apparently, the viscount can't get enough preserved lemons, but she has none on hand."

What was Torie supposed to do about *that*?

"I shall take the twins out of the house in the afternoon," she told Emily. "One of the footmen should be ready to accompany us with a purse."

Dismissing Nanny Bracknell took more than a few minutes, as the lady was determined to argue. Supposedly she had been trained for a royal household and had lowered herself to work for Lady Dorney, and then for Viscount Kelbourne. What's more, she felt very ill-used by the twins, as their conversation was unseemly and impertinent.

Torie was initially sympathetic—the children were certainly eccentric—but when the nanny declared that they weren't "normal," Torie stood up and gave the woman three hours to pack her trunk and leave.

"How dare you!" Nanny Bracknell snapped, looking as if she'd like to explode like a firework and burn the house down around her.

"You are unkind and ill-tempered. You shall leave without a reference," Torie stated, asserting herself with a vengeance.

"As if I'd associate my good name with the Dorney household!" With that, the nanny stalked out of the room. Torie followed her, finding Flitwick in the entry.

"May I be of assistance, my lady?" he asked.

"Nanny Bracknell is leaving us. I have given her three hours to pack her trunk, so I would be grateful if a footman could bring it down from the attic."

Flitwick bowed. "Certainly, my lady. Would you like me to ask an agency to send three new candidates to the house?"

"Yes," Torie said. "You might specify that we would like a young and energetic nanny who is not easily horrified."

"Very good, my lady."

"I shall meet with Mrs. Flitwick now," she told him.

She wasn't looking forward to it. When Leonora left, the cook had brought her meal plans every week, but of course Torie couldn't read them. To her relief, Mrs. Flitwick took her through the kitchen and the pantry without pulling out a single piece of paper or even discussing numbers, other than to remark how quickly wax candles burned down.

Thanks to Dominic's warning, presumably.

"The house hasn't had a mistress for years," Mrs. Flitwick said, head deep in a cupboard. She popped back out with a stack of linens. "His lordship never had time to consider such questions."

Torie smiled, trying to look as if she knew what the question was.

"These are all frayed, as you can see. If you approve, I'll send a groom down to sell them to a secondhand cloth merchant."

Her new husband didn't need the money. "I suggest we donate them to the Chelsea Orphanage," Torie said.

Mrs. Flitwick beamed at her. "May I do the same with the rest of the frayed linens?"

"Certainly."

"Shall I summon a linen merchant, my lady? A friend of mine, a housekeeper in the Duke of Lindow's household, brings an Italian man in yearly to select the new linens. It won't take more than a day to go over all the fabric needed in the house and country."

A *day*? A whole day spent selecting new linens?

Mrs. Flitwick must have read her expression because she said quickly, "Or I can do that for you, my lady. I do know what suits this household's needs, after all."

"I would appreciate that," Torie said, smiling. "My sister managed my father's house, and my mother died when I was young. I shall lean on your guidance, Mrs. Flitwick."

She couldn't have said something more guaranteed to please. Mrs. Flitwick turned pink and chattered about the difference between French and Italian linen until Torie finally managed to escape.

When she walked into the nursery, Florence and Valentine were seated at their desks, doing sums set by their tutor. On seeing Torie, Florence jumped up and sang, "She's gone! She's gone! The wicked witch is gone!"

Torie had just enough time to brace herself before Florence cannonballed into her, clutching her around the waist.

"Sorry, but I must finish," Val said, scribbling at a sheet of calculations.

Torie came to look over his shoulder, but all she saw was a page of marks that dipped to one side.

"Can you read numbers?" Valentine asked, looking up at her. "Oh, sorry!" He jumped up and bowed. "My lady."

Torie held out her arms. Valentine froze, surprised, and then stepped into her hug. "Good morning," she said, giving him a squeeze. "I cannot see numbers; they drip off the page like spilled tea."

"That is *so* interesting," Valentine said, gazing at

her forehead as if he could crack open her skull and diagnose her inability to cipher.

"I thought we might go to Smithfield Market to-day," Torie suggested.

Valentine glanced back at his calculations.

"Taking advantage of the sunshine," she said firmly. "You'll like Smithfield. I have heard that it's muddy and noisy."

"*All* things that people of quality like ourselves are supposed to avoid," Florence said happily.

"On the Prohibited List!" the twins chorused, giggling madly.

"I thought we would buy a live rabbit," Torie said. "We'll bring him home and let him hop around the nursery so we can sketch him for a few hours."

"Is that how you learned to paint their hind quarters?" Valentine asked. He waved at the rabbit on his easel, who looked vaguely like a cat with long ears. But only vaguely, as no cat had dishpan paws.

"As a child, I spent my time out of doors looking at wild rabbits," Torie explained. "I have any number of sketchbooks full of wild animals. Since Parliament is in session, we can't go to the country just yet, so the country will come to us in the form of a rabbit."

"Will he sit still long enough to be drawn?" Valentine asked. "That book you gave me, *Compendium Animalium*, shows hares leaping, just as in your painting. We've begun Latin, but we're not good enough to read the descriptions yet."

"All we can say is *do, das, dat*—I give, you give, we give," Florence agreed.

Torie hadn't even realized the book she'd found was in a different language; she'd seen it in a stall in front of St. Paul's and liked the etchings of animals. She was always looking at books, wishing she knew what was inside. They were like treasure boxes that were forever hidden from her but open to everyone else.

"Where will the rabbit sleep?" Florence asked.

"We shall sketch madly for a couple of hours and then give him to Cook," Torie said.

"Rabbit stew," Valentine said approvingly.

"Let's go!" Florence shouted boisterously.

It was more challenging to exit the house than Torie had anticipated, never having taken children anywhere without a nanny to dress them for the outdoors. Even with a maid assigned to the nursery, their coats couldn't immediately be found—until it was revealed that Nanny Bracknell had packed their velvet coats and a good deal of other clothing into her trunk. Luckily, she was still in the house when the coats were unearthed.

Flitwick kept his countenance, but the corners of his mouth tucked under when he reported the discovery.

"I didn't think about giving her her unpaid salary," Torie said. "Perhaps she was replacing lost funds?"

"You are too kind, my lady. I had taken it upon myself to pay the remainder of her salary," Flitwick said. "I might add that Viscount Kelbourne began paying her double the going wage after she complained about the move to London."

Of course Dom would have paid double.

He had the habit of easing his way with generosity, even when it would be better to refrain. Thinking of the Duke of Queensberry clowning around Bath in a pink suit with glass diamonds was irritating. Thinking of Nanny Bracknell being paid double when she spent no time in the nursery was even more so.

The twins clattered down the marble staircase and arrived before her, breathless in their matching black velvet coats, just as Dom strode into the house. Torie whirled about. Surely he had told her that the afternoon debates weren't over until—

Their eyes met. He had also told her, once, that he planned to return home at luncheon and feast on her rather than food.

"Good afternoon, viscount," she said, dropping into a curtsy.

"Torie," he said. "Wife." He caught her around the waist and kissed her until she swayed against him, one hand coming up to grasp his lapel simply to keep herself on her feet.

She pulled back with a gasp, thinking of Flitwick, the footman who was to accompany them, the children . . .

The butler and footman were staring resolutely at the wall, but now the corners of Flitwick's mouth curled up rather than tucked down. The children were staring with as much interest as they might at a zoological exhibit.

"If you're quite finished greeting Torie, we are going on an outing," Florence said to Dominic.

Torie had the distinct impression that her husband would prefer to go back upstairs. Yet that wouldn't do. There would be no going back to bed, not when the children were waiting in their nearly pilfered garments, hopping from foot to foot in excitement.

"We're going to Smithfield Market," she told him. "We plan to buy a rabbit."

The hunger in his eyes disappeared as if by magic. "You must be joking."

Flitwick's smile broadened. She hadn't realized the

butler disapproved of their excursion to Smithfield, but then, she hadn't asked his opinion.

Torie drew herself up, playing the viscountess—imitating Leonora, if truth be told. "Yes, I am serious. We need a rabbit, and I am told that Smithfield Market is an excellent place to buy livestock."

"Livestock." Dominic's voice was disbelieving. "If you wish to acquire a rabbit, tell the cook, Mrs. Cottage. She will inform the butler. My understanding is that he visits the house every morning."

"Several butchers do," the butler put in. "Mrs. Cottage feels that giving all the household custom to one butcher would encourage him to take advantage. One of the three will be able to furnish a live rabbit."

The children wilted with disappointment.

"No. We shall go to Smithfield and find our own rabbit," Torie told her husband and his butler. "It's not just about the rabbit. The children and I plan to get to know London. All three of us have spent our lives primarily in the country."

"You could come with us," Florence told Dominic, tucking her hand into his. He was wearing gloves, so his hands seemed even larger in comparison to her slender fingers.

"He has to return for the afternoon debate," Valentine said.

Torie looked at her husband. His blue-gray eyes had the perplexed look that he showed so rarely, when he wasn't certain of the right course of action. She had a feeling that she'd better treasure those moments.

"Do join us," she said. "It's not far, right in the center of London. I gather that one may buy cattle and sheep only on certain days, but rabbits are available every day."

"Yes, *please*," Florence chimed in. "We are wearing our boots in the event of mud." She stuck out one booted foot.

"Smithfield," Dominic said with disgust. "There will be mud, all right."

Torie saw acceptance in his eyes; there would be no cavorting in their bedchamber until evening, so he might as well accompany them to a cattle market.

"Flitwick, which carriage will take us on this excursion?" Dominic asked.

"The barouche, your lordship," the butler said. "I warned Mulberry to make sure his blunderbuss is primed, just in case. Simons will accompany the family, as he knows the market. His father is a cattleman."

Mulberry was Dominic's coachman, and Simons presumably one of the grooms. "Is there really a need for a blunderbuss?" Torie asked.

"Yes, because my viscountess is the most beautiful lady in London, and she is wearing silver in her hair, and pearls in her ears, and an emerald on her finger," Dominic told her, a smile in his eyes.

"Thank you, darling," she said, coming up on her toes to kiss him. Her lips clung to Dom's with a promise of nighttime delight.

He was a grumpy man, her husband, but all the same, she saw a gleam of pure delight in his eyes when she kissed him. She would never say as much, but she had the idea that he'd been lonely now and then. Occasionally.

Coming home from the House of Lords with no mistress and no family . . . just the memory of boisterous arguments to keep him company.

His mouth claimed hers again.

"I'm fairly sure kissing is on the Prohibited List," Valentine observed.

"Not if you're married," his sister countered.

"Nanny Bracknell wouldn't approve."

"The wicked witch is gone, gone, gone," Florence sang, dancing around the entry.

CHAPTER 27

*W*hy a rabbit?" Dominic asked.

Ahead of him Valentine jumped into the carriage, then leaned back and pulled his sister up by her wrist. Dominic winced, picturing a dislocated shoulder, but Florence disappeared into the shady depths of the barouche without screaming in agony.

"You yourself pointed out that the children are having trouble painting rabbits because they've never seen one alive," Torie said, as if that was truly important.

Which it was, but only in a world where accurately painting rabbits was important. Dominic caught himself before he ventured that opinion: his wife would say that rabbits were important in *her* world, and she was right.

Torie stepped onto the box that Simons had placed below the carriage door and took the groom's hand to enter the carriage. Watching her hand held by another man pushed Dominic to wrestle with a tangle of emotions, a state that he never cared for.

He wished he was bedding his wife. That was acceptable. He didn't care for her touching another man's hand. That was unacceptable.

It hinted at an unmanly subjugation to his *wife*. His father's voice in his head informed him that there was nothing more effeminizing than feverish attachment to one's wife.

"What will happen to the animal after it has been immortalized in paint?" he asked as he sat down beside Torie.

"Rabbit stew," Valentine said enthusiastically. "One of my favorites."

Torie snuggled next to him, her hand sneaking into his.

Before the morning, he might have established a manly distance and commanded the household, the way his father had taught him to do.

Now?

After she let him crush her to the bed and begged for more? After she gasped and cried and even screamed? After she licked him, and spread her legs—

He wrenched his mind away. He had no great-coat, and he was wearing pantaloons that wouldn't disguise a cock-rise.

"May I see what rapier you're wearing today?" Valentine asked.

Dominic put a hand on his glass-studded hilt and withdrew the blade just enough so that Val could see it wasn't matte black.

"May I have that one when you're dead?" Valentine asked. "It's beautiful."

"I shall add it to my will," Dominic said, thinking that the twins were altogether too familiar with the idea of death. Hopefully he and Torie would live into old age, and the children would stop thinking about inheritances and ghosts.

He hadn't been to Smithfield in a decade or more, but from what he saw through the window of the coach, nothing had changed. The huge field was dotted with pens stuffed with animals, surrounded by crowds of men smoking, brawling, and trading money. Innumerable hounds wove their way around a forest of legs, barking vociferously and

adding to the lowing of unhappy cattle. A small
herd of goats was bleating loud enough to be heard
distinctly amidst the discord.

The moment the barouche door opened, the
smell struck like a blow to the face: manure,
urine, and mud, mixed with salt, juniper, pep-
per, cinnamon, and all the other spices used to
preserve meat. Jumping down, Florence took it in
gulps; Valentine wrinkled his nose. Torie clasped
Dominic's hand to step down, turned rather pale,
and slapped a handkerchief to her nose.

Florence's boots were sinking in filth. "Ew,"
she said, pulling up one foot and examining the
clumps of reeking manure. The carriage had nec-
essarily drawn up along the same route by which
cattle were driven to market.

"I've never seen so many people," Valentine
breathed.

"You haven't been to a county fair?" Dominic
asked.

His nephew shook his head. "Nanny didn't like
us to leave the nursery because we always seemed
to get dirty."

Dominic gritted his teeth, once again blaming
himself for having no idea that his sister was er-
ratic at best in her parenting skills, if not entirely
neglectful.

The crowd surging around the pens seemed
virtually impenetrable, a ragged mob of odorous,
sweaty men bellowing and quarreling, roaring for
attention and gasping for breath amidst clouds of
brown dirt kicked up by cows desperate to free
themselves from the shoddy corrals.

"Do you see the drovers with their flat red caps?"
Simons asked Valentine and Florence. "They're in

charge of bringing the stock to market. Those with brown caps are countrymen who raise cows. Then there's the butchers, choosing a good animal to bring home and sell tomorrow. You can see them feeling the animals along the loin and rump to make sure they're nice and fatty."

"Quite a few pickpockets amongst that crowd, I'd expect," Dominic said. "Are you carrying a reticule, Torie? It might be best to leave it here in the carriage under Mulberry's supervision."

"I don't think I care to wade onto that field. How on earth would we find a rabbit amidst such confusion?"

"We needn't go into the center," Simons said. "There's only one rabbit seller. He has a hutch along the fence, close to the stalls selling pickled beef and the like. We shall avoid the crowd altogether."

"Thank goodness," Torie said. "I wish I'd brought a fan." She waved her handkerchief in front of her face.

"I like the smell," Florence said, sniffing loudly. "It's much more interesting than flowers, even more than a rosebush. Flowers are dreary in comparison."

Torie pressed the handkerchief to her nose.

"I'll take my lady's arm," Dominic said to the coachman. "Keep the blunderbuss on the ready, in case someone tries to pinch the vehicle. Simons, you are in charge of Master Valentine and Miss Florence. Do not allow them out of your sight. In fact, you'd better take their hands."

"I am so glad you came with us," Torie told Dominic as they picked their way along the fence, trying to avoid liquid puddles of muck. "I had no idea what Smithfield was like."

"Look at all the bacon!" Valentine called. They'd reached a row of stands from which hung sides of beef, pungently smelling of saltpeter, sugar, and honey; long strings of dried herbs and garlic; and bouquets of rushlights made from melted tallow from rendering mutton or beef.

"We should buy a present for Cook. Mrs. Cottage would like one of those big haunches," Florence said. "A *haunch* is the buttock and thigh of an animal," she told Torie.

"Buttock," Dominic began, but the twins interrupted him in a chorus.

"Goes on the Prohibited List!"

"We wouldn't know how to choose the best haunch," Torie pointed out.

Dominic thought his wife had turned faintly green.

"Simons knows." Florence tugged on the groom's hand. "Don't you think we should buy a side of beef? Then Mrs. Cottage would know we were thinking of her when we came to Smithfield. I'm sure she wishes she could have come with us."

"Ah, but Mrs. Cottage is *very* particular," Simons replied. "She don't deal with just one butcher. Even with three butchers visiting the house, if she can't find a chicken as plump as she'd like, she sends one of us grooms to fetch yet another butcher. Just look at all these stalls, Miss Florence. I wouldn't know how to find her favorites."

"We can just get that one, the biggest," Florence persisted.

"That's venison, not beef," Simons said. "Besides, we've arrived."

The rabbit hutch was a small building past the row of stalls. When they walked inside, they found two rows of cages full of twitching, furry animals. The smell was so strong that Torie choked and swayed. Here the stink was not merely excrement; an acid smell of blood suggested that the rabbit seller butchered his creatures on the premises.

Dominic decided that he was allowed to wrap an arm around his wife, improper though that might be. Torie turned her face into his chest and said something muffled by his coat.

He bent down.

"I love the way you smell."

Dominic only allowed his valet to sprinkle him with scent if he was headed to the Royal Court, where it was taken as an insult not to smell like bergamot and cedar.

"Leather," Torie said, just loud enough to be heard. "Musky with a hint of lemon."

"That would be my soap," Dominic said, looking down at his wife's bright head. She never powdered during the day. Today she smelled of perfume rather than turpentine. He just caught it over the reek of rabbit urine.

The children were walking down the first aisle, looking into every cage, so he held her tighter. "You smell like black currant and jasmine," he whispered.

Torie lifted her face. "My perfume is called Rosa Turchia. I'm not sure what that means."

"Whatever it is, it's captivating."

"I feel as if the stench is intensifying moment by moment," she said, looking watery-eyed. "Is that possible?"

"Torie!" Florence cried.

When they turned around, Florence was holding what looked like a mitt on her palm, the kind of thing that ladies slipped over their hands when it was snowing.

"Oh no," Torie groaned.

It wasn't a mitt, because suddenly long ears flicked up.

"Babies!" Florence cried.

CHAPTER 28

$\mathcal{H}$ell and damnation," Dominic muttered. A hare was one thing. In his experience, they had aggressive, yellowed teeth and slightly mad expressions. Such an animal could be turned into rabbit stew without a tear being shed.

But babies?

"Me name's Crouch, your lordship," a lean, filthy man said, moving toward them with a smile that put on display saffron-colored teeth not unlike those of his chosen livestock. "'Tis a pleasure to have you in me rabbit hutch, that it is."

"I didn't think there would be *babies*," Torie moaned.

"Milk-fed rabbits make the most delicate of broths," Crouch explained. "Excellent for bilious patients and famous for killing a fever. Ask any doctor. I've the mother there as well, so they're in good condition with no illnesses."

Florence had replaced the bunny she had been holding and moved to the second row of cages, following Valentine. Now the twins were shoulder to shoulder, leaning over to peer in a cage.

"They'll be looking at the runt," Crouch said, starting down the row.

Dominic arrived at the cage just in time to see Crouch respond to a command from Florence and lift a rabbit from the cage, a youngster with long ears and fur the color of fog.

"Last of his litter," Crouch said, handing over the animal. "His ears are too long for a rabbit and yet not long enough for a hare. Odd little beast. The litter came all the way from Scotland, but he was the only one so misshapen."

Florence turned to Dominic and Torie, holding the rabbit in both hands. Her eyes were huge and imploring. "We must paint him. Just look how beautiful he is!"

Dominic did not think the animal was beautiful. His ears were peculiar. One cocked up and the other hung down, almost covering one eye. Thankfully, he looked too dispirited to nip Torie's fingers.

"He traveled a long way to London," Valentine said. "At least four hundred fifty miles." The twins' new tutor had been horrified to discover that the children had only a rudimentary understanding of the United Kingdom, let alone the rest of the world. He'd set them to planning excursions and calculating miles.

The two looked at each other and chorused with delight, "Odysseus!"

"Oh, bloody hell," Torie muttered. She looked up at Dominic. "I'm sorry."

"This is going to happen, isn't it?" he said wryly. She laughed.

"How much for the lop-eared bunny?" Dominic asked.

"He's unique," Crouch began, so Dominic gave him a withering glance.

"I'll give you him for a ha'penny, as this is his third market, and I can't get rid of him. If I put him with others, they attack him, and no one wants to buy a rabbit by itself. They think he's diseased, which he ain't."

Dominic gave him a shilling for honesty, and a penny for a rabbit cage, no matter how malodorous.

"I'll wash a cage for you, special," Crouch said,

heading for the back of the shed. He unbolted a door and disappeared.

"I don't know why he doesn't keep that door open all the time and allow some air to pass through," Torie muttered.

Crouch took far too long to return, although thankfully a breeze did begin moving through the hutch. Finally he showed up with a cage only slightly less dirty than those surrounding them. Whatever he'd been doing, it didn't involve water.

"He eats veg," Crouch told Valentine, who was taking a turn holding Odysseus. "Needs water regular and fresh veg every day, mind." He tried to look virtuous even though anyone could look at his livestock and see that the poor creatures were suffering to the point of death.

"Right," Dominic said. "Let's return to the carriage, shall we?" He had an edgy feeling, his instincts warning him of danger, possibly because his lungs had taken all the insults they could manage.

No.

His instincts had been correct.

Torie and Florence walked out ahead of him.

"Dom!" Another lady's voice would be thready with fear or shrieking with terror. Not hers.

He halted, putting his hand behind him to stop Valentine and Simons, who was carrying Odysseus in his new cage. Just outside, four men were spaced in a half circle, their teeth bared in the unmistakable grins of bullies.

Directly before the door was a man with a mouth like a lamprey, a sword strapped at his hip. Then there was a moonfaced bruiser holding a club, another man wearing an incongruous scrap of pink lace around his neck, and a yellow-eyed fellow who swayed as if he were drunk. The first man—presumably the leader—opened his eellike mouth to say something, but when Torie looked him over, her lip curled, he fell silent.

"Florence, behind me," she said, pushing the girl through the door.

"Inside, Torie, children," Dominic said calmly. His eyes moved among the men's faces, memorizing their features in case any of them were smart enough to run. He'd have the constabulary on them later. "Simons!"

His groom appeared at his shoulder. "Crouch's gone," he muttered.

That blackguard had summoned his bully friends and then run off, planning to collect his share later, no doubt.

"Return to the carriage through the rear door," Dominic said.

"Shall I send Mulberry back here?" Simons asked. But Dominic wanted his coachman and blunderbuss to guard the most precious things in his life.

"No need." He put his hand on the glittering hilt of his rapier. "Can I help you, gentlemen?"

"His lordship is carrying a pretty toy," the leader said, his eyes alight with malice. "Pinkie, wouldn't you like to show that to your missus? My man Pinkie has an eye for lux'ry."

"The blade is not as pretty as the hilt, but 'twill do to take your life," Dominic said flatly, drawing his rapier. He never provoked an opponent in case they were driven to do something rash. He believed in giving them a chance to rethink or, if needed, say their prayers.

"He's holding his blade breast high," Pinkie said

scornfully. "The pretty man with a spangly blade that he doesn't know how to use. We should take it from him for his own safety, Bullet."

Bullet? The leader, presumably. A charming name for a charming fellow.

Thankfully, Dominic heard his family leaving through the back of the hutch.

In one last warning, he spun his rapier; the sunlight filtering through the fog hanging over the market caught the diamond-cut glass on the hilt.

"We can sell that for a pretty penny," Pinkie said greedily. "Course, we'll have to have it off you fore we can do that, me lordship. Now how about you give it to us, and your purse as well."

"If you do that, we won't offer any offense to that buxom lady of yours." Bullet's smirk revealed quite a few missing teeth. "A lady smells sweetest when she's on her back, don't she, Pinkie?" He drew out a battered sword with a shining edge.

"It's the fight a girl's got in 'er for me." Pinkie returned Bullet's wolfish grin. "What's the fun in tupping a naked lady if she makes it easy for you?"

Dominic's heartbeat slowed, and his entire body relaxed. "You'll meet my naked blade first."

He would have been reluctant to maim men who turned to thievery because they were hungry. Stealing to feed their families. But rapists?

"I don't like his expression," the drunk man said, a touch of fear in his voice.

Dominic looked him over with smiling eyes, cataloging the growing panic in the two men who had enough intelligence to recognize their own danger.

Bullet tensed, about to attack, so Dominic jumped forward, his rapier flicking behind the man's knee before he leapt back in one smooth movement.

The drunk watched with horror as his leader fell screaming in the dirt. He and his fellow thundered away on flat feet, leaving Bullet to his fate.

Pinkie was made of firmer stuff; his eyes sharpened to a savage glint. He snatched up Bullet's sword and spat on the ground. "You'll pay for that with your money—*and* your life."

Dominic might have relaxed with only one assailant left, but for Pinkie's casual, confident stance; it was that of a man used to thrusting his weapon through solid things. Such as men's thighs and chests. Dominic's body was lit with incandescent rage, but his hand remained utterly steady.

Pinkie was too smart to rush. He circled to the left, breathing steadily, holding his sword close.

Dominic circled the other direction until he was in place to kick the wretched Bullet in the knee. The man shrieked, and Pinkie's eyes involuntarily shot in that direction. In that instant, Dominic lunged forward, putting all his strength behind the thrust.

His rapier was not merely pretty. Spanish steel slid through Pinkie's jerkin and into his shoulder as slickly as a knife into lard. Pinkie screamed, dropping his sword; Dominic kicked it to the side. His blade came out with a nasty squelching noise.

Pinkie's eyes were bright, then suddenly pale. "You haven't killed me." He clutched his shoulder as blood oozed between his fingers.

"If I had meant to, you'd be dead."

Bullet was sniveling with fear, clutching his knee as he inchwormed away.

Pinkie crammed his filthy pink scarf into a wad and pressed it against the seeping wound.

"You'll live," Dominic told Bullet contemptuously. "You won't walk again. Perhaps you won't thieve or rape again." He let his anger flow down his body and shook it out of his fingertips, a trick his fencing instructor had taught him.

"I'm neither constable, judge, nor jury," he said, reminding himself of the truth as he said it. "You'll have your eternal reward no doubt, Bullet, but while you're still on this earth, stay away from my family." He turned to Pinkie. "If I see you again, I will cut off your pinkies and then all your other bits. Do I make myself clear?"

Pinkie grunted and kicked Bullet, holding out his hand. "Get up on your good leg."

"My blade was clean, but that rag is not," Dominic added. "I may have spared your life, but an infection won't show you the same mercy."

He had a wife and family waiting, but first he returned to the rabbit hutch. He found only the squeaks of bunnies in their filthy cages; Crouch was nowhere to be seen.

Walking to the first cage, Dominic flicked the catch, opened the door, and set the cage down on its side. Two large hares scampered out the door, gone by the time he opened the next cage.

His sister would have approved.

CHAPTER 29

Torie kept looking over her shoulder the entire way back to the carriage, praying that she'd see Dominic strolling behind them, but they reached Mulberry with no more excitement than Florence falling in the muck.

Mulberry threw horse blankets over the crimson leather seats. The children clambered in and promptly seated themselves on the floor, hovering over the cage. It occurred to Torie that a mother likely should tell her children to seat themselves properly, but she was too fearful to bother.

"I suggest you join the children, my lady," Mulberry said. "Best you're not standing here, twinkling like a lighthouse and attracting pickpockets. His lordship is a master with that blade of his, so your ladyship shouldn't worry about that."

Torie climbed into the carriage, feeling sick with worry. The men had such cold eyes, like those of dead codfish. Moreover, there were four of them, and only one Dominic.

Which was precisely when she realized that she had made two cardinal errors: taking the family to this dreadful market and falling in love with her husband.

The emotion must have snuck up on her since their wedding; she could have sworn that she wasn't in love with him yesterday. She had been coolly contemplating jilting him, and would have, if it hadn't been for the twins.

Except . . . that wasn't exactly true. She herself

had acknowledged that the twins would still love her even if she didn't marry their guardian.

According to Clara, most of polite society believed she would jilt him; their guests had arrived at the cathedral with all the relish with which they'd attend a melodrama. Her father wagered money on his certainty. Even her fiancé had walked to the altar expecting her to fail to show up, or worse, to blurt out "I don't" rather than "I do."

Whereas she had behaved with the consistency of a woman in love. She'd ignored everything and everyone, including her best friend's advice, and married the viscount.

Even though he was the most infuriating, condescending, belligerent man whom she could have chosen.

Which brought her shocked thoughts back to the fact that Dominic was even now fighting off four villains with a decorative rapier. She longed to jump out of the carriage, grab that huge gun, and run back to the rabbit hutch.

When Mulberry finally rumbled, "Your ladyship," she shoved open the door and jumped out. Simons was standing at the horses' heads, and Mulberry was on the box, blunderbuss pointing to the ground.

Dominic was sauntering toward them. She couldn't see any wounds, but she wouldn't put it past him to hide an injury so as not to frighten the children. Yet his cheekbones weren't tight, so he wasn't in pain.

When their eyes met, he smiled—*smiled*, dimples and all—as if he'd merely been taking a stroll. "Dominic," she said, the word a whisper on her lips. She cleared her throat and tried again. "Dom, are you injured?"

"Certainly not."

He had a cage tucked under one arm. Could he have purchased another rabbit? She knew from watching the glade that two rabbits quickly multiplied to twenty rabbits.

"All's well," Dominic told Mulberry. "Thank you, Simons, for escorting my family safely back to the carriage."

"Dom," Torie managed.

"One moment, darling," he said. He leaned past her and slid the cage onto the carriage floor.

"What is it?" she heard Florence ask, and then, "Babies!"

"The rabbit family is too young to escape on their own," Dominic said, returning to Torie's side. "We can set them free in one of the parks." He took her hands and brought her close. "Were you frightened?"

"Horribly," Torie admitted, wrapping her arms around his large, solid frame and burying her face in his chest. "You still smell citrusy. The children and I reek."

"I am in need of a bath." Dom leaned down and said in her ear, "And a nap."

Torie managed a shaky smile and allowed her husband to hand her into the carriage. He sat next to her, casually dusting some dirt from his breeches.

"How very tiresome that was," Torie said, managing to keep her tone light, even as her eyes widened at the sight of blood splattered on his lace cuffs.

"Please excuse my sartorial deficiencies," her husband said, stuffing the soiled lace up his sleeve. "I hope that my carriage doesn't permanently carry the aroma of this adventure. I fear for my clothing."

"We had a calamity in your absence," Torie said.
He raised an eyebrow.

"First, Florence fell down in the mud."

"Then Oddie defecated on me," Florence said
brightly. "That's why he is back in his cage. Twenty-
three little pellets. We threw almost all of them out."

"Almost?" Dominic repeated. He looked as if
he'd like to add *defecate* to the Prohibited List but
thought better of it.

Florence held out her hand. "I kept two. Torie
says that the bunny was probably not fed properly,
so we're going to give him better food and then
compare."

Dominic frowned at the squished brown pellets.
He evidently disapproved, but once a child was covered with muck, Torie didn't see that a few rabbit
pellets made a difference.

"I gather Odysseus now has a family name?"
Dominic asked.

"Odysseus is too grand, given his funny ears,"
Valentine said. "We're calling him Oddie, because
he is." He had taken the rabbit from his cage again,
and he was stroking him between his ears. "Oddie
likes this. See how his eyes close? Perhaps his
mother licked him just here."

"Who were those men, and why didn't you come
with us?" Florence asked. "Simons took us out the
back door of the hutch."

"Obviously, Father had to buy the baby rabbits,"
Valentine answered. "Didn't you hear what that
man said about broth? I'm very glad, because the hut
was not a salubrious atmosphere. *Salubrious* is—"

"I do know that word, Val, thank you," Torie
said. "I agree with you. Perhaps we can set the
mother rabbit and her babies free in Green Park.

The park has a wild wood, so likely they can make friends."

"I wouldn't mind that," Florence pronounced. "Oddie must stay with us, though. He has no family, because all his siblings were sold. He was left behind."

"Which means he wasn't made into broth," her brother pointed out. "He's the lucky one."

"Look, he's gone to sleep." The rabbit was nestled down, his nose hidden in the crook of Val's arm.

"I should like both of you to sit on the seat rather than the floor, like proper gentlefolk," Dominic said.

Perhaps that was why children were raised by two parents. After one person wearied of educating young heathens, the other could step in.

When the twins were both seated, their heads bent over the sleeping bunny, Torie slid toward Dom until she fitted against him like a puzzle piece.

"Are you truly all right?" she whispered. "Was that your blood?"

He shook his head. "Not a drop."

"I'm deeply sorry that I ever suggested Smithfield. I've only been to market fairs at home, where you can buy cows, but also whistles and rattles. I thought we could buy a doll for Florence and hear a ballad or two. We could watch acrobats or a pantomime, have some gingerbread, and come home with a rabbit."

"My fault as much as yours," Dominic said, shaking his head. "I believed Smithfield would be filthy and thought we might encounter a pickpocket at most. Not outright criminals."

Torie didn't realize she was clutching her middle until Dominic lifted away her hand and started rubbing comforting circles on her tummy.

"I put us in danger," she whispered.

"No more than I did. Next time, we'll go to Bartholomew Fair, where we *can* buy gingerbread and dolls, as well as watch a pantomime."

"I'm not sure about London markets after this," Torie said dubiously.

"We had bad luck. The rabbit hutch was isolated from the crowd surrounding the cattle sales, which emboldened those men."

"I believe they were acquaintances of that horrid Crouch," Torie said. "We saw him outside, in the back."

Dominic suddenly stilled. "Did he attempt to detain you?"

"Simons went out first, and Crouch was waiting. You must give him a reward, Dom. Simons knocked him down with a terrific blow on the jaw, kicked him around the corner, and then led the children out as if nothing had happened. They had no idea."

"Crouch was nowhere to be seen when I let all his rabbits out."

Torie nestled even closer, thinking that if she had to fall in love—an uncomfortable sensation, so far—she hadn't chosen badly. "Your father let all the bunnies go free," she said to the twins.

"Brava!" Florence cried, throwing her hands in the air.

"No, bravo!" Valentine corrected. "He is male."

"Will you return to the House of Lords?" Torie asked, under cover of a spirited discussion of Latinate gendered interjections.

"Not after this."

Dominic's feelings were in a muddle. He'd left two injured men lying in the dirt without a backward glance. He'd protected his family, so that wasn't what was troubling him.

It was her. His wife. His buxom, beautiful wife.

Blue eyes calm again, her skin as beautiful as a summer peach, her lips red where she'd bitten them.

"I shall rest instead," he said, deciding he was merely in the grip of a healthy bout of lust. "It's been an exciting afternoon." Her smile made his blood race.

"Before anything else, the entire family must take baths," Torie said, holding up her lace handkerchief. It was ripped and smeared with mud. "I did warn you that I would be a very expensive wife, didn't I?"

"My boots are particularly revolting," Valentine said, sticking one out.

"Oddie needs a bath as well. His fur is clumped in—in some areas." Florence smiled impishly. "Did you see how proper I was? The truth is that he's all matted at the rear end. Sometimes it's so hard to get at the truth because the Prohibited List has eaten up so many useful words."

"We will ask Simons to wash your bunny in the stables," Torie said. "Hopefully once Oddie has an unsoiled cage, he will clean himself."

"What about the mama and babies?"

"I have never seen a rabbit choosing to get wet," Torie replied. "If it begins to splatter, they disappear down their burrows, so I think we should leave the mama to clean her babies and herself."

"We can put her and the babies in a box and ask Simons to wash both cages," Valentine suggested.

"They can hop around the nursery!" Florence exclaimed. "The mother and babies must spend at least one night with us before they go to live in Green Park, because we need to sketch them."

She regarded Torie and Dominic with all the drama of a woman under threat of starvation. Or an artist denied her paints. "We must!"

"We have no time to go to Green Park today," Dominic said, tacitly agreeing to a night in the nursery.

"The mama rabbit is still trembling all over," Valentine reported.

"I feel the same," Torie murmured to Dominic.

He rubbed her stomach all the way home. "My poor viscountess," he murmured in her ear. "Luckily, I am certain that I can make her feel better."

Torie leaned her head against his shoulder and thought he was probably right.

Definitely right.

CHAPTER 30

The bathtub in the viscountess's water closet was made of brass with high, curving sides. It featured the astonishing luxury of running water warmed by the kitchen fire, and even better, a drain, but it was only big enough for one.

"We could put in a larger tub." Torie cleared her throat. "Perhaps I could help you bathe, the way women did when . . . when their husbands returned from war."

Dom glanced at her, eyes amused. "Without belittling your feelings, Torie, I assure you that I am a master swordsman. Those men were ignorant louts, and two of them ran off at the sight of my blade."

"Did anyone see what was happening and come help you?"

"There was no need for that," he said with irritating nonchalance.

All sorts of things went through Torie's mind, including the way a man with a pistol could take down a man with a rapier. Her breath turned ragged, and a sob forced its way up her throat.

"Torie." Dom swooped down on her, and then he was *finally* kissing her, licking at her mouth as if she couldn't open to him fast enough.

He tasted like himself. Like home and safety.

She pushed those thoughts away, because the idea of being in love with her husband was so new and perhaps merely the result of a fevered mind after the attack. Love had nothing to do with the fever gripping them at the moment.

She pulled off his coat, and he ripped her gown in his haste to take it off—not that it mattered, because she never wanted to see these clothes again. In fact, she made him dump everything, including their boots and undergarments, outside the door.

"I'll have to stay in this room forever," Dom said, his voice an aching growl. "I can't walk down the corridor to my chamber stark naked."

"I'll lend you a chemise," Torie said, giggling. "Into the tub."

"You first."

She shook her head. "Conquering heroes are bathed first. I'm sure that's what happened to Odysseus, once Penelope recognized him."

Dom's eyes took on a wicked glint that she was beginning to recognize. "As I understand it, Greek heroes were bathed and then rubbed in oil."

"I can rub you all over," Torie said. Her eyes slid over his heavily muscled thigh. "It would be a pleasure, as long as you don't mind smelling like jasmine."

"Better if I anoint you," he said, eyes somber and laughing at the same time. He began kissing her again, his tongue slow and sweet. In the end, Torie tumbled into the tub first and Dom rubbed her all over with soap, exploring every curve and dimple until she was putty in his hands. His deep voice crooned promises that would have sent a respectable matron into hysterics.

Soon she was desperate for him, moans erupting from her mouth, her eyes squeezed tightly shut so that she could concentrate on the wicked hands going everywhere. Tweaking her nipples, running between her legs, teasing her here, then there, until her skin felt as if it were on fire.

"Open your eyes, Torie." Dom's voice turned to a rough command. "I need to know if you're too sore to make love."

She rolled her head on the bathtub's curved back. "I'm fine."

"Torie."

She opened her eyes. "I could be *better*." She gave the word a suggestive emphasis.

He frowned. "Please keep your eyes open."

She tensed as a large finger pushed inside her, but the soreness melted away, and a wild cry broke from her mouth. Dom froze.

"No, no," she gasped, catching his wrist so he couldn't leave her, couldn't move that finger. "It's good, it feels so good."

He began talking again, words tumbling out in that harsh growl that she was learning to love—no, she pushed the question of love away. He was saying what he wanted and expected from her, what *she* wanted and expected.

A second broad finger joined the first, pushing deep, and pleasure wrenched her hips into an arc. He bent over the tub, kissing her mouth in a swiping caress, and Torie threw her arms around his neck, heedless of sloshing water. Dom's free hand curved under her arse. His fingers moved deeper, flexing, and that was it.

Heat shot down her body, sparking through her limbs like lightning as she contracted around his fingers. In a daze, she caught a growled "ravenous," but was he talking about him or her?

Slowly, the pleasure drifted off, and Torie came back to herself, whimpering as his fingers withdrew because she still felt empty and needful.

She lay with her head back on the tub, breathing

in gasps, boneless, her body languid with pleasure. Finally she opened her eyes. Dom's huge shoulders were bent over the bath, one hand effortlessly supporting her body.

"Not enough," he whispered roughly. "Not enough for you, was it?"

His other hand was soothing her now, gliding over her skin under the water, caressing her breasts, her nipples, the curve of her belly, the tender folds behind her knees.

"No," Torie whispered, her voice rough because she may have screamed. She couldn't remember, hadn't known.

Dom straightened, plucking her out of the bath as if she weighed no more than a child. Torie wasn't thinking straight, her mind fragmented between memories of pleasure and an aching wish for more.

She slung a wet arm around his neck. "It's your turn to take a bath."

"I'm sorry," he rasped, his voice hard. "You'll have to take me as I am."

"I like the way you smell," she reminded him.

He put her gently on her back on the bed, and Torie expected him to brace himself on his elbows.

Instead, he pulled her legs to the edge of the bed and went to his knees, pushing her thighs apart. Torie gasped and raised her head. All she could see was tousled hair and fingers gripping her thighs as he licked her.

"I can't," she protested. "I couldn't do that again. I couldn't. Not without you."

"You can," Dom stated, his voice drenched with arrogant *competence*. "You'll do exactly what I want, because you want it too. I want you to scream again,

Torie. I want you to lose your voice, because you're desperate and begging me."

"But Dom," she gasped. Heat began seeping through her again.

"I'm on my knees before you, Torie. *This is going to happen.*"

Her mouth shaped a curse that no lady would air. But then, no lady would be lying like this, legs held wide by a man's elbows so that he could lick every fold of her most private and secret parts.

"Greedy little cunny," he muttered, starting to talk against her flesh.

Her hands wound into his hair. "Like that," he ordered. "Just like that, Torie. When you're on your knees in front of me, I'm going to take your hair and move your head so you're exactly where I want you to be."

Torie had always been good at taking instructions. She pulled him closer, closer, until his tongue lashed her in just the right spot.

She did scream. And she did go hoarse. And she did do everything her husband wanted her to do.

But then, he was doing everything she wanted him to do.

CHAPTER 31

$\mathcal{A}$ week after their trip to Smithfield Market, Torie woke up to her husband trailing kisses over her face. "No session at the House this morning," he whispered. When she opened her eyes, Dom asked a silent question that she answered by wrapping her arms around his neck and then her legs around his hips, because they'd discovered that tilting her pelvis at a particular angle was . . .

Well.

"I thought I might show you the painting I'm working on," she said, once they were lying beside each other, sweaty and panting.

"Later." Dominic leaped out of bed. Making love invigorated him, whereas it made her want to sleep.

They took luncheon with the children, and when the twins departed for their daily visit to Green Park—although the mother rabbit had so far declined to show herself—Torie brought Dominic to her studio. She felt foolishly shy. He'd seen her work, after all. He thought it was meticulous, which was high praise from him.

She had begun a new study in her series on time. Rather than Persephone's dead flowers, she had chosen a black bowl full of pink-tinged Malmaison roses. In her painting, one rose was toppling from the bowl, its petals barely touching the table. In another moment, it would fall, but she was trying to suspend that moment in time.

"I know it's just a bowl of flowers," Dominic said, "but it seems to be a particularly eloquent depiction, if you could say that about roses." He turned to Torie. "Was that a stupid thing to say? I apologize."

Torie's heart was too full for words. "I'm no good at talking about my work," she managed, before she went up on her toes and pulled him close.

"Because—"

He broke off.

Even though he'd become quite skilled at disrobing a lady, they were in too much of a rush for that. Dom stopped kissing Torie just long enough to bend her over the settee, throw up her skirts, and slam inside with desperate force. She squealed with inelegant pleasure, bracing herself, pushing back against his thrusts.

After the first urgent coupling, Torie found herself sitting on her husband's lap, riding him with languid grace, silk skirts billowing around them. They made love slowly but greedily as Torie pressed kisses on his eyelids, his cheekbones, his lower lip.

For days, she'd been fighting her instincts, telling herself all the *love* she felt couldn't be real. It was merely lust. The love she felt for Leonora and Clara was so very different.

She was madly possessive about Dom. Not that she was demanding to know where he was at all hours . . .

Though she would like to know where he was.

Yet she trusted him. In the dark of night, they had even discussed Gianna, his tempestuously creative mistress. "She was not faithful to me," he told her laconically.

Torie drew the bedside candle toward the edge of the table, letting the circle of golden light fall on his face. It turned his cheekbones into blades but didn't hide the disinterest in his eyes.

"You didn't mind?"

"I was actually proud of her."

"What?"

"It's not that we didn't take pleasure in each other, but I was a job, wasn't I? I thought she deserved a lover of her own."

Torie rolled closer, tracing his mouth with her finger. "Is this like you thinking that I had the right to jilt you?"

"No. Because I was desperate to stop you, and I didn't care what Gianna did. I did hope that she'd find a different protector, but she enjoyed the notoriety of being my mistress."

Could it be love that made her admire Dom so much? Made her think that he was the most ethical, fair man she'd ever met—the antithesis of her father?

It couldn't be love.

And it wasn't, because Monsieur Eustache-Hyacinthe Langlois arrived the next day, ushering in a week that culminated in Torie's realization—once again—that her husband was an arrogant, condescending ass.

Not precisely unlovable, but she refused to consider the matter further. The smolder in his eyes when they sat at dinner together? The sweetness of his kisses? His muscled thighs? The way his sweaty chest heaved after he rolled onto his back beside her?

She loved all those things.

But the man himself?

Absolutely not. Not if she wanted to keep her self-respect.

When Flitwick came to her studio and informed her that Dominic was at the House of Lords and unable to greet their new tutor, Monsieur Langlois, Torie pulled off her pinafore and hesitated.

Perhaps she ought to go to her chamber and put on an elegant gown rather than a plain dimity. She'd met French painters. They were debonair, Gallic in their effusiveness and their elegance. At Royal Academy exhibitions, they were invariably clothed in satin, their buttons embellished with gold leaf and their lips with red salve.

They firmly believed that English ladies were not only inept painters but inelegant to boot. Given Langlois's aristocratic father, his breeches were sure to be silk and his hands free of paint.

Monsieur Langlois had been hired to teach the wife of an aristocrat and two schoolchildren how to paint "anything other than rabbits." He would be roguish and nimble-fingered, likely to be even more patronizing if she didn't head off some of his criticism by appearing as well-dressed as a French lady.

No matter how condescending he became, she had to keep in mind the rule she'd made up as a child: she could learn from anyone.

Each and every conversation offered an opportunity to learn something.

Given that it was easier to learn when one's teacher wasn't entirely scornful, she had to do a *grand toilette*. "I have need of Emily," she told Flitwick. "I must change my gown. Please escort monsieur to the nursery to meet the twins." She paused. "Does he appear to have particularly fine sensibilities? Hopefully his English is somewhat deficient, and he won't understand everything they say."

Flitwick's eyes crinkled with amusement. "I could not speak to his command of the language, my lady, but I judge Monsieur Langlois able to take the young master and miss in stride. My understanding is that the French are less devoted to decorum than we English, even finding outright vulgarity to be extremely humorous." He smirked. "The same is not true for our Queen Charlotte, of course."

"Certainly not," Torie said.

An hour later she was clothed in a gown of thick, lustrous white silk, with a transparent gauze overskirt embroidered with an enchanting assortment of forget-me-nots. The bodice was low, with puffed sleeves fashioned from the same gauze that also formed a curious roll at her neck, rather like an informal ruff. With it she wore her emerald ring and a pair of emerald earrings that she had inherited from her mother.

"You are exquisite," Emily declared. "Would you like me to accompany you, my lady?"

Torie was perfectly aware that her lady's maid wished that she would dress elegantly every day, paying calls to everyone in polite society so that her costumes and grooming could be admired. Esteem from a Frenchman was better than nothing.

"That would be very kind of you," Torie said. "I would be grateful if you could carry my reticule and fan, Emily. I'm worried I'll rip this overdress as we climb the stairs." She carefully plucked up the translucent gauze and headed down the corridor from her bedchamber toward the nursery stairs.

Now that she was properly attired, Torie was prepared for anything, from a testy Parisian who would have to be flattered into his tutoring duties to a standoffish maestro who offhandedly threw out pearls of wisdom.

When she and Emily entered the nursery, the

twins were standing by the window, focused on their easels. Langlois apparently wanted to start with fundamentals; they were scribbling with charcoal on foolscap. The Frenchman stood between them, looking intently at the twins' efforts. He was young, with a distinctly leonine yet careless beauty: tawny eyes and hair of the same hue, tied back in a simple queue.

Their new nanny rose, holding a pair of Valentine's breeches that she was mending, and dropped a curtsy. "My lady."

Torie smiled. "Nanny Grey, I do hope those are not the breeches that visited Smithfield Market."

"I'm afraid that I had to send those to be burned in the furnace, my lady. Master Valentine's velvet coat was salvageable, but Miss Florence's went to the furnace as well, along with her gown and boots."

"I'm amazed you could save anything," Torie said.

Emily and Nanny Grey exchanged nods and smiles as the two highest-ranking women in the household after Mrs. Flitwick, who held pride of place. Torie left them to have a comfortable gossip while she joined the artists.

Monsieur Langlois had turned from the easels to greet her. He was dressed without any pretensions to fashion. So much for her prediction about silk breeches. His cravat was no more than a carelessly tied length of cloth; his shirt had no frills; Torie couldn't smell any perfume, though she had to admit that Oddie's ability to produce over two hundred pellets a day—as counted by Florence—overpowered other scents in the nursery.

"Lady Kelbourne, it is a pleasure to meet you," Langlois said, bowing.

She curtsied. "How kind of you to join us, Monsieur Langlois. I am much looking forward to your instruction."

"Come look," Florence called from the window.

Torie tottered across the room, irritated by the darling shoes that matched her gown. The heels kept tipping her forward; a lady foolish enough to alight at Smithfield Market in these shoes would be stuck in the mire until rescued.

The Frenchman caught up with her at Florence's easel. "The children have put the cart before the horse, trying to paint a rabbit before they are capable of forming a circle," he explained with impeccable English. "We shall begin with charcoal and progress from there. They must develop an eye."

"An excellent plan," Torie said.

Valentine was intently drawing circle after circle before rubbing them out with a piece of toweling.

"I can't get them right," he growled, sounding suddenly like his uncle. "They are all lopsided."

"It may take quite a while," Torie said consolingly, stepping over to look at his efforts. "I expect you're already better, and if you practice every day, you'll surely achieve a circle."

"I gave up," Florence said, pointing to her easel. "Instead I drew a ghost traipsing through a churchyard after midnight. Do you know *traipse*, Torie?"

"I do," Torie said. "What are those black streaks?"

"Branches being wrenched from the trunks of trees by the howling of the wind. I'm going to do another one with a girl like me exorcizing a ghost."

"How will she do that?" Torie asked.

"She'll firmly instruct him to go away," Florence said.

Just then, Oddie emerged from behind the sofa.

In the last week, he had shown himself to be a friendly sort who liked to be part of the family.

"Come here, Oddie!" Florence called.

He obediently hopped in her direction while Monsieur Langlois jumped back with an expression that resembled a startled hare. "*Sacre bleu!*" he hissed under his breath. He shot Torie an apologetic look. "In France, such creatures live in hedgerows and never in a house."

Valentine looked up from drawing yet another lopsided circle. "Oddie is a member of the family."

Oddie halted to expel several pellets.

"Master Valentine, it's your turn to clean up after the rabbit," Nanny Grey said placidly from the side of the room. "Please don't forget to use soap when you wash your hands."

Monsieur Langlois cleared his throat. "Perhaps you could tell me something of your technique, Lady Kelbourne?"

"My technique?" Torie had been distracted, reminding herself to thank Flitwick for finding such an excellent nanny.

"Your painting technique. Though perhaps you too are beginning in the art? Do share with me your goals for my tutorship, my lady. Would you like to create watercolor landscapes? I do not know the fashionable art of painting on glass, but I am certain we could work it out if you would like to follow the newest fashion."

Florence giggled, but Torie met her eyes and shook her head.

"I should like to know more of *your* practice," she said, leading him over to the sofa.

Which was where they were when the viscount came home.

CHAPTER 32

$\mathcal{D}$ominic had spent the morning going over the tedious details of a new bill to regulate the import of cotton from Portugal. Luncheon in the Lords dining room had been irritating in the extreme; one of his peers droned on about the price of wheat until Dominic forwent the third course and returned to chambers.

Until it occurred to him that his unbecoming mood had nothing to do with his pontificating peers.

He missed his wife, which made sense because he was the luckiest damn man on the face of the earth. In fact, the next time he saw the Duke of Queensberry, he might offer to buy the fellow a new coat on the grounds that he'd robbed His Grace of a rare jewel.

After all, Queensberry had recognized a gem that Dominic had overlooked, given that his courtship of Torie had been driven predominantly by lust and a desperate need to find someone who could tolerate the twins.

Not just tolerate them but love them.

Now he knew better.

Who gave a damn if Torie couldn't read? He had concluded that literacy had nothing to do with intelligence. She was brilliant.

He found himself running up the steps of his house before he'd consciously decided to leave Lords. When Flitwick told him that the new French tutor had arrived, he climbed the nursery steps two at a time.

Now the children had a painting tutor to distract them, so he would have more time with Torie. Likely she was in her studio. He loved the simple dresses she wore under her pinafore. After unscrambling a few buttons, he could pull them over her head and—

That was the plan before he entered the nursery.

The air was distinctly odiferous, thanks to Oddie, the blasted rabbit who couldn't stop shitting, to call a spade a spade. Florence was lying on the floor with Oddie on her chest, and Valentine was at his easel. The nanny was chatting with Torie's maid over at the side.

And on the couch before the fireplace was a handsome fellow looking at his wife with an expression that Dominic recognized. In fact, he instantly resolved to bribe the artist to move to Bath before he spent even one night in the house.

Torie looked up and held out her hand, her eyes cornflower blue. "Dom, you've done such a marvelous thing in bringing Monsieur Langlois to the house! He is telling me about the accolades he has received from the *Académie Royale de Peinture*. How marvelous for me and for the twins!"

Dominic walked over and pressed a kiss on the back of her hand. Emotions of a kind he did not care for surged through him, because from where he was standing, he could see directly into his lady's bodice—that is, he could see her cleavage and the peachy shapes of her breasts, which were for him alone—as could the Frenchman.

She had dressed herself up like a butterfly, a sensual butterfly, for the delectation of the painter.

He bowed, and his voice was perhaps chillier than he would have intended. "Monsieur Langlois."

The Frenchman had come to his feet, of course, but Dominic could tell instantly that he was the careless sort of fellow who didn't stand on ceremony. Son of a baron he might be, but his standards were those of artists. The fellows in that *Académie*.

The thought was calming, because even though Torie looked as delicious as a fairy queen, she'd told him several times that she didn't care for the men who came around the House of Lords offering to make portraits. Without saying as much, she'd let him know that those painters would scorn her rabbits with mishappen rears, and likely her dying flowers as well.

Not that they'd have the chance to see them. One day when they were lying exhausted and sweaty on the settee, he'd asked whether she invited other people to her studio. "Only Clara," she'd said, which he appreciated, since the room felt like their private refuge.

Florence jumped up and took his hand. "We should show Monsieur Langlois Torie's studio."

He didn't allow himself to frown.

"You have a studio!" the Frenchman exclaimed. "How convenient. I wish all my students were as well-prepared."

"Will you start Torie with drawing circles as well?" Florence asked. Dominic was rather surprised to see that her eyes were alight with mischief.

"I'm drawing circles," Valentine called. "I'm going to draw them all night until I can get one that is absolutely, perfectly round."

Dominic went to take a look. "That seems round to me."

"Slightly flattened on the upper right," Monsieur Langlois commented.

"It's like a full moon," Valentine said. "You know how hard it is to tell if the moon is full because it could be a little bruised on one side, like a peach that fell to the floor?"

"I think Torie should try making a circle," Florence said, popping up at their side. She pulled the foolscap off her easel, revealing another sheet. "You can use my charcoal, Torie!"

"Why circles?" Dominic asked.

"Only a master can create a perfect circle without using an instrument," the Frenchman said.

Dominic had never tried it, but he was pretty sure he could make a circle.

"It *is* hard," Valentine said, scowling at another lopsided peach.

"Back in the fourteenth century, the pope sent messengers around to gather samples of the best artists' work, since he planned to commission paintings for the Vatican," Langlois said.

"Is the Vatican a church?" Torie enquired.

Dominic watched with irritation as the Frenchman melted under her smile like frost in July. "It is the home of the papal court in Rome, my lady," he replied. "The Florentine painter Giotto painted a red circle and sent that to the pope, because its simplicity demonstrated his technical skill. Of course, the pope hired him."

"Maybe also because Giotto was from *Florence*," Florence said. "You try it, Torie!" She handed over a stick of charcoal.

Dominic almost intervened. How could a woman who couldn't draw her own signature in black ink be expected to draw circles in black charcoal?

But he was proud to see Torie take the charcoal and eye the paper. It reminded him of the way she smiled at Leonora's insults. He hadn't thought much of it at the time, but now the memory of Leonora saying that Torie had a thick waist made him furious, let alone her insulting attitude toward Torie's inability to read.

Torie was a good sport. He couldn't imagine anyone else who would take disparagement from her own family members with such grace.

He cleared his throat, resolving that if he meant to defend her before the world, that included making certain that his own children didn't set her up for embarrassment.

But he was too late.

"Ha!" Florence shrieked.

"That looks like a full moon to me!" Dominic said, feeling relief prickle all over his scalp. She couldn't write her signature, but she could draw a circle.

For whatever that was worth.

"Good job, Lady Kelbourne," he continued, wrapping one arm around Torie's waist and kissing her forehead. "The best circle I've ever seen."

"I'll keep going all night long if I have to," Valentine muttered, turning back to his paper and rubbing out the peach.

"I pinned my elbow to my side," Torie said. "That might help you, Val."

Langlois hadn't said a word, but now he stepped forward and looked at the paper. Then bent in and looked so closely that his nose was likely to be dusted black.

Dominic took advantage of the man's distraction to kiss his wife. Torie wrapped her hand around his lapel and melted into him with gratifying speed.

"Kissing again," Florence said with disgust. "Come on, Oddie! Follow me!" She hopped off.

His viscountess tasted like peppermint tooth powder and tea, which was quickly becoming Dominic's favorite flavor. The touch of her tongue to his made him practically dizzy with lust. That was why he couldn't stay in Lords.

He was infected by lust, riddled with lust.

Obsessed by his sensual, circle-drawing wife.

"Lady Kelbourne," the Frenchman said, his accent suddenly three times as Parisian.

Torie drew back. Her eyes were dazed, so Dominic dropped a kiss on her nose. Even in the grip of lust, he tried to keep his head—unless they were near a bed. Torie, on the other hand, threw her entire self into each kiss. He could feel it, the way her arousal built with every touch of their tongues.

When they reached the bedchamber, he could pull up her skirts—which he wouldn't because she was dressed like a French butterfly, not his wife, but if he did . . .

She'd be wet, welcoming, delicious.

"Forgive us, Monsieur Langlois," Torie said, turning away. Dominic just stopped himself from pulling her back against his chest. "We are newly married."

"*Oui, oui,*" the Frenchman said dismissively. "May we visit your studio now?"

Dominic wanted to get to their bedchamber. "I also apologize," he said, bowing. "I must borrow my viscountess, so you will have to talk of circles at a later time."

Florence giggled some more. "Absolutely! More circles for you, Torie!"

"Perhaps tomorrow, Monsieur Langlois," Torie

said, taking the hand Dominic was holding out to her. "Children, please remember that you must ask Cook before you take any food to the mother bunny in Green Park. Mrs. Cottage was most disconcerted to find that her freshly baked tart had gone missing yesterday."

"It was an asparagus tart," Valentine explained, his right arm pinned to his side as he drew another circle. "We thought that the smell might bring her out of the woods, but it didn't."

"Lady Kelbourne," Langlois said, imploringly.

Dominic had no patience for the artist. His whole body was itching to draw Torie into their bedchamber and throw her on the bed. No, unbutton her first. Damn it, she was wearing stays. He could work around that. Get her down to the stays and chemise, and then crawl under all that starched cotton and lick her until she was ready for him.

Course, she might be ready. Her cheeks were flushed, and her eyes bright blue.

"Do you want to take Oddie with you?" Florence asked.

"No, thank you," Torie said. She nodded. "Monsieur Langlois, it has been a pleasure."

"Your studio?" he said hopefully.

The man didn't seem to be able to finish a sentence.

"I would be happy to meet you there tomorrow morning," Torie repeated. "The viscount and I are quite busy, and we are going to the theater tonight."

Dominic frowned before he remembered the plans he had for that thick velvet curtain in the back of his box. He didn't even mind if she wore that confection she had on, though Torie would probably say it was only for the day.

"I've turned into an animal," he told her when they were walking down the steps from the nursery.

She descended ahead of him since the volume of her skirts and the narrowness of the stairwell didn't allow room for anyone beside her. She tilted her head back and looked at him, her face more pointed and delicate from this angle. He couldn't see her stubborn chin.

"Animal as in rabbit?"

"I still haven't passed out," he said thoughtfully. "More practice is needed."

They had reached the landing. One of the housemaids was dusting woodwork, so Dominic forced himself to saunter beside his lady, even though the touch of her fingers on his elbow was incredibly arousing.

They passed a large gilt mirror, the two of them looking as prim as a china figurine of a husband and wife.

"Rabbits must be as frenzied as we," Torie said in a low voice. "They have so many children. Will you mind if I conceive right away?"

The image of her body rounded with his child flashed into Dominic's mind and he snapped. He scooped her into his arms, took two great strides, and kicked open the door to their bedchamber. Torie started giggling, and lord knew, that maid probably was as well.

He set her on her feet and reached out to shove the door closed before he turned her around. "Where are the bloody hooks?" he gritted out.

Torie was giggling so hard that her breasts were—

He reached around to her front and yanked down her bodice. "Careful!" she yelped. "This gauze is a work of art." But she put her head back against his shoulder.

Dominic's hands shaped her breasts, thumbs swiping roughly across her nipples.

"Oh, Dom," she moaned.

His body was feverish, his fingers trembling. Somehow he managed to undo all the intricate little buttons and hooks without tearing that wretched gauze—perhaps just a bit in the rear—and then he had her on his bed.

"I need you," he said against her lips, feeling his heart hammering against her breasts.

"Take me," Torie said, her blue eyes smiling.

He stopped, tapped her generous lip. "You look . . ."

"Happy?"

"You are often happy. You look *content*."

"I feel protected."

Dominic narrowed his eyes, trying to understand. "Were you ever in danger?" His lips went numb, his mind racing to revenge—

"No, not that kind of danger!" she said with a gurgle of laughter. "You stand between me and the world's unkindnesses, Dom. I don't think you understand what it means to me. It's bliss not to have to plan how to defuse an insult before it happens."

True, the night before they had attended a play, and during the intermission, one of her acquaintances had made an idle comment about book-learning. Dominic didn't pull out his rapier, but the lady acted as if he had, scurrying away after he scowled at her.

Torie ran her hands down his broad shoulders and powerful back. "I feel safe when I'm with you," she whispered in his ear.

"I used to feel . . . unsafe around my father," Dominic said, surprising himself. Then he came up on his elbows. "A sorry subject, and not worth talking about."

He lowered his head to her breast. Her skin was fragrant with that perfume he liked. Torie instantly started moving under his weight, shifting her legs and gasping when he began sucking one of her nipples. After he gave her a little bite, she cried out and pushed up with her hips. "I need you," she said, her breath sobbing from her lungs. "Dom, I need you."

"Do you need this?" he whispered roughly, reaching between them to grasp his aching tool and bring it into position.

A sigh that seemed to come from her heart answered him. He just penetrated her, then stopped, and ran a hand down her thigh. "How much do you need me?" he said lazily.

She opened her eyes, heavy-lidded. "Dom!"

"I'm having fun," he said in her ear, still holding off. "You said I don't have enough fun."

Torie's hands curled around his biceps, and she arched up, bracing her feet. He slid in a few inches. "Not enough," she moaned, panting as if she couldn't get enough air.

He ran his hand over her hip. She had wonderful thighs, pillowy soft, made to cradle a man's head. He sank his fingers into that soft curve and pulled her a little higher, giving her another inch.

Torie groaned, desperate. So he pulled her thigh up and thrust forward, rough and gentle at the same time. His wife threw her hands over her head and smiled as if he'd given her the world.

He couldn't have described what it felt to be joined like that, to be a part of her, to have pleasure flooding his body, to have—*fun*.

Then it occurred to him.

Safety.

It felt like safety.

CHAPTER 33

$\mathcal{D}$ominic knew it was coming: the very next morning in bed, when they were companionably eating toast side by side, Torie said, "Tell me about your father, Dom."

"I'd rather not." He put down his teacup and defensively took a huge bite of toast.

"You know everything about my father," she pointed out, turning until she was sitting beside him like a mermaid on a rock, both legs tucked to one side. "*All* my secrets are in the open. In fact, they have been for years, and I promise you that it's much more comfortable this way."

"My father had no secrets," he told her. "He was neither a drunkard nor a gambler."

Torie's thoughtful gaze felt as if she saw to the bottom of his soul.

It sent a bolt of alarm down his spine, terror that she would use her insight to control him. His father had had a seemingly magical ability to discover his small son's greatest fears and use them against him. Thinking of it, Dominic's mouth twisted into a sardonic grimace until, horrified, he flattened it away. He could not become his father, take on his cruelty. Try to break his children.

Appetite gone, he put down his toast.

Torie's hand curled around his wrist. He looked down at it numbly.

"Would I have liked him?" Torie asked.

Dominic shook his head. "Absolutely not. I didn't."

"You once mentioned that he was miserly."

"With his money and his affection."

"Eat," his wife said, holding his marmalade toast to his mouth. Then she leaned in and dropped a sticky kiss on his lips. "Why wouldn't I have liked him?"

"He would have been so rude to you."

Her eyelashes flickered. "Because I can't read?"

"He wouldn't have needed that excuse. He hated women in general, but particularly pretty ones who might distract a man from his purpose." Dominic heard his father's harsh voice in his ear, his raucous laugh. "Ladies with opinions and charm." Even thinking of his father's probable reaction to his marriage made his fists curl.

Torie was silent for a moment.

"Opinions and charm," she said, finally. "Is that why you chose Leonora? She does make a point of presenting herself as a lady without opinions. Though I think she has charm."

"Not like yours," Dominic replied. "Your allure is natural, whereas your sister's every word is deliberate. Leonora's disinclination to speak more than a few words an evening cannot be described as charming."

He couldn't abide falsehoods, and the way Torie's sister presented herself to the world was manifestly false. His wife, on the other hand, was open with everyone, no matter how much they disparaged her.

"Since I can't read, I would presumably confirm your father's worst ideas about my sex," Torie said, her train of thought accidentally following his. "Misogynists generally celebrate my addled brain."

"You don't have an addled brain!" Dominic said.

"I don't know why you can't read, but it's not a matter of that."

Torie shrugged. "I'm talking about perception. Would the late viscount have believed that an illiterate wife posed no threat to your equanimity? Was that one reason why you chose to marry me after my sister?" She eyed him, smiling over her toast. "I'm not saying that to pick a fight. I do know that whatever rational reason you had to marry me other than the twins was swamped by my enchanting—ahem—bosom."

Dominic snorted. "The late viscount would have loathed you—which, by the way, I consider a badge of honor. He would have had an apoplexy if he could see me throw myself in a carriage to come home to you, the fact we sleep together for pleasure rather than creating an heir."

"One of my favorite parts of our marriage," Torie said.

The grin on her lips sent a most peculiar lurch through him, as if the world was shifting under his feet. His father's caustic opinions had continued to burn long after his death, but now he felt an odd lightness.

As if this bedchamber, this woman, might dispel the memory of his father's edicts.

"The gown you were wearing yesterday would have brought on another fit, since he abhorred spending money," Dominic said, deciding to share all his father's worst traits. "He would have concluded that you were a spendthrift, who would obviously be unfaithful, which meant you would ruin my life."

Torie frowned. "I begin to understand Lady Dorney."

"We all seek revenge in our own ways," Dominic said, putting his empty plate to the side. "My sister chose to flaunt all his worst opinions of women. She was very proud of the fact that he died of a heart attack the morning after she danced three times at a ball with the married host and then disappeared with him for a considerable time."

"My goodness," Torie exclaimed.

"He always told me that my temper was our family legacy, though he certainly tried to beat it out of me."

"Oh, Dom." She put her teacup down with a clatter and snuggled herself against his side, wrapping an arm across his chest. "I wish I could have protected you."

"I didn't mean to sound so dramatic," Dominic said, startled. "True, my father firmly believed the adage 'spare the rod and spoil the child,' but I was never badly injured.'" He kissed her head. "And I did eventually learn to control my tantrums."

"Yet you lose your temper regularly in the House of Lords."

"I need to catch their attention."

She raised her head and kissed his chin. "If we're trading in adages, I'd suggest that 'catching more flies with honey' has some truth."

Dominic had heard as much before, but she wasn't at Lords, facing all those idiots and their waffling opinions.

Torie sat up and swung a leg over his body, sitting down. These days he woke with one part of his body standing ready, waiting for the moment when his wife would finish her tea, and he could seduce her. His tool thumped enthusiastically underneath her soft body.

"Mmmm," Torie said, wiggling.

He swallowed hard.

"I do have an important point to make, Dom."

"If you wanted to ensure my attention, you have it," he said hoarsely.

"The Duke of Queensberry—"

He put his hands on her hips and pushed down, enjoying the way her voice broke off.

"Dom!"

"Yes, darling?"

"The Duke of Queensberry is too afraid of you to take up his seat in Lords."

His hands fell away. "What did you say?"

"He's too afraid," Torie said patiently. She leaned forward and ran her hands down Dominic's cheeks. "He told me back in April, when he was courting me."

"He was trying to dissuade you from marrying me," Dominic said, steel in his voice. The hell he'd buy Queensberry another coat. Next time he saw him, he'd slash a rapier down the back of that pink monstrosity.

"I think he was genuinely worried on my behalf. He said you would surely call him a 'duffer' in public, if not worse, and that people already believed his younger brother should have inherited the title if there was fairness in the world." She wiggled again, a smile curving her lush lips. "Which there isn't, especially when you were in line to receive physical . . . endowments."

Dominic ignored that. "If I hold my temper, may we please discuss something else?"

"His Grace would be a vote on your side," Torie said. "Once you explained things to him. He's got a good heart."

"I know that," Dominic conceded. The duke had been extremely gracious when Dominic offered to pay off his debts. In fact, now that he thought about it, Queensberry had said ashamedly that Dominic probably didn't have any debts, but he himself was a nitwit who couldn't resist a lustrous silk.

Dom had silently agreed with him, since he wouldn't dream of going into debt to buy a coat. But now he saw that exchange in a different light.

Queensberry was being shamed for his intellect, something out of his control. As was Torie.

Looking down into her husband's face, Torie decided that they'd had enough serious conversation for the morning. Her painting was calling to her, but she would never be able to concentrate until . . .

"I take it your generosity is partly revenge on your father," she said, leaning over enough to nip his lower lip.

"You could say that." Sure enough, his eyes darkened.

"Perhaps you'd like to seek more revenge?"

Dominic's hands on her hips tightened, and he pulled her down again, settling her weight more firmly. "Not a bad idea. What do you suggest?" His voice was a rasp.

"We could buy every child in the Chelsea Orphanage an expensive doll, one of the ones with real china heads."

"Spending money does make me happy," her husband said. There was a suspicion of a smile around his lips.

"What else makes Viscount Kelbourne happy? And, of course, makes the ghost of his father *un*happy—perhaps even exorcizes that phantom, since Florence is certain of his existence." She raised a finger. "I have it!"

Dominic's smile grew.

She wiggled again. "Ah, my favorite clothespin," she sighed.

Her husband crossed his arms behind his head, flexing the heavy slabs that sculpted his upper body.

Torie's voice lowered. "You turn yourself over to me." She trailed her right hand over his chest and stopped at a nipple. "You let me do depraved things to you that no lady would dream of doing, especially in the morning light."

"Sunlight does make depraved things seem more depraved," Dominic agreed.

"Lie down," she commanded, shifting to the side.

His jaw flexed, but he slid farther down the bed. She ran her right leg up his thigh and cooed, "That wasn't easy, but good things will come of it." She reached back to the tea tray and picked up the little dipper that sat in a jar of honey. Golden sweetness spiraled down to the plate. She waggled her eyebrows at him and then looked at his crotch.

Dominic drew in a sharp breath. "Torie." His voice was raw.

She dipped the honey stick again.

"Lie still, Viscount."

CHAPTER 34

A few weeks later, Torie woke to find herself alone in bed. Her husband had seduced her at dawn, and then leapt out of bed an hour later, cheerful and energized, whereas she had fallen back to sleep, meaning she'd missed the best light in her studio.

That could not happen tomorrow, she decided, scowling at her own laziness as she rang for Emily. Dominic would have to come home at luncheon if he wanted to dally with his wife. She needed first light for painting.

Now she thought of it, Dom had been routinely coming home at midday, sometimes not returning for the afternoon session. His opponents had managed to push the antislavery vote off the agenda once again, with the ludicrous excuse that more information was needed about how widespread the practice was.

Despite how loudly Dom shouted that even a single enslaved person was too many, the opposition had prevailed.

Emily appeared at the door, holding a tea tray. "Miss Florence would like to pay you a visit, my lady."

She was itching to go to her studio, but . . . "Of course!" Torie exclaimed.

Florence appeared in the doorway, beaming. "I thought you might like me to read to you while you have tea. It's so boring to eat without a book in hand."

"I would love it," Torie said, patting the bed. "Slippers off."

Florence agreeably kicked them away and nestled

herself next to Torie. Thankfully the children were
finally out of mourning; she was wearing an adorable blue dress covered by a long pinafore, because
Nanny Grey had discovered that Florence fell to
her knees daily—either by accident or because she
saw something interesting on the ground. What's
more, Monsieur Langlois had the children painting
in watercolors, which tended to splatter.

"*Castle Rackrent*," Florence said, pulling a book
from her pocket. "You'll love it, Torie. The husband
is *terrifyingly* mean! A pestilent rogue!"

Torie sipped her tea, smiling. After a few chap-
ters, Florence went off for her daily trip to Green
Park—where the mother rabbit never deigned to be
seen—and Torie decided that she could not spare
the two hours needed to properly attire herself. Ignoring Emily's admonishments about viscountess
behavior, Torie pulled a wrapper over her nightgown and went downstairs to her studio.

A rose at the top of the composition caught her
eye. With sudden energy, she bundled on her pinafore and set to work. The petals were too smooth;
she wanted the swirl of the stroke to be evident. Her
still lifes never tried to capture reality. They were
about ideas, and so her brushwork had to be visible.

Two hours later, the studio darkened as rain
showers threatened. Torie began pacing around the
easel, watching how light changed the impression
that one rose was falling. Flitwick appeared with
two standing candelabras and a bowl of fruit. Torie
wasn't hungry, but she pulled out a fat yellow pear
and placed it before the black bowl, where it might
balance the falling rose.

A rap on the door made her turn around, vexed.
"I don't wish for anything else, Flitwick."

Monsieur Langlois stood in the doorway, his expression diffident . . . fascinated. In the month since he'd arrived, they had flipped from tutor to student and back again several times, finally settling on friendship.

She was a better painter than he was; in this particular realm, Torie was pragmatic rather than boastful. But he was better than she at vocalizing what she was doing. He could see into the heart of a painting, whereas she became inarticulate.

"I don't like it," he said immediately, approaching the table. "This pear, she is gauche, bold, gaudy." He snatched the fruit, waving it in the air. "She is a visit from the world of fertility and light, sensual and delicious."

A throat clearing had Torie turning to see her husband, home for luncheon.

"Torie, your brush is dripping down your sleeve," he said gruffly. "May I ask why Monsieur Langlois is talking about sensuality in the presence of my *unclothed wife*?"

She'd seen that dangerous look before, as when Dominic faced four ruffians at Smithfield Market. It must have been a particularly aggravating morning in the House of Lords; his jaw was tight and his eyes shuttered.

"The pear is sensual. *I* am clearly not." She waved at her paint-covered pinafore. "I was considering changing the composition of this painting, but Monsieur Langlois thinks adding the pear would be a mistake."

The Frenchman drew himself up and said, through pursed lips, "If you suggest for one moment that I would make an invidious advance to the viscountess, to a woman who paints like—"

Torie cut him off before he embarrassed her. "But you're right about my dressing gown, Dom. I walked in meaning to glance at my painting and remind myself what was left to be done, but that was hours ago, after breakfast."

Langlois blinked at her. "I didn't notice your attire, my lady."

No one could have mistaken his astonishment. He was genuinely uninterested in clothing, and in her as a woman, for that matter. Paint was all that mattered to him. Paint, and what one could say about paintings.

"Monsieur, may I ask you to put down your pear and leave my wife's studio?" Dominic said through gritted teeth. Apparently her husband was the one person who *could* overlook her tutor's surprise.

All the irritation that Torie generally allowed to fall by the wayside bounded into her chest. "Monsieur is my guest, invited to *my* studio," she stated, not keeping her voice even.

The Frenchman's eyes widened, and his gaze bounced between them. "I shall see if Master Valentine wishes to work on his circles." He bowed with an air of wounded dignity.

After the door closed, Torie said, "For goodness' sake, Dom! That boy has no designs on my virtue, if that's what you are implying."

Her husband gave a bark of laughter. "He's no boy. He's your age. He looks at you as if you hung the moon and the stars, Torie."

"As far as Langlois is concerned, I'm not a woman," Torie said, trying to explain. "I'm simply someone whom he can talk to about painting."

"The way the Duke of Queensberry liked to talk to you about fashion?"

Torie hunched a shoulder. His Grace had taught her a great deal about gilt buttons and the latest fabrics coming from India. "Why is that relevant?"

Dominic didn't answer. Instead he walked over to her painting. "Very pretty." He picked up the pear. "Why didn't Langlois want it in the painting?" He held it up against her canvas. "It would add a dash of color."

He had no idea that his comment felt impertinent, if not condescending. Torie took a deep breath, but all the same, a ball of resentment burned more brightly in her stomach.

"Eustache felt that the pear existed in a different world, a more sensual—"

"*Eustache*?" he cut through her sentence sharply.

"A more sensual world of fertility and light."

"Bullshit!" Dominic snarled.

Torie couldn't believe what she was hearing. "Did you just curse at me? With your voice raised?"

"Not as high as yours," he retorted.

"I didn't curse at you." She managed to suffocate a few appropriate words that were struggling to erupt from her mouth.

"*Eustache* is in love with you." His lip curled. "I'll have him out of the house by nightfall."

"He is not!" Torie cried, her stomach curdling. "You don't understand."

Dominic scoffed. "Don't be a fool."

The room went bleakly silent. Torie couldn't believe what she heard—or rather, what she didn't hear. But she knew how that rebuke ended. How could she not, having heard versions of that word her whole life, from every frustrated nanny and governess who had tried to teach her to read?

She was too furious to think clearly, but her heart

chipped and fell in two like an ormolu clock striking a stone wall.

"Don't be a fool," she repeated, trying not to take it personally. It was a common phrase, after all. She had already recognized that Dominic's defense of her didn't mean disagreement with the world's opinion.

He simply insisted that the world was not allowed to express its opinion to her face.

Yet somehow his opinion accidentally made itself known, whether he was meeting with Gianna or calling her a fool to her face.

She saw remorse in his eyes. "I apologize," Dominic said immediately. "You are correct, and I will try to . . ."

"Try to do better," she said wryly.

"Not for the first time," he acknowledged. "The insult is a commonplace that we throw at each other's heads in the House of Lords. Lord Peyrenes shouted it to me this morning."

"An admonition like that is always meant to belittle the recipient," she said. "Thus the Duke of Queensberry's reluctance to take up his seat in the House of Lords. More importantly, even if most of London didn't already consider me a fool, it would never be an appropriate insult for a husband to hurl at his wife. *Ever!*"

"I agree."

"I have always known that it's hard to keep one's opinion secret." She dropped down on the wide yellow chair, the one that Dominic had thrown himself into when he stripped off his shirt long ago. "You think that Leonora is unkind to me, but she defended me for years. Yet when she was in a rage, her opinion leaked out. It didn't mean she doesn't love me. I always forgave her, but coming from my *husband*, it feels more galling."

He sat down on the couch, obviously lining up his arguments in his head, the way he did at dinner or in Lords. "Surely you can understand that it is a shock to walk into a room and find one's wife in her nightgown talking in intimate terms with another man?"

Even if she could have understood it, she had no intention of doing so.

"Do you know *my* shock?" she demanded. "I've been stupidly thinking I might be falling in love with you . . . almost in love with you. We said we weren't going to talk of such things—or feel them, for that matter—but I don't mind telling you of my idiocy, because obviously I was *so wrong.*"

She couldn't see any response in his face, in his eyes, in his mouth. Anywhere. Except perhaps the fact that one fist was curled at his side, likely because emotions made him so uncomfortable. "You and Leonora really *were* a perfect couple," she said, tipping her head back and staring at the ceiling far above rather than his rock-hard jaw.

"I don't agree."

Torie shrugged. Her throat was aching, and her heart was aching. "I think I shall go to my father's country estate for a brief visit. I've been wanting to show the twins the glade where the rabbits play."

Dominic moved sharply. "No."

"I'm not running away," Torie said exhaustedly. "I merely need to recover my temper. Like the twins' previous governess, I would be perfectly happy to throw a clock at your head right now."

"I see."

"So you might as well indulge in all the late nights you warned me about before we married. Remember? You said that it was important to dine with important men so you could bend them to your will in a more polite manner than by emphasizing their idiocy."

His eyes flared with anger, which gave Torie a strange satisfaction. He might not be in love with her, but he wasn't indifferent either.

"I shall take respite in the country," she said, getting up. "I'll bring the children with me. You are welcome to join us, but I'm sure you have more important things to do than sprawl on the grass in a rabbit-filled glade."

His lips opened and closed.

"I *know* your work is important," she added, exasperated. "I had no intention of belittling the bill."

"That bill is delayed while awaiting reports from the Caribbean. But—"

"I know. You truly *do* have more important things on your mind than the three of us."

His eyes glittered at her. After a silence, he said in a rasp, "Langlois shall not accompany you."

Torie had the odd idea that it pained him to say that sentence. Of course, he thought a great deal of himself; it must be humiliating to imagine his addled wife taken from him by a young Frenchman.

She shrugged. "Eustache will be grateful for an opportunity to work on his painting for the French Exhibition."

His mouth flattened to a line.

"No, I am not going back to addressing him as Monsieur Langlois. He is a fellow painter. I've learned from him, and he's an excellent influence on the twins. I think Valentine might be a painter someday."

His face didn't change, so it must have been the air around him that darkened.

"Yes, just imagine," she scoffed. "Lord Dorney became a painter rather than spending his time gambling, the way his father did. What a shame."

"I would have concerns about Valentine's ability to support his estate. His father did not leave him much money."

She shook her head. "As if you aren't repairing that estate yourself. I'm sure that you have set up funds for both children. Moreover, Gainsborough's *Blue Boy* sold four years ago for thousands of pounds."

"Valentine is still drawing lopsided moons and lop-eared rabbits. I don't think we should count on his earning a living with his craft just yet."

"Painting is *hard work*," she said fiercely. "If I'd been able to read, I doubt I would be as good as I am now. I had nothing else to do. If Valentine decides to focus, he will be a very good painter, perhaps a great one."

Dominic's shoulder hitched. She didn't think he would ever respect the profession, but it was Val's fight, not hers.

"I would ask that you return in ten days."

"All right." Torie would come home whenever she felt like coming home, but she saw no point in arguing about it.

"You just made a promise," the viscount said sharply. She couldn't think of him as Dom, her Dom. Not this glowering, chilly man. Glowering, chilly, *and* jealous.

"I will return," Torie said, exhausted. The children would miss him.

WHEN SHE WOKE in the morning, she had a faint memory of strong arms around her, and there was an imprint of his head on the pillow beside hers, but he was already gone.

"Toast!" Emily shrilled, coming in the door with a tray. As Torie drank tea, her maid bustled about, packing more clothing even though she'd already sent a trunk down to Mulberry the night before.

A *trunk* for ten days in the country, where one didn't ever dress for dinner, especially when one's spouse remained in London. "Are my pinafore and paints in the carriage?"

Emily nodded. "Mr. Flitwick took care of those himself."

"Excellent," Torie said, forcing herself to finish a piece of toast. There was nothing worse than growing hungry on a long stretch of road.

"The twins are ready to go, though they had a terrible row over that dratted rabbit this morning."

"Why?"

"Miss Florence says the rabbit must accompany us, as he'll be lonely by himself. Master Valentine says if the rabbit comes to the country, the creature will run away."

"If he's in the coach with us, we'll have to be constantly throwing pellets out the window."

"I shouldn't admit it, but I am very happy to be following you in the second carriage, given the odor. I can't think how Nanny ignores that smell in the nursery, but she says one gets used to it." Emily turned up her nose. "That would never happen to me. Oh! I forgot to tell you that Lord

Kelbourne intends to return to say farewell after the morning session in Parliament."

"Unfortunately, we're leaving directly, as I informed him yesterday," Torie said, climbing out of bed.

Emily opened her mouth, but Torie caught her eye.

"Yes, my lady," her maid said.

"I should like to leave within the hour, since the children are ready. I'll wash at the basin and wear a plain dimity."

"Within the hour," Emily echoed with a gulp, starting to rush about.

The three of them were loaded in the coach on time, with Oddie in his cage on the floor, Mulberry and Simons on the box, and two liveried footmen in the rear.

"His lordship's orders," Mulberry said when Torie suggested the two footmen could travel in the second coach with Emily and Nanny.

"It will be so dusty and uncomfortable."

But Mulberry shook his head. She could see the blunderbuss stored at his feet.

As they were about to set off, the coach door suddenly opened again, and Mulberry's face appeared. "The Duchess of Huntington, my lady." He withdrew, and the cheerful face of English's top steampipe designer appeared in his stead.

"We were coming to see you!" the duchess said. "Hello, twins."

Florence and Valentine jumped up to curtsy and bow, Valentine's head just grazing the top of the carriage. "Good morning, Your Grace," they chorused.

"I'm afraid that we are on the very point of going to the country," Torie said smiling, because grim though she felt, she genuinely liked Her Grace.

"I want to commission you to paint my red steam engine."

"I'm afraid that isn't my forte," Torie said apologetically.

The duchess waved her hands. "Yes, so your husband said. He thinks you can't do anything more than flowers and kittens."

Torie ground her teeth. Dominic had *seen* her paintings. Surely he knew that she was *choosing* to paint flowers, rather than being confined to that subject. But then, she'd never wanted to boast, had she?

She just kept hoping that one day he would stride into her studio, look around, and recognize that she was a real artist, not a lady dabbling in a hobby.

"Kelbourne said that he would get you a tutor, and you might be able to manage a locomotive in a year. Didn't want me to ask you before then in case you were embarrassed."

"I see," Torie managed, even though her throat felt thick. Actually, *Dom* was embarrassed. That's what it came down to.

"I made a few inquiries amongst my friends about your painting ability," the duchess continued, a distinct note of triumph in her voice.

Torie felt herself turning a little pink.

"She can draw a perfect circle!" Florence said.

"Precisely," Her Grace said, taking that comment on board without flickering an eyelash. "Your stepmother can certainly paint a steam engine. I suggest that you all come to Huntington Grange. My husband and I were just stopping by to commission the painting before we left for the country. Your coach can follow ours. We'll stop midway and spend the night in a nice inn."

"We were going to watch rabbits playing in a glade," Florence objected.

Torie made a mental note that somehow she had to impress upon Florence that young girls were expected to be seen and not heard, especially in the presence of a duchess.

"We have rabbits!" Her Grace said, thankfully showing no signs of affront. "More rabbits than you can imagine. We've taken to leaving the front door of the Grange open, and now and then one hops in for a visit. A few months ago, a wild boar wandered straight into the main hall."

Valentine looked up at that. He was trying to finish his hour of practicing circles before the coach made it impossible.

"Did you kill the boar?" Florence asked with relish. "Shoot it with an arrow?"

"Of course," Her Grace said with aplomb. "I wasn't personally involved, but the boar was cooked in the fireplace and served for dinner. Four footmen brought it in, with a ruff around its neck and a velvet hat adorned with pearls on its head."

"Why?" Valentine asked.

"Why what?" Her Grace looked confused.

"Why a velvet hat? Was the boar a female?"

"I have no idea. Why shouldn't it wear a velvet hat? I added a tiara on top of the hat."

Florence clapped her hands. "I shall write a story about that boar!"

"Excellent," the duchess said. "You may read it to my children. I haven't had the time to hire another governess since the last one left."

"Neither did our mother," Valentine said cheerfully. "I expect we shall get along with them very well. Do you think this is a true circle?" He held up a sheet.

"No," Her Grace said. "It is a shade flattened on the upper left. When one is designing machinery, even the smallest details count. Now, shall we leave immediately?"

One of the reasons Torie had gotten along with her husband until this point was that she had the ability to see another person's viewpoint. Right now, it was crystal clear that the duchess would not be angered if they didn't pay her a visit, but she would be hurt.

After all, "we're going to watch rabbits" wasn't a very compelling excuse.

"We must inform our butler," Torie said.

"Of course," the duchess said, her head disappearing.

"Would you like me to write a note for Father?" Florence asked. "I know you usually ask Emily, but she is already in the other carriage."

Torie felt color spilling into her cheeks. "No, thank you," she managed. "I'll just let Flitwick know where we've gone, so the viscount doesn't worry."

"He won't worry," Valentine said. "He knows you're with us."

Flitwick appeared at the door of the carriage.

"We shall pay a visit to the Duchess of Huntington," she told him. "Please tell Lord Kelbourne, as well as Emily and Nanny Grey. I would be grateful if you would inform the viscount that the Duchess of Huntington has commissioned a painting of her steam engine. I shall try not to embarrass him, even given my inexperience in this area."

The butler disappeared, and the carriage trundled away.

"Father would never be embarrassed by your paintings," Florence observed.

"I was feeling cross, or I wouldn't have said it," Torie admitted. "I *shouldn't* have said it."

Val was frowning. "I can't imagine any reason he would ever feel embarrassed by you, other than perhaps your inability to read."

"Which doesn't matter," Florence said. She pulled out *Castle Rackrent*. "You have me!"

CHAPTER 35

Dominic strode out of the main chamber of the House of Lords the moment the session was called. Around him, peers were clustering, discussing where to eat.

He blew past them, ignoring the sideways glances and the way a few pestilent cowards cringed as he strode by.

Yes, he had a temper.

And he could be . . . mean.

He couldn't stop thinking of the crushed look in Torie's eyes when he implied she was a fool. He didn't mean it. All morning, the evidence of her intelligence had marched through his mind like soldiers on parade, their brass buttons glittering. The way she quoted everything from the Bible to obscure Shakespeare plays. The way she countered his arguments, often in more complex and twisty ways than anyone in Lords had ever come up with.

Even the way she painted.

He knew the house was empty the moment he drew up his curricle. The two large carriages had been standing in the street that morning, but now it was empty. His butler jerked open the door and came down the steps; obviously he'd been watching from the drawing room window.

"Flitwick," he said grimly.

The man bowed.

"I gather that Lady Kelbourne has left for the country. Was my wife informed that I planned to return after the session?"

"Yes, my lord."

Flitwick's confirmation made his chest hurt, as if his heart was too stiff to beat.

"But my lady left with the Duchess of Huntington en route to Huntington Grange," the butler said quickly. "They had to begin immediately, since they hope to reach the Bell & Parrot Inn."

Dominic couldn't have heard correctly. "What did you say?"

"Lady Kelbourne and the twins were invited by Her Grace to pay a visit to Huntington Grange." Flitwick's chest puffed out, more than a hint of pride in his voice.

"Did Lady Kelbourne indicate how long she intends to remain at Huntington Grange?"

"My lady plans to return in ten days. She says that you are aware that the duchess planned to commission a painting of a steam engine."

Dominic frowned. Didn't he explicitly ask the duchess to give Torie time to learn some new skills? It was a good thing he hadn't sent Langlois off with a flea in his ear. The man would have to stop waving around pears and get Torie focused on machinery, now that she'd accepted the commission.

"I see."

Flitwick hesitated.

"Did the viscountess leave another message?"

The butler winced and then repeated, "'I shall try not to embarrass him, even given my inexperience in this area.'"

Stinging silence fell between them. Dominic gave him a nod and strode into the house, throwing his greatcoat and gloves at a footman. He went to his study, shutting the door behind him. Once there, he dropped into a chair and buried his head in his hands.

He loved Torie—yes, *loved* her more than anyone else. More than the mother he never knew, his angry, flighty sister, his horrible father. More than the twins, fond though he was of them.

He felt as if Torie had carved a door in his heart and stepped inside, creating a space that was only hers. Even in the maelstrom that was debate in the House of Lords, taking a breath and thinking of her would ground him.

Yet he'd betrayed her. First with Gianna, though he hadn't been sleeping with the woman, and then again with this stupidity. Together with every single day that he didn't tell the world how brilliant she was.

Every single one of those days was a betrayal.

His hands curled into fists thinking about it. *He* prided himself on his moral superiority? *He* was the fool. The men bumbling around the House of Lords did their best to get their minds around the ramifications of grain imports from Portugal and sugar from Jamaica. They were ignorant, most of them, but they went home and treated their wives with kindness.

The point that made his throat burn was that *he* had been dismissive, in thought and deed, of his astonishing wife. Of his brilliant, funny, creative wife. Look how he'd gotten rid of the Duke of Queensberry, so that she wouldn't have a duke to run to.

Immoral. Irreverent. Unkind.

He'd hurt her.

And now she was gone. It felt as if his heart had cracked. He wasn't even sure where she would sleep tonight. He didn't know if miscreants like Pinkie and Bullet would covetously eye her emerald ring, her beauty, and—

The thought tore at him, and he lunged out of

his chair and charged back to the entry. "Flitwick, she set off with Mulberry, Simons, and two more grooms, didn't she?"

"Yes, my lord," Flitwick said. "Mulberry had the blunderbuss, but Simons also had a pistol, just in case they encountered a highwayman. *Very* unlikely, as you know, my lord. They'll be following the Duke of Huntington's carriage, and he let me know that he travels with four outriders who will guard all three vehicles."

"I should have sent outriders," Dominic said hollowly. "Why didn't I think of outriders?"

"Because her ladyship was only going five hours down the road," his butler said patiently. "Overnight is a different story, but since His Grace travels around the country with that steam engine in tow, he's used to being prudent."

Curses were pounding through Dominic's head, but he forced himself back into his study. Where would Torie sleep tonight? Would they reach the inn in time? Would she be safe?

She would be fine. The children would be fine. Mulberry was steadfast and deeply loyal. Most importantly, Dominic couldn't scamper after her as if she held a leash. His father's thundering voice reminded him to be a man.

Every night in the following week he lay awake, staring into the darkness, knowing in his bone marrow what it meant to love a woman—and lose her. It felt helpless: the worst emotion he could imagine—but one he recognized.

Helpless was what a little boy felt when his father's temper was like an arctic wind. When that father was impossible to please, and his whip always ready to hand.

That father's voice resounded through space and time, telling him what a *bloody fool* he was. Telling him that there had never been such a stupid viscount in the history of the Kelbournes. The same voice that told his sister over and over that she had a jezebel's heart and a slut's hips.

As the days passed, Dominic began to delay his return to the silent house until late at night—and why shouldn't he, since he couldn't do any of the things that made Kelbourne House a home? He couldn't throw open the door of his wife's studio and snatch her into his arms. Couldn't run up the stairs, find Torie at her dressing table, and banish giggling Emily. Couldn't listen to ghost stories in the nursery, meeting Torie's amused eyes over Florence's head, or carefully assess Valentine's latest lopsided circle.

One morning Dominic came to a simple realization: he needed to be where his family was. He would try not to hurt Torie's feelings ever again. He would sit in her studio and beg her to explain why a pear didn't belong in a painting. He would inform society about his wife's brilliance.

He would never listen to his father's voice again.

He just didn't know how to convince Torie that he truly loved her, not when he kept disrespecting her.

A far-fetched idea came to him, an idea that might be possible with enough money to grease the way. He would go to that bloody Royal Academy. He'd pay them to let in women, and insist they elect Torie, same as they did those fellows like Gainsborough, whom she admired so much.

Thankfully the man was dead, or Dom might truly have competition for her affection.

Torie had said she was *almost* in love with him.

He'd take it. He'd take it, and take her, and throw enough money at the Royal Academy to make her feel confident and happy about herself and her work.

He'd even let that Frenchman stay in the house.

After querying Flitwick, Dominic tracked down Monsieur Langlois in Torie's studio. He was standing before the largest window, coat off and shirt-sleeves rolled up, wearing a pinafore not unlike Torie's. A bowl of fruit sat on the table to the side. He was dabbing at his canvas, dripping paint on the floor of the former breakfast room, but Flitwick had long since given up that battle.

When Dominic entered, Langlois threw a distracted glance over his shoulder and looked back at his painting. Dominic strolled over and surveyed the painting. "Interesting," he said.

"*Pas bon,*" Langlois groaned. "Not good, not good!" He threw his brush to the floor, and orange paint splattered in all directions.

"What's the matter with it?"

The Frenchman moaned and clutched his hair in a Gallic frenzy. "You are a philistine, so I shall not waste my time. Why are you here? This is a sanctuary." He picked up his paintbrush.

Dominic looked at him. "A sanctuary?"

"She is here, she is everywhere, she works *here.*"

Bloody hell. "You're in love with my wife." The words came out like bullets, but there was a limit to what a man could take.

"Philistine!" Langlois screamed.

He didn't resemble a man in love. Queensberry's eyes had had longing in them that Dom was pretty sure could be seen in his own eyes now. To the contrary, Langlois looked outraged.

"*You* are in love," the Frenchman snorted.

"*L'amour* is not for me. I am a man of great seriousness, I!"

His English was disintegrating. Langlois turned his back and started vigorously swirling his brush around, mixing colors before he darted at his canvas.

It wasn't unlike how Torie painted. Sometimes Dominic walked in and found her staring at her easel. Then she would fly at her colors and swoop over the painting and . . . do something to one leaf, or one petal.

But when he tried to ask what, she brushed him off, saying that she couldn't explain it.

"Langlois," he said.

That earned him a Gallic stare.

"Explain this painting to me." Dominic pointed to the painting hanging on the wall, the wilting flowers Torie had given him for their wedding, but never really given to him. It had gone up on the wall of her studio, and sometimes he found her peering at it, almost as if she intended to wipe it with turpentine and start over.

He should probably rescue it.

Twenty minutes later he was as bewildered as if the Frenchman was talking of pears. Not flowers, but time. Not just time, but time passing, time dying, time caught in time. "*Le temps qui passe,*" Langlois concluded, picking up his paintbrush and going back to his hapless pear.

CHAPTER 36

As soon as they arrived at Huntington Grange, the duchess helped Torie set up her easel and paints before the red locomotive. The duke dragged out an overstuffed chair from the drawing room himself, for there was no butler. In fact, there were almost no servants at all.

That first day, Torie just stared at the machine: walking around it, then returning to her seat. The machine had no life or sense of time beneath its red paint and shiny curves. But it did have *purpose*, which was interesting.

She wasn't alone, as the duke and duchess were busy implementing ideas they gained while meeting other steam enthusiasts around the country. They ignored her, darting here and there around the engine.

The second day, Torie began to sketch, trying to decide which angle to paint from. Not straight to the side, because somehow she had to give the painting a feeling of speed.

Nanny Grey—who had an almost saintlike patience—came outside to tell Torie that she thought the ducal children weren't being bathed as much as they might. "No nanny and no nursemaid. The boy, Master Silvester, makes certain his sisters are fed and in bed, though of course I've taken charge during our visit."

"Oh dear," Torie said, trying to envision mentioning the state of the nursery to Her Grace.

"I'm scrubbing that room down tomorrow with

caustic soap." Nanny bustled away, looking surprisingly cheerful.

Torie went back to her drawing, finding herself thinking absent-mindedly that everyone needed to feel needed. She put down her pencil again.

Dominic needed her. He might not realize it, but he did.

It wasn't until the third day, when she began blocking in the locomotive's shape and thinking about color, that she realized the most fascinating aspect of the locomotive was not its color, but its creators.

Once she got the locomotive blocked in, she sketched the duchess on top of the engine, throwing her hat in the air, with the duke down below, laughing up at her.

"I like it," Valentine said on the fourth afternoon of their visit. He was still doing his daily practice making circles, though it was difficult to measure one hour, as they had discovered that no clocks in the house functioned.

"Come here when the sun begins to sink," Torie had advised him. "When the sky turns purple, your hour will be up."

He squinted at her. "How will I know that it's sinking?"

"Pay attention to the light."

The next two days, he didn't show up at the proper time, but on the seventh day, he appeared at precisely the moment when twilight began. And his circles were much improved.

After Val ran away, Torie sat down in her chair and looked at her sketch. She had managed to give the locomotive a sense of motion: the duchess was nearly flying off the top, and the duke was caught in mid-laugh.

Florence showed up and wedged herself into the chair. "You can see how much he cares for her."

"He?"

"His Grace," she said obediently. "It's hard to remember that he's a duke." She lowered her voice. "His shirt is ripped, and I saw a bit of his belly at luncheon."

"I noticed that," Torie said. "Do you think I ought to put that detail in the painting?"

"Yes," Florence said. "He's the only duke with a ripped shirt. Did you know that none of their neighbors will visit, because they think the duke and duchess are too strange?" She jumped out of the chair. "I don't want to leave."

Huntington Grange was an odd, mad household, but like Florence, Torie felt entirely at home.

The only problem was Dom.

She lay awake at night, aching for her husband as if a part of her body had gone missing. Finally she brought up a branching candelabra that she found in the neglected ballroom and started sketching something quite different from roses or rabbits or steam locomotives: Dom's face.

She gave him that look of leashed energy that he took with him through life. His eyes were fierce, but also tender. The dimples appeared.

Two days later, she was quite sure about her own drawing: she had captured a man in love.

Interesting.

CHAPTER 37

$\mathcal{T}$he Royal Academy of Arts was in Somerset House, a palace that used to be the official home of Queen Elizabeth—though from what Dominic remembered of his history lessons, the queen spent most of her time jaunting around the country, dragging a household of three hundred courtiers on monthlong visits to her favorite noblemen.

His Elizabethan ancestor was not so favored. In the midst of a temper tantrum, the former viscount had turned his back on Her Majesty—whereupon she threw a slipper at his head and declared she would never grace his home with her presence.

Which saved the family fortune from being bankrupted by a royal visit.

That legacy of temper had come down through the generations, along with the Kelbourne estate, a hunting lodge in Scotland, and the London townhouse.

Dominic drove his curricle up to the gate of Somerset House, threw the reins to his groom, and strode through the imposing courtyard. He was impatient to get this over with and set out for Huntington Grange.

Never mind the fact that the House of Lords was still in session.

"We were founded by King George III in December 1768," the director of the Royal Academy said, once Dominic had presented himself. The man had eyes like shiny sea pebbles and a boastful manner.

"Only the very best artists are allowed to join,

naturally. Our first president was Sir Joshua Reynolds . . ."

Dominic let the man's voice wash over him as he was escorted into the first of three exhibition halls. Paintings went from floor to ceiling in a dizzying array. The ones at the top had been tipped forward so they could be seen.

"Surely that is dangerous," Dominic said, pointing to one that appeared ready to crash to the floor.

The director looked at him disdainfully. "Art must be seen."

"Right. So who is the president?"

"King George III's official painter, an American gentleman by the name of Benjamin West. Here he is now."

Benjamin West had a slender nose and black hair that curled up over his ears. He was surprisingly young to be running an academy that—according to its director—was the most prestigious academy for design and art in the world.

Hopefully West had witnessed American women trampling their way into male strongholds and was open-minded enough to allow Torie to join the academy.

"Good afternoon," Dominic said, bowing. "I am Viscount Kelbourne."

On meeting Dominic, people generally looked nervous—if his reputation preceded him—or awed, depending on where they were in the social hierarchy.

West bowed and said, "Good afternoon." In short, he acted like a duke, not a plain mister.

But, of course, he *was* American.

Dominic had given some thought to his strategy. He'd decided to lead with an offer of largesse and follow it up with a demand. "I would like to make a substantial donation to the academy."

West brightened up and looked more interested.

"In honor of my wife," Dominic added.

They made their way through two more exhibition rooms into West's office, a gracious room, its walls covered with art.

"Is this yours?" Dominic inquired, looking at a painting that depicted a couple of fellows in togas walking through a crowd.

West joined him, nodding. "Socrates. The power of expressing historical events in painting—with perspicuity—is one of the most impressive powers that can be given by man to convey useful lessons to others."

"I see," Dominic said, moving to the next painting.

"Caesar just after being slain by Brutus," West said. "Note the exquisite columns in the background. Rome holds the sources of true taste."

"No flowers."

"No."

The finality in his voice suggested that the Duchess of Huntington had been right: flowers and kittens were considered feminine, whereas Caesar covered with blood was masculine. Dominic had a sinking feeling that West might not be amenable to his request.

He had to switch tactics. He'd make the request first and follow it up with money. As he originally conceived the bargain, West would take the bait before giving in. But this man was *all* about art.

West acted like a duke because presumably he *was* a duke in the world of art. After all, his office was in a royal palace.

When they were seated on red velvet chairs picked

out in gilt—definitely worthy of a duke—Dominic began with a simple question. "Has the Academy ever considered accepting women painters?"

Unsurprisingly, West's face expressed disapproval. He leaned forward, and Dominic reminded himself that he had no intention of losing his temper fighting with this bantam cock from the former colonies.

"The Academy has ladies among its ruling members!" West stated. "Angelica Kauffman is an esteemed history painter. Mary Moser is known for her portraits. And floral paintings." He sat back, satisfied. "The vulgar world may consider women to be the inferior sex, but here the only qualification is talent. The art world is a meritocracy."

"I should like my wife to be a member of the Academy," Dominic said, putting his cards on the table. "I am prepared to make a substantial donation to the Academy's endowment in order to facilitate her entrance."

"Impossible," West replied dispassionately. "Did you not hear what I just said? *Talent* is the only means of entry to the Academy."

"You believe a viscountess could have no talent?"

West's face twitched, registering the way Dominic's voice had dropped. Perhaps it also occurred to him that a viscount had direct access to his patron, King George.

Yet he had the courage of his convictions, and he leveled a stubborn American chin in Dominic's direction. "Talent is possible at any rank. What does your wife paint? Historical scenes, perhaps? Mythological depictions?"

"Flowers and rabbits," Dominic said. "With the odd kitten, though I haven't seen any of those."

The president winced. "With all due respect, my lord, ladies make charming paintings the way cows make milk. More is required of still lifes than to be pretty. Mary Moser is considered the first significant British floral painter. Her work conveys depth and emotion."

"My wife's are excellent." Dominic fixed West with a basilisk stare.

"I applaud your loyalty. If your wife would like to submit a painting for the Summer Exhibition, I will make certain that it receives a fair viewing by the Royal Academicians."

"Is that the best exhibition?"

"It is the world's oldest open submission exhibition," West told him. "We began in 1769. Your wife's sex would not be a factor."

His face said clearly that Torie's talent would be the problem.

"Will Mary Moser judge the exhibition?"

"She takes an active role, yes."

Dominic had a sudden idea. Most men bought their wives a gem to soothe over a marital battle, but given the way Torie left that emerald ring around the house—though it was worth three times the diamond he'd given Leonora—she would be unimpressed.

But a painting?

"Do you have any paintings by Mary Moser for sale out there?" He jerked his head toward the exhibition hall.

"Those paintings are not for sale." West rose from his chair, a cardinal sin in a world in which he ranked so far below a viscount. Dominic stayed where he was.

"How much would one of Moser's flower paintings sell for?"

"I could not speak to the cost of her paintings; you'd have to contact the lady or her agent. The *Times* reported that Queen Charlotte commissioned Mary Moser to create a floral decorative scheme for one room in Frogmore House. She paid nine hundred pounds."

Dominic was stunned.

As a duke, West oversaw a lucrative empire.

"If you will forgive me, my lord, I must return to the academy proper, where students are sketching from life."

Dominic raised an eyebrow.

"A naked man. Art is the representation of human beauty, ideally perfect in design, graceful and noble in attitude," West said, diving suddenly into eloquence. Then he added, more prosaically, "Our female academicians are not invited to join those sessions, nor do they attend committee meetings and dinners. Of course, they have no wish to find themselves among so many men."

No wonder Torie had avoided these pompous idiots.

Dominic caught himself. How often did he label people fools and idiots?

Frequently. He had to stop.

He rose. "Thank you for your introduction to the Academy, President West."

West looked gratified by the use of his title. "May I have the viscountess's name? I'm afraid in my world we do not memorize Debrett's." He tittered.

"My wife is Viscountess Kelbourne."

West managed to stop himself from rolling his eyes. "Yes, but how does she sign her paintings?"

"Sign?"

"In the lower right corner, generally, but sometimes on the back."

"I have no idea. Would she sign with her given name? Victoria."

"Her full name," West prompted. "Mary Moser, for example. The artist is married, but she exhibits under the name by which she became famous."

Dominic didn't like the idea of Torie using any name but his. Still: "My wife's maiden name is Victoria Sutton."

West said in quite a different voice, "You are jesting, Lord Kelbourne."

"I assure you that I am not," Dominic replied. He turned away, taking another look at the room and its paintings filled with restless groups of men. He preferred Torie's roses. Hell, he preferred Valentine's rabbits and Florence's deranged trees.

"I wish you good afternoon," he said, bowing.

"Viscount!" West's voice was incredulous and shrill. "Your wife—your wife is *Victoria Sutton*?"

Dominic froze. "Yes."

"Who signs her work V. Sutton?"

"I have no idea," Dominic said. He kept his expression calm only by a fierce exertion of will. "I gather that you do know my wife's work."

"The Academy issued an honorary invitation to Miss Victoria Sutton when the lady was not yet seventeen," West said flatly. "Since then, she has exhibited in every Summer Exhibition, as well as any others when we can persuade her to honor us with a painting."

Dominic's voice emerged weightless from his chest. "I see."

"You came here to try to buy entry for one of the greatest floral painters in England, likely *the* greatest, given that Mary Moser is losing her eyesight," West said. "I thought you were speaking of a witless woman who paints daisies onto the back of a piece of glass."

Dominic remembered his vow. "Those ladies are not witless. They are not encouraged to paint Caesar. They are only taught to paint daisies."

"With apologies, Lord Kelbourne, *you* are the witless one, given your ignorance of your wife's genius!" West snarled, with all the fury of a queen whose courtier had rudely turned his back. "I have personally begged your wife to meet the Academy students for a mere half hour, to explain her current work on time."

"Time," Dominic repeated, thinking of the three petals he had labeled "meticulous."

"Miss Sutton will not sell her works. She claims that she will only give them to people she loves. I personally conveyed an offer of two thousand pounds from an American collector, and she turned him down. I know of only one artist— *one!*—who has had the luck to carry out extended conversations with her. What Monsieur Langlois reports of her thoughts on time dazzles and amazes."

"I see."

"You don't. I myself try to capture a moment, say the moment when Caesar dies. I give the depiction as much reality as possible. I try to put history on a canvas. Miss Sutton works with ideas: rather than the precise moment a flower dies, she paints its suspension in time."

In Dominic's opinion, this particular duke would never get closer to admitting that there was a queen in his world.

And he, Dominic, was married to Her Majesty.

"Constraints are visited on aristocratic women that the rest of us will never endure." West looked Kelbourne up and down. "One of those is presumably marriage to a man with so little respect that he doesn't even know whom he wedded!"

"I agree," Dominic bowed. "Good afternoon, President West." He turned around and walked out.

CHAPTER 38

On the way to Huntington Grange, Dominic didn't sleep overnight in an inn, as his family had done. He drove himself in his curricle, changing horses every ten miles throughout the night. Luckily it didn't rain, and the miles spun by under his wheels as he followed the road by the light of the moon.

He thought hard the whole way about the word *fool* and what it had meant to him as a boy—and to Torie as a girl and then as a woman.

He also thought about her extraordinary achievements.

And his own.

Since that long-ago relative insulted Queen Elizabeth, his ancestors had taken no part in guiding the country from which they benefited so much. His father didn't even take up his seat in the House of Lords. The most important bill of Dominic's career appeared doomed for the moment, but he had championed other bills that protected the nation's justice system and its finances.

Neither he nor his wife were fools, far from it. And yet the word *fool* had played a heartbreaking role in both their lives.

The moon paled quickly as his horses plodded up the final hill leading to Huntington Grange. At the top, he looked down onto a building that appeared to have been built in a haphazard way around a medieval castle, which made the shiny red steam engine even more conspicuous.

The groom seated beside him made an odd

sound. "The door," he said urgently. "The door is open, and I don't see anyone up and about."

Dominic's heart stopped in his chest. Could the house have been attacked?

His children. His wife.

He drew in the horses only after reaching rusted gates; thereafter he slowed, because his light curricle was in danger of flipping over as he steered around pits in the road and drove over two shining steel tracks, perfectly maintained.

As he neared the engine in front of the house, Dominic caught sight of his wife.

"You're smiling," the groom blurted out. And hastily, "Forgive me for the impertinence, my lord!"

Dominic jumped down, thinking that he should bury the memory of his father mocking his dimples, along with the memory of everything else that benighted man had ever said.

He walked around the locomotive into a courtyard littered with paints and easels. His wife was standing before an easel, wearing a pinafore over her nightgown, hair in a messy plait.

He strode toward her, feeling an acute, sharp longing that would be with him for life.

"Hello, Dom," Torie said quietly, putting her paintbrush into a jar.

"We have to—" he said.

"We must—" Torie began at the same moment.

They both stopped.

"My father often excoriated me for being a fool," Dom said. "That is not an excuse for what I said to you. But I hope it is an explanation. I am more used to my father's unkind language than the opposite."

Her response was . . . a growl. She looked infuriated and understanding at once. He was already in love with her, but he tumbled even deeper, because she was still angry with him, but she was also livid at his father. Somehow, magically, he caught both those emotions in her eyes at once.

Dominic stepped forward and brought her hands to his mouth, the fragrance of turpentine making him irrationally happy. "I promised myself that I will not only *try* to do better; I will do better."

"Perhaps we should just put our first marital fight behind us," Torie said. She gently pulled her hands from his and slung her arms around his neck, reaching up to brush her lips over his.

A groan broke from his throat. "Darling."

"Kiss me," she whispered.

But Dominic felt anguished to his bone marrow, and kissing would merely delay the conversation they needed to have. "Do you remember what I thought was the bedrock of any relationship?" he asked instead, eyes searching her face. "The one attribute I hoped my wife would have."

Her brows drew together. "Fidelity?" she guessed, stepping back. "I have never had the *slightest* improper thought about Langlois, Dom."

"It was honesty. That replaced all my foolish notions of what I wanted in a wife."

CHAPTER 39

$\mathcal{T}$orie barely stopped herself from gaping at her husband. "I haven't lied to you." She realized she was tugging on her braid and looked down at her clothing in dismay. She had slept poorly, lying awake thinking of the moment when she told Dom that she could never love him.

That had been a lie.

Loving him was like breathing: she couldn't stop doing it, no matter how much she wished she'd fallen in love with a gentle duke.

She wanted her ferocious, burly viscount, with his fiery eyes and even fierier rhetoric.

"Do you mind if we go upstairs?" she asked. "I don't want to be caught in my nightgown by the duke, who rises early."

Dominic glanced down at her bare toes, then nodded. He followed her silently into the huge, echoing entry hall of Huntington Grange.

"The duke roasted a wild boar in that fireplace," Torie said, desperately trying to figure out why her husband was accusing her of dishonesty. She rarely lied. She'd had enough of prevarication in her first Season, while pretending that she could read.

They climbed the stone steps leading to the first floor of the old castle, then turned right and walked down a windy corridor and through a door that had been unceremoniously knocked in the stone, leading to a newer building.

Not *new*, since Torie thought it might date back to the current duke's grandfather, but at least it wasn't medieval.

Up another flight of stairs, then around a circular flight of stone steps leading to her bedroom. *Their* bedroom, if her husband recovered his temper.

Torie walked in. "I have no chairs."

Dominic stood in the doorway, his eyes traveling from the cobwebby ceiling high above them, to the shuttered windows, to the huge bed that jutted from one rounded wall. The only other furniture was a rickety-looking table holding a basin and a soap dish.

"It is an insult to place my viscountess in this dusty attic," he snarled, eyes flaring, clearly about to pull out his rapier and stomp downstairs to blast the duke for disrespecting his wife.

"No!" Torie said quickly. "I chose the turret chamber for its view." She went to the window and pushed open the shutters, letting in a grass-scented breeze before she turned back to him. "Are you going to tell me why you're so angry?"

"I am not angry." Dominic sat down on the bed. She would have taken that retort as defensiveness, but he sounded bereft.

She came over and sat beside him. "I cannot think of a lie I told you."

"No?"

His eyes fixed on hers.

"Truly," Torie said in some bewilderment. Then, after a pause, "That's not entirely true." She summoned up her courage. "I was in a rage when I said that I could never love you. It wasn't true. I am in love with you. I hope you can come to love me in time, or perhaps you already do. But I can't let you believe that I don't love you." A wave of intolerable, itching embarrassment went over her body.

"I do love you," Dom said flatly.

"Oh." Her mind reeled from that matter-of-fact statement. His voice didn't invite celebration. "I still can't think of any lies I told you."

A shadow crossed her husband's eyes. "You promised that you would never present yourself as someone you are not."

"I'm incapable of pretending to be ladylike the way Leonora does," Torie said, nodding.

"Actually, I would say that you are far more expert than your sister in the art of pretense."

"What?" Torie asked, dumbfounded. "What are you talking about? I feel as if I've been tried and sentenced, and no one has told me my crime!"

"Roses, rabbits, and the occasional kitten. Do I have the subjects of your paintings correct?"

Torie felt the instinctual caution that small animals must feel when a hawk circles overhead. "I don't actually paint cats."

Dom's face was as hard as marble. "Strange, given that your father introduced your artwork by talking of kittens. Baby animals are ladylike subjects for painting, are they not? Subjects that a gentleman might discount for their association with femininity?"

Torie scowled at him. "Some women painters—"

"Such as Angelica Kauffman? Her historical paintings are renowned."

"Why, yes, they are," Torie said, surprised. "You have heard of Miss Kauffman?"

"*Is* she Miss Kauffman? I understand that Mary Moser is listed as a Royal Academician under her maiden name."

Torie stared in bewilderment at her husband, seeing the tightness in his cheekbones, the vibrating intensity in his eyes. He wasn't in the grip of anger; it looked more like he felt betrayed.

An idea struck her like a hammer. Did her painting embarrass him?

"You don't want your wife to paint because it's not ladylike?" she said, dread plummeting to the bottom of her stomach like a rock.

"No!"

"It's too late," she told him, hearing a queer echoing in her ears. "I cannot give up painting, Dom. I *cannot*." Despite herself, her voice broke. "It is the only thing—well, one of two things—that I've ever been any good at."

"I didn't mean 'No' as in I don't want you to be a painter."

She drew in a shuddering breath. "Oh."

"I recently learned that you are a Royal Academician. As a matter of fact, I was informed by the president of that academy that you are the best floral painter in the United Kingdom."

Torie froze. "You met Benjamin West?"

"Indeed. I went to Somerset House hoping to convince the Academy to add a woman to their roster. I was informed that hierarchy in the art world is based not on birth but merit."

"That is partially true," Torie said, biting her lower lip as a sinking feeling came over her. "What a kind gesture on your part."

"I should have asked you more about your work," Dom said, raw honesty darkening his voice. "That's my fault. But you . . . you pushed me away, Torie. You dismissed your own painting by letting me think that your father's characterization of you painting kittens was correct."

Torie swallowed hard. "I've never spent much time with cats, so I don't paint them."

"This is not about cats," Dom stated. "It's about

the way you hid your true self, just as your sister did. I was hoodwinked by both my fiancées. In fact, hiding your talent and letting my ignorant assessment of your work stand is worse than Leonora's bad temper."

Torie saw exactly what he meant. She had hidden the importance of her ideas about time behind society's notion that women painted frivolous subjects, in the same way that she had hidden her passion for art behind being a silly butterfly.

"I do love you." His voice rasped. "I'm in love with you. I went to Somerset House because I wanted to do something to show you that I valued *you*, no matter the disparagement of your work in the eyes of polite society."

"Oh, no," Torie breathed, her gut twisting. "What did you propose?"

The derision in his eyes was directed at himself, not her. "I tried to talk the president of the Royal Academy into allowing my viscountess to exhibit a painting of kittens in the Summer Exhibition."

Torie's eyes rounded. "In the *Summer Exhibition*?"

"The same." The corner of his mouth curled up but without humor. "I was prepared to bribe him handsomely. West was horrified—until I informed him that my wife's maiden name was Victoria Sutton, and yes, she likely signed her paintings V. Sutton. You can imagine how quickly his expression changed."

Alarm shot through her. Her viscount was bad-tempered—and *proud*. West would dine out on this story for many a night, and Dom knew it.

"I misled you," Torie admitted, twisting her hands together. "I do hide behind kittens when my paintings are discussed."

"Why? Why not just inform the polite world that you are a great painter? Or if not them, why not tell *me*?"

"My father approved of my painting ladylike subjects," she said, faltering. "I failed him in so many other respects."

"His judgment of you stemmed from your inability to read, not your painting. As I recall it, he boasted of your ability when you first met the twins."

Torie took a deep breath. "He doesn't mind that I can't read. If you'll remember, he thinks that women have no need to read. Yet if I, an illiterate ninny, tried to paint historical scenes, the mockery would have been deafening. My inability to read is always taken as an indication of ignorance. No one criticizes a lady who paints adorable animals. Do you see what I mean?"

"I think your father is contemptible, and I do see the parallel between talk of kittens and the jests you offer in ballrooms, hoping to head off criticism based on your illiteracy."

"I suppose you're right," Torie said, never having thought of the two in parallel. "My point is that a woman who paints kittens is not trying to rise above her station. The subject itself admits her presumed foolishness."

Dom bit off a curse before she heard the whole word. "That wretched situation doesn't explain why you concealed your artistic success. I gather you could have sold one of your paintings for two thousand pounds or more. Surely Sir William's lack of interest reflects his ignorance of their worth."

Guilt was burning in Torie's gut, but now resentment was prickling to life. "Of course he would have been interested. If I sold a painting, the money would have been Sir William's, not mine. As his daughter, I had no claim to money made from my own work."

"Nor have you as my wife." Dom's jaw was steel. "Are you saying that you concealed your artistic success fearing that I would confiscate any money you might earn, as your father undoubtedly would have done?"

"No!" Torie cried. "I never thought that. It had simply become a habit. It takes me months to finish a painting, and sometimes I abandon it in the middle. If my father saw my work as a source of money, he would have expected me to churn out a painting a week."

"I understand."

"If you—we—ever need money, I would be happy to sell every painting I make. I didn't mean to hide myself from you. I genuinely never thought of it that way. Ladies don't . . ." She faltered. "I was taught not to boast."

"Sharing yourself, your passions and successes, is not boasting." Dom ran his hands through hair already tumbled by a long drive in an open carriage. "Your lying by omission hurt because you're everything to me: my family, my lover, my best friend."

A sob rose in Torie's chest.

"Standing in front of Benjamin West, realizing that I deserved his mockery because I didn't know my own wife, felt like a knife twisting in my gut."

"Oh, Dom, I'm so sorry. I didn't mean to!"

"All those afternoons after we made love on your settee, you never thought of telling me about your work? You never considered sharing your talent, your ideas about time, your fame . . . nothing?"

Torie swallowed hard and shook her head.

"Why not?"

She told the truth. "It didn't occur to me." She looked down and saw his hand curl into a fist, white-knuckled. Not rage but sadness.

"Yet you shared it all with Langlois." His voice was even.

"He already knew," Torie said, trying to explain. "Not at first, but after he came into my studio, he recognized the painting I gave you."

"How could he recognize it? I thought no one visited your studio?"

"My work is recognizable to other artists. I truly didn't mean to speak to him and not you," she said, her voice trembling. "I don't *like* talking to other artists. I can't talk fluently about what I do, the way Langlois does. I avoid the Royal Academy."

"He's of your world," Dom said huskily. Uncompromisingly. "I feel like such a fool. I don't know you, and yet I love you." His eyes were dark with betrayal.

Torie pressed a fist against her stomach. She *was* sorry, but a germ of anger was growing inside her chest. "To be honest, I didn't think you were interested."

The words hung in the air between them.

"I deserve that."

With a quick movement, she swung off the bed and went to the window, looking over the unkempt garden, the weedy lake, the fields that stretched into the distance.

Behind her, always the gentleman, Dom rose as well.

Torie turned about and leaned against the window, allowing the breeze to cool her neck since she felt as if she had a fever. "I was protecting myself," she said, the words wrenched from her raw throat.

"From me?"

"From your judgment."

A muscle ticked in his jaw. "I know nothing of the art world. Calling a painting worth thousands of pounds 'meticulous' shows my ignorance. I would have . . ." He cleared his throat. "I would have loved to learn, had you chosen to tell me."

"It's not about my art," Torie said baldly. "You think *I'm* silly, Dom. *You* think that, my husband. I know it, and while you may not have allowed yourself to realize it, you do as well."

"I disagree." He folded his arms over his chest and gave her a ferocious scowl.

"I love the fact that you offer to fight duels against those who insult me," Torie told him. "But warding off society's unpleasantness is not the same as disagreeing with their judgment. In your world, a world of letters and education, a person who can't read is a fool."

"That is not true."

"It *is* true! When you tell someone in Lords not to be a fool, you say it because you believe he *is* stupid. *You* told me that those men refuse to read accounts of the slave trade, so logically, when you told me I was a fool, you meant it."

"They are fools because they are unethical and immoral," Dom stated. "They could read the accounts, but they choose not to, making them fools as they have no desire to learn."

"I agree with that, but reading is not the only way to learn, Dom."

"I've learned that from you, because you are one of the most intelligent women I know." His voice was uncompromising, his eyes fixed on hers. "You have an eidetic memory. Your argumentative skills are wilier than mine. I take the commonplace route when analyzing the *Odyssey*. You offer judgments that are fresh and new. I don't think you're foolish, Torie. Not at all."

He didn't? The label he'd hurled at her stuck in Torie's memory, and she stared at him mutely.

"What I said was inexcusable," Dom continued. "*I* was the fool between us. I must learn to think before I speak. That insult comes quickly to my mind because my father often disparaged me with that same word. I am trying to banish his voice from my memory."

Torie's lips parted in surprise.

"He told me repeatedly that I was a fool, that I couldn't allow a woman to control me, that my dimples were effeminate, that I was too weak to be a real man."

Tears pricked her eyes. "That's absurd! You are everything a man should be."

"I will always defend you, Torie, because I can't bear to think of you being *hurt*. I know how that feels." The words rasped in his throat.

Torie felt anger draining out of her.

"In that moment, my father's voice came out of my mouth."

She took a step toward him, but Dom shook his head. "I need to tell you the whole of it. From the moment I left the nursery, he controlled me absolutely, and yet he loathed everything about me, from my smile to my walk. I couldn't fight back when he said I walked like a woman. I chose to fight with the rapier, thinking that the skill would prove me manly." His eyes were dark with pain. "He died before I realized that his opinion was worthless."

A tear ran down Torie's cheek.

"I was terrified that people—that you—would gain power over me the way he had." His voice hitched. "On the drive here, I realized that it's too late. Even if you don't love me enough to share your art, even if you never give me a painting of my own, you have me. Every part of me."

Torie threw herself at him, wrapping her arms around his waist. "How could you think that I don't love you? I already gave you my most recent painting, and you can have every single one that I make for the rest of my life. I will spend hours explaining them, as long as you understand that I'm incoherent on the subject."

"I knew that you give paintings to people you love, but—"

"I love *you*!" she interrupted, smiling through her tears.

"I was waiting," he finished. "I kept hoping you would take it off the wall and truly give it to me."

"I made something even better," she said, turning to her bed and reaching under the pillow where she kept her sketchbook. "In case you don't think I love you . . ." She opened to a page that would have horrified polite society. There was her viscount in the naked flesh: burly, rough, masculine. The look in his eyes wasn't gentlemanly.

Not at all.

Neither was the rest of him.

Dom looked in silence for a moment and then burst out laughing. "That's no clothespin. It looks like me, doesn't it?"

She nodded. "I'm good," she said with satisfaction. She tapped the sketch. "You're laughing." Her eyes blurred with tears again. "I make you happy."

Dom wiped the tears away and then cupped her face in his large hands. "I love you so much, Torie."

A sweet buss on the lips wasn't enough for either of them, so she tossed away the sketchbook and went up on her toes, pushing her fingers into his disheveled curls and drawing him into a stormy, fierce kiss.

When Torie finally pulled back, breathing hard, she was on the bed, sitting in Dom's lap. "The twins won't wake up for an hour or two." She licked the strong column of his neck. "Mmmm. *Parfum de* dust."

Dom rolled sideways, his weight settling over her. "I must bathe before I make love to you."

"There are no baths," Torie said, smiling at his appalled expression. "The duke only has a few servants, and Emily can't carry more than a pitcher of water up all these steps."

"I brought grooms with me."

"So did I, but the tub—the only tub—rusted out last year." She put a finger across his lips. "No, we aren't moving to an inn, because the children are happy here, and so am I."

He nipped her lower lip. "What about all this dust?"

Torie felt joy swirling through her. "Come look at my view."

"What?"

At the window, she leaned against Dom's chest and pointed to the lake, shining limpid blue in the early morning sun. "The duchess swims there in her chemise, so the children and I have been joining her."

Dom bent his neck and nipped her ear. "I see water."

She smiled up at him.

"And willow trees so thick that the shore can't be glimpsed from the castle."

CHAPTER 40

Torie couldn't stop giggling as Dom ripped the top sheet from her bed, snatched her soap, and drew her down the stairs and across the back lawn, through the willows that edged the lake.

"Nightgown," he ordered when they stopped under the shade of a huge tree, his voice as urgent and intent as his gaze.

"I can't be naked outside!" she protested, shrugging off her robe. "I swim in my chemise." She glanced down at the dimity cotton of her nightgown. "This will do."

Watching her with hungry eyes, Dom wrenched down his breeches and threw them on top of his boots. "Why not take it off? I am naked."

Torie's eyes drifted down his chiseled stomach to his tool, straining toward her. Desire surged between them like a living presence.

"I'm going to wash the dust from my body," Dom announced. "Then I plan to make love to my wife in the lake. After that, I shall make love to my wife on the shore, followed by making love to her in that rickety old bed, hopefully without destroying the frame. Then I'm going to sleep for three days, except when I'm making love to her. Because without her, I can't sleep."

She managed a wobbling smile. "I haven't slept much, either."

"You broke my heart by leaving and then broke my heart again when I realized you hadn't shared your greatest passion with me—but none of that matters. Nothing matters except you." Dom swept her into his arms and walked straight into the water.

"*You* are my greatest passion," Torie said.

She squeaked as cool droplets splashed her legs, but Dom unceremoniously put her down in water up to her waist.

He dunked himself, standing up and rubbing his hands through his hair. Torie swallowed hard as streams of water ran down the slabs of muscles that made up his chest. The light cotton of her nightdress billowed around her legs as she unraveled her braid before she ducked underwater.

Just as she realized how fascinating it was to see morning light swirling through shallow lake water, her husband caught her hands and brought her upright. Greedy eyes fastened on her breasts; a growl broke from his throat as he pulled her against his chest. He wrenched up her sopping nightdress with his left hand as his right slipped over her breasts, then down her stomach, between her legs.

"Are you sure no one can see us?" she gasped, blood thumping in her veins, her legs quivering.

"Even if someone were on the top of the turret, they couldn't see through the willow trees."

Torie threw her arms around his neck and kissed his jaw. "I love you, Dom. I'm sorry I didn't tell you about my paintings. After this, I'll bore you to tears talking of them."

"Nothing about you bores me." The anguished words seemed torn from Dom's chest. "I keep thinking about ravishing you—when I'm not thinking about arguing with you, because I love that too, Torie. You are my finest debating partner, the only one who matters."

The next hour came back to Torie later in flashes,

as if acute pleasure frazzled her memory. In the lake: her fingers skating over the hard curve of his arse, pulling him closer. On the shore: Dom's dark, wet head between her plump thighs as she lay back on the crumpled sheet. Her hands twining into his hair, holding him in place as filthy promises tumbled from his lips. The sound of his harsh breath in her ear as he pumped deep inside her, the sound of her own gasps. The moment when he said desperately, through gritted teeth, "Be mine, Torie. Be mine. I'm jealous and possessive, but damn it, I love you so much that I can't—"

He broke off, kissing her desperately, overwhelmed by his emotion.

Pleasure and joy seemed interchangeable: knit into her essence by his kisses, by his love for her. By hers for him.

"You're mine too," she whispered. "*You*, the most intelligent man in London, the most ethical and generous person I've ever known."

The sun was warming the surface of the water by the time he drew her to her feet and bundled her back into her robe.

He sank to his knees in front of her.

"Dom!"

"I can't atone for what I did, for the way I treated you."

"You needn't! I was wrong, too. We were both wrong."

She was surprised to see laughter in his glittering eyes. "I decided that the best way to exorcize my father's ghost is by horrifying it."

Torie let out a startled giggle.

"I'm on my knees in this bloody uncomfortable pile of leaves because my wife owns me," he informed the air around them. "I am hers, and I always will be. If she leaves me, she takes my heart with her."

Torie smiled, her heart full. "Done?" she asked.

"Never." He drew her down to him, nudged her legs apart, and grinned at her, a pirate's smile. "I shall never be done with you, love. One touch on my arm, and I'm hungry. You know what the worst is?"

She shook her head, feeling airy as a soap bubble.

"Turpentine," he admitted. "I smell it, and I get an erection." He lowered his head and kissed her thigh. At her giggle, he served up a mock indignant scowl. "Not just any erection, Torie: the agonizing kind. The out of control, desperate kind."

The last word was muffled because he was kissing his way up her inner thigh, so Torie lay back and watched a cloud drift across the pale blue sky far above. She was thinking dreamily that perhaps she would paint a sky with luminous gold edging around the clouds, as if angels were lounging on the other side, just out of sight.

The thought evaporated because Dom licked her delicately, like a cat with a saucer of cream, so her eyelashes fluttered shut. She could smell river water and healthy man and mown grass. Hunger washed over her even though they had just made love, and she had been so *replete*. Satisfied.

He moved back, sitting down, and held out his arms. Torie curled her legs around his waist, discovering that making love twice, not to mention exorcizing a ghost, hadn't quelled his desire. Waves of heat melted her from the inside out.

"Your generosity and your loyalty are at the top of the many reasons why I love you," she said.

His arms wrapped tighter around her. "Even I would have called my loyalty into question after Vauxhall."

"That was idiocy," she said impishly. "You see, I think it's fine to call an *action* idiotic, just not a person. Even when you thought I painted kittens, you strode into the Royal Academy to demand that they put my felines next to Benjamin West's dying Caesars."

One side of his mouth curled up. "He's created more than the one dead Caesar he showed me?"

"He does them all the time," she said dismissively. "They sell in buckets to Americans. My point is that if you had known I was an excellent painter, it would have meant less than you stamping into Somerset House and demanding that my rubbishing kittens be recognized."

"I don't follow."

"I was used to my father belittling me and my work. He does it with affection."

He leaned forward and kissed her. "Mine did the same but without affection."

"But you fought with me. You *only* fight when the battle is important, and the opponents worthy. You fought for my kittens too, even though the cats didn't exist." She drew his head down to hers, smiling through the shimmer of her tears. "You are the only man who has ever offered to defend me and my ladylike paintings. That means everything to me, Dom. Everything."

"Consider my father exorcized," he said, his voice cracking. "I'll never hurt you again."

She shook her head. "We are both imperfect. I expect we will insult each other again—and forgive each other. That's what marriage is."

"And what love is." Dom smiled at her, his dimples showing. "Because we do love each other."

"Dom, do you know what they call a baby rabbit?"

He was kissing her and didn't answer.

"A kitten," she whispered . . . and then burst out laughing.

EPILOGUE

$\mathcal{T}$he Summer Exhibition at the Royal Academy was honored by the arrival of its greatest patron, King George himself.

"His Majesty is standing before your painting!" Dom said to Torie when they entered the chamber. "Let's go speak to him before West bores him into an apoplexy, and he has to leave."

"He doesn't suffer from apoplexies," Torie said, feeling a quiver of anxiety. "What if the king doesn't like it?"

"If so, why would he stand there staring at it?" her husband asked with perfect logic. "Here, give the baby to Nanny Grey." Nanny had reluctantly bowed to the fact that the viscount and viscountess most oddly chose to take their baby wherever they went. She managed to stay close, even while keeping an eye on the twins.

Earning, as Torie often told her husband, every penny she was paid.

"My lady!" Nanny Grey said urgently, reaching out for the baby at the same time she nodded toward the far wall.

"Oh, bloody hell," Dom said, setting off through the crowd in the direction of the twins, who had begun chatting with the King of England.

Torie made sure that her darling Charlotte was comfortably curled against Nanny's shoulder, her fist clenched on Nanny's pinafore, before she turned to follow.

By the time she joined them, the conversation was in full swing. His majesty was bent down, listening carefully to Valentine. Thankfully, Val was at his most respectful.

"If Your Majesty looks carefully at these figures," he said, gesturing toward the portrait of the Duke and Duchess of Huntington atop their steam engine, "you'll see that they are caught in motion. Her Grace's arms are twirling in the air. That is most difficult to achieve."

"I see," His Majesty said, nodding. "As opposed to this one here, eh?" The work hanging next to it was Benjamin West's depiction of the death of Nero.

Valentine's lip didn't curl, but his restraint clearly took some effort. "Precisely so, Your Majesty."

Torie sighed. Val didn't know that Benjamin West was King George's chosen portraitist.

"It's not all about movement," Florence piped up. "The Duchess of Huntington said that it's the only likeness she has of her husband that caught his personality."

The king looked up and saw Torie. "Here is the artist herself."

Torie dropped into a deep curtsy. "Your Majesty."

"A great work," he said. "I knew the duke since he was a boy. His death was a loss to the nation, as well as his family. This portrait captures his joy, doesn't it?"

"I hope so, Your Majesty."

"Viscount Kelbourne," King George said. "Heard the bill was voted down yet again. Maybe next year, eh?"

Dominic bowed. "I hope so, Your Majesty. The Quakers have done much to advance its success."

"Good people, those," His Majesty said somewhat vaguely. One of his courtiers popped up at his shoulder. "I'd like a portrait of myself and my family," he said to Torie. "All of us."

Torie dropped into an even deeper curtsy. "It would be an honor, Your Majesty."

"Depicted like that," he said, nodding at the Duke and Duchess of Huntington on their engine. "I always heard your paintings were about time, but they're not, are they?"

"They aren't?" Torie asked cautiously.

"That one's about emotion," the king said. "Joy. Love." He looked around again. "Where's my queen?"

"I'll take you to her, Your Majesty," his courtier said, drawing him away.

Avoiding the crowd that was swirling ever closer to Torie's painting, eager to see the work that King George liked the best, Dom drew her to the side of the room. "Where's my queen?" he asked, putting his arms around her. "Oh, here you are."

"Dom!" Torie protested, but her husband had long since decided that he didn't give a damn about the opinions of polite society. He especially disliked the rules that adjudicated the behavior of married people.

"I love you," he said huskily, turning his back to the room. "My wife, painter of kings."

"And viscounts," Torie reminded him. She put a finger on his lower lip.

He grinned back at her. "Perhaps you need to do another life study, since they won't allow you to do it at the Academy."

Torie's smile was so wide that she thought her heart might burst with happiness.

But somehow, it never did.

A NOTE ABOUT BUNNIES,
SUGAR PLANTATIONS,
AND OIL PAINTINGS

*T*he genesis of this book was my memories of my mother curling her lip. She was a brilliant writer and a loving mother, but her insecurities led to her to readily label people "fools" or "ill-bred," while assuring her children that they were exceptionally intelligent. I can only speak for myself, but I knew perfectly well that I was middle-of-the-class rather than the top. I managed to end up with degrees from Harvard, Oxford, and Yale; years later it occurred to me that I turned those Ivy League names into a flimsy dike before a tsunami of disparagement—which promptly arrived the first moment I wrote a book containing "that sex stuff," as she called it.

I don't mean this note to read like some sort of retrospective therapy for my younger self, but I do want to call out how damaging careless comments like "Don't be a fool" can be. Torie and Dom both made brilliant contributions to their (fictional) world. Their parents' disparagement was unfair and untrue, and I hope that every single reader of this book makes the same distinction between unkindness and truth.

So let's discuss my decidedly-not-foolish hero's and heroine's professions. Dom was not successful at passing a law outlawing slavery in the colonies; that wouldn't pass until many years later, in 1834, when the ruling class finally realized that maintaining slavery overseas was too expensive (if you're interested, you might enjoy Tom Zoellner's *Island on Fire: The Revolt That Ended Slavery in the British Empire*). I wanted Dom to be an abolitionist—as was Jane Austen's brother—but I also wanted to acknowledge the reality that the government's final decision was not moral but economic. I also wanted Dom to be fighting a losing battle. His father would have mocked him as a failure, but one can still be a success while fighting the tide.

When I began thinking about Torie, I didn't envision her as a member of the Royal Academy. I knew that she couldn't read, and that she claimed to be painting kittens and roses. As I learned more about women painters in the era, though, I couldn't resist giving her that distinction. The two women painters mentioned here, Angelica Kauffman (1741–1807) and Mary Moser (1744–1819), were indeed founding members of the Royal Academy—established by King George III, whose personal painter was Benjamin West (I should add that West's more ponderous statements were adopted from the historical record). I wanted to balance the pejorative response to Torie's dyslexia with a world in which intelligence, birth, and gender were not paramount—though, of course, both Kauffman and Moser fought sexism throughout their lives. Another woman wasn't invited to the Academy for years, although one particularly enterprising young woman did win entry to the school by signing her application drawing "LH," rather than "Laura Herford."

Speaking of enterprising young women, I owe a debt to my daughter, Anna. Her ghoulish stories, written when she was around nine or ten, appear here as Florence's. I still think she may become the next Stephen King, but at the moment she prefers the art of baking. If you read my memoir, *Paris in Love*, you may remember Anna at that age.

Finally, Oddie would have been one of the very first lop-eared rabbits in England. The English lop is the oldest version of our modern lop-eared rabbits. They were selectively bred in the 1800s until the Victorians turned them into a popular household pet rabbit. Lop-eared rabbits are distinguished for being particularly fertile, giving birth to up to fifteen kittens at a time. So for the sake of the nursery, for baby Charlotte, Nanny Grey, and the twins, Oddie stayed single, and the mama rabbit moved to Green Park.

Don't miss Eloisa James's next book,

HARDLY
A
GENTLEMAN

Available Spring 2025

more from **ELOISA JAMES**

NOT THAT DUKE

Bespeckled and freckled, Lady Stella Corsham at least has a dowry that has attracted a crowd of fortune-hunting suitors—which definitely doesn't include the sinfully handsome Silvester Parnell, Duke of Huntington, who laughingly calls her "Specs" as he chases after elegant rivals.

And then—

The worst happens. Marriage.

To the duke. To a man marrying her for all the wrong reasons.

How can Silvester possibly convince Stella that he's fallen in love with the quirky woman he married?

THE RELUCTANT COUNTESS

Giles Renwick, Earl of Lilford, has never made a fool of himself over a woman—until he meets Lady Yasmin Régnier. Yasmin is ineligible for his attentions in every way: not as a wife, certainly not as a mistress (she is a lady!), nor even as a friend, since they vehemently dislike each other. Her gowns are too low, and her skirts are dampened to cling to admittedly lovely thighs. She loves to gossip—and giggle.

She isn't dignified, or polite, or even truly British, given that her father's French ancestry clearly predominated. Not to mention the fact that her mother had been one of Napoleon's mistresses, a fact she makes no effort to hide.

So what—in heaven's name—possesses him to propose?

And what will he do if she says yes?

HOW TO BE A WALLFLOWER

Miss Cleopatra Lewis may be the granddaughter of a viscount, but she has spent the last few years tending the enormous fortune her father left her, which stems from the sale of toilets. Her mother's last wish is that she meet her grandfather, who immediately announces that he will introduce her to society. She will need an entirely new wardrobe, so she makes her way to a costume emporium—and ends up buying the establishment.

Jake Astor Addison is an American financier in London to buy the Emporium, with a ring snug in his pocket ready to offer to the lady of his choice back in America. But when he walks into the business that he intends to transfer to New York, he discovers that a British lady has bought it out from under his nose.